CW01102856

Anna Mantovani

The City of the Dragon

Trilogy of Europa
Book 2

© 2020 Anna Mantovani
Editing: The Mantovanis

PROLOGUE

Kathleen Anderson entered the small meeting room where the main representatives of the government were gathered.

The parliament building had been built a few centuries before and had been designed to accommodate large plenary meetings: the large semi-circular room that she had crossed vaguely resembled an ancient Greek amphitheatre, which was supposed to welcome hundreds of people and had excellent acoustics.

Kathleen was sure that her heels ticking on the floor could be heard on the other side of the room.

Of course, it hadn't been used for its original purpose for many years: the idea of parliamentary assemblies had fallen into disuse in the previous century.

Now the places that had been created for the deputies were occupied by employees who were working in front of terminals; there was really no need for all that space when all the decisions were taken by a handful of people.

The same people who now looked fearfully at her, Kathleen noticed with a thrill of satisfaction.

They had already met in her previous life (so she had started to think about everything that had happened before being reunited with the dragon), but they had always been brief encounters, in which she had to wait long hours before being received, and all she did was listen and then utter a few words of approval.

Now, instead, she was returning as their equal, or even their superior. *That's how it should be.*

President Hartmann greeted her warmly: *good old Hartmann, so affable and useless*, she thought.

With his Santa Claus looks, it was impossible not to love him: however, beyond his social skills, he had never taken a decision in his entire career.

Seated to his right, slightly separately from all the other ministers, were Stefan Lange, Chairman of the Board, General Chardon, the minister of Defence, and the head of the secret services, Christian Voigt.

That trio were the ones who really ruled.

At least for the moment.

Lange shot her a smile, wide and obviously fake: "Dr Anderson, it's so good to see you. Please come, have a seat," he invited her, indicating a place at the big table of fine wood in which all the other ministers were seating.

Kathleen merely greeted him with a nod and took a seat.

A deferential-looking secretary hastened to bring her a cup of tea.

Such a luxury, she thought.

"I gather you wanted to talk to me?" she asked.

Chardon and Lange exchanged a glance: "Indeed we do," Lange confirmed, "We had news that you began a massive production of vaccines for DH16N10 in your laboratories."

Kathleen sipped her tea: "That is correct," she nodded.

"May we ask you why?"

"You may," she granted. "But it's a pretty useless question, isn't it? You already know that I have decided that it's finally time to give the vaccine to the population."

A murmur spread through the room.

"It's common opinion that the time is not yet ripe for this step," Lange declared.

Kathleen almost had to laugh at their audacity.

She set the cup on the table: "When you say 'common opinion' do you mean *your* opinion? Well, I'm sorry but I don't care. I created the vaccine, and I'll be the one to decide what to do with it."

"Kathleen, there is no need to arrive at a clash..." Hartmann said. "In the past, you have also agreed with us..."

"I didn't agree at all," she interrupted him. "I went along with your decisions because I wanted to get something from you, that you covered and supported me in my research. Now, this has happily come to an end, and there is nothing you can offer me for my silence."

"Dr Anderson, please think this thoroughly," Voigt said. "We know that you have no sympathy for the group of infected rebels led by Cain…"

"Cain is no longer a problem, as I've already told you," she cut him short, "and without him, I am convinced that the group of insurgents will soon disintegrate. Besides, if the vaccine is distributed there is no reason why they should be emarginated."

Lange chuckled: "Please doctor, you must be joking. Even if the entire population was immune, the idea that those creatures could walk freely down the street…" he shook his head. "It will never happen."

Kathleen just smiled. Lange probably did not understand that she had far more in common with some of those creatures than she had with him.

We'll keep it in mind.

"The risks linked to contagion are now at a minimum," Lange said. "There hasn't been any real case for… months now, maybe even more than a year. Why spread the vaccine now? It would do nothing but create more chaos."

"Chaos? I don't believe so. It would raise the spirits of the population, it would create confidence. Also keep in mind that those infected continue to have dragons, at least six of them!" she said with passion.

Voigt smiled condescendingly: "Dragons are the least of our problems. The infected themselves have never been able to use them effectively in an offensive. They surely look the part in the old videos used on the news, but apart from that they are more a problem for them than they are for us."

"The real enemies of Europa are on the inside," Lange continued. "Subversives, troublemakers… and the people who live in the underground! We are the last bastion between the citizens of Europa and those folks. They would only bring trouble. The fear of the plague gives us a slightly bigger range of action without getting lost in the bureaucracy, that's all."

"That doesn't mean that we don't appreciate your work of research," Voigt pointed out. "We know that you hired a team of people to search for a cure."

Kathleen felt uncomfortable for the first time: *damn Voigt and his secret services*. She had thought she could keep that information to herself for a while longer.

"This is an initiative that we greatly appreciate," he continued. "In fact, maybe we could come to an agreement... more money, more resources to continue your work, do you think you could use that?"

Kathleen scoffed. She had not gone there to beg for a few cents; they needed to understand that they were no longer in charge.

She stood up: "I'm sorry, but this time there is nothing you can bribe me with. I will spread the vaccine, and there is nothing you can do about it."

She had started to leave when Lange's voice stopped her:

"Dr Anderson, you don't want to have the government of Europa as your enemy," he warned her.

Kathleen laughed: "Don't I? Perhaps it's you who better not have me as your enemy. Think about it."

She almost desired to stay to enjoy the expression of outrage on those old, over-fed faces, but it was time to go.

She briskly walked out of the building, to a large courtyard surrounded by lawns and flower beds.

There she found a group of police officers waiting for her.

One of them came up to her.

"Dr Anderson, you are under arrest for subversive activities. Please follow us with no resistance."

Oh dear, they made up their mind quite quickly, she thought.

"Otherwise?" she asked sweetly.

The policeman looked confused: "Otherwise we would have to use the force," he said.

Kathleen smiled.

A moment later, a warm breeze slapped her face, and fire enveloped the courtyard.

The dragon was on the police in a moment, attacking with flames and with its jaws.

Some tried to run away, burning like torches, but the dragon grabbed them and threw them between his teeth.

He had already eaten of course, because Kathleen made sure he was always well-fed, but in his mind she could feel the particular pleasure he felt in being nourished with an alive, wriggling prey.

When each of these men had been wiped out and the yard was nothing but a large charred open space, Kathleen stepped close to the dragon.

"Let's go home, darling," she said, "I think that's enough for today."

She felt a sense of dissatisfaction: *they could enter the old parliament, search for men who had offended them, hunt them down... they were the ones who had to pay, not those whose bodies now lay burned at her feet... it would take so little and it would be such a great pleasure...*

But no, not now.

They could wait. They had all the time in the world.

With a graceful leap, she climbed on his back and, in a few seconds, they were nothing but a dark dot in the milky sky.

CHAPTER 1

Fever arrived on the twenty-eighth day since Sophie had fished Cain's unconscious body out of the water.

In the time between her discovery to be infected and the appearance of the first symptoms of the plague, Sophie had fluctuated between different states of mind: she had tried to convince herself that maybe the sensors were not accurate and that there was hope that she wasn't infected at all; she had looked for all sorts of information among survivors to understand how they had overcome the acute phase of the disease, without coming to any final revelation; she had spent long days without wanting even to get out of bed (what was the point? She would die anyway); at the end she was so tired of waiting that she had almost begun to hope that the fever started to rise, just to get it over with.

But when she found herself shivering from the fever chills, under multiple layers of blankets that could not appease the cold she felt, she discovered she was terrified.

She was in the basement of a decrepit house in the eighth ring.

The rebels usually moved in the underground tunnels when they were in town, but they were accommodated in real flats. Living in the middle of the underground city would have been unwise: the contagion would spread too easily.

They did transport Sophie through long tunnels, completely wrapped in the protective clothing that she had been using on the island; except that, at that point, they were no longer needed to protect her, but everyone else, she thought bitterly.

They no longer had a headquarter in which to meet, as the island where she had lived in the previous months used to be.

Famke had reckoned that the risk that Emma, or Kathleen, or whatever her name was, could locate the other island, which had been prepared as a headquarter, was too high.

Now all the infected were distributed among various places in Europa that were considered relatively safe.

The house where Sophie was living was the largest agglomeration, because it was in an area sparsely populated and little known by the authorities. In the same building, several floors below the ground, there were also the cages of the dragons.

Sometimes, late at night, when all was quiet, Sophie could hear their cries and the tugging they gave to their chains, in the vain hope of being released.

Sophie thought it was unwise to keep them all in one place: but Famke seemed the only person who knew how to deal with them, and she was there. So, in the end, there wasn't much choice.

Even Cain was in the same house, in a room not far from hers.

Seeing him lying on the bed, motionless, Sophie thought him dead at first glance, but getting closer, she could see his chest rising and falling in rhythmical breathing.

After the first few weeks, he no longer needed a respirator, which at the beginning had seemed encouraging. Cain, however, had not given any other sign of improvement.

His wounds were healing, but he kept sleeping.

When she had arrived at the hideout, Ken had told her something that, despite the circumstances, had made her happy: Amanda, with the help of James, had escaped from the hospital where she had been locked up.

"Will she come here? Can I see her?" Sophie asked.

Ken shook his head: "Not yet. The city is plastered with posters with her identikit, and we're still not quite sure that she's not being followed."

"But will she come here before... before..." *Before I die*, she meant, but she didn't dare to admit it, even to herself.

Ken looked at her with pity: "I hope she does."

He had patted her shoulder in a comforting gesture, which earlier would have made her wince. She had spent so much time carefully avoiding any physical contact with others, that it was hard to remember that she had nothing to fear now. After all, the worst had already happened.

After turning over in the bed for a long time, she managed to fall asleep.

When she woke up, she had an ice bag on her head, and Famke was trying to make her drink something with a straw.

She felt confused; she wasn't seeing clearly.

"Come on, you must re-hydrate yourself," Famke said.

Sophie took a sip: "I'm fine. I'm drinking regularly."

Famke looked puzzled: "You haven't woken up for two days."

Sophie felt dizzy: "What's my temperature?"

"Forty-one point eight. Drink now, we'll give you something to lower it."

Sophie felt very weak. She closed her eyes... and when she opened them, there was someone else with her, or at least she thought there was. She could no longer see properly and saw only confusing shadows and lights.

"I can't see!" she screamed. "I can't see anything!"

"I know, I know, it's normal," Ken's voice said. "Stay calm."

"What's happening?" she screamed. "What are you doing to me?"

"It's the disease... calm down, now."

Sophie tried to get up, but strong arms held her down.

I must get out of here, she thought. She had to get away, had to...

Her eyelids grew heavier and she lost consciousness again.

She could no longer distinguish wake from sleep: everything had become a succession of shadows, lights, confused thoughts.

How long had passed? She couldn't distinguish days from minutes.

At some point, it was the pain that woke her up: it was like a flame that burned every single inch of her skin.

She ran her hands on her arms, trying to get rid of the source of the pain and discovered to her horror that her skin didn't feel like skin anymore. It was only a single expanse of painful pustules, rigid as stone.

She began to scream, while around her some frantic voices bundled up.

"Please calm down, Sophie."

A different, harder voice. *Gregor, perhaps?* "God, that's gross. That one's good as dead."

They had to do something, anything, just to make the pain stop... she wanted to speak, but she was only able to scream incoherently.

"Can't we give her a good dose of morphine and be done with it? At least she could go away in her sleep, it would be a merciful gesture."

"You know that it wouldn't work. Besides, she could still make it."

"Not with this temperature: it went past forty degrees long ago."

The world around her was made of pain and panic...

Then, she suddenly felt a familiar, yet vaguely alien emotion: the image of a closed cocoon, a thick and pleasantly warm liquid around her. Distant lights, as through a very dark glass.

Were they hallucinations? They had to be, there was no other explanation.

The comforting feeling quickly faded, as she was thrown into a tub full of cold water.

She felt her body shaking violently, in fits, then she lost consciousness again.

"Oh, damn."

"I told you it wasn't a pretty sight."

Sophie tried to open her eyes, but she could not take it. What was the point anyway? She was blind.

Her skin was still burning as if it had been punctured with hot needles. She wanted to cry, but she didn't have the strength.

But she felt a different voice closer to her: more energetic, so familiar... *Amanda!* She was there!

"Kidneys and liver's functions?" she asked.

"Dunno," Famke's voice answered. "Lost days ago, I'd say," she sighed. "I don't think that she will pass the night."

"Well, we'll see about that."

Sophie squirmed, trying to make them understand that she was awake.

A cool hand, covered with a latex glove, held hers.

"Hey, Sophie, what have you done? I can't leave you alone for a few days that you catch the plague."

Sophie wanted to answer, but again she was overcome by foreign sensations: the liquid that she had felt around her body was moving, the walls around her were trembling.

Did she have to hit them? What was happening? She wanted to stay inside the warm cocoon, and, at the same time, she felt she had to get out.

"Sophie? Sophie, can you still hear me?"

"There's something in my head..." she managed to gasp. "I see... things..."

She had no breath to elaborate further.

"She's hearing a dragon!" Famke exclaimed.

"At what stage is the egg? There is one more, right?" Amanda asked.

"It's been looking like it's about to hatch for some days."

There was a long pause.

"Bring it here, as quickly as possible. And light the fire, bring the heaters, we have to raise the temperature. Give me other blankets."

"But so far we have tried to keep it low as possible," Famke objected.

"It makes no sense to try to cure her as a human being, she's doomed. But if we take the dragon out, she can make it."

Sophie saw brighter lights around her: the hot liquid was choking her, it was time to get out.

She looked down and saw that her hands were pale with translucent claws.

Then again, she found herself in the dark room, on her sickbed.

She felt shaking from the inside: she was having fits again.

"Hurry up, she's having another attack..."

Sophie began to cough and realized that a hot gush, probably blood, erupted from her mouth.

"Come on, there is no time! Sophie, hold on, just a few more minutes... Sophie, Sophie... can you hear me?!"

She saw a bright crack widening more and more in front of her until there was nothing but blinding light.

CHAPTER 2

Erik opened the door of his old office and, despite everything, he felt comforted by the familiar environment.

He had arrived in the early morning, before any of his other colleagues, just to stay a few moments alone.

After a rest period prescribed by the psychologist of the medical police, Erik had received official communication that reassigned him to his job at the police headquarter.

Maybe it was Hoffman who had requested his reinstatement, or maybe it was the psychologist that believed that he could benefit from a well-known and reassuring atmosphere; in any case, there he was again, at the same old desk where he had always sat.

He had never left much in his locker at the custody hospital, and, at the same time, he never unpacked the items that had been taken from his desk when he was transferred, so that morning all he had to do was take in the same box that he had thrown in the closet a few months before.

He pulled two chipped cups out of the box and rearranged them in the exact spot where he had always kept them, and did the same with a spare t-shirt, whose place was the second drawer of his desk.

When he found himself staring at the framed picture of Thea, Maja and Peter, the feeling of calmness that had invaded him since he had entered the headquarter quickly vanished.

He could not stop thinking of the bullet that sunk into his wife's chest, and her eyes, losing their light as she was dying in his arms.

And the pain of the loss was exacerbated by the knowledge that it was all his fault: if only he hadn't been in such a rush that night... if only he had stopped to think before concocting that stupid trap... or, even better, if he had never gone to the hospital that night, his only problem now would be a not so exciting career as a guard, and he could go home every day to his family.

He would never forget the moment when he went home and had to break the news to Peter and Maja.

If Peter had been devastated, Maja immediately demanded to have more details and had instantly sensed his participation in the whole thing, although he had tried to minimize it.

"Even if you never suspected that Mum was a spy, how could you risk taking one of us into a trap full of snipers ready to shoot?" she accused him.

"No, I would never have imagined that it could be one of you... I thought, perhaps... Marc Werner."

"So you would have had Marc shot?!" she had exclaimed. "And if you really thought he looked so sketchy, why didn't you even think of talking to me?"

The truth was that no, he had never thought about it. He had continued to think that every member of his family was a delicate creature to be protected from the evils of the world, without realizing that each one of them, even young Peter, had gone on with their lives making decisions independently of him.

After that heated discussion, Peter had gone to his sister's house, and since then he had settled there.

He had seen them at Thea's funeral, but they had refused to talk to him.

That day had been the worst of his life, even more painful than when she died.

The memory alone was enough to bring back tears in his eyes and...

"Erik! So it's true that you're back!"

Lara Meyer's voice shook him from his dark thoughts.

Erik turned: "Yep, here I am," he confirmed.

"I wanted to give you my condolences. I wanted to come to the funeral, but then I thought that..."

"Thank you," Erik interrupted her. "That's fine."

"How do you feel?" she asked. "You don't look great."

Erik shrugged: "Uhm, I feel pretty... well... to be honest, I feel like crap," he finally admitted. "But I'm glad to be back to work."

It was the truth: anything was better than wandering around his empty apartment with the sole perspective of the meetings with the psychologist.

At that moment, Laurent and Janssen also arrived and greeted him with big pats on the back and an exaggerated camaraderie. Erik suspected they didn't really know what to say.

Who knows what strange gossip had circulated: the fact that his wife had been killed during an attempted arrest, that she was a spy, or that she wasn't...

People were probably telling many contradictory accounts.

Once the pleasantries were over, the three colleagues looked hesitant, as if he could have a nervous breakdown right in front of them.

How embarrassing, Erik thought. He could not stand being treated that way.

"Have you heard of Anderson, Erik?" Laurent said, probably to change the subject. "Lately no one talks about anything else."

"No!" Erik replied, grateful. "Who is that?"

"You never heard of her, really?" Janssen became animated. "There are the strangest rumours about her. She has started to spread a vaccine against the plague, in a medical centre in the second ring. Completely free! Some say that it works very well and that so far the government has kept it secret, and, for this, they tried to kill her with a dragon. Others argue that it is all a plot to inject all of us with a substance that controls our thoughts."

"Shut up!" Meyer laughed.

"Well, I admit that maybe it's a bit far-fetched," Janssen granted. "But, think about it for a moment: how come this vaccine has only been released now and no official source talks about it? There is something very strange about it..."

"Did I hear correctly, you talked about a dragon? Since when has the government had a dragon?" Erik asked.

"It's a hoax," Lara snapped.

"Oh, this isn't just a hoax, there is at least a grain of truth to it," Laurent pointed out. "There was a newsletter about a month ago, to aeronautical control: until then, the order was to fire on sight of any unauthorized flying object, living or inanimate. With that new order, they were ordered to keep the living flying object, which would be a dragon, under control and fire, but not to shoot until they have the authorization."

"That's a long shot from saying that there's a dragon who isn't controlled by the rebels!" Meyer objected.

"And the accident at the parliament?" Janssen jumped up. "Erik, surely you have not heard of this, they put everything to rest. But it seems that a full squadron was incinerated, just like this, *poof!*" he snapped his fingers. "Officially no one said anything, but here everybody knows."

"Another attack, perhaps?"

Janssen shook his head: "But then why the secrecy?"

Laurent shrugged: "However this Anderson lady looks like a nuisance for the government. It wouldn't surprise me if they tried to get rid of her."

Erik had a chill, thinking back about the uninfected locked up in prison, apparently dead for the rest of society, when they had simply been made disappear...

"Has any of you been vaccinated?" he asked.

"Definitely not!" Janssen exclaimed. "I don't intend to let them inject me anything suspicious, thanks a lot."

"I'm going to do it," Laurent declared. "I spent the best years of my life living in fear of the plague. It's time to stop."

"What about you, Lara?"

Meyer shifted her weight from foot to foot: "I don't know... for now it's just rumours. I'd like to go to see for myself and learn something more."

Erik nodded: "I agree."

At that moment Hoffman arrived, greeted Erik and told him to go to his office to 'receive updates.'

Erik sat in the chair in front of the boss's desk, looking around and seeing that nothing had changed. The same piles of paper, the dusty terminals, the same metal shelves that had always been there.

It was a comforting feeling, but at the same time it was alienating too: how could it be all the same when he felt so different?

"So Persson, do you want to talk about your... feelings?"

Erik looked puzzled: he didn't really want to have a heart-to-heart conversation with Hoffman.

Did he really expect him to start telling him about all his misery?

"I mean," his boss elaborated, "I received a note from the psychologist who is treating you, about your health state..."

This makes me sound like an asylum escapee, Erik thought.

"So, do you feel like going back into service? On-field, I mean?"

Erik opened his mouth, intending to say that yes, of course, he wanted to start again, then stopped.

He had not really taken the time to think about what it meant to return to his previous role until then.

Would they make him arrest 'alleged infected' again, like Amanda Solarin?

And if he couldn't trust the information he received, how could he go and get those people, knowing what awaited them?

He realized that Hoffman's question didn't have such an obvious answer.

"To tell you the truth..." he said, "I would like to have a less operational role for a while. If that's possible."

"Sure, of course!" Hoffman nodded. "Naturally, I completely understand. In fact, I have thought about a project to which you could devote yourself to..."

The 'project' turned out to be a boring report compilation and the filing of paperwork that probably had been left aside for months, waiting for some poor soul that would take on the worthless task.

However, Erik was grateful to Hoffman. That unchallenging job was just what he needed.

"I was thinking..." he said, before returning to his desk. "Do you think Zoe Hernandez will be reinstated to her old role?" he asked.

Hoffman stared at him: "Hernandez? Why?"

"Well, I thought that since it was established that she was not responsible for the information leak..."

"Hernandez's problem was mainly disciplinary," Hoffman cut him short. "The fact that she had nothing to do with the mole doesn't change this situation."

"I see," Erik said.

He didn't think Hernandez deserved that relegation, but apparently Hoffman was not going to change his mind.

He then returned to his seat and set himself to start the work: if nothing else, he would have something to think about.

CHAPTER 3

Sophie laboriously opened her eyes and squinted, dazzled by the dim light bulb hanging from the ceiling.

Her first instinct was to close her eyes and go back to sleep: around her, all was warm and soft, and for a moment she basked in the torpor of the awakening.

To her surprise, she discovered she was feeling well... no, she was feeling *great*, as after a restful night's sleep.

The events of the previous days seemed no more than a dream.

A nightmare, she corrected herself: terrifying but also curiously unreal.

Had she really had the plague? Was she now a different person, an uncontrollable creature? She didn't feel that different from before.

The thought made her bolt upright, and at that moment she realized she was not alone.

On the camp bed on which she had slept, amid the tangle of sweaty sheets, there was a squamous bundle, about the size of a small dog. Sophie stared at it: it was a dragon!

His eyes were closed and he was breathing regularly in his sleep.

Much like Taneen, Nadia's dragon, when he was little, this one also looked like a bird: he had a long snout and a slender body, so that she could see his ribs rise and fall rhythmically. The front and rear legs, however, already had well-defined muscles, even if they were small and delicate-looking. The wings were paper-thin, almost impalpable, and seemed as fragile as a paper tissue, although the bones that linked them to the back were very solid. His tail was almost as long as the whole body.

The dragon was almost entirely white; perhaps the colour of the scales was yet to be defined.

He was just... *beautiful*, Sophie thought. He looked like a miniature painting.

When she reached out a finger to stroke his little claws, the creature opened his eyes.

His pupils were elongated, the irises a golden brown. When he saw her, he gave an excited, strident shout, and Sophie felt invaded by a wave of emotions that did not belong to her entirely: confusion, joy… love.

Was she feeling them, or was it the dragon?

"Hello little one!" she said. "Where have you come from?"

The creature gave another happy shout and rubbed the tip of his muzzle against her hand.

He's so cute, she thought.

The door opened: "You're awake," said a familiar voice.

"Amanda!" Sophie exclaimed, motioning towards her.

"Hey, stop!" Amanda warned her. "No more hugs, you're contagious now."

"Ah… that's right," Sophie said, taken aback.

She noticed that Amanda had the gloves on and was completely covered in clothes that could prevent the infection.

"It's nice to see you on your feet again," her friend continued. "When I arrived, I thought that you were more dead than alive."

"So did I," Sophie confessed. "My memories of the last few days are all mixed up."

As she spoke, the little dragon climbed on her back, up to her shoulders.

Sophie gave him an affectionate pat.

"Amanda, thanks for saving me," she said. "I don't know what would have happened without you."

"Oh, I didn't do anything!" she laughed. "It was this young one here," she indicated the dragon, "that saved the day. You were in cardiac arrest and didn't breathe anymore. I feared that we had lost you, but as soon as you made contact with the egg…" she spread her arms. "What can I say? It was a miracle. I've never seen anything like it. Within seconds your breathing resumed, beat became steady and temperature stabilized, although it never quite lowered."

The dragon began to nibble Sophie's ear, delighted.

"Do I have a fever?" Sophie asked. "I feel good."

"Of course you feel good, this is your normal temperature now. You are officially a survivor."

Sophie looked down at her own hands, and only then she noticed the dark scales that crossed their back and disappeared under her sleeves.

She touched her own face and felt a different texture beneath her fingers.

"Haven't you seen yourself yet?"

"No…"

Sophie left the room and walked down the hall to the bathroom.

The mirror was old and cracked in several places, dotted with dark spots.

Even so, she could not avoid noticing the signs of the plague on her face.

Sophie had to hold back a gasp of horror when she saw her own reflection: two rows of scales crossed her face at the cheekbones, and others from her forehead and temples rose to hide under her hair. Raising her head, she could see other spots of scales on her jaw and neck.

Some infected had so few obvious signs that a little bit of foundation was enough to confuse them with the uninfected population: she apparently wasn't among the lucky ones.

As for the vast majority of the survivors, her face got disfigured.

She had no idea of the state in which her skin under her clothes was, and she preferred not to think about it. She would discover it at her first shower, she decided.

"It's not terrible," Amanda minimised. "You just have to get used to it."

Sophie frowned: she appreciated her encouragement, but she didn't see how she could ever get used to seeing that… *thing*… in the mirror.

"Look, a few days ago you were much, much worse. You were covered with boils that were just plain disgusting… and let me tell you, when they started to burst, there was pus everywhere…"

"You know, that doesn't really make me feel any better."

"I'm serious, we couldn't even look at you, you didn't even look like a human being anymore…"

"Ok, ok, I get it," Sophie snapped. "I'm lucky I'm alive."

"That's the spirit!" Amanda agreed. "Ah, and you also don't have to worry about your period, sanitary napkins, tampons and all that jazz anymore."

"Oh," Sophie said, puzzled.

Of course, not having to worry about her menstrual cycle was a nice convenience, especially since she had found herself in a community of people where she was the only one to have this issue.

However, this also put an end to any future prospect of motherhood; she had never thought it through, but perhaps within herself, she had always assumed that one day...

Well, it didn't make sense to think about it anymore, she decided. At that moment, it was the least of her problems.

The dragon moved in her arms, trying to catch the light that was reflected in the mirror.

Sophie felt a new wave of enthusiasm.

It was true, she was contagious and covered in scales, but she finally had a hope of a different life... maybe not the one that she would have chosen for herself, but a life nevertheless.

She wondered briefly if this sudden optimism stemmed from herself or the dragon... but all in all, it wasn't so important.

She smiled at Amanda: "I'm hungry. Is there any food in here?"

They crossed the hall, then climbed the set of stairs to the top floor.

Sophie realized that between the depression and the disease she never got out of the basement where they had accommodated her.

Above, the windows were covered or frosted, but daylight still managed to enter the room; after weeks spent only in the light of the light bulb dangling over her head, it was a really good feeling.

Amanda led her to a room where three people were bent on a computer.

"It's true, you're alive!" Famke welcomed her. "Nice scales!"

Sophie smiled, uncertain: was it kind of joke between the infected? It was all new to her.

"I'm glad to see that you are well, we feared the worst," Ken said, formal as ever.

Gregor merely raised his gaze from the computer: "Don't even think of letting that little beast in here," he said, pointing at the dragon.

The very idea of closing the puppy in a cage in the basement made Sophie shudder.

The dragon, as perceiving her thoughts, squeezed her more tightly.

"I'm holding him, don't worry," Sophie said.

"Are you?" he scoffed. "You'll keep holding it even when it'll start to spit fire and burn down the whole house?"

"He won't," she assured, feigning confidence that she didn't actually have. She had no idea if the dragon was already able to breathe fire, or what could induce him to do so.

"Really?" he argued as if reading her mind. "And how can you be so sure?"

"Give it a break, Gregor!" Famke chimed in. "It's just a puppy, it can't do any damage."

"Cain wouldn't..."

"Well, Cain isn't here, is he?"

Famke's statement was followed by a silence full of discomfort.

"Do you have any food? It seems that Sophie has recovered her appetite, which is a good sign," Amanda said, perhaps to break the ice.

"Yes, there is something, "said Ken and deposited in front of her a polystyrene box containing a standard ration clearly coming from the food distribution: boiled rice, corn, and a protein substitute burger.

Sophie wolfed down the food, pausing only to try and give the dragon bites of burger, but he spat them out in disgust.

"Don't worry about him, I have meat downstairs," Famke assured.

"Are they carnivores?" Sophie asked, interested.

She didn't know why but the idea of a steak, preferably rare, made her even more hungry: it was peculiar because she had never eaten much meat in her life and also during her time on the island, where there was in abundance, she had never really taken a liking to it.

Was it a side effect of the plague?

Famke nodded: "Oh yes, definitely. They can survive for limited periods of time with other foods too, but not for long. And, if possible, they prefer to hunt for themselves."

As if he had understood, the dragon jumped off the table and began to observe the walls, sniffing around.

Sophie saw that Gregor's gaunt and pale face was tense, but he didn't say anything.

"So, any news?" Amanda asked.

Ken sighed: "Apparently we can abandon the idea to move to the second island. Our cameras recorded landings, so it is as we feared: Kathleen Anderson knows about it. She probably saw the maps when she was with us."

Sophie blushed: she felt guilty for bringing Emma, or Kathleen, right in the heart of the infected headquarters. She had been in good faith, but the consequences of her actions had been disastrous.

"Do we have any other option?" Amanda asked.

"Cain occasionally spoke about crossing the quarantined territory, but... well, external borders are very guarded, although we don't know exactly why. From there, nothing goes in or out. It would be suicide."

"And beyond the sea?" Sophie asked. The idea of a long journey on a boat didn't excite her, but the alternative was to resign themselves to live hidden for the rest of their lives. There had to be an alternative. They had been at sea before, it would not be difficult to reach the Atlantic. And on the other side of the ocean there could be anything.

Gregor looked at her as if she had asked a very stupid question: "It's been centuries that the Atlantic is unnavigable, the currents and the tidal waves are too violent. Our ships are not even remotely able to deal with it, and certainly not the helicopter," he said, bored.

"So we're stuck here," Ken summed up. "At least until further order."

Amanda seemed disappointed: "Apart from seeking another place, what can we do?"

"Our people are keeping us informed about new infections, but there hasn't been any new case for several months," Gregor said. "There are still some infected in the hospital where you were too, but I don't think we would be able to organize other escapes for a while. Added to this, there is the problem that it's difficult to find safe channels of communication since we are all scattered through Europa."

"James said he was able to visit one of those centres where doctors administer the vaccine. And for free! The authorities are not happy, they are doing everything to spread alarming news. But it really seems to be working."

Sophie remembered Kathleen's words: *'I will distribute the vaccine immediately if it's so important to you.'*

She was really doing it. Was it a message for her, or would she have done it anyway? She had no idea.

"It looks like it is," Ken confirmed. "This might be a good thing for us. Maybe, in a few years, we could live peacefully in the city; after all, we wouldn't be dangerous for anyone."

There was a note of disbelieving hope in his voice that it was impossible to ignore.

"Yeah, go figure!" Gregor snorted. "Do you really think they will say 'Oh yes, we spent fifteen years trying to exterminate you but now we can be friends again?'" he shook his head. "Listen to me, don't even think about it."

"There's a lot of uninfected people that are supporting us," Ken insisted. "People who are not happy with the government..."

"But that's the point, that's precisely the reason why they'll never leave us alone!" Gregor exclaimed. "Don't you understand? We are a nuisance. And it's much safer for them to continue to try to get rid of us."

"What should we do, then? Resign ourselves to always live in hiding? Infecting all those we can?"

"Ah, that's fine by me. Cain always said no, there would be too many victims... so now, *we* are the victims," Gregor concluded.

They don't have the faintest idea of what they are doing, Sophie thought.

She realized then that the rebels, without Cain, were in complete disarray.

The new order mentioned by Ken would never come.

"What about the dragons?" she asked.

Famke seemed surprised: "What do you mean?"

"Will they have to remain imprisoned here?"

"Sophie, we have to contain them..." she explained. "I don't like this solution either, but we can't walk them around the block on a leash, don't you think? "

Sophie noticed that the dragon had started to casually chew the tip of her boots.

"What if..." she began hesitantly, then she stopped. Maybe it *was* a stupid thing to say.

"What were you going to say?" Ken gently pressed.

"Well, I also think it's very unlikely that they'll let the infected live quietly in the middle of the city."

It was strange to speak of the infected now that she was a part of them.

"But Kathleen Anderson is a nuisance for them too, and she has a dragon. And we have the dragons, too! In short, wouldn't the government have every interest in establishing a truce with us? They can't fight on two fronts."

Amanda looked doubtful: "I believe that they will find an agreement with Anderson. They are not that different."

Sophie, however, was not convinced. She remembered what Kathleen had told her: 'They won't be able to deny me anything.' Any agreement would always be overcome by a new arrogance from her. They would have to choose whether to submit to her will or clash, and Sophie did not doubt what they would choose.

"Maybe Cain will wake up. He could come out of the coma tomorrow for all that we know." Famke said, hopeful. "Amanda, isn't it so?"

"Yes," she nodded. "Technically it's possible."

No one commented.

As much as no one could exclude that possibility, they couldn't rely on it.

Sophie realized that in that moment, all the people in that room missed Cain as never before.

CHAPTER 4

The office hours spent doing administration work were long and tedious, but they were still the time of day that Erik preferred.

Staying home alone was more than depressing.

After Thea's death, the police had turned the whole flat inside out looking for evidence, clues and generally anything that might have provided additional leads to identify the network of informants of the rebels.

Many of their personal belongings were never returned (his cell phone and his tablet for example), and the rest was left in disarray in the apartment.

Erik knew he should tidy everything up, and perhaps check Thea's clothes and belongings and decide what to keep and what to give away, but he had never managed to find the courage to do so.

He had merely stuck all he had found in his wife's side of the wardrobe, and he had not opened it ever since.

The areas of the house that he used regularly, like the kitchen and the bathroom, were clean and tidy, but he hadn't even opened the door of Peter and Maja's rooms and he knew that everything in there was still as the police had left it.

So, when Laurent announced that after work he would go get vaccinated, and asked if anyone wanted to accompany him, Erik volunteered.

He was not sure if he wanted to be vaccinated or not, but, in any case, he was interested in learning more so he could choose on an informed basis. Besides, there was no point in denying it, any excuse was good not to go home.

Lara Meyer also wanted to go with them, but that day she was busy, so, in the end, only he and Laurent set out to go to the medical centre of the second ring.

Janssen tried to dissuade his colleague: "Don't do it, Laurent!" he urged him. "You don't know what sort of stuff they will inject you with… the vaccine has not been tested enough, it gives terrible side effects and no security against the plague!"

"Please, stop, I've decided," Laurent cut him short. In the past days, he tried to bring some convincing arguments to Janssen, but soon it was evident that the more the two discussed, the more each of them became more adamant in their position.

On the train, Laurent chatted all the time about Janssen's conspiracy theories and others gossips about their colleagues, and Erik had the impression that he did it mainly to cover his long silences and avoid topics that would stop their conversation or make it too personal. In any case, he was grateful for the distraction.

The medical centre was very large, and, even in the modern and stylish second ring, seemed luxurious. The symbol that hung over the building was a stylized version of the rod of Asclepius, the snake-entwined staff.

On the ground floor, there were large windows, from which he could see the crowd of people that were received by nurses with a functional and immaculate white uniform.

As they entered, Laurent received a serial number, and soon he was called at the acceptance.

He answered a series of questions about his health, and he signed a release form.

"Janssen would never have done this," Laurent chuckled nervously.

Even if he was sure of his decision, now that he had come to the point Laurent seemed a bit anxious.

"Do you have any questions?" the acceptance employee gently asked him.

"Actually, I do," Laurent said. "I heard some alarming rumours about the vaccine's side effects, and I would like to know how often they occur and what they consist of."

"Of course," the employee replied, with a professional smile. "It's a very common question. Here are some brochures that explain clearly what can happen and what to do." Erik and Laurent took the booklets, made of expensive glossy paper, whose cover showed two people smiling confidently to a nurse who was about to inject them with a syringe.

"In short, the most common side effect is a simple fever, which occurs in one-third of cases, sometimes accompanied by a minor skin rash, which usually resolves within twenty-four hours. We recommend you to take paracetamol and drink a lot," the employee continued. "In a very low percentage of the vaccinated, less than one per cent, on the injection site there can be a small lump that persists for a few weeks..."

While the possible side effects (all very negligible), and their percentage, were listed to Laurent, Erik let himself be distracted from the brochure he had received. On the back cover, there was a picture of a woman in her seventies, with a serious and competent look, portrayed with a white coat over an elegant dark suit.

The caption indicated that it was Dr Kathleen Anderson, the creator of the prodigious vaccine.

Erik looked at the picture: he was sure he did not know her personally, but there was something distinctly familiar about her face, something he could not identify but which led him to continue to stare at that image...

"Here's the number with which you will be called, please wait your turn in the waiting room, end of the corridor on the left," the employee concluded, shaking him from his thoughts.

Erik and Laurent moved into the indicated room and sat down on a bench to wait.

"So, what do you think?" Laurent asked. "Will you get vaccinated too?"

Erik shrugged: "This place is undoubtedly impressive, but I want to hear also the other side of the argument."

"That sounds reasonable," Laurent agreed.

Since the vaccine had begun to spread, many rumours about rare syndromes that the vaccine would unleash had begun circulating.

The claims were not supported by official sources, but, because of this, they were all the more convincing, given that they presented themselves as unwanted information that Anderson and the government would try to silence.

The brochure that had been delivered to them clearly stated that there was no correlation between the vaccine and the diseases, and, in general, it was a big hoax, but it was hard to tell whom to believe. The majority of the population, including Erik himself, didn't have the knowledge to understand what the truth was.

Sure, maybe getting vaccinated was a risk... but the idea of being able to finally be free from the spectre of the plague was very tempting.

Erik wondered if his work would still make sense if the vaccine would have reached the coverage needed: in fact, did it even make sense to talk about medical police in a world in which the plague was no longer dangerous?

He looked around the medical centre: there were people of all ages and social status.

There were children accompanied by their parents, employees just emerged from their offices, students, workers who probably came from the outer rings. Everyone wanted to get rid of the nightmare.

Erik remembered that Laurent had not been asked for documents or cards, so even those living on the margins of society, like the inhabitants of the tube tunnels, had access to the vaccine.

At that moment, however, he didn't see anyone with such a look and a lack of personal hygiene to suggest that they came from the underground city.

Suddenly he saw a crowd of people who exited a lift. They all seemed very agitated, but Erik could not see what catalysed their attention.

Since Laurent was about to be called in for the injection, Erik stood up for a better look, and, within the group, he noticed Dr Anderson.

In person, she was more attractive than in the picture, he thought. She had a confident demeanour, which made her look younger, and she seemed to radiate a sort of *energy*.

Her hair was cut at her ears and her face...

"Emma Lemaire!" he exclaimed before he could stop himself.

Dr Anderson turned around.

Of course, that's why she looked familiar: Kathleen Anderson was identical to Emma Lemaire, the woman who he had been looking for so long with Zoe Hernandez.

It was more than a resemblance, he concluded: they were undoubtedly the same person.

The reaction of the doctor, then, confirmed it. Although at that moment she had recovered her calm and professional expression, Erik had noticed the nervous gesture with which she had turned in his direction when he said the name of the fugitive.

"And you are..." he began, while Kathleen Anderson merely looked at him with an air of polite incomprehension.

"Excuse me?"

Erik knew he would never get explanations in that waiting room full of people.

It would have been easy for Anderson to deny everything, and to make him look like a lunatic. He had to be able to talk to her in private.

The investigation which he had carried out to find her had started the chain of events that had destroyed his life... he had to know.

"Excuse Me, Dr Anderson, I am officer Erik Persson, from the medical police," he introduced himself. "I think we have a mutual acquaintance, Mrs Lemaire. Emma Lemaire. She told me so much about you," he said, trying to sound significant, and hoping that she would cooperate.

Dr Anderson looked at him, and for a moment Erik was sure she would call security and she would have him thrown out of the building.

But after a moment she smiled: "Of course, dear Emma," she said, shaking his hand. "How is she?"

"It's been quite a while since I last saw her," Erik said. "Sometimes it looks like she's disappeared."

He thought he had caught a flash of humour in the eyes of the doctor.

"Now that I think about it, she told me you would pass by. Would you be kind enough to wait for me in my office? I'll be with you in a moment."

"Er... yes, of course."

Erik was escorted by a diligent assistant to the top floor of the building, where the offices were located.

Dr Anderson's office was big and bright, full of shelves, file cabinets and several computers.

In fact, there was a bit of confusion, with several folders open on the desk and even a cup of tea, now cold, next to a terminal.

Despite the corporate appearance of the medical centre, Erik knew that was a scientist's work, not a manager's.

For some reason, he liked that.

There was also a small meeting room next to her office, and the assistant left him there.

After about twenty minutes, in which he tried to remember everything he knew about Lemaire's case, he was joined by the doctor.

"Agent... Persson, you said? Excuse me for the wait," she said.

"No problem," Erik said. He wanted to ask her for explanations immediately, but instinct told him it would be better if Anderson spoke first.

She must have had the same idea because for a moment there was nothing but an uncertain silence between them.

"So..." she finally said. "How did you come in contact with Emma Lemaire?"

"I was one of the officers who arrested Amanda Solarin," Erik explained. "Then I was involved in trying to track down her assistant and the disappeared patient."

"I see," she nodded thoughtfully. "I thought the police had received orders not to continue with the investigation."

"Yes, well, actually it was more like a personal initiative," Erik admitted.

"I'm sorry to have wasted your time, that was a necessary deception," she said, sounding sincere.

"May I ask you why?"

"Well…" she sighed. "It's a long history, but you have the right to know. You see, for years I struggled with the government to get the authorization to spread the vaccine, but to no avail."

Erik's eyes widened: the vaccine had existed… for years, even?

"I understand your dismay… and believe me, I agree with you. But my hands were tied. Even if I always wanted to share my discovery with Europa, I was never able to obtain authorization to do so. Eventually, I realized that I had to bring something else on the plate, something even more valuable than a vaccine."

"What?"

Anderson leaned forward: "Think about it: what did those infected have that we did not?"

"The plague?" Erik tried.

"No," she said "Dragons!"

There was an almost feverish excitement in her eyes.

"Thanks to the vaccine I knew that I would be able to control a dragon. Oh, don't worry," she added, noticing his alarmed expression. "That was an experimental version of the vaccine, very different from the one which is being injected to the population right now. None of them will ever have any side effects related to dragons. However, they accepted and I infiltrated among the rebels, with the fake identity of Lemaire, and eventually managed to rob them of a dragon."

Erik thought about the rumours that he had heard at the office: so it was true, there was a dragon in the hands of the government! Or in Anderson's hands? It wasn't clear.

"However, even that wasn't enough for the men in power. They didn't want to have the population vaccinated… they want to keep us docile and frightened, so we won't ever raise our heads to face them. Even now, this denigrating campaign being conducted against my vaccine…" she shook her head. "And there are people who are believing it! It's so frustrating!"

Erik thought of Thea: would she think it was right to oppose a cruel power, that was leaving people to die and chasing the infected? What would have she thought of Dr Anderson?

At that moment, more than ever, he would have liked to ask her for advice.

"Well, now you know the truth," Anderson concluded.

"I guess you'll want this to remain private…" Erik started.

"Oh no," she answered. "Not at all. Feel free to talk about it with whomever you want. Talk to your colleagues… Let them know for whom they are really working."

She got to her feet and Erik knew he was about to be dismissed.

Kathleen Anderson looked into his eyes: "Agent Persson, you look like a reasonable, committed person. We need people like you. I want to create a new city, a new world. Do you want to continue to support the people who have brought Europa to the brink of collapse?"

"Uhm, I…"

Erik felt dazed. It was too much information to elaborate in a few minutes.

Anderson reached into her pocket and pulled out a business card.

"This is my number. Think about it"

Erik shook her hand, and then looked at the card on which the telephone number of the scientist was marked.

Even the card bore the symbol of the rod of Asclepius he had noticed that on the façade of the building. Looking better, Erik realized that the snake looked more like a dragon.

CHAPTER 5

Sophie thought that her disease had very bad timing: when she was on the island, the infected could live freely and she had to implement every precaution not to catch the disease; now that she was the contagious one, they were in the city, so she still had to remain segregated in one of the houses controlled by the rebels.

Yet, even though she had to live as a prisoner and there were still no signs of improvement from Cain, all worries vanished when she was with her little dragon.

The puppy followed her everywhere, and his proximity filled her with enthusiasm and good spirits, the same feelings the creature felt in front of the new things he encountered every day.

"You should start leaving him in the cages with the others, at least at night," Famke had suggested. "The more you wait, the more difficult the separation will be."

Sophie knew she was probably right, but she couldn't find the strength to do so.

Nadia was right when she spoke of the bond with her dragon, she realized: at the time she had thought that her friend was overly melodramatic, and that Cain wasn't entirely wrong. The dragons, after all, were dangerous animals, not pets.

Yet, now that she was in the same situation, she realized how intense the relationship with them could be. She felt she was sharing the puppy's thoughts, feelings, emotions.

There was nothing in her previous life that had prepared her for such intimacy.

At that moment she was missing her friend very much; she had the feeling that only someone like her, who had been through the same experience, could understand how she felt.

Ken had told her that Nadia was fine and that she was in another ring with Karla.

Apparently, with the commotion that had followed the night in which Kathleen and the dragon escaped, no one had thought it was necessary to keep her captive. She was still separated from Taneen, though.

Sophie also realized that, even though she was locked up in that sort of bunker and had never crossed the threshold of the building, she was enjoying much more freedom than Nadia nor any other infected in contact with a dragon ever had.

Cain had applied an iron discipline on the relations with the dragons: Sophie shuddered at the thought of what Nadia had to go through, forcibly separated from Taneen for most of the time. No wonder she was always so angry or prone to violent mood swings.

Despite herself, she was surprised to feel a sort of sympathy for Kathleen and her actions... but then she scolded herself for such an absurd thought.

Kathleen had almost killed Cain, and she would never forgive her.

Now that Cain was in a coma, all the rebels seemed to wander aimlessly, unsure of what to do.

Amanda seemed to try to keep the ranks of the organization, but it soon became clear to Sophie that the other infected were not very prone to listen to someone who didn't share their condition.

Maybe it was overly paranoid, but Sophie was beginning to understand why they felt that way: after all, Amanda could always abandon them, go on her way, even betray them.

They, on the other hand, were forced to stand together and protect each other forever, because no one else could understand their marginalization. It was a sad but powerful bond.

The trio that had been close to Cain, Famke, Ken and Gregor, had difficulty finding a common line of action and a strategy to follow.

The situation was far from rosy, but the upside was that no one cared how Sophie and the dragon passed their days.

Only Famke, who had always taken care of the dragons and from which Sophie used to go to get food for herself, knew for certain that she was not following the rules that had been standing until then, but, apparently, she was willing to close an eye, or perhaps she simply had more important things to think about.

In any case, Sophie was not going to investigate: she was afraid to draw attention to herself.

"What's his name?" Famke asked her one day, giving her a bloody steak on which the puppy jumped hungrily.

"I'm not sure... They have a numeric sequence, right?"

She remembered that Nadia had said something similar about Taneen.

Famke raised her eyebrows: "You know what I mean. Nobody remembers those silly acronyms. What's the name you gave him?"

"Well, I thought... I'd like to call him Pasteur," Sophie confessed.

"That's a strange name for a dragon."

"He was as a great scientist!" Sophie protested. "His discoveries changed the world!"

Famke shrugged: "As you wish."

She patted the dragon's head, busy devouring the steak with his sharp teeth: "Good boy, Pat!"

"Don't call him Pat, come on, it's a stupid name!" Sophie laughed. In spite of herself, however, she had to admit that the diminutive suited him much better.

"I believe that a dragon should have an ancient name, as a great legend, like... Fáfnir," Famke added, sounding suddenly a bit sad.

"Who is Fáfnir?" Sophie asked.

"My dragon..."

Sophie was surprised: she had never seen Famke being interested in one of the creatures more than in the others.

"Which one is he?"

Famke ran her gaze on the cages where the dragons were locked: "He's not here, not anymore. We tried to use the dragons in battle, a few years ago but..." she shook her head. "We were never able to control them. The outcome was disastrous," she explained sadly.

"I'm so sorry."

"Thank you. But Sophie..." the woman sighed. "You must trust me when I tell you that you should start trying to keep him under control. Your Pat is used to get around as he likes, but it won't always be that way. How will he react when you'll need to lock him up here with others?

Sophie averted her gaze.

Why did they all speak of control and containment all the time? She didn't need to bring him under control... their wills were united. To make him do something, she only had to want it.

"Couldn't there be... I don't know, another way?" she tried.

It was Famke's turn of sounding uncertain: "To be honest it has been discussed in the past..."

"What do you mean?" Sophie asked, interested.

"Oh, you know, it was so long ago, but... well, there was a time in which, as I said, we thought that we could use them as a weapon, you know, in a battle. We have these huge and deadly beasts that spit fire, we said, certainly they could help. Some people, including, I must admit, myself, believed that we should have taken advantage of our relationship, deepen it. Cain has always been against it. But you know, his authority wasn't so strong back then, and we eventually decided to attempt.

At first, all went well, but when we were in the city, in front of the cops..." Famke sighed. "We didn't manage to hold them. It was like the smell of blood had made them mad. They just wanted to kill, destroy, shatter everything, and not just the police... Almost all the telepaths like me died: I saved myself because I managed to get away in time. I left Fáfnir..."

Her voice broke, and Famke was silent for a moment, her eyes glistening.

"I thought I wouldn't survive, you know. It was such a shock... for months I wasn't even able to get out of bed. It seemed that nothing made sense anymore but, in the end... I mean it, Sophie," she said at last. "Sooner or later you will have to start thinking about how to put a bridle on him."

Sophie looked over her shoulder, where Pat had climbed once his lunch was over. He too stared at Famke with his big golden-brown eyes, as if he understood every word.

Famke's story had given her the creeps, but something didn't quite add up.

"Your dragons were not used to trust you," Sophie objected. "They had spent years imprisoned and shackled. If you had kept them free from childhood, from birth..."

Famke shook her head: "I don't know Sophie, I really don't know. I would like to have all the answers, but I don't. Cain had always been so sure of his opinion, and so far the facts have always shown that he was right."

Sophie didn't know what to say, but at that moment she felt certain that Cain had always been wrong.

Later she went upstairs to look for something to eat for herself.

She was so hungry that she could have bitten the meat Famke had given Pat... in fact, it was the sight of that very steak that had made her hungry.

From the small kitchen, she could hear an unusual noise.

Sophie opened the door and she found a familiar figure with Ken, Gregor and Amanda.

"James!" Sophie exclaimed. "You're back!"

"Sophie? Damn, I almost didn't recognize you!" he said, stepping back to give her a better look.

She shrugged, embarrassed: "Yeah. My new plague look."

Even if the other infected didn't seem ashamed of their appearance, Sophie wasn't yet used to her new scaly face, and the fact that all those that met her did nothing but comment about it made her feel very uncomfortable. Of course, she winced even more every time she looked in the mirror over the sink, but she didn't want to think about it.

"Yes, that's not bad," James laughed. "But I'd say you look great in general."

She couldn't say the same about him. He looked unusually gaunt and tense as if he had suddenly aged since the last time that she had seen him.

"I'm not on my deathbed anymore, yay," Sophie replied, raising both thumbs without great enthusiasm. Enough of talking about her scales, she decided. "Where have you been all this time?"

"Here and there. I was- Wait, what the hell is that?!" he suddenly exclaimed.

Sophie realized that Pat had climbed on her shoulder again. He did it so often that she had stopped noticing.

"I call him Pasteur," she explained, stroking his head.

James still looked troubled: "And... what is it doing here?"

Gregor snorted: "Our little princess here thinks it's fun to carry it around like a chihuahua in a bag," he spat out. "You know, a cautious thing to do, reasonable, totally safe."

"Oh, by the way..." James changed the subject, much to Sophie's relief. "We had to move from the seventh ring north. There were too many cops around... I don't know if it was a coincidence, but the area was no longer safe."

"Shit," Gregor commented.

"Heinrich and Jane?" Ken asked.

"They went to the fifth ring. They have cell phones, but I think they should pass through the underground city, therefore they might not work for a while."

There was a moment of silence.

"So, how did it go?" Gregor finally asked, turning to Amanda.

Sophie noticed only at that moment that the latter was dressed in a different way than usual and she wore a wig of long hair, which made her look curiously demurer and more vulnerable.

"Done. I did it," Amanda said, smiling. "They didn't ask me anything, I only had to sign a paper. I used a fake name, but no one checked."

She took off her wig, rolled up her sleeve and showed them a patch with a piece of cotton secured to the arm.

Sophie took a moment to understand: "You got vaccinated?"

"Yes," Amanda confirmed. "It's so weird, I've been with you so long that I thought it wouldn't change anything but..." she chuckled nervously. "I have to admit that I feel so much better since I did it. It was like a boulder has been taken off my chest, if you know what I mean!"

Sophie gave a strained smile, and she noticed that also all the others didn't know what to say.

Rationally she was happy for Amanda, but, at the same time, she felt bitter because she would never have the same security that her friend had. For all of them, now, the hope of a normal life was over.

"It should have been our vaccine," she said, a little disappointed.

"Ours might not be ready for years," Amanda answered. "And this one is already here, nice and ready and even free…"

Sophie shrugged: "Yes, well, I understand that you must have been so afraid to stay in the same room with us…" She suddenly felt very annoyed, and she didn't understand exactly why.

Was it for all the useless work they had done in the past years? Or was she jealous because in the end Amanda was able to overcome the epidemic unscathed and she didn't?

Pat began hopping nervously from one of her shoulders to the other.

"What are you talking about?" her friend asked. "I've never been afraid of the infected, you know it. But you also know that… oh, really, you're trying to guilt-trap me because I took an entirely reasonable precaution to protect my life?" she snapped.

Sophie suddenly wanted to leave the room: "I… no… I don't know!" she admitted. She realized that her heart was pounding, and she was breathing heavily. She felt very stupid and irrational, but she couldn't calm down.

"Someone is starting to have a bad dragon day, huh?" Gregor said, apparently amused.

Sophie felt she hated him.

"Go fuck yourself!" she exploded, then left the room.

The dragon gave a belligerent bark and followed her.

CHAPTER 6

The meeting with Kathleen Anderson had left Erik very upset.

Although it was the doctor herself who had urged him to talk to his colleagues about what he had discovered, Erik had not yet said a word to anyone.

He didn't feel like talking about it until he had wrapped his mind around it.

At one time he could have asked Thea for advice... but he tried to dismiss the thought.

Even his attempts to contact Maja and Peter had not borne fruit. They ignored his calls, pressing the voice mail button on the first ring.

At least that way he knew they were all right, Erik thought sadly. If sometimes the phones had not been ringing for minutes, he would have had the doubt that they had been disconnected.

He wanted to show up at Maja's flat and force them to talk to him, but he also thought that perhaps the best thing at that time was to leave to his children their own space and time to mourn the death of their mother.

When his thoughts were not troubled by the thought of Maja and Peter, they kept going back to what Kathleen Anderson had told him.

On one hand, it seemed incredible that his whole life had been a lie: he had spent twenty years waging war to the infected when the vaccine had always been available. For years he had taken pride at the thought of doing something that could save the lives of his family and all the inhabitants of Europa, and now he had been told that it had been nothing but a farce.

The idea was so shocking to make him dizzy.

Yet, Kathleen Anderson had spoken of a new Europa, a new world. Surely, she was trying to create a world free of the scourge of the plague.

Would that be a better one?

However, to make up his mind about the vaccine, he also started to read about the therapies that Janssen and the other detractors of Anderson proposed as an alternative.

Although the vaccine was distributed free of charge, they said, it was just a perverse strategy to maintain the economic interests of major companies such as Anderson Pharmaceuticals.

The plague was in remission, according to them, and the vaccine was nothing more than a useless palliative to psychologically enslave the population, making them believe that Anderson had their best on her mind, when in fact she just wanted to get richer and richer.

Some said that, along with the vaccine, the company injected some psychotropic substances to control the mind of the community.

Others claimed that the vaccine contained toxic substances that would generate a disease in a few years, in order to make people dependent on medical care that Anderson herself would sell them.

Janssen had also passed him some very illegal documents showing that the doctor was still studying a cure for the dragon plague.

"Why would she still seek a cure if the disease could be eradicated by the vaccine?" he asked. "It's clear that even she doesn't really believe in this hoax. Don't you understand? She just wants the government to lower their guard on the security measures of the plague, so she can sell the cure to the future infected!"

Besides being the basis of these long-term strategies, the colleague claimed, the vaccine also had dangerous side effects that Anderson Pharmaceuticals persisted in denying: in some cases it had triggered terrible immune reactions, leading to anaemia, asthma, kidney failure and even unsightly pimples.

Erik didn't know what to believe: both Anderson's revelations and those of her detractors sounded like fiction to him.

The government, on their part, gave no official response, but they weren't even doing anything to oppose the campaign against the doctor and her vaccine. Everyone had expected decrees and laws to encourage their population to be immunized, but they had never arrived.

Since he had gone to the medical centre with Laurent, he agreed to accompany Janssen to a meeting of anti-vaccination activists.

Laurent obviously refused, and even in that case Lara Meyer refused to participate since she thought that it was, in her own words, 'a bunch of nonsense.'

"You won't be disappointed, believe me!" Janssen, instead, had assured him. "These people have opened my eyes."

The meeting took place in a poorly lighted, humid basement.

Erik was not entirely sure of the degree of clandestineness of the association: technically there was no reason to keep everything so secret. But, he thought, maybe the air of subterfuge fed the attractiveness of the meeting, giving the participants the impression that they were acting against a conspiracy bigger than themselves.

In the room, there were about fifty chairs, almost all occupied, and a desk where the speakers sat.

The participants did not look particularly subversive, Erik marvelled, realizing with embarrassment that he had imagined a crowd of misfits like the inhabitants of the underground city.

Instead, much like his colleague Janssen and himself, they were normal people; indeed, many of them had the distinguished and tidy look of the inhabitants of the inner rings. They all seemed quite young, he noticed, about twenty-five, thirty-years-old.

Erik noticed that almost all looked as if they knew each other, greeting amicably and exchanging small talk about their families.

He sat in the back rows, only willing to listen.

The speaker, a man in his forties with a beard, asked who was there for the first time, and only Erik and a couple that looked like newlyweds raised their hands.

"Welcome!" the speaker said. "If you are here it's because you don't let yourselves be deluded by the comfortable lies that the real criminals of Europa are trying to spoon-feed us, so let me congratulate you!"

Erik merely gave a polite smile, while all present eyed him with approval.

"First," the speaker continued, "we will be distributing some studies that I just received from sources very close to the health ministry. It seems that the government wanted to spread them to deter all the citizens of Europa to continue with this madness of the anti-plague vaccine, but Dr Anderson is putting everything to silence."

An angry murmur filled the hall.

"I know," the bearded guy nodded. "That woman has a sprawling power, even our institutions are not safe anymore."

Erik was passed a pile sheets photocopied and stapled together with a paper clip, with alarming-looking titles: 'VACCINE: HERE'S HOW ANDERSON PHARMACEUTICALS IS POISONING EUROPA' or 'VACCINATED TODAY, SICK TOMORROW: AND IT'S ANDERSON WHO PROFITS'. This article was accompanied by a grotesque caricature of Kathleen Anderson, who was represented as a witch who stretched her clawed hands on the city.

"At the bottom, you can find the summary of the abstract of the study that I found. It is an incontrovertible proof that not only the plague vaccine does not immunize against the disease at all, but rather only serves to expose your body to all kinds of inflammation, which will cause you to contract many more diseases and then to buy more medicines!" he declaimed.

Next to Erik, Janssen shook his head, and the rest of the audience seemed to have a similar reaction, as if what the bearded man had said merely confirmed the suspicions that they had always had.

Erik flipped through the file to the designated part, but he had the impression that the evidence was not as decisive as the speaker argued: firstly, there was no information on the size of the sample population studied, nor the method by which it was conducted; furthermore, the conclusions looked a bit too hasty. Erik was not an expert in medicine and research, but he knew that it was difficult to reach such certain results with no error margin, especially in such a short time.

"Also, do you know what is in one dose of the vaccine, like the one that right now, before our very eyes, that is being injected to lots and lots of unsuspecting people?" the bearded guy continued "Formaldehyde!"

The audience seemed disgusted.

"Yes!" the speaker nodded. "The same substance that is used on CORPSES!"

Many gasped, shocked.

Erik could not help himself and spoke: "Excuse me, but a vaccine, like any medicine, contain preservatives, otherwise they could not deploy it on a large scale... if they prepared it and injected it within a few hours, it would be very impractical," he said. "The discriminating factor is the dose used, isn't it?"

The bearded man looked at him with contempt: "Oh, the usual objection. You feel comfortable letting yourself be injected with a toxic substance? To your own body? To one of your children?"

"Well... Yes?" Erik tried, a little taken aback. "Well, this is a low dose, even when we take a simple medicine for high temperature..."

"I would never use medicine for high temperature!" a woman declared. "Fever is a natural reaction of the body's defence, which must be left to drain and then heal completely."

"Yeah, ok," Erik admitted. "But if it rises above a certain threshold..."

"Worst case scenario, you can apply cold compresses," she conceded. "Nature has thought of everything," she concluded, with a confident smile.

The rest of the onlookers nodded.

Erik had the impression of being in the middle of an assembly of lunatics.

"The real question is: why should we compromise our health by letting ourselves be inoculated with the principles of disease topped with poisons and all sorts of crap? Why should we take that risk?" the speaker asked again.

Erik couldn't restrain himself anymore: "Have you ever seen an infected who contracted the plague?" he scoffed. "Have you ever seen the boils, have you ever heard their screams? You all look very young, maybe you don't remember the first wave of the plague, the worst one. People were dying in the streets... families were destroyed, institutions collapsed... do you have any idea of how easily it could all happen again?!"

He realized that he had screamed.

Everyone looked at him as if he was insane, including Janssen.

"Come on Janssen, you of all people!" Erik urged him. "How many infected have you seen since you joined the police?"

"Ah, you are from the police?" the bearded man asked. "It just so happens that you come here to try and discredit our arguments, that's rather suspicious, isn't it?" he pointed out.

Erik realized that the way in which the audience was looking at him quickly went from baffled to openly hostile.

"I wasn't discrediting anything!" Janssen exclaimed. "I share your views... I'm on your side!"

"Oh, sure, you surely can't blow both your covers!" another guy jumped up.

"Cover? That's ridiculous!"

The crowd began to roar, and finally the bearded spoke again: "I have to ask you to leave," he said.

"But I didn't do anything!" Janssen protested.

"Both of you, before we throw you out!"

Erik got up, very happy to get the hell out of there.

When they were outside, Janssen twisted his arm and faced him: "Hey, what's gotten into you? Why did you have to make a scene? Now they all hate me!"

Erik was shocked: "What are you talking about? Those are lunatics! Don't you see it?"

"Ah, *they* are the lunatics?" Janssen scoffed. "And you, who spend your days staring into the void? Every time someone tells you something it looks like you're about to have a nervous breakdown! No one ever knows how you will react!" he shouted. "Who's the lunatic now, huh?"

Erik stood still, not knowing what to say.

Was this what his colleagues thought of him? It was true, after Thea's death he never felt completely like himself, but he didn't believe...

Janssen took a deep breath too and seemed to calm down: "Look Persson, I'm sorry, I..."

"It doesn't matter. Stop," Erik interrupted him.

"Really, I didn't mean..."

"I said it doesn't matter. Now I just want to go home."

He walked to the train station, without looking back.

At first, he was afraid that his colleague would follow him, but soon he realized that Janssen had left him alone.

Not only what was left of his family despised him, but also his colleagues regarded him as an unpredictable psychotic, he thought.

He wondered if that was the reason why Meyer, although she had said she wanted to know more about the vaccine, never wanted to accompany him in his research.

While waiting for the train that would bring him to his empty house, Erik realized that there was only one thing he could do.

He picked up the phone and dialled the number that was on the card that he carried in his pocket since the day he received it.

"Dr Anderson, this is Erik Persson. I hope I'm not disturbing you... I wanted to know if your offer is still valid."

CHAPTER 7

After the first burst of anger after Amanda's vaccination, Sophie discovered that it was more and more difficult to control her aggressiveness.

This difficulty was growing together with Pat's size: if, at first, he looked like a little dog, now he was much closer to the size of a calf or a pony.

He had not started to spit fire yet, and when he was with Sophie his mood was usually playful, but in front of strangers he became defensive, and Sophie herself found it very difficult to curb her negative emotions.

For this reason, she continued to spend most of the time alone with the dragon: she had the impression that only he could fully understand how she felt, and he was the only one who never said or did something that made her upset.

She tried to avoid all other people as much as possible, including Amanda. They had almost always gotten along until then, but, at that moment, it seemed that everything her friend said had the power to make her feel angry and misunderstood.

She couldn't always avoid leaving her room, but she tried to limit her movements to when she didn't hear any noise coming from the corridor. It wasn't particularly difficult since everyone seemed to be moving chaotically, running from one refuge to another without knowing exactly what to do and how to move.

Every so often, she heard voices about the government that was getting increasingly weak and Kathleen Anderson that was acquiring a growing segment of supporters, people who felt she had to be the one to rule Europa.

That she didn't like, but it all seemed so far away from her concerns that she didn't have the patience to be interested.

One day she left her room cautiously, closely followed by Pat, as always, with the intent of going into the kitchen and have her lunch.

She had heard the front door close just moments before and since then there had been only silence, so she was reasonably sure there was no one around.

Unfortunately, she was wrong.

"Oh, you're still alive. We thought that by now the rats were devouring your corpse." said a contemptuous voice behind her.

Sophie turned: it was Gregor. He moved silently, and he was always the most difficult one to detect, Sophie thought, cursing to herself.

She had not seen him since the day she had told him to go to hell. She had even considered apologizing, but, now that he was before her, she discovered that she would have liked to insult him again.

"I was going to eat something," Sophie muttered, hoping to get him out of the way.

Gregor instead stepped in front of her, blocking her way.

"And then you'll disappear again?" he asked. "Do you think that if you stay locked in there long enough everyone will forget that you have a dragon out of control?"

"I'm doing great. Now let me pass," she tried to cut him short.

But Gregor didn't seem willing to give her a break: "You can't even control yourself."

He walked towards her, looking threatening, and she stepped back.

Why didn't he leave her alone? Sophie felt a fury growing inside her. Pat began to growl.

"Let me pass," she repeated.

Gregor instead stepped further towards, forcing her to retreat.

"Or else?" he challenged her, giving her a shove on the shoulder.

Sophie looked away, not wanting to argue with him... but she was feeling more and more angry, more furious...

She took another step back and felt the wall behind her.

He gave her another nudge against her shoulder: "What will you do? Will you make me attack by your giant chicken?"

Sophie felt trapped, while Gregor loomed over her, with his infected pale face closer and closer to hers.

She felt an icy chill run down her back and remembered how he had shot Nadia without batting an eyelid.

"Leave me alone," she murmured again.

"Otherwise? Huh?" he teased her.

"I said LEAVE ME ALONE!" she shouted, and, before she realized what she was doing, she attacked him.

A second later she was on top of him, hitting him with all her might with kicks and punches, while Pat too tried to scratch his face with his sharp claws.

Sophie could no longer think straight: she only felt anger, desire to hurt him, to get him out of the way...

We can kill him, tear him to pieces, we can destroy it, we can...

"That's enough," Gregor said. A moment later, Sophie felt she was being tipped over, and with one quick movement, Gregor forced her to the ground, with one knee pointed to her chest, while his hands nailed Pat's neck against the wall.

Sophie struggled for a moment, shouting all her frustration with inconsistent groans, while Pat hissed and tried to cough puffs of black smoke.

After a while, however, she felt the anger wane away as it had arrived, until she just lay on the ground out of breath, feeling very embarrassed.

"Do you understand what I mean now?" Gregor simply asked, standing up and letting go of Pat, who crouched near Sophie.

She just nodded, sitting on the floor.

Had it been her who had attacked Gregor so brutally? She felt like what had happened a few minutes before was enveloped in a hazy mist as if she hadn't been quite herself.

"I'm sorry," she said, after a moment of silence. "Usually I'm not... like that," she tried to explain.

Gregor sat down beside her.

"You are now. It's a part of you that will always be there," he said. "We've all been there. But you have to do something to learn how to control yourself, or you'll be a danger to yourself and us too. And as long as you are with the dragon, it will be even more difficult."

"I don't want to be apart from him," Sophie said, absently stroking Pat's back. "I can't do it... I don't believe that there can't be another way."

Gregor shrugged: "Cain always said that aggressiveness that we feel comes from dragons and keeping them away would help us overcome it."

"But this theory doesn't work, does it?" Sophie objected. "Even all the infected who are not in telepathic contact with a dragon have these outbursts. And I don't think the problem has disappeared for those who have held the dragon at a distance."

"This is what Cain said," Gregor insisted. "For him, it worked. You saw him, didn't you? He was always very self-possessed."

Sophie thought about what she had heard from Kathleen Anderson, that night... Cain hated the dragon that he heard in his mind, and he had spent his whole life striving to silence him.

But if someone had used the same way to improve the communication, rather than eliminate it...

Only it wasn't possible to talk to him. Cain was still in a coma, only the empty shell of his old self.

"I don't know how Cain did it," she admitted. "I don't even know where to begin," she added disconsolately.

She didn't see how locking Pat up in a cage in the basement could help her, but if she couldn't find an alternative sooner or later she would have to. For now, only Famke was on her side, and she seemed more worried every time she looked at the dragon almost visibly growing.

"Come on, down with that long face," Gregor urged her. "Maybe I have something that can help you."

He got up and led her into the next room, where mobile phones (antiquated handheld models), maps and a stack of dusty boxes were messily piled up.

Pat immediately began to nibble at a metal box in the corner.

"This is Cain's stuff," Gregor explained. "When we evacuated the island in a hurry, we brought with us everything that he had already packed. It isn't exactly what I would have chosen to keep," he added with a grimace, "but maybe it can be useful to you," he said, dropping a heavy box in her arms.

Sophie opened it and found a series of books, all dealing with meditation, breathing, guided relaxation.

"Try to calm your mind, and perhaps, who knows, in the end you'll be able to control that dragon of yours too," Gregor said.

"Thank you," Sophie said, flipping through the volumes. They had evidently been read many times and for a long time; they showed signs of wear, ears on the pages and underlined sentences.

Was it Cain who had read them so much? She ran her fingers through the pages, wondering how many times he had done the same.

"I hope you don't expect me to stay here to watch you do the double lotus pose or some crap like that," Gregor shook her from her thoughts. "In case you hadn't noticed we have an emergency here: we had to give up two shelters in a hurry. We are getting busted out like newbies. Ten years of this and we are still a bunch of fucking amateurs," he added, more to himself than to Sophie.

"What did you do before you got infected?" she asked, suddenly curious.

Before she got the plague herself, she had always considered all the infected as if they were more or less the same, as if everyone was born with the disease and there had been nothing before.

It was disconcerting to think that all of them must have had a normal life before, like herself.

"I used to work with that asshole, Christian Voigt," Gregor replied.

"Secret services? Really?"

He looked at her with disdain: "Who do you think organized the whole network of informers that allowed us to survive up to now? Cain? Think again."

Now that she thought about it, it wasn't hard to imagine Gregor as a spy or a secret agent. Even with the signs of the plague, he had an anonymous, ordinary face. He always stayed in a corner, as if wrapped on himself, so that it was easy to forget that he was there until he spoke.

"Were you a big shot then?"

"Not big enough for the vaccine, it seems," he replied.

"Is there where you learned that ninja move you used before? Can you teach me?" Sophie asked eagerly. "That'd be useful."

Surely it couldn't require much physical strength, because, much like herself, Gregor was neither tall nor especially strong-looking.

"First try to learn not to have a fit whenever someone contradicts you, and then we'll think about the 'ninja moves'." he scoffed. "Seriously, keep the beast at bay. He's learning to breathe fire, you don't have much time."

In the following weeks, Sophie studied the books she had received and tried to do the exercises that were described.

It was much more difficult than it seemed since the authors did not foresee the possibility of having an overly enthusiastic puppy in telepathic contact that hindered her throughout the meditation exercises.

She didn't know what to expect, but if the aim was to create a vacuum in the mind and hold off Pat's thoughts, then was failing miserably: the more she focused, the more the bond with the dragon became intense and deep.

In addition to his more superficial emotions, now, she could also perceive his increasingly articulated thoughts.

It was not the only side effect.

Sophie remembered what Kathleen had said about her dragon, that since they had reunited, she had felt stronger and healthier than ever.

She, too, was feeling this kind of change: not only was she feeling physically stronger, but it also seemed like she was able to think and react with greater speed.

This, however, often gave her a severe headache, and she needed many hours of sleep to fully recover.

She was, in fact, sleeping when Ken woke her with a start.

"You must come immediately," he said. "It's Cain. He's having a crisis."

Sophie immediately felt alert and rushed into the room where Cain was, always attached to the machines that were monitoring his conditions.

His body was shaken by violent convulsions, and Sophie thought he looked smaller and gauntier than ever.

She had to remain calm, however: she checked the status of the pupils and the pressure.

"He could be having an aneurysm... we should get an MRI."

"We can't do an MRI here," Ken objected.

"I know, I know..." Sophie said, frantically trying to think. What should she do? If it was an aneurysm, she would have to perform a surgery, but she had never done such an operation before, not to mention the fact that she didn't have any specific equipment and...

"Where's Amanda?" she asked. "We must call her, she must come at once..."

"She's on the other side of the city, it will take at least a couple of hours to get her here."

Could they wait that long? Probably not.

But, if she performed a craniotomy, she could compromise his brain functions... she was not a qualified surgeon.

She could paralyze him, give him coordination issues, or make him lose all memory... she could damage him forever.

But if she did nothing, he might never wake up at all...

"Sophie? What should we do?" Ken pressed, in a panic.

She took a deep breath.

"Ok. Let's do the surgery."

CHAPTER 8

Erik was darting through the streets aboard a large black car with tinted windows.

The new job as head of security at Anderson Pharmaceuticals had a number of significant benefits, such as the use of a company car.

Although he had felt very sad about leaving the police, where he had worked for more than twenty years, he was more than ever convinced that he had made the right decision.

Besides the fact that managing security for Anderson was far more stimulating than having to cope with all of Hoffman's bureaucratic work, as well as more profitable, the aspect that Erik preferred was the feeling that he was doing something useful and good for the whole city.

If Anderson had made an impression on him at their first meeting, she had now definitely conquered him.

Erik admired her enthusiasm, her strength, the energy she put into her projects.

He was convinced that if there had been someone like her in a position of power, Europa would change for the better: they could have a city without the threat of plague, managed without corruption, in which the government dealt with the problems of real people instead of hiding everything under the carpet, or, in that case, in underground tunnels.

He was not the only one to think so: if at first managing the personal safety of Kathleen Anderson seemed a secondary aspect of his new job, Erik soon realized that it was becoming his biggest challenge.

In addition to Anderson's bodyguards and all the personnel involved in the protection of her medical centres, every day enthusiastic people who wanted to support her in her mission showed up.

Perhaps she wasn't aware of it, Erik thought, but the truth was that she was gathering an army.

It was vital to try to immediately remove suspicious individuals, probably sent by the government to check on them.

Not that she had anything to hide, Erik was certain: since he had been there, Kathleen had done nothing but lavish all she could to others, continuing to study a cure for the plague and dispensing her free vaccine. While following her closely, he had never seen her engaged in shady or vaguely criminal activities: she had never asked for money or favours, nor had she ever met any of the corrupt personalities that populated the political life of Europa.

She was a true benefactor, Erik reflected: besides, she didn't need to compromise with anyone.

Besides having considerable financial resources of her own and growing popular support, Anderson had a weapon that was the object of many rumours, but few had seen live: her huge dragon.

Erik had seen it many times, but only from a distance, in the large park surrounding the doctor's mansion: it was an impressive, dangerous-looking creature.

He had already seen one of the rebels' dragons in action, but he felt that it had nothing to do with Anderson's one.

The latter could eat a cow in one mouthful, Erik had estimated.

The doctor, however, approached it fearlessly, called it 'Fuzzi' and cuddled it as if it was a big puppy. As responsible for her safety, he had tried to urge her to be more cautious, but she had only laughed off his concern.

"He could never hurt me," she had explained. "He and I are one thing."

The only sacrifice that he had to make since he was hired was to drastically reduce his cigarettes: Anderson could not stand that he smoked in her presence because, in her opinion, it was a suicidal habit, which damaged others too.

Erik knew she was right, but he suspected that part of her aversion was also due to the fact that the dragon was exceptionally alert when he was near a flame or any flammable material, as he had noted the first time he had tried to use the lighter in its proximity.

However, it was not a sacrifice that burdened him as much as he had feared.

Thea would have been happy, she had always urged him to stop smoking.

A few days before he was finally able to get news of Peter and Maja: ironically, the only one who agreed to talk to him was Marc Werner, Maja's boyfriend, whom he had found so obnoxious in their first meetings.

He was still slimy and over-smiling, but Erik had never been happier to receive a call.

He had told him that Maja and Peter were fine, although they were still 'quite shaken.' Peter didn't even contemplate talking to him, as he had very tactfully made clear, but Maja seemed more open to discussion. Erik had plans to try again to call in the following weeks and hoped that for once she would respond.

Meanwhile, he had given Marc all his new numbers (he had to return his phone to the police when he resigned).

He parked in front of the train station and went inside: it didn't take long to identify the agent he was looking for.

Zoe Hernandez was doing the usual routine checks to all the people passing by.

She looked very bored and kept carrying out her task, rarely raising her eyes from the sensor.

"Hello Zoe!" he greeted her.

His face lit up when she recognized him: "Erik! What are you doing here? You look dapper," she said, observing him. He was wearing a suit with the symbol of Anderson Pharmaceuticals on the breast pocket, which was definitely more formal than the hospital guard uniform and also than the regular clothes he usually wore at the police headquarter.

"I changed jobs," he told her. "Can you take a two-minute break?"

"I think so."

Zoe nodded to one of her colleagues, who replaced her, so she could get away with Erik.

Erik asked her what she had done in recent months and saw her bitterness in describing the abrupt demotion that Hoffman had imposed.

Then it was his turn to tell her briefly about his decision to resign from the police and about his new job with Dr Anderson.

Erik didn't even try to hide his enthusiasm for his new employer, but Zoe seemed a bit sceptical.

"So you don't believe all the strange rumours that circulate about her?" she asked.

"Like the fact that the vaccine is unnecessary and causes other diseases? Absolutely not," he replied.

He had got vaccinated shortly after deciding to accept the proposal from Dr Anderson: apart from a slight fever the day after the injection, he was fine.

"Well, not only that," Hernandez elaborated. "They say she experiments on people forcibly taken from the underground city, and none of them come out alive..."

"Oh, come on!" Erik laughed. "I assure you that I've never seen anyone being dragged in the laboratories! Don't tell me that you believe this nonsense."

"This is what they say," she defended herself. "They also say she spread the plague to steal the properties of all the dead infected, and that's how she became so rich."

"If you met her, you would be sure too that it's nothing more than a squalid slander," he assured.

"And also that she has a dragon and he and she killed an entire squad of policemen at the parliament," Hernandez said.

Erik hesitated: "Well, there is a dragon," he admitted, "this is true. But I can't believe that Kathleen could ever do such a thing!"

"Ah, 'Kathleen'... already calling her by her first name, huh?" Zoe teased him. "Anyway, are you serious? That woman has a dragon? Wow," she commented, impressed. "That I'd like to see."

"And what if I told you that 'that woman', as you say, has an urgent need for a bodyguard and I'm looking for someone I can trust? Would you be interested?" Erik proposed.

Zoe looked at him in surprise: it was evident that she hadn't expected it.

"Well, I understand that your heart bleeds at the very thought of leaving all of this behind," he joked, pointing at the decrepit station around them. "But perhaps the offer may interest you."

He took out a bunch of papers in which the job offer was detailed. Although he did not know in detail about Hernandez's current wage, the one offered by Anderson was a much higher salary than the one that his former colleague probably earned.

Zoe flipped briefly through them: "Do you think I would leave the police to be the bodyguard of a mob agitator with a sinister reputation for a few extra credits?"

"Well, yes."

She shrugged: "You're right. When do we start?"

CHAPTER 9

Cain had been moved from the operating table to his makeshift bed and kept sleeping, seemingly oblivious to everything that had happened.

Sophie felt exhausted, yet she still had too much adrenaline in her system to be able to fall asleep.

Even Pat tossed at her feet, trying to bite his tail.

She kept wondering if she had taken the right decision, performing a craniotomy on Cain.

On one hand, she was convinced that yes, there had been a brain haemorrhage and Sophie believed that she had been able to isolate it completely with long and delicate work.

On the other hand, she had run a huge risk: what if she had damaged some areas of his brain?

Maybe she had left him paralyzed, unable to speak or...

She felt tears pricking her eyes at the thought.

Amanda had arrived late at night and had helped Sophie in the last stages of the operation when she was about to close the incision.

At the time she had just helped to complete the surgery, but once Cain's skull bone had been set back in its seat, she had pulled her aside: "Sophie, what on earth got into your mind?" she had asked her. "This is a delicate operation, in these conditions... it's a miracle he didn't die on the operating table."

"If I had waited, it could have been much worse!" Sophie had protested.

"Or maybe not. We could have started with the anti-oedema, and then try to limit the embolization... My God, Sophie, you've got to think twice before you open a person's head!"

"I... I did," she defended herself.

Now that Amanda was saying that, Sophie felt very stupid.

What had she done?

Yet a part of her was intimately convinced that she had done the right thing. The drugs would not be enough, she knew. And, deep down, she knew that she had carried out the surgery in the best possible way.

She had worked long hours, but at the time they had seemed like a few minutes: she had been careful, very concentrated. Even too concentrated for her normal ability... Had it really been her credit?

At times she thought she perceived the presence of the dragon in her mind as if to help her by providing more energy and all his powers of concentration. It was as if they had acted together.

She wondered whether it was right.

Surely, at that moment, it was a huge advantage, because in good conscience she didn't think she would have been able to work alone and in those conditions without his help; but shouldn't the meditation exercises have helped to isolate her mind from Pat's?

Why did she feel him more and more present in her mind instead?

In any case, Cain was now breathing freely, his heartbeat was regular and the pressure had dropped to acceptable levels.

There were clips of metal on his skull, where she had to shave him completely.

It was a shame, she thought, he had such beautiful hair, so soft and thick... but it would regrow, she thought, even more beautiful than before.

She wondered in which state he would be when he would awaken and could not help but wonder if it would ever happen.

The more the time passed, the more the possibility seemed unlikely; and yet she knew it didn't mean anything, there had been many cases in which patients awoke even after years.

Someone knocked on the door, then opened it without waiting for an answer.

"Come in the other room," Gregor ordered. "There are problems, you have to listen too."

"What problems?"

She was too tired to withstand another crisis: she just wanted to get to sleep and possibly forget the possibly disastrous consequences of her actions.

"Get a move and come, I don't want to explain the same thing twenty times," he replied, preceding her in the hallway. "And leave your chicken in your room, please."

Amiable as ever, Sophie thought, rolling her eyes.

She brought Pat to her room, then followed Gregor.

The room that served as living room, meeting room and management centre of what was left of them was more crowded than usual; other than Famke, Ken, James and Gregor, there were also some infected that Sophie had seen little of: a couple named Heinrich and Jane, a curly-haired man named Paul and a short and plump woman that she believed was called Marie.

Amanda was not there, she noticed. It was probably considered a meeting for plague bearers only.

In one corner she also saw Brit, looking gloomy as usual.

She gave her a nod, but the elderly looked away.

Apparently, not everyone had decided to forget the fact that she had been the one to bring Kathleen Anderson in the heart of their headquarters, she thought.

Sophie went and sit next to Famke.

"I will get to the point right away," Gregor began. "Turns out that those we thought were safe havens are actually not. There are people, probably undercover agents, who are patrolling the surrounding areas."

He pulled out a map of Europa on which several points were marked with red circles.

"This one's gone," he said, drawing an X on a black circle located in the seventh ring. "As Jane was telling me, they were forced to flee in a hurry."

"They knew we were there!" Jane confirmed. She still appeared shaken. "They started checking around, but they had a precise idea of what they were looking for. Fortunately, Heinrich found a way through the underground tunnels, or else…"

"Right," Gregor snapped. "Anyway, we had to leave those too," he explained, marking most other points with an X. "This, this and this…" he continued, always drawing black signs on the map. "Essentially only this house and another in the fourth ring remain. But if they know the others, it's likely they will soon come here too."

"How did this happen?!" Famke exclaimed. "Gregor, you said you had the situation under control!"

"I thought I did!" he defended himself. "And none of our informants in the police and secret services seem to know anything. I don't know how it's possible, but..."

"Maybe these informants of yours are not as trustworthy as you say," Famke accused.

"Why, do you have others? No? Then, please, shut up."

"I'll shut up when you will too!"

"Please, this is not the time to argue," James interrupted them. "The point is, where do we go now? Where can we accommodate nine hundred people without letting the police discover us?"

No one answered.

"Gregor?" James tried again.

He sighed: "I can still get you maybe ten abandoned flats, but no more. And we can't hide in there by the dozen, it would be too suspicious. Three, four persons per house at max."

"And the others?"

Gregor shrugged and looked down.

"The underground city? But it's too dangerous!" Famke protested. "The risk that even a single person may get infected..."

"I don't like the idea either, but I don't see any alternative."

Sophie was opening her mouth to ask a question when she was preceded.

"Where are we putting the dragons?" Marie asked.

Sophie noticed that some of them, like her, seemed very alert; others, especially Ken and Gregor, appeared uncomfortable. Famke didn't seem able to look up from the ground.

"Well..." Ken began. "I know it will be an unpopular proposal but... I think we should consider the idea of not taking them with us."

"What? Are you kidding?" Marie was shocked. "How can you think of leaving six, no, seven dragons roaming in the city?"

Ken looked at James, who looked away.

Sophie shivered when she realized what they were suggesting. "No!" she shouted. "You can't do it... It would be inhumane!"

"You want to kill them?" Jane gasped. "Have you gone mad?"

Heinrich and Paul also began to protest vehemently, and it took James quite a while before he could calm them down and speak again.

"Look, we must speak clearly. The dragons are wonderful, and I know how much you all love them. But they are dangerous, and we don't know how to control them. And we have nowhere to hide. If we are around them, the risk of being caught increases exponentially..."

"Rather than let you kill Cosette, I prefer to surrender to the medical police myself," Marie growled softly.

"Please try to be logical for a moment..." Ken tried.

"I agree!" Britt, who until that moment had been silent, exclaimed. "Those beasts have never done anything but damages."

"I'm leaving, and I'm bringing my dragon with me," Heinrich announced, standing up. "Just try and stop me."

"Good idea Heinrich, I like that," Gregor said, sarcastic. "Just tell me, where are you going? Oh, wait, it seems you know a safe place, unknown to the police, with ample space to keep a big flying beast, don't you?"

"I know it," Sophie realized at that moment.

Everyone turned to look at her.

"Where would that be?" Ken asked wearily.

"In the underground city... there is a cathedral, underground," Sophie explained. "I was there last year, while I was running away from the police. There's plenty of space, it's huge! There was a flood, they had to go in a hurry... but maybe it's still empty, maybe they haven't returned and..."

"There are a little too many 'maybes' in your proposal," Gregor pointed out.

"But it's worth checking, isn't it?" Marie supported her. "It would be the perfect place for our dragons!"

"Yes, indeed!" Sophie confirmed. "I can find it, I'm sure!"

She wasn't. She remembered passing through a manhole and walking for a long time, completely blind, in dark tunnels full of mice. But she would find it, she promised herself, at the cost of spending days and days wandering in those dark tunnels.

Anything to keep Pat safe.

"Alright," James nodded. "Let's try. I say that we should go on ahead and check."

"I'll get you there right now."

"I'll go with her," Gregor offered. "I know the city best."

Sophie would have preferred James's reassuring company rather than Gregor's, but she had to make do.

Reaching the cathedral took them several hours, many more than Sophie had imagined.

The fact that she took the wrong way three times certainly didn't help.

Sophie was grateful for the presence of Gregor, without whom she probably would have been completely lost and would have wandered in the tunnels for weeks; but she would have preferred that he wouldn't underline whenever she decided to go back with remarks like 'I see you have a great sense of direction' or 'I can find it, I'm sure... yeah, right.'

When at last, after a long walk in an endless tunnel, they crossed the metal door, no longer guarded by Korbinian's thugs, Sophie had the satisfaction of seeing him gape.

The cathedral, empty and apparently abandoned for months, was even more impressive than she remembered, and definitely more ghostly.

The downside was that it was completely flooded, and the water reached up to their ankles.

Some public maintenance man had probably identified it as a loss and insulated the tubes that had been hijacked by Korbinian's community, but not before the water had continued to inundate the whole area.

Sophie noticed the remains of mattresses, blankets and other everyday objects floating on the surface.

She wondered what had happened to Jeanne and her sons, or to Edmund Harris and Korbinian. Despite everything, they had been nice to her. She also felt a bit guilty, because, if she hadn't brought Kathleen there, they would still have a home too. Then she remembered that they had held that infected captive: if they met again now, maybe they would try to do the same with her. Suddenly she felt far less guilty.

"This place is a mess," Gregor said, shaking her from her thoughts.

"It needs a fix," she admitted. "But it's perfect. Look at that tall ceiling! They might even fly in here!"

The idea of leaving Pat free to spread his wings gave her great joy.

Who knows when he would start flying? He was much smaller than how she remembered Taneen, but he already tried to jump off the furniture shaking his wings.

"All right, I think this time you saved your chicken's life," Gregor granted.

Sophie beamed; at that moment, it seemed the best news she had ever received.

"Now let's go and tell the others."

They were about to turn around and go back when a mocking voice surprised them from behind: "Well, well, well... haven't we just found our old friend?"

CHAPTER 10

The afternoon air was cold and damp, and Erik thought that it would rain soon, perhaps even snow. It didn't snow very often in the territory of Europa : the temperature was too high due to the layer of pollution. However, sometimes it did happen.

At that moment, however, the cold was the least of his thoughts: soon, for the first time in months, he would see Maja.

Thanks to Marc's intercession, his daughter had agreed to meet Erik, and he hoped that they could make peace.

He had gone to pick her up at the computer services company where she worked part-time; in the rest of the time, she followed a course in the same field.

Erik felt very nervous: at that moment he would have given all his belongings to still have a cigarette. As he often did lately, he threw a piece of chewing gum into his mouth. It was not quite the same thing, but the act of chewing gave him a bit of relief from the tension and the abstinence from nicotine.

At least it was a much less expensive habit, he thought.

Finally, he saw Maja exiting through the door of the building: she had longer hair, he noticed, and generally seemed older, now an adult, perhaps because he saw her with the office clothes and the badge hanging from her neck with a colourful strap.

They greeted kissing on the cheeks as always, even though they both were stiff and embarrassed, then they sat down on a bench.

"So, uh, how are you?" Erik asked.

Maja shrugged: "Alright."

"And Peter?"

"He's fine too."

There was an uncomfortable silence.

"Marc told me that you've changed job," Maja said.

"Oh, yes."

"That's quite a change. I can't imagine you out of the police," she smiled.

"You're right, it was a bit of a shock, but I had the impression that the place wasn't right for me anymore. After what happened…" he stopped. Maybe it was better not to dive into that topic so soon. "Well, I needed a change," he simply concluded.

"So you sold yourself to the private sector," Maja teased him. "Marc wasn't sure for whom you're working."

"For Anderson Pharmaceuticals. I work directly with Dr Anderson," he explained with some pride.

Maja's smile died on her lips: "Ah."

Erik realized, disappointed, that Maja was giving credit to the slanders that had been spread about Kathleen.

"But I assure you that we do nothing sinister, like dissecting people or spreading new diseases," he tried to joke.

With what seemed like a great effort, Maja managed a tight smile.

"I've almost finished the courses. In six months, I will be able to work full time," she changed the subject.

"Congratulations, that's amazing!" Erik was thrilled. "You've done great!"

"Thank you."

"Now they'll have to give you a nice pay rise!"

Maja shrugged: "I hope so!"

"By the way, soon Peter will finish high school. Has he told you what he wants to study?"

Maja looked away: "Well, I don't think he wants to continue with his studies. He's pretty sure, actually."

Erik was shocked: "What? But why? He's a bright boy, why shouldn't he keep studying? We can afford it, I…"

"Dad, you know, he… he's not cut for an office job. He's kind of… more practical," Maja explained.

"I understand, but higher education gives access to more opportunities. Now it may seem like a waste of time, but it could jeopardize his future. I can't allow him to do such a stupid thing! He must listen to me, how do I talk to him, how…"

"I don't think that at this moment he's very inclined to listen to you, to tell you the truth," Maja interrupted him. "Besides, *he* has to choose what he wants to do with his life."

Erik took a breath, trying to calm down.

He went to the appointment with the idea to show that Maja that he wasn't the intrusive and controlling person that she had accused him to be, but it wasn't going very well.

"I'm sorry, I... you're right, of course. Peter must decide by himself."

'Although it would be in his interest to listen to the advice of those who know more,' he wanted to add, but he bit his tongue.

At that moment the most important thing was that make peace with the kids. Peter's studies could wait.

"How is the cohabitation with Peter going?" he asked, changing the subject.

Maja grimaced: "Er, okay, I think. Let's say we have some divergence on domestic work."

Erik smiled: knowing Peter, that probably meant Maja had to fight just to get him to wash his breakfast mug. Oh well, if his sister got him a bit in line it could only do him good.

"You could say that we don't do anything but argue," Maja continued, with fervour. "Can you believe that I even tell him to pick up his socks off the ground? If it were for him, he would leave them there!"

"I know!" Erik laughed. "And how's it going with the food?"

"A disaster! He always says that he will clean up 'later'... but in exactly which geological era would this 'later' rank?" She rolled her eyes: "He makes me so mad! Thankfully there's Marc at home, because if it wasn't for him to make peace between us..."

"Now Marc lives with you?" Erik asked, upset.

Okay, maybe that guy was not the slimy spy of a criminal organization, and yes, he was grateful for his help to reconcile with his daughter, but now, living together... it seemed far too early. How long have they known each other? Three months, six? Why were they in such a hurry? Maja was so young, she should have been thinking about his studies and then, maybe, much later…

He had to restrain himself once again to keep his opinion to himself.

"Yes, he's been so close to me in these months, and, in any case, we were always together, so…"

"Ah, um… that's good news," Erik commented, trying to sound sincere.

He mustn't lose sight of the goal: to make peace with his kids. Everything else was a minor issue.

"Yes!" Maja nodded enthusiastically. "Marc is fantastic, I don't know what I'd do without him."

"How marvellous," he said through clenched teeth. Time to change the subject, he decided.

"I'm glad to hear that you are doing good. I was very worried about you two and… well, I missed you," he explained with sincerity.

He took courage and decided to tackle the subject: "What happened to your mother… There isn't a single day in which it doesn't torment me, thinking about what I should have done but I didn't. Not only that night but even before… if only she had trusted me enough to talk about what she thought of the police and the rebels, if I had caught the signals, perhaps we…" he shook his head. "I thought about it for so long that I can no longer distinguish reality from what I believe to remember," he admitted.

"Even we never imagined that mom could be involved in *that*…" Maja admitted. "I keep trying to recall the details that were supposed to make me understand, I continue to think of her gestures, or conversations to see if she had tried to tell me something, but…"

"I know, I do the same," Erik nodded. "But you and Peter must believe me when I tell you that I never wanted your mother to be hurt… I am so sorry, and if I could go back in time…"

He realized that his eyes were shiny.

"But I think she wouldn't want me to become a stranger for you. Although she probably didn't approve of my work, this doesn't change the fact that we have always been a family."

Maja also appeared emotional.

"You're right," she said. "I only want you to trust us more, without being so controlling… that's it."

"I'll try," Erik promised. "Please try to understand me, though: for years I had the constant feeling that we were all in constant death danger because of the plague and the infected…" he shook his head. "But, fortunately, things are changing, and everything will be different, too. The mere fact of having the vaccine and that we can no longer be infected is like a weight that's been lifted off my chest…"

"Actually, we haven't been vaccinated," Maja objected quietly.

Erik's heart sank: "Why not?"

"There are a lot of risks associated with the vaccine, and I don't trust that woman," she said defiantly.

" 'That woman' would be Dr Anderson? Maja, don't be fooled by the disinformation campaign they are waging against her… the vaccine is safe, you must do it! Don't you understand that the risk of the plague..?"

"Dad, I know that you work for her and obviously you trust her, but I don't like what's going on. Her supporters are scary. Didn't you see what they did to government's seat?"

A few nights before, in fact, a group of Anderson supporters snuck into the government's seat and had vandalized some rooms with graffiti praising Anderson and promising the imminent end of the dictatorship.

It was the last and most dramatic of a series of episodes that testified how much Kathleen was gathering support.

"Those people have nothing to do with Anderson. They certainly have nothing to do with the vaccine. Come on, Maja!" Erik grew impatient. "Don't tell me that you got duped by those stupid flyers with ranting conspiracy theories?"

Maja blushed: "No, but… well, perhaps not all of what they say is true, but if only there was a grain of truth, why should we take the risk of injecting us with a mysterious substance that comes from this woman who is distributing it for free, with no government control…"

"Because the plague is worse!" Erik exclaimed. "Because if you catch the plague you die, immediately, almost for sure!"

"Now there's no need to shout," Maja protested, and Erik realized that he had raised his voice more than he intended. Looking around he noticed that some passers-by were staring at him perplexed.

"Please, listen to me," he continued, his voice more controlled. "The fewer people vaccinated, the higher the risk is of a new outbreak. I just can't think that just you and Peter are so at risk... I... please, just promise me you will get vaccinated!"

Maja shook her head: "I'm sorry dad, I can't do it. I don't trust either Anderson nor those fanatics that support her."

"I support her! Do I look like a fanatic?"

"You work for her, that's not quite the same."

"I would support her anyway!" he argued. "And it's crazy to continue risking catching the plague, that's irresponsible, you absolutely can't..."

"No Dad, I can!" Maja said, now yelling herself. "You keep saying that you've changed, that you want to respect my choices, that you trust us, but, in the end, you continue to tell me what I should do! You can't make me vaccinate, the choice is mine, and mine alone! And that counts for Peter too!"

Erik felt incredibly frustrated: how was it possible that she, his own daughter, didn't understand the risks that she was running? He wanted to be able to drag her to the nearest medical centre, give her the damn shot and then give her a candy as he used to do when she was small, but it wasn't possible.

He had to get her to see reason, she had to trust him.

"Fine. You're right," he admitted. "But at least promise me you'll think about it and won't take everything you read at face value. Keep yourself informed, please, try to listen also to those who you think are wrong."

"I will," Maja sighed, rolling her eyes.

Despite that small victory, Erik had the impression that the meeting didn't go as he had hoped.

Once he bade Maja goodbye, he went back to the office.

Outside the headquarters of the Anderson Pharmaceuticals, he found a crowd of people who were hoping to see the doctor. Lately, it happened more and more often; there was always a small group of onlookers waiting for her at the office and near her house. Sometimes they were just passers-by who stopped a little more in the hope of seeing the woman whom the whole city kept talking about, sometimes they were more organized, with signs and megaphones.

His instincts told him to disperse those people, but Kathleen never wanted to hear about it.

Even though they were huge fans of the doctor, Erik continued to find them disturbing.

Zoe also agreed with him.

The former agent had set well and was enthusiastic about the new job.

She also got along well with Kathleen Anderson, which undoubtedly was important for her role.

"She's great," Zoe had said a few days earlier, referring to the doctor. "She's so intense and full of energy... even if sometimes she speaks to herself," she added laughing. "It took me a while to understand, I thought she was talking to me."

Upon entering the building, Erik realized that, although the crowd seemed quiet, in case of a riot the security officers at the entrance would be far too few.

He made a mental note to increase surveillance at the entrances.

By his initiative, as well, the system of distribution of the vaccine had been made more controlled, and entering the medical centre had become long and laborious. This had created long lines and even longer waiting times, but Erik thought it was a fair price to pay for the added security of the doctor.

That day it seemed that there were more people than usual.

He must increase surveillance throughout the building, he decided. There were several entries on the back and side of the lab. Until then no one had tried to sneak in from there, but caution was never too much.

He decided to go talk to Kathleen immediately. He met Zoe, who was returning home, tired after a twelve-hour shift. The other bodyguard, a tall, muscular guy named Alan, was at the door of Anderson's office.

Alan was more threatening-looking than Zoe, who by comparison looked harmless, but Erik was convinced that in an emergency the girl would have been more than ready and would keep her nerves firm.

The doctor was in her office, and as always welcomed him with politeness.

When he explained that he needed to employ more people, she raised an eyebrow, puzzled: "Is it really necessary? Certainly, these people are not a threat to me, they are on my side."

"That's correct," Erik granted. "But we don't know how many potential murderers can hide in the middle of a cheering crowd. You're becoming more and more a public figure, we can't run any risk."

Kathleen shook her head: "I don't think I'm running any risk, but... In any case, you are the security expert: I trust your opinion on the subject."

"Thank you," Erik replied, relieved. It was good that Anderson trusted his judgment. The possibility of organizing the surveillance as he thought fit made him feel better.

"Excuse me if I'm being intrusive, but are you well? You look a little upset," Kathleen asked.

"I... Well, I've just had a discussion with my daughter," he admitted.

Anderson looked surprised: "I didn't know you had kids."

"I have two, Maja and Peter."

He explained that lately their relationship was a little strained, avoiding going into details of the circumstances of Thea's death, but explained her their reserves to get vaccinated, and how this had almost generated another quarrel between them.

"When the government responded to my vaccine with this silly scaremongering campaign I didn't bother, but now I realize that it might have done more damage than I thought. Many people don't want to get vaccinated, but, until we reach the sufficient immunization coverage, we can never definitively eradicate the plague..." Anderson commented, annoyed.

"I'm sorry that your daughter has been exposed to those ridiculous theories. But look, why don't you offer her to come for a tour here? She could talk to our doctors, read our material, visit the labs... I will be pleased to meet her myself if she wants to."

"Well... That would be very kind of you," Erik said, grateful.

It was an excellent suggestion: Maja definitely couldn't turn down such a reasonable request, and Erik was certain that, once she would see with her own eyes how the doctor was working, she wouldn't pay attention to that bunch of incompetents anymore.

"Don't worry, that's a pleasure," Anderson assured.

Suddenly Alan knocked on the door: "Your car is ready at the entrance, doctor."

"Ah, thank you, I'll go downstairs immediately," she said.

Erik frowned: "How come it's at the entrance? You should leave from the parking lot downstairs."

"They are doing maintenance work to the piping line," Alan explained.

"Why didn't I know anything about it?" Erik protested.

He didn't like the news: all those people at the entrance, the confusion...

"I just have to get to the car," said the doctor, as if reading his thoughts. "It's only a matter of minutes."

Erik nodded, but he decided to accompany Kathleen too. He wanted to evaluate those people with his own eyes.

When Kathleen Anderson came out of the gate, escorted by Alan and Erik himself, the crowd erupted in a roar.

There were cheers, chants, and mere screams that were difficult to interpret. In any case, the love for Kathleen was evident.

Within seconds all his men were in serious difficulty to rein in the multitude of people pushing to shake hands with Kathleen or just to see her.

"Kathleen, please, sign me an autograph!"

"Dr Anderson, I'm here, I'm here!"

"You are the salvation of Europa!"

"Don't you ever stop!"

Anderson dispensed smiles, handshakes and autographs, perfectly at ease, but Erik continued to feel anxious.

There was too much confusion, it wasn't safe.

He took the arm of the doctor and steered her towards the car.

"I'm sorry, but we have to go, we are too exposed here."

"Just a moment," she said, still smiling to a mother with a small child in her arms.

Suddenly, Kathleen found herself next to a man, strangely motionless throughout the agitated crowd.

Erik shivered, without knowing why.

A moment later, the man leaned over Anderson with a crazy look.

"Death to dragons," he murmured, pulling out a gun.

Erik grabbed Kathleen by the shoulders and pushed her down, trying to shelter her, while behind him a shot was fired.

CHAPTER 11

Sophie and Gregor turned around: in front of them, there were five men who wore goggles with a greenish glass. Two of them had rifles that looked old and battered, but still dangerously functional.

Seeing their faces, they all instinctively made a step back.

Coming across an infected always made a certain effect, Sophie thought, for once happy about her new condition.

However, the newcomers continued to watch them menacingly.

Apart from one, small and skinny, they were all very tall and strong.

Gregor knew how to defend himself and Sophie also suspected that he had a gun, but could he beat five armed guys, four of which were twice his size? She doubted it.

He too must have come to the same conclusion because he stepped forward and raised his hand to better show the scales.

"We have the plague, step back," he ordered. "We don't want problems. Now we're leaving, and no one will get infected."

The five looked at each other, then began to giggle with contempt.

Sophie shivered: that wasn't a good sign.

"You know," the skinny one said, "until yesterday it might have worked."

He raised an arm to show a piece of cotton fixed with a band-aid: "But now we are all fresh out of the vaccination centre. So how about you come here and give us that nice gun you have under your sweater?"

There was something familiar in the guy's voice.

Gregor looked uncertain, but, eventually, he pulled out the gun he had on his left side and laid it on the ground.

One of the men came forward and took it.

"Much better," the guy said. "And now explain to us what the fuck you're doing in our territory."

Sophie suddenly recognized him: "Alois!"

It was one of Korbinian's men, one of the first she had met when she had stepped into the cathedral the first time.

He stared at her, or at least she thought he did, since he was still wearing the infrared goggles.

"It's you. The doctor who flooded the cathedral. I thought it was you, from a distance, but then the scales..." he grinned. "You got your face ruined, eh?"

"It wasn't me who caused the flooding!" Sophie objected.

"Oh, wasn't it? But you'll admit that's a bit of a coincidence: we live peacefully for years and then one day you arrive, you and that old lady, and suddenly the pipes explode, our infected runs away, we have to leave the place and..."

"Ok, it wasn't a coincidence," she admitted. "But I assure you I had nothing to do with it. It was my friend... well, it turned out that she wasn't really my friend at all."

"Spare me your sad story," Alois snapped. "What do you want now? You've come back to finish the job? You came looking for your other infected friend?"

Sophie felt a little guilty because it had never even crossed her mind that the man who had been tortured for years by Edmund Harris could use some help.

Who knew if he was still alive? But now it wasn't the time to worry about him.

"I... Well , we..." she stammered, taken aback.

"You know what, now I'm taking you to Korbinian. He'll decide what to do with you," Alois said.

One of the men with a rifle pushed her and Gregor forward with the tip of the weapon, and they were forced to move through a dark tunnel. Korbinian's men put themselves in front of them and behind, being careful never to touch them.

Despite their boasting about the vaccine, they still had qualms about directly touching an infected.

Sophie noticed that, despite not having the goggles, the tunnel wasn't completely dark, or perhaps a side effect of the plague was a better night vision too.

Gregor beside her appeared alert, although his expression was unreadable.

"You didn't tell me that you had flooded the cathedral and now these guys hate you," he hissed at her ear. "Don't you think you could have mentioned it, between a wrong turn and the other? Something like 'By the way, Gregor, we're going to a place full of people who want to take revenge on me, my deadly enemies, we probably won't get out alive... well, turn right here, so we take the wrong way again.'"

"I told you it wasn't me!" Sophie protested. "I didn't even believe they would accuse me..."

To be honest, she hadn't thought of that. Gregor was right: it was incredibly reckless of her to go there without a shred of a plan that wasn't just seeing if the cathedral was still standing.

What had she been thinking? She had always been so reasonable and cautious, how come that lately she kept being so rash?

"And did I get that right, are they leading us to Korbinian?"

"Why, do you know him?" Sophie asked.

Gregor looked at her as if she was stupid: "I've heard of him. He's one of the many criminal leaders of the underground city. Perhaps not the most important, or the evilest, but one that wouldn't hesitate to stick a bullet in our forehead. Damn, Sophie, I can't believe you didn't warn me about anything..."

"No talking, you two!" one of the men ordered them, sticking the tip of the gun in Gregor's ribs, who gave her one last murderous look.

"I'm sorry," Sophie whispered, feeling dumb.

He rolled his eyes but didn't answer.

She wondered how Pat was doing. She tried to reach him with her mind and felt a sense of confusion and dismay.

She had never left him alone for so long.

I wish you were here with me, she thought.

She could only hope to see him again.

After a short walk that took them deeper, they came to a metal door that looked a little shaky. Alois opened it and they found themselves in a large room, which originally was probably a tube control room. On the walls, the remains of old electrical panels, now unused for centuries, could still be seen.

Inside there were many people, camped as best as they could on the sides of the hall.

Sophie realized that there were much, much fewer people than those who had inhabited the cathedral: space was smaller, and they seemed dirtier and more ragged.

She remembered that once they had unlimited access to hot and drinking water and electricity; now they probably didn't.

At that moment she began to understand with fear why Alois looked so furious with her.

Everyone turned to see them on their arrival, looking at them with curiosity.

When they saw the scales, the crowd turned instinctively aside, crowding against the walls.

A few moments passed, in which the henchmen fled to alert the boss. All the people seemed too scared to do anything to them.

Sophie recognized in the corner Jeanne, who stared at her with her big moth eyes wide open.

She wondered if she had recognized her.

Finally, from the back of the room came Korbinian: apparently, he had to give up the private suite he had in the church, but the area had been summarily divided from the rest of the room with curtains.

When Sophie had seen him the first time he looked as relaxed as a mouse in cheese, but now he was pissed off.

He looked strained, his face was more tense and gaunt. His eyes were still underlined with black eyeliner, but if once it had given him a mysterious look, now it just made him look haunted.

"Alois, what the hell were you thinking?" he shouted. "Bringing infected in here? Are you crazy?"

"Look who it is," he said, pointing at Sophie.

Korbinian stared at her, then remembered: "Why, if it isn't a surprise. You have some nerve to show your face down here," he said.

"Um, yes. Well. About that... it was all a misunderstanding," Sophie began with a collaborative smile.

"I'm sure it was," he replied.

"Yeah. Do you remember the lady who was with me here? I thought she was a poor innocent persecuted woman but..." she quickly explained, "you see, it turned out that, instead, she was Kathleen Anderson, yes, the very one, and that her plan was to infiltrate among the rebels and free a dragon, and now she has the dragon and I got the plague and... well, she was the one who flooded your church, not me."

Korbinian just looked at her with mild curiosity: "Oh, it was Kathleen Anderson. The famous scientist. This explains everything."

Sophie realized that her story sounded like a bunch of nonsense, every claim more far-fetched than the next... but it was the truth!

She felt a cold sweat: if Korbinian didn't believe her he would kill them, and until then she hadn't been able to say anything particularly credible.

She didn't want to die, she thought frantically. She didn't want to die without seeing her dragon again...

"I know it sounds absurd, but you have to believe me," she begged.

"And you came down here to tell me this pretty story?"

"To tell you the truth we came here for the cathedral," she explained. "We needed something like that and I thought... uh, we can offer you a deal. To use it, you know."

Korbinian grinned mirthlessly: "I changed my mind: you don't have chutzpah, you just want to die. Now tell me why I shouldn't shoot you immediately."

"Because we are not the only ones down here," Gregor interjected before Sophie could speak. "Our friends are nearby. If they don't see us return, soon you will have your pretty house full of plague victims. I don't think you'd be too pleased about it, would you?"

"They will never find you down here, it's a maze," Korbinian said.

"Oh, we know how to communicate," Gregor tapped his temple with his index. "Do you think the scales are the only side effect of the plague?"

Korbinian appeared uncertain: on one hand, it was clear that he didn't want to let them go, especially now that they knew where he was; on the other Gregor's words had instilled doubt in him.

"You know what I think? I think you say a lot of bullshit," he finally said. "Inside this place, we had an infected for years, and had any of you ever come to take him back? No. So maybe your communication is not as reliable as you say."

His words were defiant, but he didn't look as confident as before.

Sophie realized that perhaps they would be able to get away for the moment, but this meant that they definitely couldn't come back. It meant giving up the cathedral which was the only place they could hide Pat and the other dragons.

She couldn't allow that... there had to be another solution.

"Korbinian, listen to me," she said on impulse. "Why must we be enemies? Why can't we reach an agreement? We are not so different after all."

Korbinian looked disgusted.

"We are two sides of the same coin," she insisted. "We must hide because we were outlawed; they hunt us because there is no place for us in the world they have created in the city above.

Why should we make war between us? We have a common enemy. It would make much more sense to join forces and try to take back the surface. You also have much to gain by collaborating with us." She paused, to give him time to process the idea. "You have a safe space that we need; we have many resources... a network of informants, the possibility to insert ourselves in the main computer systems. Think of what we could do together!"

He said nothing, and Sophie knew he was considering her proposal.

Gregor looked stunned, as if he wanted to ask what had gotten into her mind, but she avoided meeting his eyes.

"We can negotiate, can't we? You could go back to being what you used to be, and even more! I mean," she looked around, "the loss of the cathedral was a blow, wasn't it? You seem to have lost a lot of what you had earned and…"

The expression on Korbinian's face changed quickly, and Sophie realized she had made a mistake.

"What do you mean?" he thundered. "What do you mean 'I lost?' You come here to disrespect me in front of my men, and you expect me to spare your life?"

All the people of the cathedral were staring at them, their gaze that passed quickly from one to another, and Sophie knew that she had it all wrong, again: she should have talked to him in private, where he could admit his weaknesses...

"I didn't mean to..."

"There is nothing more to discuss," Korbinian gestured to one of his men, and Sophie's heart sank, while the guy raised his gun against her head.

At the same time, in the confusion, Gregor drew Alois closer and pulled out a knife from his right boot with a rapid movement, then pointed it against his throat.

"Enough with the bullshit," he said. "Now we're leaving. Or should we infect you all?"

Korbinian seemed shocked: "We are vaccinated..."

"Oh yes? Everyone? Even that kid over there?" Gregor asked, pointing to one of Jeanne's sons. "You know, right, that no one under puberty has ever survived the plague?" he reminded him with a sweet voice.

"Let me go, please, get your hands off me..." Alois begged.

"What are you afraid of, you're vaccinated," Gregor scoffed. "Of course, what if it wasn't as effective as they say..."

The boy seemed on the verge of tears.

"Let go of Alois or I'll shoot her head off," Korbinian ordered, indicating Sophie.

"And then? You know what happens if I can just touch one of them?" Gregor challenged him, indicating the families who retreated in the corners of the room.

Sophie was desperate: she didn't know how they could get out of there alive.

Korbinian was afraid to show weakness, and this usually led to do some very stupid actions, and his henchman's gun was still pointed at her head.

And then, she didn't want those innocent people to die. Would Gregor intentionally infect those children? She didn't want to know.

Her thoughts went again to Pat... what would she give to have him at her side. Who knows where he was at that time.

I'm here.

Sophie's mouth opened in surprise, and awareness made its way into her mind.

"Gregor, get down!" she ordered him.

"What?"

"Down!" she repeated, and fortunately he instinctively heeded.

A moment later, the gate metal darted over their heads like a bullet, while Pat burst into the room spitting flames.

The dragon flew next to Sophie, and stepped between her and Korbininan's men, keeping them away with violent flames.

He looked like he was even bigger than the previous day.

Around them, everyone was screaming and trying to reach the exit.

Gregor approached Pat, settling himself strategically under one of his wings, while the dragon opened its jaws against Korbinian.

"Wait, wait!" he begged. "Please, don't! We can negotiate!"

Gregor laughed: "Ah, now we can? I wonder what made you change your mind."

He turned to Sophie: "We have already lost too much time here. Let's roast these hobos and let's take the cathedral if you care so much about it."

Sophie hesitated: the temptation to retaliate against those who earlier had threatened them was very strong.

They would not have scruples at reversed roles, she thought.

But that wasn't the only reason: there was also a dark, primordial desire, to destroy, to tear them apart... she could do it if she wanted to...

"No," she decided, with great effort. "I don't want to spend all my time looking over our shoulders. If we want to move all of ours down here we can't fear retaliation. We should make a deal."

Gregor shook his head: "Would you trust the word of these people? They were going to shoot you in the head, my goodness! They are unreliable, like beasts!"

"That's what they think about us infected!" she insisted. "I didn't lie when I said that we are more alike than it seems. We can't always be alone against everyone else... we need allies!"

"Cain didn't think so."

Sophie shrugged: "Cain is not here. Maybe he never will. We must go on," she urged him.

Pat gave a frustrated growl.

Good boy, she thought. *It's all right. Now we are together.*

Reluctantly, the dragon calmed down, and crouched against her knees, quiet again.

She turned then to Korbinian.

"It's OK. We are ready to negotiate... what do you offer us?"

He stood up with some effort. He had a few strands of burned hair, and his face very red, but he did his best to appear self-possessed. Sophie, despite herself, had to admire his nerve.

"I believe I understood that you were interested in the cathedral," he said nonchalantly.

CHAPTER 12

The bullet had hit Erik at the centre of the shoulder.

It was a crippling pain, such as he would never have imagined.

He had confused memories of the moments that followed, of how the crowd had screamed, the confusion. He remembered a voice saying he would have to lie down on the ground and not move, and Dr Anderson who wanted to bring him back into the building to visit him immediately.

Eventually, with his last strength, he ordered Alan to bring both of them inside the car and then to the hospital.

His first thought was to remove Anderson from danger, but later discovered that it was unnecessary. The man who had fired at her had been attacked by the screaming crowd, unarmed and, he discovered to his horror, lynched on the spot.

The police had arrived too late.

It had all been so sudden that it was no longer possible to learn what had motivated his gesture: had it been the action of a psychopath who had taken the propaganda against Anderson too seriously, or had someone hired him?

Erik was more inclined to believe the former, but he would never know the truth for certain.

Despite the anger he felt towards him, however, he could not help but cringe at the thought of the fate that the wannabe-killer had met. How could those cheering people transform within minutes into an uncontrollable horde that had torn a man apart?

He remembered vividly the face of the woman who was holding her son so that he could greet the doctor, her bright and protective eyes. Had she, too, turned into a killer to beat a man to death? It was a disturbing thought.

Anderson's car took him to the nearest hospital, where he was immediately hospitalized and operated to reconstruct his left collarbone. A metal plate had been inserted to hold together the bone fragments.

He had always had the crazy notion that a gunshot wound to the shoulder wasn't a serious injury.

Although during his training days he had been told a thousand times that every bullet, no matter where it hit the body, was life-threatening, he believed that wounds not on the head or abdomen were little more than dodged.

He had seen some of his colleagues in the past with their arms in a sling or with crutches, but, very foolishly, he had always considered them minor accidents, things that can happen during the service.

Now that he had the experience under his belt, he discovered that reality was quite different.

On the way from Anderson Pharmaceuticals to the hospital, which were no more than a few blocks apart, he had lost so much blood to require an immediate transfusion to keep him from bleeding to death.

In the car he had started shaking violently from the cold, in shock.

The doctor who was treating him had told him that he would need months of physiotherapy, and at the beginning it would be difficult even to just lift his left arm.

And in all this, the hospital staff kept telling him that he had been 'very lucky' because the bullet had not adversely affected any vital organs.

He would spend a few days in hospital: Kathleen Anderson had gone to see him in person and had also paid for a private room in the building, a thoughtful gesture, since in normal circumstances Erik would have to pass those days in a dormitory with about ten beds.

Erik felt weak and certainly needed rest, but getting stuck in the hospital was extremely frustrating, especially because in the days following the attack on Anderson, the situation in Europa had precipitated quickly.

Supporters of Anderson had accused the government of having ordered her execution, and since then there had been continuing uprisings.

The police had been sent to quell the riots, but this had made the protesters and the supporters of their cause even more aggressive.

Also, it seemed that many of the policemen sympathizes with the crowd and refused to proceed with the arrests.

The government seemed in shambles. President Hartmann had spoken on television, saying he was confident that the citizens of Europa would not be fooled by these dangerous revolutionary tendencies which were undermining the harmony that the government had worked so hard to get.

His confidence, however, was misplaced.

Some districts of the city, between the second and third ring, were now in the hands of the supporters of Anderson, so much so that the police didn't even try to enter them.

The doctor, from her part, had spoken publicly, urging the crowd to demonstrate peacefully, to respect the law as she had always done; but she had never asked the protesters to disperse or to give up their action.

Erik was confused, because he had never thought that Anderson really wanted to take the power in Europa; when she said she wanted to build a new world he had thought that she would do it by helping to ensure the health of every resident of the city.

However, the more he thought about it, the more the idea of Anderson as president seemed natural. She had already saved many lives by giving the vaccine to the citizens; she was smart, efficient, passionate. He could not imagine a person who would be better suited to lead the city to a bright future.

In any case, he had spent all his days of convalescence attached to the phone, trying to keep the movements of Anderson under control and organizing the staff to make sure that another attack couldn't happen again.

He had ordered that all the cars with which the doctor moved were equipped with bulletproof glass, and there were always at least three bodyguards to accompany her.

Fortunately, Zoe Hernandez had, like him, a feeling for danger acquired during the past years in the police, and she helped him to handle the situation.

Nevertheless, he couldn't wait to be able to go out and take care in person of the organization of the security in those critical days.

On the last day before being released from the hospital he heard am uncertain knock at the door of his room.

"May we come in...?"

Erik's face brightened: it was Maja and Peter.

The kids seemed puzzled to see him in bed in pyjamas and a bandage that immobilized his upper back, and hugged him with great caution.

Peter looked slightly more adult, as if his face was losing the roundness of adolescence to become harder, more angular. But the impression was dispelled when his son gave him his usual smile.

"Sorry if we only came today," Maja began. "But apparently the hospital did a bit of a mess with the numbers to call in case of emergency. Zoe Hernandez called from your office and..."

"It doesn't matter, that's ok! How are you?"

"We're fine," Peter said. "You're the one who got shot. Does it hurt?"

"No way, I'm a real bodyguard, brave and daring, the bullets just tickle me..." Erik joked. "No, to be fair it hurts like hell," he added more seriously. "It takes me ages just to button up the pyjama top! It's very difficult to do it with just one hand."

"Zoe said that you launched yourself in front of the bullet, and then in spite of the wound you rescued two people..."

"I wish! I just fell on the ground like a ripe pear!" Erik laughed. "It wasn't like in the movies. In fact, I hardly had time to realize what was happening."

"Who would have thought that, just when you leave the police to do a theoretically quieter job, you would get shot," Maja said.

"That's ironic," Erik agreed. "Have you had problems to get here? I've been locked in here for three days, but I have heard that there are blocked roads, rail service suspended..."

Peter shrugged: "From the news it seems that the city was set on fire. Actually, we came here without any problems and our neighbourhood is very quiet."

"Well, yes," Maja admitted, glaring at his brother. "However, we are being careful, because it wouldn't be sensible to underestimate those fanatics."

"That's good, always be careful," Erik nodded. "You want me to call a car to get you home?"

"A taxi?" Peter asked, amazed.

"Actually, I was thinking of an Anderson car."

"No, thanks, that's ok," Maja answered quickly before Peter could say anything. "The train will do just fine."

Erik would have felt more comfortable knowing that they were on one of his secure and anonymous car, but he preferred not to insist. Apparently, Maja's contempt for everything that had to do with the Anderson Pharmaceuticals had not lessened.

"Is it true that Anderson is planning to attack the government, leading the protesters on her dragon's back, and then make him eat President Hartmann?" his son asked.

"What? Of course not! Where did you hear this nonsense?"

"I heard it at school. That sounds pretty cool to me," Peter said.

"Look, Dr Anderson is a normal person, although very bright and smart... she's not a Joan of Arc who hears voices in her head."

For a moment he thought of Zoe, who told him about Kathleen talking to herself, but he drove the thought away immediately, feeling almost guilty.

"Maybe not," Maja conceded. "However, she scares me. And those who follow her too. And now you got shot..." she shifted her weight from foot to foot. "I don't know... are you really sure you want to continue to work for her?"

"Maja, it was one of her haters who shot me, not one of the supporters," said Erik. "Don't worry, Kathleen knows what she's doing. However, I agree with you on one thing: it's better to stay away from the riots. The protesters are probably good intentioned but..." he thought about the man who had shot him, and the crowd, which closed on him while Erik fell to the ground... "It's better not to take risks," he concluded.

"I'm sure *Kathleen*," Maja emphasized the name sarcastically, "knows what she's doing, but to me it seems that she's trying to overthrow the government."

"Maybe she is," Erik granted. "Would that be so awful? For years, since you went to high school, I've heard you complain about the government repression, corruption and food rationing... and now that a person who could solve all this comes, you become the champion of the institutions? I don't understand."

"Of course I want to change things but... not this way! I think we are about to go from bad to worse!" Maja heated up.

"I hope that if Anderson becomes President she will open the borders. Next year I want to travel... I want to know what lies beyond the quarantined areas," Peter said.

Maja assumed an exasperated look, as if she had heard that many times, while Erik stared at him.

"Beyond the quarantined areas, there are... well, other quarantined areas. You've seen the documentaries," Erik said cautiously.

"Yes, they say there are only deserts and stuff like that," his son answered nonchalantly. "But I don't think that's true. It doesn't sound very believable."

"Yet you're ready to believe that my employer wants to barbecue the President, now that's so believable, isn't it?" Erik commented before he could stop himself.

Peter assumed a wounded expression.

"Never mind, I can never talk to you," he muttered.

Erik felt guilty. For days he had done nothing but hope to see Peter, and, now that he was there, he only made fun of him.

"I'm sorry Peter... maybe you're right, who knows, maybe there is something to explore out there," he tried half-heartedly.

"Yeah, that's it!" Peter nodded. "After school I want to go to work in the fields of the eighth ring. That's the closest place to the borders," he said enthusiastically.

"You want to work on a farm?!" Erik asked.

Peter became defensive: "Yes, what's wrong with it?"

"No, no it's just that... well, it's a very hard work, you're aware of it, yes?"

"Of course I am," Peter said, very unconvincingly.

"Because if you are interested in agriculture, you know that Anderson Pharmaceuticals has immense crops of plants that are used for the active ingredients? But they come from intensive, specialized agriculture, you have to study to get there," Erik suggested.

"Ah... so what?" Peter didn't look like he was figuring out where the speech was going.

"So nothing," Maja snapped. "When you'll finish school, you'll choose what you want to do."

In that moment a nurse came in to let them know that the visiting hours had ended.

Erik was not sure that the reconciliation with the kids had gone as he had hoped. But, he thought, he had to make do for the moment.

Erik was finally discharged on the next day, and he was able to return to work.

The trip to the headquarter of Anderson Pharmaceuticals was very quiet: as Peter said, there weren't signs of riots.

When he arrived before the building he gaped seeing a sea of people who had camped in front of the door.

He had to struggle to get to the entrance, and when he finally managed to arrive there, he discovered that Zoe had taken charge of the situation and ordered that the vaccines wouldn't be administered for the day; those who wanted to be given the injection were diverted to the peripheral health centres.

However, even after this announcement, the crowd hadn't dispersed. They all looked like they were waiting for Kathleen Anderson.

"What the hell is going on today?" Erik asked when he managed to reach his office.

He received conflicting information; however, they all agreed that the uprising in the city had increased.

A few minutes later Kathleen herself summoned him in her office, where she was watching a small screen placed on the boardroom table.

Zoe was standing next to her and greeted Erik warmly.

"When I heard that you were back, I had you called immediately," the doctor said. "I hope that your shoulder is doing better."

"Much better, thank you," Erik said, then turned his gaze to the screen. "What is it?"

"These are images coming from the Strasbourg area. It looks like a crowd of people is trying to occupy the seat of government and ask my appointment as president," she explained quietly.

Erik was shocked: "What are you going to do?"

"Naturally I have to go there too."

"Well, of course, but you must be cautious. Arranging safe transportation at this time is complicated, since it seems that all of the first ring is completely blocked and…"

"Don't worry about transportation. I have already taken arrangements. But I must talk to the people who are there for me," the doctor said. "At what time do you think you can bring your staff there?"

"How many of them?"

"All those at your disposal. Just leave someone guarding the headquarter."

"I don't know…" Erik ran a hand through his hair. "A couple of hours at the earliest…"

"Fine. I shall see you at the old parliament in two hours. Zoe, you won't need to come with me," Kathleen declared.

"Doctor, it would be more cautious to come with us."

"I told you it isn't necessary."

"Can I at least ask you how you plan to get there?"

"No," she smiled. "You cannot."

Getting to the seat of government was easier than Erik had imagined.

It was enough to show the car with the symbol of Anderson Pharmaceuticals, the rod of Asclepius with the dragon coiled around it, to make the crowd open as they passed.

Once he arrived, he discovered that the army had betrayed the government, passing to Anderson's side: General Chardon, the Defence minister, had personally conducted the deposition of Hartmann, and had had Lange arrested.

The crowd in front of the old parliament waited for Kathleen.

"When will Dr Anderson arrive?" the general asked. "I thought she was with you."

"Well..." Erik began, but he didn't have time to answer.

The noise coming from the outside ceased abruptly, while thousands of people fell silent and stared upward.

Erik went to the window and looked out, just in time to see a huge creature landing on the roof of the parliament.

It was Kathleen Anderson's great dragon, and she was riding it.

There were thousands of people in the square and the surrounding streets, but an eerie silence reigned. Slowly, Anderson stepped down from the dragon, and approached the edge of the roof. Her hair danced around her face, and even from this distance, Erik could see that she looked transfigured, ageless.

"Citizens of Europa," she said in a firm voice. The silence was such that she didn't need microphones to be heard. "Today I am here to officially become the President of our great city. I am only here because of you, and thanks to the love you have shown me. When I decided to donate my plague vaccine to all of you, I ran a great risk. The powers that ruled the city didn't want me to do it... they did everything they could to get rid of me.

But when the government which was in charge until a few hours ago tried cowardly to silence me, sending an assassin to kill me, they discovered that they were struggling with a force that was too great for them. It wasn't an army, nor weapons or even a dragon, but yourself! It was your love to protect and avenge me!"

Kathleen looked at the audience and Erik knew that everyone felt that she was addressing them personally. Behind her, the dragon appeared motionless, like a giant and realistic gargoyle.

"And it's from this feeling I want to start to create a new city, a place where each of us can be free to live in harmony with others, without being enslaved by fear and suspicion. In part, this objective has already been achieved: without the fear of the plague we can live in peace with others, be closer, without the fear of infection. But we can't really trust each other if we have the constant fear that our neighbour is stealing our livelihoods.

Until now, the most vital and primary goods have been sipped with arrogance and greed by cruel tyrants. Well, this will stop! The first thing I'll do is to abolish the food rationing."

The crowd still didn't speak, but each of the faces reflected joy and disbelief in equal measure.

"The rationing was necessary only because the richest could live in comfort and luxury at your expense. I will not allow this corruption and inequality to continue!

And because there is plenty for all, I have already studied a program of intensification of agriculture that will recover the territories suitable for cultivation beyond the eighth ring. Europa will never suffer hunger anymore!"

At last the audience exploded in a roar of screams and applause.

Kathleen smiled satisfied, then gestured them to be quiet, to be able to speak again. Only when the dragon behind her gave a mighty roar, the audience fell silent again.

"I won't stop there. To be able to live happily with each other, it is necessary that the human and social relations are cultivated in sunlight, according to the laws and rules of civilized life. Unfortunately, now it is not so: thousands of people are living underground, like rats, feeding on crime and theft.

I cannot allow this to continue, not in the city I dream of and I want to build. This is a message to the underground city: abandon your old life. Come out... everyone will find a place in my new world. Those that still want to live in the shadows and thriving in subterfuge, know that I will have no tolerance or mercy towards them. From this moment, the underground city has only few hours of life left."

The audience applauded again, more and more delighted.

"This also applies to the rebels who survived the plague," she continued. "They keep living among us, undermining the fragile balance that we have created with the vaccine. Unfortunately, thousands, perhaps millions of people are still not vaccinated, and the presence of the rebels is like a time bomb just waiting to explode."

The crowd, terrified, caught its breath.

"But I'm not completely merciless. Many of these people had no choice, they were victims of events. I know some of them can communicate with a dragon, just like myself. I want to say this to them: come to me. Bring your dragon. I can teach you how to control them, to live with these wonderful creatures. Come to me, and I'll receive you as my own brothers and sisters."

Her expression seemed reassuring, almost maternal.

"Today everything has changed. Forget your old existence, the compromises that you had to undertake to survive. If you are on my side you will have a new life, richer and more peaceful than you have ever known up to now. Otherwise..." suddenly her face changed almost imperceptibly, becoming fierce, "let it be known that from this moment we are at war. And that there will be no mercy."

The dragon spread his wings as the crowd erupted in a roar again, applauding Kathleen Anderson.

CHAPTER 13

Sophie had followed Kathleen Anderson's speech on a small television that Ken had installed in the living room, announcing that 'they had to see this'.

She and Famke were preparing to move the dragons to the cathedral. In the past days they had managed to drain all the water from the floor: the place remained very humid, but it wasn't bad for the dragons. It would balance nicely the effect of their flames, Famke claimed.

When Sophie and Gregor had returned with the news of the agreement, they were all very surprised: James and Ken had seemed a bit offended that she had made the decision without consulting them, but the others had appeared relieved that someone finally was doing something, anything.

Heinrich, Jane and Marie, then, were excited by the idea of being able to finally free their dragons from their chains.

Sophie had silently watched the screen which was broadcasting the triumph of Kathleen.

Seeing the one that she had considered her closest friend for months was disconcerting: a part of her still considered Emma Lemaire and Dr Anderson as two separate peoples, as if the first had died when the other was born.

Hearing her voice and seeing her face destroyed this illusion: it was the same person, the one that she had always been. And she had been deceived like a fool.

At least she was not the only one, she thought. Even Europa had fallen victim of the same deception: all the people who had brought her to power and now were chanting her name under the illusion that she cared about their well-being, but she was sure it wasn't so.

Kathleen Anderson only cared about herself and her dragon.

She didn't know what she wanted to get now that they were together again: power? She had it already. Greater power? And what would she do with it? She wasn't sure, but one thing was absolutely certain: this woman, whoever she was, was a terrible danger.

"Sophie, I knew that allying with Korbinian was a mistake!" Ken said, appearing quite desperate, once the speech was over, and Sophie and Famke exchanged a glance, uncertain of what it meant for their future.

"Why?"

"Didn't you hear what she said? It's the end of the underground city! And that's where we're going!"

"Actually, I think it's a sign that we chose well," Sophie replied. "The city is no longer a safe place. They are all crazy for her, and we will be hunted as never before. In the underground city, however, they are as desperate as we are."

Ken shook his head: "She'll hunt us down like rats. We're going to die!"

"Ken, get yourself paper bag to breathe in, you're hyperventilating," Gregor suggested in a bored tone. Sophie turned surprise: she hadn't realized he was there, too.

She realized that as she watched the speech on television, James, Amanda, Heinrich, Marie and Jane had also arrived in the room.

"Now is not the time for your humour!" Ken exclaimed. "Didn't you hear what that woman said?"

"We all heard her," Famke assured him. "Now we must decide what to do. Do we want to move to the underground city or not?"

"No!" Ken exclaimed.

"Yes, we do," Sophie insisted. "We can't stay here much longer. And the dragons can't be locked up for a long time. It can't do them good."

Ken grimaced: "Ah well, of course, your first thought is that the dragons can exercise. Good thing you got your priorities checked."

"If she indicated the underground city as a target, that just means she knows it's out of her control," Sophie continued. "Moreover, we must move now, while the city is still in confusion... in the next few days it will become increasingly difficult. We have to get there tonight."

"She's right," James said, exchanging a look with Amanda. "If we must act, we must do so as soon as possible."

His voice was uncharacteristically low and weak, and Sophie briefly wondered what was wrong with him; however, she had more pressing matters to worry about.

"All we need to accommodate the dragons is ready," Famke declared. "I don't know what we're going to do with the cages, but..."

"There will be no need for cages," Sophie interrupted, earning herself a look of clear approval by Marie. "In the cathedral they will have all the space they need."

"No, no, this is another madness!" Ken snapped. "Aren't you listening to yourself? We should trust a small-time crook and let the dragons free to do harm? Cain would never let this happen," he spat out angrily. "If he was here now, he would never let you go ahead with this stupid plan!"

There was a moment of silence, in which all avoided looking at each other.

"We don't know what Cain would do," James said reasonably. "The circumstances have changed a lot since he... since his accident."

Ken looked around, looking for support, but everyone seemed to avoid his gaze.

"Gregor!" he finally called. "At least you, I beg you, say something!"

Sophie gasped: everyone seemed to agree with her, but Gregor's sharp words were always very convincing and, she realized, could be the one to tip the scales.

If he continued to defend Cain's line of action, what would happen to Pat? Was he still in danger? The solution seemed so close...

Gregor sighed: "I'm sorry Ken. I'm with Sophie," he said. "Risky as it might be, the underground city is still our best bet."

Sophie felt a pleasant warmth spread in her chest: she had done it.

Preparations for the move quickly became frantic.

Gregor, with Korbinian's help, had identified a number of underground passages that connected the basement where the dragons currently were to the tunnels leading to the cathedral.

Unfortunately, it wasn't possible to use any vehicle there, and it would be a long walk.

Others would use the cars, traveling at night as a precaution.

Gregor was impressed with how the underground city was organised.

"I thought I knew Europa well but these people... well , they sure know what they're at," he had commented, appearing unusually struck.

Reluctantly, Sophie had to say goodbye to Cain, who would be moved with a car to one of the last remaining safe houses.

"He can't live down there, he would never be able to recover," Amanda said. "His health is precarious enough. Such changes in temperature and humidity would only risk to add some other infection that would be fatal to him."

After the operation that Sophie had carried out, there had been no improvement in his condition. In fact, after the first aneurysm, Cain had continued to have other crises: his pressure could rise sky-high unexpectedly, he had had more episodes of seizures and on one occasion he almost went in cardiac arrest.

In Amanda's words, who was cautious and tactful in a completely uncharacteristic way, Sophie realized that she had to start preparing for the worst.

Perhaps that would be a farewell.

Was it her fault? Had it been a mistake to operate him in those conditions? No one would ever know for sure, she thought.

Sophie ran her hand on his head, where the rough hair that had begun to sprout pricked her fingers.

"We'll take care of him," Amanda promised. "Should there be some emergency... you'll be the first to know."

Sophie nodded.

She had helped Amanda and James to load his stretcher in the car, and she had watched the vehicle go away with tears in her eyes.

However, there hadn't been much time to process the event.

Suddenly, it seemed that everyone had to ask her what to do and where to go.

After a few hours, she had hidden in her room, ostensibly to bring food to the dragon.

Pat, always sensitive to her moods, that day was gloomy and a bit confused.

Come on, Pat, she thought, stroking the puppy, which was becoming more and more massive and had started to take a nice dark mahogany colour. *Soon we will be in a new home, with many new friends.*

One of the reasons why she was anxious to leave that house was the fear that someone had seen him when he had launched himself to her help.

She had found her bedroom window broken: it was from there that he had gone out, and presumably flown outdoors until he found an entrance to the underground city.

She hadn't seen fit to emphasize this in front of the others because she feared the usual sort of discussion about how unwise it was that Sophie didn't keep him in check as the others.

She left him in his room with the lunch, which consisted of an unidentified bloody carcass.

As the months passed, finding fresh meat had become increasingly difficult.

When she came out, she saw Heinrich and Jane who were waiting for her, slightly apart from all others.

"We'd like to talk to you," Jane began.

"Sure, do tell me," she said, perplexed.

"Uhm, it's a bit of a delicate subject, but..." Jane exchanged a glance with Heinrich. "You've heard what Anderson said about the dragons, haven't you?"

Sophie began to understand why the two looked so furtive. The symbolic olive branch that Kathleen had tried to present to the telepaths didn't seem very attractive to her, knowing her duplicity, but she realized that for the others, who had always been cruelly separated from their dragons, it might seem a good alternative.

"Sophie, she is like us!" Heinrich said warmly. "She understands! Perhaps it's true, in the past she did questionable things, but... well, she had to find her dragon! I do not approve, of course... but I can understand what led her to do it."

Sophie hesitated for a moment: she thought of Kathleen telling her to go with her, and imagined Pat free, flying in the sky without fear... but then she also saw the knife plunging into Cain's throat, his eyes wide with surprise and the blood...

My God, all that blood.

She blinked: "We can't trust her. I know what she says may sound convincing, but you can't really believe any of her words. She's very good at saying what we want to hear, but once she gets what she wants she won't have any scruples."

Heinrich and Jane looked at each other: "It's just that..." Jane said. "We don't believe that she would force us to stay away from our dragons. Instead here..."

"It won't be like that anymore!" Sophie exclaimed. "You think that's what I want for Pat? No, no... I promise you that when we'll get down there, and we'll be safe, you'll be able to be with your dragons all the time. Indeed, I want to encourage you to do that... I want you to build a strong relationship with them, so that they will trust you completely!"

The two still seemed uncertain.

"I'm sure you want to," Heinrich said. "But will you be able to convince everyone else? Cain has always been so strict..."

"Trust me, please," she said, trying not to sound too imploringly. It was important that they remained united; without the dragons they would be over, she was sure. "I won't let this torture keep being carried out. I promise you."

"Ok," Jane finally said. "I believe you. But please don't disappoint us, otherwise we will have to... well Kathleen said..."

"I won't," Sophie promised.

After that conversation she darted to Gregor: "Where are Nadia and..." she tried to remember the names of the other dragon telepaths. "Paul and...?"

"Marie?" he suggested.

"Yes, her. I want you to contact them immediately and send them all to the cathedral by tonight, before the dragons get there."

Gregor stared at her puzzled: "Isn't it too dangerous to put them all together?"

"No," Sophie said firmly. "They must stay close. It's the only way they can control them. And we must let them right away, before they decide to all go on Anderson's side and take away their dragons."

"But Cain..."

Sophie felt that if she heard someone mention what Cain said again she would scream in frustration.

Perhaps he would have done something completely different, but in that moment he wasn't there with them and the thought did nothing but make her feel worse.

"I know, I know... Cain would have a bloody fit if he knew," she snapped. "I understand. I thought we had already moved on from this..."

Gregor thought about it: "Whatever. You're the boss," he said, shrugging. "Now get out of my way, I've got work to do," he added, then began typing something on his tablet, ignoring her.

Sophie was stunned: was she really the one making decisions now?

CHAPTER 14

Since Kathleen Anderson had taken over the government, Erik's days had become a whirlwind of rapid changes he struggled to keep up with.

Following the appointment of Kathleen to the presidency of Europa, the status of Erik and his men had changed too.

What used to be just an office dedicated to the security of Anderson Pharmaceuticals had in fact become a state body which had replaced the presidential guard.

Anderson, in fact, said she preferred to be protected by a trusted person.

This meant that overnight Erik had received an official commission from the government; he was no longer an employee of Anderson Pharmaceuticals, but a representative of the new government of Europa.

For a good chunk of his time he had to work closely with Christian Voigt, the chief of secret services.

The latter was a large, balding man, with a slimy smile. He was already head of intelligence with the previous government, but he had agreed with Anderson to keep his place, as general Chardon did too.

In fact, this was a big advantage for her, because no one knew how to control the complicated gear of the secret services like Voigt.

Erik, however, didn't like the guy.

He found his smug way to inform him of what he thought he should know particularly irritating, as if he was doing him a favour while it was simply his job.

He liked to be coaxed, as if it was necessary to extort from him the information that he had obtained from his agents.

He reminded Erik of a fat spider in the middle of its web. He would get along with Hoffman, he thought. Or maybe not: it would be like having two roosters in the same henhouse.

In addition to the work of prevention of possible attacks against Anderson, a part of his work also involved recruitment: from a hundred people employed by Anderson Pharmaceuticals, the presidential guard had been ordered to grow to a thousand units.

The majority was made up of former soldiers, but there were also many enthusiastic volunteers that Kathleen had decided to enlist.

Erik would have preferred more former policemen, as himself and Hernandez, because civilians were inexperienced and disorganized, and military, in his opinion, were too often prone to brutality.

Unfortunately, Kathleen Anderson didn't seem particularly successful in attracting officers from the medical police, perhaps because her research was slowly undermining the very reason of existence of the institution.

The highest grades of the new presidential guard had been indicated by Kathleen herself with the help of General Chardon.

Erik had obviously accepted it without problems, but unfortunately for him he was to be surrounded by people that he didn't especially trust.

Zoe, at least, continued to be the personal bodyguard of Anderson.

If he had had the possibility to choose, he would have rather made more efforts to look for some more medical police officers... but Kathleen Anderson was in control, not him, so he had to trust her judgment, which until then had been impeccable, Erik thought.

Although it was an advancement in his career, Erik noticed that the news of the change in his employment status was not greeted with much enthusiasm by his kids.

In fact, Peter only asked him if he would have access to all the secret files about contacts with aliens or with the governments of the states of southern Europe that had segregated from the city, now that he was working with the secret services.

"Probably not," Erik replied through gritted teeth, trying with all his might to hold back a snide comment about the kid's beliefs.

Peter seemed disappointed, but he didn't comment further.

Maja, however, seemed to find his new work arrangement very disturbing.

"So now Anderson got herself a private militia," she said.

"It's not like that," Erik objected. "The point is that now she's even more exposed than before to attacks and other plots. And it's normal that there is someone in charge of defend her."

Maja had looked away and changed the subject, but Erik knew she wanted to add something.

Once he would have urged her to speak, but since their relationship was still too tense, and he didn't want the discussion to degenerate into a fight, he hadn't insisted.

It was true that Dr Anderson was always at risk, but in fact the population of Europa was for the most part in love with her.

Kathleen didn't hesitate to implement the promises she had made during her inaugural speech.

The food rationing had been abolished, and, thanks to a new and more efficient system of redistribution of resources, shops full of goods that costed much less than what was once taken from the taxes to finance the food distribution had sprung.

Moreover, given the sudden competition, retailers were doing their best to make their products attractive and tasty. Bakeries, fruit and vegetables stalls, and cheese shops had started to open.

Meat was still very expensive, and it was considered a luxury, but apart from this, Europa was experiencing an abundance that they hadn't known for years.

Despite the cold and pungent winter, people seemed to want to get together and celebrate, especially in the improvised bars that sprung up in every street corner.

Sometimes it was just a handful of tables and chairs, evidently coming from the owner's house, arranged haphazardly on the sidewalk, and it was impossible to order anything more elaborate than a beer or a soda, but it was nice to spend a few hours in a conversation with a friend while sipping something refreshing.

When spring would come, Erik thought, it would be even nicer.

In addition to this, Anderson had reorganized agriculture, devoting many of the territories beyond the eighth ring to grow food, thanks to the techniques patented by her company, and had built greenhouses and nurseries in record time.

It was still a bit too early to reap the benefits, but the first shoots of wheat, corn, beans and vegetables had already started to sprout.

For the first time in years, Erik, like most of his countrymen, he had begun to feel optimistic about the future.

Kathleen Anderson didn't even lie about her strategy to eradicate the organized crime of the underground city.

Despite her offer of reintegration in the social structure of Europa to all those who had decided to leave their old life of crime of their own free will, only a few inhabitants of the tunnels had decided to take advantage of that possibility.

From what Erik had understood there was a kind of atavistic distrust of the institutions of the city, regardless of who ruled them; besides, many of them disliked the idea of being 'filed'.

Living in the old underground, despite being uncomfortable in many ways, looked like a solution more in line with their philosophy of life to them.

But, of course, it was no longer possible to tolerate that situation.

A few days after she had taken office, Anderson had sent teams of anti-riot police in the main meeting points below the city and had arrested all those they found.

In a matter of weeks, the prisons had begun to overflow with inmates.

Proving her proverbial intelligence and efficiency, Dr Anderson had arranged that all prisoners were used as labour in the recently inaugurated fields.

"After many years of living off the citizens of Europe as parasites," she had said, "it's only right that they finally contribute to the sustenance of everyone."

Erik couldn't help but agree with her.

During the first raids some infected were also arrested, and they were immediately isolated and secured. No doubt they had tried to infiltrate the population to further spread their virus, taking advantage of the fact that few inhabitants of the underground city were vaccinated, the doctor had declared.

A board meeting to address their strategy about the problem of the rebels had been called, the first in which Erik participated.

He felt a bit nervous: did Kathleen expect him to give an active contribution? Or maybe he only had to listen to be informed of the decisions? Erik wasn't sure of what his role was, so he hoped he could see what others were doing and behave accordingly.

He felt like a schoolboy on the first day of school, he thought with a hint of embarrassment.

Beside him, the meeting was attended by the ministers and the most important personalities of the government: the new ministers of interior, agriculture, transport and services, as well as general Chardon and Christian Voigt.

Once the meeting began, however, he realized that there was no need to worry: Anderson took all the decisions and he had the impression that she didn't really expect to be contradicted.

"Our campaign of recovery of the underground city is giving very promising returns," Kathleen began. "However, I received information that suggest that the infected that were part of the resistance once led by a man named Cain now are right here under our feet, taking advantage of the labyrinth of tunnels under the city."

Erik shivered, and realized that he was not the only one.

Even despite the security given by the vaccine, the infected continued to arouse an instinctive fear.

"Moreover, it seems that this time they brought the dragons with them. During my personal reconnaissance last year, I found that the rebels have at least seven dragons, including an egg, four small ones and two medium-sized ones. Contrary to what they did in the past, it seems that this time the rebels have decided to use them for guerrilla warfare."

Bystanders appeared troubled, and Kathleen nodded to Voigt, to her left.

He cleared his throat: "A small dragon was spotted a few weeks ago… at least four times in different points of the city within an hour," he announced with fluting voice, observing the effect that his words had on the group of ministers in front of him.

"Here you can see an image picked up by a surveillance camera of the seventh ring."

Voigt clicked on a remote control and, on the wall opposite him, a slightly blurred image of what looked like a big black bird appeared, darting across the sky between two buildings.

Despite the fact that the photo itself wasn't very impressive, what it implied was all the more alarming, Erik thought.

"During the past few days, through cross-checks, we have come to identify a house in the eighth ring which we believe served as the headquarters of the rebels."

Voigt clicked several times on the remote control and on the wall appeared the image of some decrepit and unkempt interiors, with everyday objects thrown haphazardly on the floor, apparently abandoned in haste.

The next pictures showed an eerie basement with cages, chains and chewed remains of animals.

From the photos it was unclear if the dragons or the infected themselves had been living there.

As an expression of disgust was painted on general Chardon's face, Kathleen spoke again: "It has always been my intention to eradicate any possible outbreak of rebellion within the city, but never has the issue become of such vital importance until now." Her intense gaze seemed fixed personally on each person at the table of the meeting. "My hope was that, once eliminated Cain, the rebellion would extinguish naturally. Unfortunately, that was not the case. Indeed, the rebels seem willing to use all the weapons at their disposal in a last desperate attempt to destroy us... even those that they cannot control, like the dragons.

Unlike the previous government, I gave them an alternative. They could surrender, and live again in our society, but they decided not to.

I don't see any alternative but to try to destroy them all, to the last man or woman."

The fleeting image of Thea passed before Erik's eyes, as she had been the last time he had seen her: pale, bleeding and dying.

Erik frowned: he shouldn't have been thinking of Thea in that moment.

But he couldn't help but wonder what his wife would have thought of Anderson's decision. She had died for her collaboration with the rebels. But at the time they hadn't been given them any choice: all the infected were executed. What would Thea think of the fact that, now that they could live in peace with the rest of the city, they had decided not to do it?

Meanwhile, General Chardon nodded: "I assume that we must also consider the dragons as an objective," he said.

"NO!" Anderson roared, with a fierce voice that didn't even sound like hers.

Erik was startled and realized that some ministers seemed perplexed.

"It isn't necessary," the doctor continued, in a quieter tone. "The dragons are not to blame for the reckless decisions of the rebels. They are complex and fascinating creatures, and it is our duty to preserve them. In addition to this, they are a powerful weapon in the wrong hands... but useful and beneficial in the right ones. Our hands."

The general nodded quickly: "Why, of course. I didn't mean..." he stammered. "It will be our priority to escort them to a safe place," he concluded.

Kathleen nodded: "No one must hurt them. That's the priority."

After the meeting, Erik was ready to go back to his office. He still felt uncertain about the orders relating to infected.

Once he would have had no doubt that Anderson's hard line was the best, but his time at the custody hospital had softened his attitude.

He had had occasions to see that the infected were much more human than what was commonly believed.

It was true that, despite Anderson's invitation, none of them had surrendered but... well, until a few days before they had been chased and executed by the police. The fact that they didn't trust the institutions was at least understandable.

He was immersed in these thoughts when he realized that Anderson was beside him.

"I'm glad to see you, Persson," she greeted him. "I haven't had the opportunity to give you an official welcome within the executive. How do you like your new job?"

"I am adjusting to the new role," Erik admitted. "I'm trying to establish a fruitful collaboration with Mr. Voigt," he added, looking at him askance, but he was at a distance.

Everyone except himself and the new president had left the room.

"He's got a bit of a big head, hasn't he?" she laughed. "But what can I do, he truly *is* useful. He's been covering that role for twenty years, and he would be very difficult to replace."

Erik frowned: "So that's why he likes to be a law upon himself. He knows he's untouchable."

"I said difficult, not impossible," Kathleen pointed out with a soft smile. "Apart from his personality, however, I think that Voigt knows where he's at. Actually, I wanted to talk to you about something quite different," she added. "I saw you were troubled as we talked of the actions against the rebels. Is there something that worries you?"

Erik realized that the feeling he had when Kathleen spoke, that she individually watched each person in front of her, was right.

In front of others he could pretend and keep his doubts to himself, but he knew that Kathleen Anderson would listen impartially.

"To tell you the truth I was wondering if it wasn't... uhm.... perhaps a bit of a hasty decision, stopping trying to collaborate with them. After all they have a good reason to be afraid to surrender to the authorities," he explained.

Kathleen nodded thoughtfully: "It was a long time that I had in mind to talk to you about this, but..." she sighed. "This is a very personal subject and I wouldn't want to make you uneasy."

"No, I... do tell me, please," Erik said, puzzled.

"Well, when I decided to hire you, of course I did some research about you," she explained apologetically.

Erik felt a little troubled by this invasion of his privacy, but rationally he said to himself that he had nothing to reproach her. She had entrusted him with her safety and her life... the fact that she had wanted to know who the man in front of her was perfectly understandable.

"I found out about... your wife, and the circumstances of her death," Kathleen continued.

"Oh," Erik said, not knowing what to think.

"I know that, when she was alive, she used to be a spy for the rebels."

He nodded gravely. He still felt guilty about what had happened, but at that time, the familiar poignant pang in his chest had been joined by a new kind of anxiety: perhaps Anderson thought he was a naive simpleton not to have sensed what was going on under his own roof? Or maybe she thought that he might have been involved?

As if reading his thoughts, Anderson said: "I already knew all these things before I hired you, and please, don't think that I would judge you for that," she hastened to reassure him. "But I must admit that I wondered what could bring a healthy person, moreover, someone who was married to a medical police officer, to cooperate with that scum. I did some research about Thea Kron..."

Anderson took a file from her bag and Erik thought that his heart was missing a beat: what could Thea still be hiding from him?

"... and I found out that, about twenty-seven years ago, she had been treated by a psychiatrist. Did you know?"

"I... No, I didn't," Erik admitted, shocked. "She never told me."

"I see," Kathleen said sympathetically. "Post Traumatic Stress Disorder. It seems that a person that attended the university with her, this..." she checked on the dossier, "Baumann, an architecture student, had contracted the plague, and she had warned a doctor. It was the first wave of the epidemic, and of course Thea didn't know what that would entail. She thought he would have been taken care of but..."

"It wasn't so," Erik completed.

"No. He was taken away from what would become the medical police, and Thea soon realized that she would never see him again. Following that incident, she had a nervous breakdown."

Erik said nothing: it wasn't hard to imagine the guilt that his wife had experienced.

But what did that mean for him? Their marriage had been a fallback, a second choice? Or the death of her boyfriend was simply an episode from her past that she had finally moved on from?

Anderson handed him the dossier: "Take this home," she suggested. "Read it. The infected are not a bunch of desperate people only trying to pull a living. They have a plan, a strategy, and a network of informers," she said, looking intently at him. "I am convinced that those people have approached Thea knowing of her past. They relied on her empathy, her guilt, to manipulate her. It was them who put her in the forefront, to make her risk everything because she had the impression to make amends for her past sins. They put her in the line of fire."

Erik grabbed the file with trembling hands: he felt that part of him wanted to read it immediately, and the other was tempted to put it in a drawer and never open it again.

Kathleen put a hand on his arm, and he felt absurdly comforted, as if with that touch he was receiving forgiveness for all his past mistakes: "Your wife was a victim, Erik," she said. "Now you have the opportunity to avenge her."

Erik could do nothing but nod.

CHAPTER 15

The infected had left the temporary headquarters in the eighth ring just in time.

Gregor confirmed that, a few hours after they had moved the last dragon to the cathedral, the secret services agents had raided the place, fortunately only finding empty rooms.

This news had consolidated Sophie's approval among the infected, since she had insisted that they move as soon as possible.

Nevertheless, Ken continued to be very negative and critical about the new housing solution; however, his protest gathered little support.

Apart from the small group that had remained on the surface in the safe houses found by Gregor, as Cain and others who couldn't stay underground for health reasons, all other infected had been placed in the territory of Korbinian, a vast underground area that included various large rooms connected by a labyrinthine network of tunnels.

At first it seemed impossible to navigate: Korbinian then showed them a series of signs painted on the walls that at a first glance looked random and incomprehensible. It was a sort of road signalling system that ultimately made the move quite simple, once they had memorized the code.

All the people who lived there had become vaccinated in the days before their transfer; they had made it just in time, because the following week Kathleen Anderson had made the vaccine mandatory and a requirement to access any kind of service within the community, from taking a train to be treated in a hospital. This had caused the need for a certificate of vaccination, which was an official and personal document. It was no longer possible to just show up at one of the medical centres and get the vaccination done without fuss.

One of the innovations that made Sophie happiest was that Nadia was back. Her friend was well and had recovered from the blow to her shoulder; when she saw her face covered with scales, she laughed and hugged her.

"Karla told me, but I couldn't believe it until I saw you with my own eyes," she said with enthusiasm. "Now you're really one of us!"

For once, Sophie didn't feel gloomy about her new status.

Nadia had told her briefly what she had done since they had last seen each other.

Cain had her locked up on the island, apparently with the idea to inflict her some sort of punishment at a later time, but then with the evacuation and his coma, the whole business was more or less forgotten and no one bothered to follow up. In the end everything was resolved in a half day of captivity.

She had spent the last few months with Karla, in a number of houses between the fifth and seventh ring, and it was clear that she was sick of it.

"I was going crazy to see only the same old two or three rooms all the time!" she told Sophie. "And nobody would tell me anything about Taneen. I even feared that they wanted to get rid of him!"

Sophie had felt a little guilty for all that time in which she never thought to send her a message or a letter. She had never even thought it was possible.

Nadia, however, wasn't mad at her: on the contrary, she was radiant because she had finally been reunited with Taneen. The latter had finally stopped growing, settling on a size similar to that of a bear, or a big bull. It was clear, however, that he was no longer a puppy.

Sophie had taken the opportunity to talk at length about what had happened the night Kathleen Anderson had revealed herself and nearly killed Cain.

She realized that, apart from the disjointed story that she had given Famke the first night, and the questions that she had answered feeling indifferent and numb as she waited for the arrival of the symptoms of the plague, she had never really talked to someone about it.

Nadia was shocked as she heard about Emma's identity, and she seemed even more surprised to learn that Sophie had jumped into the sea to save Cain.

Unlike her, Nadia hadn't been very impressed by the sad story of his origins.

"I think you should have left him there," she said, shrugging. "You would have avoided yourself a lot of trouble."

"Well... I didn't know he wouldn't wake up anymore... I was hoping he would be alive and awake," Sophie defended herself, with a small pang of realizing that everyone, even her, now spoke of Cain using past tense.

Nadia made a face: "All the more reasons not to jump."

It was not worth arguing with her: she had never hidden her grudge against the former rebel leader, and now, unfortunately, it no longer made any difference.

The dragons were doing well in the cathedral: even the two biggest ones could easily spread their wings and fly. Although at first sight they had seemed huge, now that she had seen Anderson's dragon, Sophie could see that they were actually much smaller specimens.

One of them, she discovered, had been linked to Elias Visser, an infected who had died in prison some time before. Even his dragon, in fact, didn't look good: despite the considerable size, he appeared weak and emaciated, moved little and had a greyish colour.

Sophie wondered if dragons could suffer from depression too.

Now that all the creatures could be looked after by the person to whom they were linked, Sophie had suggested to Famke to take care only of Visser's dragon.

She thought that since then the great dragon appeared a little less sad.

Although now they were no longer chained or locked up in cages, all except Pat and Taneen seemed reluctant to take off. Most of the time they continued to remain crouched in a corner as they always had, even though they chains weren't there anymore. Sophie was very sorry for them, and she hoped that soon they would recover.

The arrival of the infected in the underground city coincided with the beginning of the attacks by the new government.

Kathleen had given orders to purge the city from the "rats" who lived underground, and until then she had achieved good results: thousands of people had been arrested and sent to work somewhere beyond the eighth ring. No one knew anything about their fate.

Many sinister rumours were circulating about what happened to the prisoners, but Sophie suspected that they were mostly false. She imagined that they probably weren't doing great, but that they were alive.

Gregor agreed with her: "Of course they don't write home!" he exclaimed, exasperated. "How could they? These people have no addresses or phone numbers, not to mention the fact that their location would be discovered if they could be contacted."

However, there was still a lot of fear for the police raids.

Korbinian's territory had not yet been reached yet, but there had been attacks in some superficial tunnels not far from them.

Korbinian seemed quite sure of his locations, and he was convinced that the police would never come to them.

Sophie was in the cathedral with Nadia: Pat and Taneen were flying in front of them, or at least they were trying.

Although Pat was much smaller, he appeared surer of himself on his wings than Taneen, who was clumsy and uncertain.

Surely it depended on the long period spent in chains, as Nadia never failed to point out.

Sophie had the impression that she was a bit competitive about the performances of their dragons.

The other dragons were quite indifferent to each other, but Pat and Taneen often sought each other to play fight.

Sophie wondered what was the true nature of these animals, if left in their habitat: were they solitary creatures or moved in packs?

Gregor suddenly materialized beside Sophie.

"You must come with me," he ordered.

"Damn, how come you always catch me by surprise?!" Sophie protested.

She was sure that his ability to move quietly was useful, but it could be very annoying.

Gregor looked at her sternly: "Because you never pay attention to what surrounds you."

Nadia merely observed him with her lips tightened in an expression of disapproval.

She didn't like Gregor, which wasn't strange considering that he had shot her, Sophie thought.

"Why?" she asked.

"It's about that Korbinian guy," Gregor answered. "I found that he has kept receiving requests from other leaders of the underground city to talk to us, but he never told us anything."

"What?" Sophie exclaimed. "Why?"

"I don't know why," he scoffed. "But you must do something, he can't keep putting us aside. It's a matter of authority."

Sophie felt bewildered: she had no idea of what she should say. Threaten him? Coax him? Order him to go find the people whom he had sent away?

"Cut one of his arms off and feed it to Pat," Nadia suggested, seeing her hesitation. "So he'll learn, and meanwhile you'd also solve the dinner issue."

Sophie frowned: "He would make a poor snack, didn't you see how skinny he is?" she pointed out. "I don't know anything about diplomacy... what should I do? What would Cain have done?" she asked, seriously, to Gregor.

"He would have made a big mess," Nadia replied. "You think he was diplomatic? More than ten years of resistance and everyone hates us, what do you think?"

"Sure, because when your enemies create a body of police with the sole purpose of hunting you down and killing you, your problem is popularity," Gregor hissed.

"In any case," Sophie interjected, hoping to cut off the discussion, "maybe Cain would know how to deal with Korbinian. But I don't."

Nadia didn't pick up the hint and looked at her critically: "Sophie, look, I think you've idealized his memory a little. Don't you remember what he really was like? He was not a perfect and angelic creature as you describe him. Cain was an asshole!" she exclaimed.

"That's not true!" she protested, blushing. "It's just that he had a tragic life and…"

"Oh, then he was an asshole because his mother never loved him as a child, poor thing…" Nadia interrupted her. "That doesn't make it right that he almost had me shot in the head."

"In the shoulder," Sophie objected. "He just wanted to stop you, not to kill you."

"Actually, I was the one to target the shoulder," Gregor pointed out. "He just said 'shoot', without specifying where."

"Oh, thanks a lot, what do you expect? A round of applause?" Nadia snapped.

"No, it was just for the sake of accurateness," he said, shrugging.

"You're not helping," Sophie muttered.

"Because Nadia is right," Gregor replied, exasperated. "Cain *was* an asshole! The point is that he was an asshole who did what he had to do."

Unlike me, Sophie thought.

She got up to go talk to Korbinian then, on second thought, she decided to bring Pat.

A dragon always did a certain impression, she thought.

For safety, she addressed to Pat the thought of trying to look as terrible as possible and the dragon puffed up his crest and spread his wings, appearing bigger and fierce. She thought she felt a twinge of amusement and wondered if dragons could have a sense of humour.

In fact, when Korbinian saw them coming, accompanied by Gregor who was already disturbing enough of his own, he stepped back, and suddenly seemed to get smaller.

For Sophie, who had always been physically small and unthreatening, being able to inspire such awe with her mere presence was a vaguely rewarding feeling.

"Sophie, it's such a pleasure to see you," Korbinian said, with a slimy smile.

"Enough with the pleasantries," Sophie ordered, trying to sound strong and authoritative. "I heard that people have come to talk to us, and you sent them away."

Korbinian paled: "Well, I didn't want to disturb you..."

"Let us decide what disturbs us or not," she snapped. "Next time someone asks for us or comes to you for something that concerns the infected, I want you to make them talk directly with me."

Gregor cleared his throat.

"Or with Gregor," Sophie added resolute. "Or send us a message if we're not there. Or leave us a note..." Gregor's expression told her that it was better if she stopped there.

"All in all, don't take decisions on our behalf," she concluded.

Korbinian didn't look very pleased: "But you've made a deal with me," he protested. "You're in *my* territory. If others come here to ask for protection, it is I who should decide..."

"Protection?" Sophie asked, puzzled. "What do you mean?"

"Against the police raids," Korbinian elaborated. "People from Misha's and Lisica's have already come. Once they would never have bothered to send someone to me. The poor, insignificant Korbinian, all locked up in the bowels of the earth..." he said bitterly. "They had the best territories for trade, the ones closer to the surface. And now they have the courage to crawl down to me, what chutzpah! Imagine that only last year..."

Sophie reflected, as Korbinian went on to list the various harassments that he had to endure during his career.

If all the clans, as they were called, joined them, they could fight against the police, against Kathleen...

But if they were isolated, sooner or later they would be driven out. Would dragons be enough at that point? Probably not, she thought.

"You must contact those two who came here immediately," she ordered Korbinian. "Misha and..."

"Lisica?" Korbinian completed, appalled. "What?! Didn't you hear what I said?"

"Not only them but also all others. All the clans that are still in the underground city," Sophie explained. "We must all unite and find a strategy against Kathleen Anderson."

Korbinian laughed: "Look, sweetie, you don't know anything about how things are going on here. We are mortal enemies! There are some offenses that can't be overcome, stuff from years ago that…"

"I'm sure there are more important things than your wounded pride," she interrupted him. "If we don't face the danger together, we're all as good as dead."

"What if I didn't want to do that?" Korbinian asked defiantly.

Sophie was exasperated… how could he not understand?

"I'll cut off one of your arms and feed it to the dragon," replied Gregor, sounding deadly serious. "So you'll learn, and meanwhile we'd also solve the dinner issue."

Pat snorted a warning flare.

Korbinian grew pale, and Sophie realized that he had believed it.

"In this case," the criminal said, with as much dignity as the situation allowed him. "I can arrange the delivery of your message."

It took a week to be able to bring together all the criminals in the same place at the same time.

Sophie had the impression that many did not accept the first proposal for a meeting, and made excuses, just to give the idea of having a thicker schedule of commitments than they actually did; but she knew they had to be desperate.

The underground city, apparently, had rules of conduct of its own, that Sophie found incomprehensible and a little frustrating.

Eventually, however, they managed to be in what Korbinian had explained was a 'free zone', a part of the underground city where none had jurisdiction, and where it was forbidden to enter armed.

Korbinian had however advised them to keep a small gun or a knife because 'you never knew'; and in any case everyone would have done the same, he added with a shrug.

Apparently convincing those people to work together and to have mutual trust would be more complicated than expected.

Fifteen people had showed up, mostly accompanied by a small group of thugs.

They were a very mixed crowd: they wore strange clothes that Sophie had never seen, had very long or short hair, with bizarre cuts, and even tattoos.

In there even the plague scales wouldn't stand out so much, Sophie thought: however, when she, Nadia, Gregor, James, Amanda and Famke entered the meeting place, everyone fell silent and looked at them with fear, perhaps also for the presence of Pat, who functioned both as a weapon and as a representative of their delegation.

Sophie had decided not to bring Ken, because in recent times he seemed to oppose all that she said on principle, and she needed support.

Gregor had turned his nose up when Sophie had decided to extend the participation to Amanda, because he continued to consider those who hadn't been infected as outsiders that couldn't be trusted completely; Sophie, however, thought that the presence of Amanda, as well as being useful because she appreciated her opinion, would send a positive message to the people of the underground city, making it clear that they shouldn't fear their presence.

Sophie was indicated about who were the most important criminals: Misha, she discovered, was a burly man with a thick dark beard, who sat in the middle of the room as if he was on a throne.

Lisica instead was an elderly woman with orange hair; she stood in a corner silently, but carefully observed everything.

Besides them there were others whom she had never heard of: Farkas, Sinsonte, Królik, Had...

Korbinian had insisted to speak to first and explain their proposal, which he did after a lengthy introduction that Sophie found unnerving:

it seemed, however, that going straight to the point would be considered a rude gesture.

When he finally explained that he wanted everyone to collaborate to fight the arrests performed by the police, there was a murmur of protest.

"Just asking me to ally myself with those people," said Farkas, a man with a grey hollow face, indicating the area where Misha was, "is an insult to the memory of my brother!"

Misha spat: "Your brother got what he deserved," he said with a booming voice. "When he robbed my property…"

Shortly, everyone started arguing with each other, bringing up past sins.

It didn't take long before Sophie realised why Cain never tried to ally with them.

"It's not going very well, I'd say," Nadia observed.

James also seemed disappointed: "They will never get along, they've spent all their life at war."

"Why do they keep spitting?" Gregor asked with a grimace. "It's gross."

Amanda leaned toward Sophie: "We must do something, otherwise this will go on for hours," she advised.

Sophie nodded, and her thoughts turned to Pat.

The dragon gave a roar and a powerful blaze, which had the power to instantly stop every word in the room.

While the characteristic pungent smell of smoke was spreading, Sophie watched one by one the people in front of her.

"I know that between each of you something unpleasant happened in the past, something that under normal circumstances you would never forgive or forget," she began. "And you really don't have to: I'm not here to force you to make peace, because I know it's impossible."

She thought that all the faces had an unreadable expression. What were they thinking?

Would they accept her proposal or would they reject it with indignation?

"But I want to ask you to consider a truce," she continued. "At this moment we have a greater and more dangerous enemy to fight, someone who in a short time has started to destroy everything you've worked for in the past."

Maybe 'worked' was a bit of an improper term, she thought fleetingly, but surely they had put resources and effort in it.

"As far as I'm concerned you can continue to hate each other. You can keep your resentment for past abuses. You can use this time to study each other and identify their weaknesses. But as long as Kathleen Anderson will be in power you have to cooperate with each other... At least, if you want our protection. They might have more weapons and more men, but we have dragons." Sophie put a hand on Pat's head. "And you have the territory, a complicated and ramified area that, unlike the police, you know well. If we can overcome our differences, we have a chance."

There was a long silence.

In the end, a hoarse chain-smoker voice came: "What's your proposal?" Lisica asked.

Sophie felt exalted: it was a very cautious opening, but it was a start.

"Uhm, well, first of all we should have access to all of your territories. Ideally, we should have a single map that..."

She didn't manage to finish the sentence, because again there was a chorus of protest.

"A map? Never!"

"Don't even think about it!"

"If I gave you my territory what would I be left with?"

Korbinian approached Sophie: "It would have been better to say this later," he explained softly. "We are strong when we are the only ones to know the tunnels... giving away this knowledge is like giving up our most precious treasure."

"How can we coordinate attacks if we don't know where we're going?!" she asked.

Korbinian shrugged: "Yeah, this could be a problem, but that's the way it is."

Sophie rubbed her temples: she was getting a headache.

It took several hours and some persuasive blaze by Pat to convince everyone, though very reluctantly, to deliver to Gregor a map of all the tunnels linking their territory to the other: the details of how the inner areas were articulated could continue to remain secret, they agreed.

"It's useless this way! If we must stop the police we must at least know how to move in all directions," Gregor complained.

Sophie shrugged: "You're right, it is an incomplete solution, but at least we have something. The rest we can ask later... for now the fact that they have agreed to this is quite a result!"

Gregor kept appearing discontent: "I can't stand them anymore. I get sick at the very thought of having to fight together with these people."

"I'm not enthusiastic either," Sophie sighed. "Especially the guy at the bottom that squeaks so much... Fan... Fab..."

"Fa'r."

"He's so annoying!"

"Every time he speaks, I contemplate enlisting in Anderson's guard," Gregor said grimly.

Sophie chuckled, and Gregor appeared offended.

"Yes, you laugh, because in the end who is it that will have to put up with these barbarians while you happily frolic around with your dragon?"

He seemed genuinely disgusted by those criminals, at least as much as they were by the infected.

"I don't frolic around!" Sophie protested, but her attention was diverted again to the meeting.

Fa'r, which was a little man with an elusive expression and a thin, scratchy voice, stood up again and informed them that they would leave that infected people and others to circulate freely in their territories, but only if that all weapons and assets recovered by policemen who died in their burrows were the exclusive property of their clan.

"For the umpteenth time," Sophie said exasperated. "We don't want to kill them, just to make sure they are locked. If all goes according to plan, there won't be mountains of corpses to strip!"

"Here, this I don't agree with," Misha thundered. "They kill us without mercy, why should we do differently?"

Sophie had the impression of repeating the same things over and over: "Because we don't want to destroy all those who live in the city above, nor all the cops. If we go on like this, we will always be war."

"Ah, that's fine for me," Fa'r commented with his squeaky voice, earning a murmur of agreement. Sophie felt the urge to give him a slap.

We could do it, said a voice inside her.

She imagined how nice it would be to hit him, to take that grin away from his face... indeed, more, to sink her claws into his throat, tearing his flesh to shreds.... It would be so satisfying...

Beside her, Pat gave a low and ferocious growl.

Sophie blinked: was she really thinking about those horrible things?

She patted Pat reassuringly, and at the touch of her hand he calmed down instantly.

Sophie was then able to bring her thoughts back to the subject of the conversation.

"Do you understand that if the entire population of Europe considers us murderers and terrorists Anderson has already won?" she insisted. "We don't have any hope this way. We must defend our survival, not to become criminals!"

"It's just that they already are," Gregor whispered through clenched teeth.

Several hours later, after the meeting, Sophie felt exhausted.

She just wanted to take a long sleep, and possibly forget everything about the police and the underground city.

Amanda joined her, her expression serious.

"Look, I thought about what you said about the opinion of the citizens of the Europa," she announced gravely.

"And you don't agree," Sophie anticipated her.

"No, actually I'm with you!" Amanda said. "Cain has always said that it was useless to seek the support of the population because most of them would always hate the infected. Perhaps he was right, but I think the situation has changed since there's been a vaccine. But striving not to be violent is not enough. We have to let everyone know what the police is doing, instead."

Sophie thought about it: "You're right. But how can we do that?"

"I have an idea," Amanda said. "And I think Ken could help us with the IT part."

"Ken isn't excited about our new line of action," Sophie warned her.

Amanda shrugged: "He'll come around, you'll see."

While Sophie gave Pat, who looked even more tired and nervous than her, his evening snack, she reflected on how difficult it would have be for the infected and the criminals of the underground city to collaborate.

The meeting of that day had shown that it wasn't only a matter of different origins or class: the underground city had a completely different mindset from them, who in their previous life had been ordinary citizens of Europe.

Maybe everything would just end up in a disastrous defeat.

Sophie had no idea whether her strategy had any hope, or if she was actually handing the underground city over to Kathleen Anderson.

CHAPTER 16

The file about Thea that Kathleen Anderson had handed over to Erik had become crumpled for having been leafed through so many times.

Erik had resisted half a day, removing the stack of paper from his sight and trying not to think about it: in the end, however, he had capitulated, and with a lump in his throat he had carefully read the material he had received.

They were documents about Thea: information about her work and her family, mostly things he obviously already knew well. But above all, there were the transcripts of the sessions she had done with a psychiatrist, Dr Cohen, years before they met.

Even in the arid pages on which their conversations were reported, it became clear how fragile and desperate Thea had been, torn apart by guilt and eager only to get her hands on some medication that would make her feel better.

How could that be the same happy, positive person he loved?

Was the Thea he had met just a mask?

Rationally, he knew that there was a very simple explanation: so much time had passed. Back then, she was just a little girl, even younger than Maja. It had been a lifetime since then, and Thea had had plenty of time to get over what had happened and come to terms with her ghosts.

At times, Erik thought he should bury that file, forget it, and appreciate the many good memories he had of his wife. He wanted to remember her as she had been all their lives together: funny, happy, passionate.

Yet there was another part of him, a part that continued to feel betrayed, that wanted to get to the bottom and know exactly what had happened.

As much as Erik tried to silence it, that voice inside him kept haunting him.

Unfortunately, or fortunately, he didn't have much free time to brood over the past.

After a very exciting start, in which the police had collected one success after another in the purging of the underground city, the local underworld, helped by the infected rebels (or so they said) had evidently begun to organize a counter-offensive.

Those rats were smart, Erik had to recognize with frustration.

They never openly attacked them, but they confused them.

They drew the cops into tunnels and then collapsed them in front of them, forcing the rest of the team to spend hours moving the rubble to free them.

At other times they would be chased for miles in the labyrinth of tunnels, and then suddenly disappeared: the policemen advanced for a few meters to find out that they had returned to the starting point.

And what was worse was that they started covering up the police with ridicule.

They had never killed any agents, nor seriously injured anyone; however, they often bombed agents with bullets of colourful paint, or glue and confetti, forcing them to go out into the street amidst the laughters of bystanders.

At first, the citizens of Europe looked at the policemen with respect and also, why not, a certain fear.

Erik was not a person who enjoyed being feared, but he was convinced that the police should have some authority, otherwise it was useless.

When they had carried out their first raids in the old subway, their inhabitants had been taken out in handcuffs, and people had watched approving, happy with the efficiency of law enforcement and impressed by their strength.

In a few weeks the situation had turned upside down: every time the teams were getting ready to enter the tunnels, immediately a flock of curious would appear, eager to see in what funny conditions the agents would emerge.

At first, Erik thought it was a foolish and childish strategy, but now he realized that, even if it could not continue forever, it was subtly undermining the power and authority of the institutions of Europa themselves.

The repression had become fiercer. When the cops managed to get their hands on a rebel, they were usually already frustrated and angry, and they certainly didn't let them get away.

Yet, that joke of resistance had also managed to exploit this fact: Erik didn't know how, but the rebels had begun to document each of the arrests that were made, taking pictures every time the agents let themselves go and beat someone up.

The same photos were then scattered throughout the city, attached to the walls, doors and light poles.

It was impossible to ignore them.

And, of course, the photos never showed the thousands of arrests that his former colleagues had made in perfect professionalism, limiting themselves to handcuffing people and escorting them to the buses used to transport them to the detention facilities.

No, only the most shameful and brutal episodes appeared in those images.

In particular, one picture had become viral: it represented a woman, with red, congested eyes because of the gas that had been spread in the tunnels, who was hit by a policeman with a baton and gas mask.

The photo had circulated so obsessively that it had even been painted by some vandals on a wall of the second ring, right in front of the Anderson Pharmaceuticals headquarters.

In a very short time, public opinion had begun to change: Anderson was still adored, without a doubt, but people had begun to wonder why she allowed these episodes of incivility to occur.

A delegation was even sent to the government, calling for respect for human rights in the underground city.

Erik found that whole story absolutely paradoxical: of course, the cops were wrong when they let themselves go to violence; Erik thought he was a person of a peaceful nature, but he knew too well the reactions you could have when you were subjected to that mix of fear and frustration that was often generated during field operations. He didn't justify those agents, but he understood them.

However, he could not understand how Kathleen Anderson could be held responsible for these episodes: she had only ordered the eviction of the underground city and the arrest of those who did not want to cooperate, which all the citizens had agreed was a necessary measure.

Did they already forget all the good that Anderson had brought them?

People are so ungrateful when their bellies are full, he thought bitterly.

Kathleen called an emergency meeting of the strategic council, and Erik went to the government headquarters, eager to know how the new president intended to address the issue.

Outside the door of the boardroom, he found Alan taking over for Zoe Hernandez, who had just finished his shift. The former agent looked tired and worried.

"You really need a good night's sleep," Erik joked.

"Yes," she agreed. "Look, Persson, can I talk to you for a moment? In private," she added, looking around.

"Sure," he replied, perplexed.

They left the room and entered a small office, which was deserted at the time.

"What's going on? Are you okay?" Erik asked.

Zoe nodded: "Yes, yes, I'm fine. It's just that..." Zoe nervously bit her lower lip. "Okay, I don't know how to say it... but you think that Anderson might be... sort of... going crazy?"

"What?" Erik laughed.

"I almost feel guilty talking about it," Hernandez continued. "I mean, she's fantastic, and you know that I support her in everything..."

"Of course. Go ahead."

"Well... the thing is, sometimes she's so weird. As a bodyguard I must follow her everywhere, and... more and more often she speaks to herself."

Erik looked at her indulgently: "That's it?"

"I know that saying that sounds like nothing..."

"Because it *is* nothing! It doesn't mean she's... What did you say? Going crazy? Come on!"

Zoe kept looking worried: "I can tell the difference between a person thinking out loud and someone who's losing their marbles," she insisted. "Anderson has whole conversations on her own! With different opinions, quarrels, recriminations!"

Erik raised an eyebrow: "Could it be that she's using her mobile phone headset and you haven't noticed?"

Zoe hesitated: "I... well... I haven't checked, actually."

"Well, then! It's probably the headset," he minimized. "You panicked for nothing."

"They didn't sound like phone conversations at all," Zoe mumbled, but she appeared less self-confident.

"You did the right thing coming to tell me," Erik reassured her. "I'm glad that you closely keep an eye on Kathleen, it does give me confidence. But maybe this time you were too alert?"

"I don't know... it's just that..." Hernandez seemed to be struggling for words. "It's so disturbing..."

"What's disturbing?" Kathleen Anderson asked, entering the room.

Zoe froze, and Erik made a dismissive gesture with his hand: "Nothing important…"

"We're waiting for you at the meeting," Anderson informed him. "Zoe, are you all right?" she added, with an indecipherable smile.

"Yes, madam," Hernandez lied without blinking.

"I'll be right there," Erik said, just to end that moment of embarrassment.

He said goodbye to Zoe and followed the president into the boardroom.

Zoe's concerns were exaggerated, he thought: Anderson always looked so reasonable and self-confident. He couldn't imagine anyone looking of healthier mind.

The meeting focused, as planned, on the new strategy to adopt towards the inhabitants of the underground city and the rebels, who for the first time were considered as a common front.

Kathleen Anderson, of course, was not satisfied with the turn of events, and had asked the chief of the medical police, Seidel, to improve the organization of raids in the underground city.

"And for heaven's sake, stop beating up the rebels!" she exclaimed "It's quite enough that half of Europa is laughing with them, all we need is for them to sympathize with that scum!"

Erik looked at her with attention: even though Anderson always seemed controlled, the weight of power had begun to leave traces on her appearance.

Compared to a few months before, when she was not yet president, Kathleen appeared much more tired: her face was tense and more lined, and her skin had begun to take an unhealthy complexion.

With everything she had achieved in a short time, Erik thought, it was no wonder she was a little weary.

Seidel defended himself by saying that the medical police did not have the resources to explore all the tunnels of the underground city: the place was a maze, it would take months, maybe years, to map it all.

"Certainly, if we had the army with us..." he cautiously suggested, "we could definitely move forward more quickly."

"The army could intervene if the state of emergency were declared," General Chardon pointed out.

Kathleen's gaze went from one to the other.

Erik was puzzled: it was clear that the police, alone, was having enormous difficulties in dealing with the new strategy of the rebels.

On the other hand, the idea of the army in the streets of Europe... was that really necessary? he wondered, upset.

The last time this had happened was during the first wave of the plague, before the establishment of the medical police.

What would have happened to the quiet and optimistic atmosphere that had been created in the city in recent months?

It would certainly collapse, as would the cautious economic recovery that had begun.

Kathleen seemed to read his mind: "No, I don't think it is appropriate for the army to invade the city," she declared. "It would be a shock for the population, and it would increase the protests. We must show superiority, also from a moral point of view."

Erik nodded, as always in agreement with her.

"But I can give further support to the medical police. Persson, do you believe that the presidential guard can provide additional resources and assistance in the purge of the underground city?"

"We, umm... yes, of course," Erik declared, caught a little off guard. It was the first time he'd ever spoken in those meetings.

Anderson nodded: "Good. It's settled, then."

At the end of the meeting, Erik took a dark car with Seidel that carried them to the station.

It was strange how, despite the fact that less than a year had passed, his situation had changed so radically.

Only a few months earlier, he had walked through that door, happy to have returned to being a simple agent, and now he was about to have a meeting with no less than Seidel, the boss of the boss of his old boss's boss.

All thanks to Kathleen, he thought with gratitude.

Despite being satisfied with his new working condition, Erik felt nostalgic passing in front of the hot beverages machine where he had spent so much time with his former colleagues.

"Erik! Is that really you?" a familiar voice called.

"Lara," he exclaimed, recognising his favourite colleague. "How are you?"

"I'm fine," she replied. "But you, on the other hand... you left without warning anyone," she added reproachfully.

"Well, you know, it was all so sudden." Indeed, he had used holidays to cover the months of notice, and, after that unpleasant afternoon in the company of Janssen, he had never returned to the station.

"You're looking good. I hear you've become a big shot in the Anderson government, congratulations!" Meyer congratulated him.

"Not really a big shot," he laughed. "A very small shot, actually. But I don't have to share my desk with Janssen anymore, that's a priceless advantage."

Lara laughed: "The poor guy felt terrible when you left. He kept saying it wasn't his fault, but no one listened to him. Laurent looked at him askance for at least a month."

"Serves him right," Erik, commented, but at that moment he discovered that he missed all of them, even Janssen.

"How are Maja and Peter?"

"Good," Erik replied. "Peter has finished high school."

"Oh, what is he studying now?"

Erik sighed: "He has decided to go to work in the plantations of the eighth ring, one of his crazy fixations... I hope it's only a sabbatical year."

In fact, Erik had to ask for some favours to make sure that his son was hired as a laboratory assistant and not as a simple labourer.

He wasn't proud to have used his position for personal purposes, but he was shocked by the idea that his son should go to work elbow to elbow with all the dissident prisoners who had been picked up during the raids, and in the end he decided to make a small exception to his principles.

Seidel looked impatient next to him, so he had to cut himself short.

"Perhaps when I'll finish this meeting we could go and get a beer... now that we can! That way, the dramatic confrontation between Laurent and me can finally take place."

"That'd be great, but we've all been called for another one of those stupid subway raids," Lara rolled her eyes. "Last time I got lost in a tunnel and it took five people to get me out, it was so embarrassing..."

"Ah, never mind then," Erik said, a little disappointed.

"Come on, next time you come, send me a message, let's organize it," she said. "I was glad to see you."

"Yes, me too..." Erik noticed that Seidel seemed more and more bored, and it was clear that he would have liked him to hurry up. "Now I have to go."

"See you soon, Erik!"

Erik watched Lara move away, admiring her hair dancing on her shoulders, as he had done so many times before.

CHAPTER 17

Sophie mentally thanked goodness for finding Cain's meditation books, while she appealed to all her self-control not to tell Misha and her clan to go to hell.

Despite the good results obtained against the police, all the leaders of the underground city were very unhappy, and they would have liked to adopt a different strategy.

The complaints were of various nature: collapsing the tunnels damaged their territory; they had not managed to get any kind of booty from the trapped agents; they would have liked to take some more violent action because according to them, that way of fighting was useless and did not show any strength.

Even if Sophie was inclined to ignore most of their complaints, that last point threatened her confidence a lot... especially because she didn't know what she could do as a next step.

The defeatist attitude of the underground city, however, bothered her a lot: it was true, with her method they did not get any financial advantage, nor did they take away land from the police. All she had done so far was protecting people from brutal arrests: since they started to coordinate, the police had not been able to make mass arrests, and they had gone from arresting thousands of people a day to a few hundred a week.

But it was also clear that the wishes of the criminals were not realistic: Kathleen Anderson would never abandon the idea of regaining the territory under Europa. She had exposed herself too much in that sense, and she would never decide, as they hoped, to let go and abandon the tunnels to their jurisdiction.

"You fill our heads with a lot of talk about your dragons," Misha accused, looking at Pat with contempt, "then why don't we use them? Let's be the ones to attack for once!"

To Sophie's disappointment, the proposal raised a murmur of approval.

"We should make a nice little attack on their people" Misha continued "Maybe to the seat of government, or Anderson Pharmaceuticals… let's see how she likes to see her life's work destroyed" he proposed, poisonous.

"And then what would happen?" Sophie objected, for what seemed to her to be the hundredth time. "Do you think that she will go in front of the rest of the government and say 'You know what, attacking the terrible Misha was a bad idea, let's just give up and not think about it anymore'?"

"Well, for sure next time she will think twice before putting herself against us!"

Sophie shook her head: "There will be no next time. Anderson cannot show weakness in front of the rest of the city… there would only be an escalation of violence."

Although her objection seemed very reasonable to her, the leaders of the underground city continued to protest.

At the end of the meeting, Sophie felt demoralized. The alliance with a group of criminals seemed more and more problematic and difficult to manage.

"I have the impression that we're not going anywhere," she told James, who had accompanied her, tirelessly. As always, she had brought Pat with her, even though the shock factor was getting more and more exhausted, as everyone was getting used to seeing him around by now.

James shrugged: "No one here has any idea what they're doing."

It was a diplomatic response, but she didn't find it very encouraging.

She returned with him to the lodgings that Korbinian had made available to them.

Although dragons could enjoy more space and freedom in the underground city, the same could not be said of humans: Sophie and about twenty others were crammed into a room that probably used to be some kind of subway maintenance room, where they had placed sleeping bags and makeshift cots. At first no one had complained too much, also because of the fright they had taken in discovering that they had been tailed by the police, but now Sophie too began to show signs of intolerance for this complete lack of privacy.

Fortunately, she could spend a lot of time in the cathedral, which, despite the dragons, was a much more private and quieter environment.

Sophie took the opportunity to bring back Pat, so that he could spread his wings. There she found Famke, who was trying to get the dragon that had been Visser's up in the air.

After a few attempts, the beast finally spread its wings and rose a few meters.

Famke rewarded him with a mouthful of raw meat and a gentle pat on his head.

Sophie was happy that, although they didn't have a telepathic connection like the others, the new couple was also doing well.

Paul arrived to feed his dragon, a six-year-old specimen with blue-golden scales, not very large but stocky. Paul was also short and robust: Sophie often had the impression that in addition to sharing a telepathic bond, humans and dragons often ended up resembling each other physically.

Paul also brought two boxes of polystyrene: like most telepaths, he preferred to eat with his dragon.

"Want one?" he offered.

Sophie realized that she hadn't touched any food all morning and accepted gladly.

There were vegetable patties in it with tomato sauce and spicy rice. It was all very tasty and Sophie ate it with pleasure.

"What is it?" Gregor said, arriving suddenly and stole her last patty before she could stop him. "Good," he commented.

"Hey, that was mine."

Gregor ignored her protest and sat next to her: "I spent all day putting up explosive charges in a tunnel with a guy who probably hasn't showered since the first plague epidemic," he said with disgust. "It's a miracle that my appetite isn't gone forever."

"Is it just me or has the quality of food improved lately? I haven't seen a protein substitute burger in a month," Sophie observed, thinking about it for the first time.

"Yes, Anderson had the sense to abolish the food rationing. We agree that she is a psychopath who has practically killed most of the city, creating a deadly disease... but, between us, if I weren't infected now, I would be quite happy with her government," he confessed.

"How can you say such a thing?" Sophie flared up. "She tricked me, she exploited me... she cut Cain's throat! She's just a fake, a hypocrite..."

"Ah yes, instead your attitude is not hypocritical at all," he replied. "Coming from the same person who complains all day because those guys from the underground city can't forget their past quarrels."

Sophie blushed: "Wait, it's completely different-" she began, then stopped.

Was it *really* that different? Or did she, like Misha and Lisica, have difficulty letting go of her personal grudge?

"Let's give credit where it's due: food rationing was bullshit," Gregor continued. "In the first ring there has always been food of all kinds in abundance."

Sophie rolled her eyes: "That's what they say... but to be honest I don't believe that even the wealthiest classes did that well, after all..."

"No, no, I assure you, they did," he said. "I lived there, I remember it well."

"In the first ring?" she asked, impressed.

Sophie looked at the worn-out sweater, too wide for his thin chest, the hint of a grey, uncultivated beard covering his cheeks and the dark earth stains he had on his hands and trousers, probably from digging in the tunnels.

At that moment, it was difficult to imagine Gregor in the luxury that distinguished the inhabitants of the richest and most institutional area of Europe.

"You had some bad luck, getting the plague," Sophie commented.

It was well known that, while the disease had spread like wildfire to the less well-off quarters, the first and second rings had been almost untouched by the epidemic: it was usually said that this was due to better hygienic conditions, but Sophie was rather convinced that the main reason was the lesser contact between people.

It was much easier to get physical contact between a hundred people pressed into a railway wagon than between the two passengers of an institutional car.

Gregor laughed mirthlessly: "Bad luck, sure. You can also call it that."

"How did you get infected?"

"It was a goodbye gift from a colleague of mine. Thoughtful, isn't it? There are those who receive a clock, there are those who receive a beautiful plate... Voigt decided to give me the plague."

"Christian Voigt is infected?" Sophie asked, dismayed.

Gregor shook his head: "Look, since we're here, might as well tell you the whole story. I had been hired by the secret service, and I was doing just fine. I was an agent for a few years, then I moved to the offices. I was pretty ambitious, you know, I wanted to get ahead. Fact is, I started working with Voigt. He wasn't the boss at the time, just a young man with high hopes. They were the first years of the plague, when the medical police had just been established. At one point we were in competition for a promotion: the post of deputy director of the seventh ring was at stake."

Sophie tried to imagine a younger Gregor, all dapper in suit and tie, but it seemed an unrealistic picture to her.

"We were both very close. We used all the cards we had: we asked for support, offered favours, exchanged information... in short, it was a fair fight. At a certain point Voigt started thinking that I had stabbed him in the back, causing him to make a complete fiasco in an operation that he had coordinated."

"Ambition had made him become paranoid," Sophie commented in a wise tone.

Gregor thought about it: "Yes, there was that... and also the fact that it was true."

"Oh."

"One night, Voigt asked me to stop by his office, and he told me he heard the promotion would be mine. The next day it would have been official. I was so happy... I mean, it was a good shot. He gave me a good speech, with congratulations, no hard feelings, the best man won...and then he motioned to shake my hand. When I grasped it, I felt a sting."

Gregor stared at the palm of his right hand, where there was a large scale from which other stripes radiated.

"You know what that asshole did? He immediately picked up the phone and called the medical police, saying I was infected and threatened to infect him. I was upset, I could not believe what he had the courage to do..." Gregor ran a hand on his face, appearing suddenly very tired. "Luckily, I realised I had to escape before the police arrived. After a month, the first bubbles arrived... and here I am. I never saw Voigt again. He was probably one of the first to get the vaccine, which explains why he was so bold as to inject me with the disease without fear of being infected. What a bastard... I'm not surprised he's had such a career," he commented.

Sophie nodded: "I bet he and Kathleen are getting along splendidly."

"You know, when Cain put together the first group of rebels and I joined them, I only had one condition: that I could infect Voigt with my own hands and then watch him die of the plague."

Sophie thought of Kathleen, and how she wanted to cut her throat with her own hands, and how Kathleen wanted to kill Cain, and how the leaders of the underground city hated each other, in a vicious circle of resentment that seemed to never end.

"Do you think it's a mistake to continue to use my diversionary tactic against the police?" she asked him point-blank.

Gregor turned to look at her. "Yes," he answered.

Sophie's heart missed a beat: Gregor did not have James' diplomacy, but at least he spoke clearly, and he was brutally sincere.

"You're right when you say that agents and civilians are innocent and have nothing to do with this war that has been created. But if you want to win you can't avoid getting your hands dirty forever," he pulled a face. "This, at least, I learned from Christian Voigt."

"I know, I just... I wish I had more time," Sophie confessed. "I don't want to hit at random, just to cause as many victims as possible. I would like people to get used to seeing us as something different from beastly and irrational creatures... I was one of them until recently, I know how they think. For them, all we want is to infect or kill them, and they find the underground city simply terrifying."

Gregor raised his eyebrows: "They're not entirely wrong there."

"OK, yes," Sophie admitted, "but the point is that it's not an uncontrollable and destructive force. I am convinced that there is a way in which we can all coexist," she sighed. "The fact is that Kathleen is always stronger than us. She has the police, and her presidential guard, and even a dragon! What do we have in comparison?"

"More dragons?"

"Yes, more dragons and more people," she agreed, "but we are disorganized, and I think that in a direct confrontation we would still lose."

Gregor remained silent for a while, immersed in his thoughts.

"You know, once there was a Roman politician, Fabius Maximus, who thought just like you," he finally said, thoughtful. "To stop Hannibal, who was a Carthaginian general trying to invade Rome with a huge army, he understood that they mustn't go into direct contact with the enemy, otherwise they would lose. They were much stronger, they even had elephants, which in those days was a bit like having dragons. Fabius Maximus's fellow citizens, however, thought that he was a coward or even a traitor, and they called him the 'delayer' with contempt."

"How did it end?"

"Well, in the end he won. But the Romans, while on the one hand they were taking time, on the other they went to wage war to Carthage directly, forcing the army that was attacking them to retreat. No one can stall forever," he concluded, getting up.

"How do you know all these things?"

"I studied them when there were still schools worthy of the name." Gregor pulled a face: "I'm going to use all my classical culture to fill a tunnel of dragon dung to be spilled over the cops. Ah, how times change..." he mumbled, leaving.

Sophie remained silent, thinking of Gregor's words.

In the end, she thought maybe she knew how to unblock the situation.

CHAPTER 18

The support given by the presidential guard to the police for the purging of the underground city had caused Erik an exponential increase in problems related to the discipline of his men.

When it was a small group of bodyguards, he had never had difficulty keeping everyone in line, but, with the growth of staff and their involvement in armed actions, there were also many more episodes of violence on duty, which Erik could not contain.

Despite all the warnings, sanctions and even dismissal in a couple of cases, the men in the presidential guard seemed even more inclined to use weapons and brute force than their fellow police officers with whom they worked.

Erik was convinced that the problem was not so much in its management as in the very origin of the people he had hired: too many civilians without adequate training and ex-military with past disciplinary problems.

He had ordered all his subordinates to use the utmost severity in punishing those who did not follow his directives, but he suspected that they were themselves the first to turn a blind eye when one of their men used the baton a little too liberally.

Returning to his office, he felt increasingly exhausted and bitter: he had the impression that he was not cut out for that role. When he was an agent, everything was simpler. Perhaps, all things considered, he was nostalgic for when he could only follow orders and not make decisions.

The seat of the presidential guard was unusually deserted: Seidel had organised a particularly intensive raid and most of his men had been called upon to provide support.

Erik was coming from the abandoned subway station from which most of the agents had entered the underground city: he had been there all day and the operation had been unusually quiet.

They had managed to arrest a handful of people and there hadn't been many deportations, or childish tricks to ridicule the agents.

Perhaps the underground city was running out of imagination, or the last attacks had affected their grotesque sense of humour.

Fortunately, also because of the lack of resistance, it seemed that the arrests were being carried out in a peaceful and orderly manner.

Erik turned on his computer, intending to deal with correspondence: another downside of his new institutional role was that he received an enormous number of messages and letters, and everyone seemed very annoyed if he didn't respond within an hour or so.

Finding more than four hundred unread messages in his mailbox, Erik made a disconsolate sigh; he would be spending the whole night at the office.

Maja continued to live with Marc, and Peter had settled into the eighth ring. He had spoken to him over the phone and every now and then he got an e-mail from him, but Erik couldn't tell if he was doing well or not.

Peter was not usually particularly inclined to tell what he was doing, even if he lost himself in long speeches on topics that interested him, and, on the phone, he was decidedly laconic.

Apart from some unenthusiastic mumble or some "everything okay," he had not managed to snatch many details from him.

Erik had decided to visit him as soon as he had the chance, but for the moment he hadn't succeeded yet.

He hoped that Maja would know more, but his daughter was also unusually untalkative: Erik knew that she found his work and everything that had to do with the presidential guard disturbing, but he didn't want to argue. In the end, many conversations ended in an embarrassed silence.

If it hadn't been for Anderson, Erik would have been tempted to give up everything and find a quieter job that would allow him to stay close to his children and put the pieces of his life together.

But he could not abandon the person who had done so much for him and Europa; it would not be correct on his part, not to mention the fact that the most irrational and vindictive part of him wanted to get to the bottom of that matter of the infected who had recruited his wife.

Using the new channels he was given by his position, he had researched Dr Cohen, the psychiatrist who had treated Thea years earlier, and discovered that he was still practising.

He had asked for the lists of his patients and colleagues to be checked, but for the time being nothing had emerged about his possible involvement with the rebels.

Erik had asked to continue investigating, but he almost hoped that nothing would be found… maybe that way he would have been able to give up all that affair and try to move on with his own life, if for no other reason than for the sake of Maja and Peter.

With a certain effort of will, he decided to focus on the mail to be sorted: he opened a couple of messages and discovered that he was only one of the recipients in copy for information; a third was to be trash, and the next was the first of a long conversation.

Perhaps he could have asked his assistant Charles, a young boy fresh out of graduation who had joined them at Anderson's side, to sort the messages before they got to him; yeah, he thought, but at that point, his mailbox would no longer be private, was it appropriate? He could ask him to help him in that situation, though: it was late, and he didn't want to spend the whole night reading emails that probably were mostly of very low priority.

He left his office to head for Charles' desk, which was in an open space with others.

The boy jumped up when he saw him coming: it was something he always did. This military approach was certainly gratifying for Erik's self-esteem, but when he went back and forth several times and saw the poor guy jump up all the time, Erik found it both funny and irritating.

"Yes…um…just sit down," he began. "I must ask you for help in sorting my mail…"

Suddenly, his attention was attracted by a shadow that stood out against the window: Erik turned and saw a dark silhouette, similar to that of a large bird or maybe...

The shadow moved, and an object was thrown through the window, breaking the glass.

The half a dozen people left in the office shuddered, and Erik heard someone scream out of surprise.

He approached to see what had been thrown and was amazed to recognize a tear gas candlestick.

"Stay down!" he ordered, and a fraction of a second later the candle exploded, causing a cloud of gas to invade the office.

Erik closed his eyes and held his breath, taking off his jacket and putting it in front of his face as a filter.

Around him, he heard cries of pain and confusion as someone threw up.

Further away, he heard more glass breaking and more candles exploding.

Erik knew about the effects of tear gas, but he had never happened to be the target of it, without having the gas mask or the protective suit that was used by the cops.

They were under attack, he realised, but how was that possible? Was it the rebels?

They must have stolen weapons and equipment from the police.

Were they using dragons to throw the gas candles?

Despite some of the gas coming out of the window whose glass was broken, the air remained saturated with it, and next to him Charles and a girl who worked in administration, whose name Erik did not remember, coughed heavily.

They had to be able to reach a bath: the water would help them to remove dust residues from their faces and mouths.

He approached Charles and, through his jacket, instructed him to follow him.

The boy didn't seem to be able to move, continuing to cough and spit, so Erik had to drag him by the arm until he got up. The girl from the administration had managed to cover her face with a handkerchief, so she was slightly better.

Around him there was a thick, dark cloud, and he couldn't spot the others, even though he could hear their complaints.

First, he had to take Charles and his colleague to the bathroom, then he'd get the rest of them back, he decided.

He also had to rinse his eyes, which had begun to tear despite having tried as hard as possible to cover them with the fabric of his jacket. The skin on his hands burned excruciatingly.

Proceeding slowly and almost completely blindly, Erik managed to guide the two to the bathroom and closed the door behind him, then rushed to wet towels and put them in front of the door crack.

Coughing, he rinsed his face, hands and eyes, which were congested and injected with blood, while the two kids did the same.

"What's going on?" the girl asked, terrified. "This stuff... it burns... I don't understand..." she stammered. Erik saw that blisters were beginning to form on her arms.

"Stay calm," Erik said. "They've launched tear gas. Now I have to go outside and take the others here to rinse their eyes..."

"But... but if we open the door the gas will enter..."

"No, it's leaking out of the broken windows," Erik assured, even if he wasn't so positive. However, he knew that the people left in the room should have access to water as soon as possible, they could not lock them out.

The girl opened her mouth to say something, but at that moment the door was opened with a kick: three people with a gas mask and rough protective clothing broke in and, without too many compliments, grabbed them and dragged them back into the office.

"Come on, out, out..." they urged them, with the muffled and metallic voice that the masks emitted.

Erik was hit by the remains of the cloud, and, as he couldn't cover his face, he felt he was choking.

He tried to hold his breath but, after a few seconds, he was forced to inhale the toxic gas, which crept into his nostrils, throat and lungs, leaving a burning and painful trail.

He bent in two and began to cough, but one of the rebels shook him and forced him to keep walking.

Soon, he could no longer see anything: he would have liked to protest or at least try to reason with those people, but he couldn't do anything but cough and spit.

After a journey that seemed endless to him through the building invaded by gas, he realized that he had been taken to the hall, where he collapsed.

The air there was clean, but Erik continued to cough because of the residue of the gas he had breathed.

Other people with gas masks and heavy protective gloves were tying all the people they had found in the building. They had rifles and machine guns in their hands.

Erik tried to look through the tears to see who they were. From the clothes and the characteristic smell of unwashed body, he assumed they came from the underground city.

Were there infected with them, he wondered, feeling fear grabbing his stomach. He was quite sure that all those who were part of the presidential guard were vaccinated, but if for some reason someone from the offices had not been vaccinated…

Erik noticed that Charles was not far from him, and he recognized several other people.

Everyone was coughing and crying, and several had burns on their skin.

Suddenly a guy grabbed him by the shoulders and forced him to pull himself upon his knees, then began to tie him down with a rope.

"Wait a minute… who do we have here?" the metallic voice coming from the mask asked. "Isn't this the director, the general or whatever the fuck his job is?"

Another one approached him and grabbed his face, tethering it towards him: "Yes, it's him. Perlmann, Peterson, something like that…"

Erik called to all his strength to be able to speak: "My… name… is Persson. If you take me to whoever is… at the head… of this action, I…"

The guy grabbed him by the throat, further cutting off the little breath he had: "We do not have a 'head.' You don't know shit about how it works with us," he said. The angry tone was perfectly discernible even filtered by the gas mask. "We don't take orders from anyone, and we certainly don't want to take orders from you."

He suddenly let go and Erik fell to the ground, slamming his face on the floor. The pain radiated from his chin to his skull, and Erik feared he would fall unconscious.

"Are you the one who ordered all the raids in our territory?" the guy asked him again. "It's not so pleasant when we do the same thing at your home, eh?"

He kicked him, and Erik felt the tip of the combat boot dig into his stomach. The desire to vomit became even more intense.

The other rebel lifted his head "This is for having my girlfriend arrested, asshole," he informed him, then punched him in the face.

They were completely out of control, Erik thought, dazed for the pain and lack of oxygen.

They had no civilization, they were beasts, rats… Kathleen was right about them, he thought while he was being hit by another fist, she was always right…

"What the fuck are you doing?" a cold voice behind him asked, and the blows stopped.

With the last of his strength, Erik lifted an eyelid and saw a man without a gas mask. He was thin and pale, and, at first, Erik mistook him for a policeman, before noticing the line of scales that climbed from his neck to his skull. An infected, he thought terrified, there, among them…

"Didn't you hear when we said no beatings?" the newcomer continued in an exasperated tone. "It's not difficult to understand!"

"But this is their leader here…" the other rebel protested.

"Ah, splendid, and why not fill him with punches instead of discussing the release of some prisoner?" the infected said. "Bravo, great idea, aren't you a top negotiator."

"I don't like your tone, half-lizard shit," the other said, taking a menacing step towards the man with the plague, which was almost a foot shorter than him.

However, the latter didn't even flinch, and, in response, he pulled out a gun and pointed it at the rebel's forehead: "And I don't like your stench, but for now we must bear each other. Now get out of my way before I get some strange reptilian killer impulse."

The two rebels who had hit him moved away, and Erik breathed a sigh of relief.

His head was spinning, and his breathing was getting harder and harder. He wondered if that kick had broken his ribs.

The images and sounds around him became confused.

He heard the voice of the infected man bending over him: "Look at what the fuck they did... Ah, there you are, just in time," he said, perhaps addressed to someone else. "Take a look at this one here, I found Misha's henchmen punching him. I swear that if I have to deal with one of those again I will have a nervous breakdown, I feel like I'm just talking to myself..."

It was probably a delirium given by the pain, but Erik had the impression of hearing the voice of Amanda Solarin: "Erik? Erik Persson," she asked, upset.

He felt fresh fingers touching his neck, a strangely pleasant and comforting sensation.

For a moment he felt absurdly happy to see her and opened his mouth to say something; then he had a coughing fit and lost consciousness.

Erik opened his eyes and found around him the reassuring aseptic environment of a hospital room.

Was it the same place he'd been a few months before? Maybe so, but those rooms all looked a little alike.

He tried to prop himself up, but he was stopped by a stabbing pain in his chest.

He couldn't breathe well: he ran a hand over his face and noticed that his nose was medicated and bandaged.

He also felt that his face very swollen, and he had a patch on his forehead.

Suddenly he remembered the attack to the presidential guard, the gas, the rebels who beat him up.

A nurse entered the room: "Don't move too abruptly Mr Persson, you have a broken rib."

Erik lay back on the bed: "How did I get here?" he asked, then he was struck by a terrible thought: "The people who were at the seat of the presidential guard... were they captured? What happened?"

His voice was ridiculously nasal because of the bandaging.

They had probably broken his nose again: he would look like a boxer, he thought in dismay.

"They're all OK," the nurse assured, then he thought again. "Well, let's say that there are no casualties or serious injuries. Some people have gas poisoning and almost everyone has a terrible stomach-ache, very inflamed eyes and skin lesions, but they will recover," he explained. "Many are kept here in observation, but most are already at home."

"Didn't the rebels take hostages?" Erik asked.

"I don't think so," the nurse replied, while checking Erik's chest. "They released a video saying that today was just a demonstration action, or something like that. To tell you the truth, I didn't have time to see it, it was a very intense day..." he admitted tiredly.

Erik nodded: from the open door of his room he could see that the hospital corridor was crowded with people waiting, some on stretchers, others sitting on the floor.

"How long have I been here?" he asked.

"About four hours. You were one of the first to arrive with the ambulance... we just had to give you some stitches and change the dressing on your nose."

"Change it?" Erik asked. "Had the paramedics already treated me?"

The nurse stared at him, perplexed: "Actually, I wanted to ask you. You seemed to have already received first aid on-site, but not from hospital staff. Don't you remember?"

Erik tried to recall, but the events of that afternoon seemed a confused fog to him.

He only had blurred flashes: the feeling of something cold, a hand holding his head, Amanda Solarin's voice so close to his ear... was it really her? Or was it a hallucination? He wasn't sure.

Every breath caused him a lot of pain, and he didn't dare to think about the state of his face.

Damn rebels, he thought angrily. If only he had gotten a hold of them without being tied up and intoxicated by the gas, if only...

"Do you want something for the pain?" the nurse asked.

"Yes, please."

Erik received two tablets of paracetamol, which he gulped down with a little water, whose taste seemed metallic to him. Now he just had to wait for it to take effect.

"Your daughter is outside," the nurse informed him. "Normally it would not be visiting time but she insisted a lot and..."

"Please let her in!" Erik exclaimed.

The nurse nodded: "OK, but only ten minutes. She can't stay here all night, there is already too much confusion..."

When the man walked away, Maja entered, looking very worried.

As soon as she saw his swollen face, she burst into tears.

"Oh no, Dad, what have they done to you?"

"Come on, don't cry," he told her, trying to appear cheerier than he felt. "It looks worse than it is," he assured.

In fact, when he had been shot, the aftermath had been more painful, but perhaps it was not worth pointing this out.

"What happened?"

Erik briefly told her about the attack on his office, trying to omit the most alarming details, such as his fear of the brutality of those two men who seemed to want nothing but to bring violence.

"Is it true that the rebels have broadcast a video?"

"Yes," Maja confirmed, sniffling. "It has been inserted in all the television channels about ten times, at half-hour intervals. They called my boss to send a technician to check the system, they still haven't figured out how they breached the security protocols," she explained.

"What does it say?"

"Do you want to watch it?" Maja proposed, pulling out her handheld. "By the way, this should remain between us. Technically, I shouldn't have a copy," she confessed. "They're all very annoyed by this intrusion. My boss said that the people in the government were very angry..."

"I get it, don't worry."

He didn't remind her that he was part of the government too.

When he returned to work, he would surely see it anyway, but he was curious and didn't want to wait.

Maja started the video.

In the first scene, Erik saw films showing arrests and infected suspects: Erik recognized the images of the institutional videos he had often seen in the police.

In this case, however, the image stopped on the faces of the arrested, drawing attention to their expressions of fear and despair.

"For the past twenty years, the government of Europa has systematically tried to eliminate all people who have the misfortune to contract the DH16N10 virus, commonly known as the plague. Those who manage to survive are then persecuted, even if they have had no guilt, except that of getting sick and not dying."

The video showed the face of the person speaking, a tall man with dark skin and the face marked by plague scales.

"That's James Solarin!" Erik recognized him.

"You know him?"

"Yes... he broke my nose some time ago."

Maja raised an eyebrow: "Oh, him too?"

Erik made a dismissive gesture: "Long story."

"For almost twenty years we had to hide, fearing for our lives. We found ways to contain the contagion, so as not to be a threat to the citizens of Europa. All the stories you've heard about our willingness to infect as many people as possible are false: we've never wanted to hurt innocent people."

In the video, a woman looking a lot like James Solarin appeared.

"Amanda!" Erik exclaimed. So it was true, she was with the rebels.

"Do you know her too?"

Erik nodded: "Yes, I..."

He thought of her penetrating dark eyes through the glass of the hospital cell, her fresh hands on his skin, her voice telling his brother not to shoot him.

"We have met," he concluded.

"Anderson Pharmaceuticals' vaccine has changed everything," Amanda said in the video. "For the first time in twenty years, I can fearlessly hug my brother again.

For years the plague has divided thousands of families, leading to death, destruction and suspicion, but now we have a chance to put an end to these tragedies."

On the video images of Anderson's speech on the roof of parliament appeared.

"Kathleen Anderson declared that she would bring peace to our city, but for us, that wasn't the case," said the voice of James Solarin. "She claimed that she would welcome every survivor, but then did not hesitate to try to tire us out with brutality and violence."

On the video, the famous image of the policeman who beat the defenceless woman appeared, followed by many other pictures showing the arrests in the underground city, the explosion of tear gas and people collapsing in fits of coughing.

"There can be no peace until all citizens are granted the same rights," Amanda continued. "The right to security, to food, to the company of their loved ones. In a nutshell, the right to life. This applies to all of us, even to those of us who have been infected by the plague, and those who for various reasons have ended up outside the system."

On the screen, the images of the policemen beating the people arrested in the underground city continued to stream.

"Today we attacked the presidential guard, but unlike the police, we did not take victims or hostages," James said, as the video showed a line of people tied up in front of his office building.

Erik shuddered to see that dragons were flying around the building, with small human silhouettes on their backs, probably some infected. He was also surprised to see himself, unconscious and lying on a stretcher, not far from the other prisoners.

"If you think that this action was violent, know that it is exactly what has been happening every day, for months, in the underground city. If you think this is fear and chaos, know that this is nothing compared to what the infected have had to endure for almost twenty years."

James and Amanda appeared together on the screen: their faces, so similar and so different, and the contrast between the similarity of their features and the difference given by James' vaguely reptilian appearance made for a striking effect.

"This is a message for Kathleen Anderson," Amanda said. "If you want these clashes to end, we are willing to negotiate. We want guarantees that the rights of all will be protected and that the persecution of the infected will end. You cannot bring indiscriminate destruction and stand as the champion of justice. You can't make a desert and call it peace."

Her dark, intense eyes seemed to burn across the screen, Erik thought.

"But if you really want a new Europa, founded on harmony and respect, the next move is yours," James said. "We are here, and we will continue to be."

CHAPTER 19

"What the fuck have you done?!" Sophie screamed, pushing Amanda against the wall. "How dare you send that video without telling me anything?"

"Let me explain, I..."

"No!" she shouted, angrier than ever. "No! You offered Anderson to negotiate! I don't want to negotiate! I want to kill her, tear her to pieces, I want her dead, I want..."

Her fingers closed on Amanda's throat, tightening more and more, until someone grabbed her arms from behind, immobilizing her.

"Get yourself together," Gregor's cold voice hissed in her ear. "Are you still able to discuss like a civilized person? Or have you become like those thugs from the underground city?"

"Let me go! Leave me alone," Sophie ordered, trying to wriggle away with all her might, to no avail. Anger made her uncoordinated, and, despite his unathletic appearance, Gregor had a very firm grip.

After a few moments, she felt her anger diminish, and the crisis passed, leaving her exhausted. Finally, Gregor let her go.

James, meanwhile, had helped his sister to get up.

"I had to do it, Sophie," Amanda said in a reasonable tone. "Come on, think about it for a moment. What else can we get? I don't want to be at war forever."

"We can't trust her," Sophie retorted. "She always lied to us, she killed millions of people..." her voice broke, "she killed Cain…"

"Technically, Cain is still alive," Gregor pointed out.

Sophie looked at him askance: as if it made any difference...

"You are the one who keeps telling Korbinian, Misha and all the others that they have to overcome the past, unite for the common good and so on..." Amanda continued. "Why do you refuse to do the same with Anderson?"

"She killed Cain!" Sophie repeated.

"Oh, come on!" James exclaimed. "Do you think that Cain's life was worth nothing to us? You were on our island for less than six months,

I've been his friend for more than ten years. Do you think I'm happy to ally with the person who cut his throat? No, I'm not, and yet I can see that's the only thing we can do."

"She ruined your life! She ruined it for all of us, she created the plague! It's not just about Cain, She has so many more people on her conscience, and..."

"Am I the only one who remembers that Cain isn't dead? Just so I know," Gregor asked, without receiving an answer.

"Yes, it's true, Anderson created the plague," said Amanda, pragmatic. "If she wasn't born at all, the world would have been a better place. But she's here, as is the plague, and we can do nothing to change the past. But, Sophie, be reasonable, we can't go on with this guerrilla warfare forever. Anderson's stronger than we are on all fronts. Now we have good leverage, it's the right time to make a deal. The more we go on, the weaker we will be."

Sophie opened her mouth to answer but found out she didn't know what to say. Amanda's position made sense, even she realized it. Her aversion to the idea of reconciling with Kathleen Anderson's government was moral and personal, not strategic.

"Think of all the other infected people," Amanda continued. "They deserve to have a life as normal as possible, don't you think?"

"How can we possibly trust her word?"

Amanda nodded: "Now, this is a reasonable objection," she admitted, "but I think that by bringing this thing before all the inhabitants of Europa, we have tied her hands. She has exposed herself too much as a champion of peace and prosperity to risk losing all her consent by taking her word back. And for what? She's not personally at war at any of us; if anything, she had a grudge against Cain. Her authority is undermined by those who are beyond her control, but if we manage to make her look good, like the woman who managed to bring the whole of Europa together, we cease to be a danger, indeed, we become her success."

Sophie did not like the idea of being responsible for Kathleen's success, but she said nothing because she would have sounded even more childish.

"And then think of Pat," Sophie looked up when she heard the name of her dragon. "Do you want him to be confined in the underground for the rest of his life? Thanks to Kathleen he could fly in the sunlight, have much more freedom than you can give him."

Sophie thought about it: the idea of seeing Kathleen again, to consider an ally made her stomach twist...and yet, the prospect of Pat having more space...

He was so happy when they finally went out into the open, to attack the presidential guard's palace. Sophie had personally thrown gas candles through the windows, just as the police had done before while arresting people in the underground city.

Pat had squeezed his vertical pupil eyes when he had finally seen the sun, but then he had cheered at the warmth and light pirouetting happy in the air.

Was it worth biting back on her grudge and agreeing to deal with Kathleen for him?

Probably yes, Sophie thought eventually.

"I understand your reasons, Amanda," she said. "But I still would have liked you to talk to me about it before, instead of confronting me when the whole thing was done."

"I had to act quickly, the surprise effect was pivotal," Amanda replied.

"Yeah, well, I think that's bullshit," Gregor said. "I mean, I'm with you about peace and everything else, Amanda... but, if you don't mind, we're the ones who are infected and I don't think you should have spoken on our behalf," he snapped. "So, thanks but next time mind your own business."

Amanda raised her eyebrows, surprised: "Well, James is also…"

"James should have talked about it with us first, not with you," Gregor cut her short. "And don't come and tell me that there was no time. I saw the video. You didn't put it together in ten minutes. I know that you've been working on it with Ken for at least a month."

"A month!" Sophie exclaimed. "Really?"

"Um…" James began, embarrassed. "Only the part with the videos, not our speech…"

Gregor looked at him contemptuously: "Because you improvised the speech, right? You think I'm completely stupid?"

"Now, stop using that tone –"

"Oh, so, I'm the one who should stop? When you two go around making decisions that affect our very survival and…"

"How dare you imply that my sister who is not one of us?" James thundered, standing up and towering over Gregor. "She ended up in prison for us, she was tortured!"

At that moment, Nadia arrived in a hurry: "Turn the TV on!" she urged them. "Anderson is answering!"

James hastened to turn the screen on, and Kathleen Anderson appeared, speaking into a microphone with a magnanimous expression: "… and it is with great pleasure that I accept the possibility of handing over an olive branch to these people that my vaccine has made not a threat but a future opportunity for a lifelong friendship…"

She's so fake, Sophie thought, staring at the TV with hatred. As if she hadn't tried to do them all in…

"You look like someone who wants to tell her where to put that olive branch," Gregor whispered to her. "The ideal state of mind for a future opportunity for a lifelong friendship."

"If a representation of the people who survived the plague virus will accept," Kathleen continued, "I am ready to receive them in seven days from now, at the seat of government."

Kathleen's message ended, and the news went on with other information.

"This is great news," Amanda exclaimed. "We have to prepare some conditions, and ask for guarantees… meanwhile, we must decide who goes and…"

"Look, Kofi Annan, thank you for the interest but it's *us* who should decide whether to go or not, don't you think?" Gregor hissed. "Sophie, what do you say?"

Sophie took a breath: "Amanda is right," she decided, reluctantly. "Let's do it."

If it had been difficult for them to agree on a course of action towards Kathleen, it was downright impossible to reach an agreement with the leaders of the underground city about who they wanted to send as an emissary.

Each of them would have liked to go in person or send one of their henchmen; at the same time, no one trusted the others. After having tried for a long time to propose Korbinian as a possible representative (mostly because he looked like the most presentable one), Sophie had to acknowledge that they would never agree. The proposal was rejected, and, eventually, they decided that none of them would go.

Sophie was given several lists of conditions to propose, one more unacceptable than the other: in fact, they wanted the government to leave the underground city behind, and all decisions to be left to them. Kathleen would never have accepted anything like it, Sophie was sure, but she decided not to insist too much. All in all, the fact that she didn't have to carry any of those unpredictable figures with her made her much more confident.

On the day of the meeting, though, Sophie felt very anxious. In the end, they had decided to go in three: herself, Amanda and Gregor. Besides the fact that they were the least alarming looking ones (Amanda was healthy, and Gregor had far fewer scales than most of the infected), Amanda was definitely the most suitable person to negotiate the conditions, and Gregor always thought of aspects that no one else ever considered; moreover, in the absence of Pat, Sophie felt more secure with him at her side. After having thought about it for a long time, in fact, she had decided not to show up with the dragon: even if his presence would make an effect, she was afraid that he might be in danger at the seat of government. Anderson's men probably knew how to immobilize and capture him, as they were dealing with her huge dragon.

Even if they had arrested her, at least Pat would be free; for the same reason, it was decided that James would remain in headquarters, so that, in case the meeting was a trap, there would always be someone reliable to lead the rest of the infected.

Gregor had verified that everyone at the government headquarters seemed ready to receive them early in the morning: apparently, there were snipers all around the building, helicopters flying over the area and presidential guards everywhere.

A growing crowd of curious people had also gathered and camped in front of the parliament.

According to Gregor, the best thing was to hurry up and try to get in before too many people arrived and the situation got worse.

"Are you ready?" Amanda asked Sophie.

"No," she answered sincerely. "Do you think snipers are a good sign? 'Cause, you know, to me it doesn't look very encouraging..."

Amanda shrugged: "I wouldn't have expected anything less. In any case, however it goes," she continued. "This is the first time that someone in the government has agreed to discuss the possibility of recognizing the rights of the infected... I mean, it's a huge thing. We can be proud of ourselves."

"If we don't fuck it up," Sophie objected.

"We won't," Amanda assured. "Just try to keep the anger under control, OK? If you feel a crisis coming, make a sign and Gregor... well, I don't know, he'll give you a soporific grip on your shoulder or something like that."

"Shall we go?" Gregor urged them, arriving at that moment.

Sophie noticed that, shaved and with clean clothes, he looked surprisingly normal. Despite the sad story of how he was infected, Sophie was a little envious that he could hide the signs of the plague so easily. Her scales, on the other hand, were impossible not to notice; on the way to parliament, in fact, she had to cover herself with a hat, scarf and, obviously, gloves.

They came out of a manhole in the sixth ring, then took trains to the first ring, changing often; this would make it much more difficult to try to identify their origin using the security cameras scattered around the city.

The area in front of the government headquarters was filled with a crowd of people waiting for them to arrive.

Sophie noticed that some people expressed their disagreement with the idea of a truce: they had signs praising the killing of all the infected who had caused so many victims in the past years. Others, however, she noticed with surprise, supported their rights and denounced the inhumane treatment they had received up to that moment. And it looked like there were a lot of them. She found the thought oddly comforting.

When they arrived, they took off their hats and advanced towards the entrance to the building.

The crowd silenced for a moment, shocked, then the screams began.

Sophie, Amanda and Gregor were brought in quickly, always held under fire by snipers and guards, while, behind them, the demonstrators began to discuss with each other.

As the door closed behind her, Sophie saw that the police seemed to be about to intervene and disperse the crowd.

With her heart hammering in her chest, she crossed several corridors: she was so nervous that she didn't pay much attention to the building, which was surprisingly large and luxurious.

She tried to look calm and resolute and noticed that Amanda and Gregor were doing the same, or maybe they were genuinely less anxious than her.

Finally, she found herself in front of her: Kathleen Anderson, or, as she had known her, Emma Lemaire.

The traces of her previous identity, however, had been almost completely wiped out: the old-fashioned hairstyle with a knot of grey hair at the nape of her neck had been swapped with a short cut that made her look younger and classier; her demure attitude had been replaced by a safe and confident air. She no longer looked like the sweet old woman Sophie had believed she had to protect, but neither did she resemble the crazy fanatic who had cut Cain's throat.

When Kathleen saw her, she widened her eyes in surprise.

"Sophie!" she exclaimed. "My dear girl, you were infected... but you survived."

"So it seems," Sophie replied, surprised at how firm her voice sounded.

"I had no idea that you were going to come here today," Kathleen smiled. "What a wonderful surprise."

Kathleen turned to the group of people, ministers or so Sophie imagined, who surrounded her: "Sophie Weber and I met about a year ago when I carried out an undercover mission to the infected. She was a valuable help, as was Amanda Solarin, who allowed us to meet. I couldn't imagine better conditions for our negotiation," she added, with what seemed like sincere enthusiasm.

The ministers nodded politely and looked at them with interest and slightly less fear.

Sophie found it terribly annoying that Anderson was nonchalantly talking about how she had deceived them all, as if it had been a curious anecdote to tell at a party, but she had to keep her frustration to herself.

"Shall we proceed?" Kathleen said, leading the way. "We can go to the council room. I have already gathered all the representatives..."

"No," Gregor interrupted her. "We want a private meeting."

Kathleen seemed perplexed: "But, surely, the contribution of the rest of my government..."

"We are but a small delegation, we want an adequate interlocutor."

Sophie nodded: if Kathleen had the support of all her ministers, she would have a definite advantage over them, not to mention the intimidating effect.

Anderson left to talk to her associates.

"Do you think she'll accept?" Sophie asked Amanda.

"Of course she will," she replied. "So she'll also have the excuse to decide everything for herself."

Sophie hadn't thought about this, but it did make sense.

Kathleen came back shortly afterwards, accompanied by a guy with a uniform full of grades and another who seemed to have recently had an accident, since his face was in a dreadful state.

He and Amanda looked at each other intensely, but they said nothing. Did they know each other? Sophie wondered. It was hard to say.

"General Chardon, Minister of Defence, and the director of the presidential guard Erik Persson," Kathleen introduced the newcomers. "They will assist me during the meeting."

They moved to a smaller office. Now that there were three against three, Sophie felt less intimidated by the situation.

"I would say that I can start with our proposals," Kathleen began in a practical tone, after the pleasantries. "First of all, we ask you to lay down your arms and stop any illegal activity, both in the underground and outside the city. We want you to turn yourself in and to be registered, after which you will be guaranteed accommodation and adequate support for your health conditions."

They were only small concessions, but it was a start, Sophie thought.

"You're asking us for unconditional surrender," she said, halfway between unbelieving and indignant. "We need a few more guarantees, of course."

Kathleen simply waited for them to present their conditions.

"First of all, the personal freedom of all the people who survived the plague must be guaranteed. None of them may be arrested or held in custody against their will," Amanda declared.

"Unless they obviously commit a crime," Anderson specified.

"The rights of the infected cannot be guaranteed if the crime of spreading the infection continues to exist, and if there is even a government body dedicated to chasing them," Amanda said, "We want the medical police to be dismissed."

To Sophie's surprise, Kathleen nodded: "The medical police will be integrated into the ordinary police force and will no longer deal with questions relating to the plague."

She had the impression that the president appeared satisfied: perhaps it was something she too would have liked to do from the beginning but feared to trigger an uproar?

She never was a big fan of the police, since she had even created her own guard, she reflected.

"And we can't be registered," Gregor added.

This triggered a long discussion: according to Kathleen, registration was necessary for reintegration into society, while they saw it as a possible weapon of oppression.

In the end, they found a compromise: registration would not be mandatory but, instead of the vaccination certificate, the infected would have to submit a declaration of infection issued by a medical centre to use public services such as offices or hospitals.

The question of dragons remained unresolved, and Sophie felt more and more nervous.

"Shall we take a break?" Anderson asked.

Sophie looked at a clock hanging in the room and was amazed to see that more than three hours had already passed since they had arrived.

The Minister of Defence left the room, while Persson was tinkering with his handheld, appearing stressed.

Sophie, Gregor and Amanda looked at each other, uncertain about what to do. In the end, Gregor and Amanda headed to a table where hot drinks had been put, and Sophie asked where the toilet was.

Once there, she realized that she hadn't used a clean and well-maintained toilet for months: the bathrooms in the underground city were only makeshift accommodations.

While she was washing her hands with a pleasantly scented soap, Kathleen entered.

"Sophie," she said, placing herself in front of the door. "I was hoping to be able to talk to you alone."

Instinctively, Sophie looked around, looking for another way out, but there was none.

The idea of being alone with Anderson made her uneasy. She couldn't avoid thinking back of the swift gesture with which she had sunk the knife in Cain's throat, the tug she had given, the blood spilling out.

"I'm happy that you survived the disease," Kathleen said gently. "I've often thought about the events of that night... I would have liked things to go differently, you know."

"Me too. For example, I'd rather you didn't slit anyone's throat."

Anderson appeared impatient: "You despise me for what I did, I understand. What can I say? That's your prerogative. But the only reason we are here today, why we have the chance to bring peace, is because Cain is dead. You know it, too."

"Cain isn't..." Sophie started, but then held her tongue. It was more cautious not to specify that he was still alive. She did not know what Kathleen might decide to do about it, she thought with a shiver.

"All he wanted was revenge. He would not have been able to move on, as you are doing."

Kathleen got closer and took her hand, looking at the scales.

"You feel it now, don't you?" she whispered. "I immediately understood, as soon as I saw you."

"What...?"

"A dragon!" Anderson said, her eyes shining. "You can feel one too, I'm sure."

Sophie didn't know what to say, so she just nodded slowly.

"I knew it!" Kathleen exclaimed, triumphant. "I know that you are still angry with me, and I understand. I respect that. But I know that inside you, you can understand me now. Now you know what a bond like the one we have with dragons means..."

Sophie opened her mouth to answer but found out she couldn't. She wanted to deny it, but it would be a lie, she realized. If she had been in her place, separated from Pat... No, she wouldn't think about it. She was not like Kathleen, she would never have been so ruthless.

"We are more similar than you think," Anderson continued, as if she were reading her mind. "Trust me. We're going to do great things together. Me, you, and especially the dragons. When I say that we can create a different world, I mean it."

Sophie was confused: once again she didn't know what to say.

"Now we have to go back that way. You'll see, we'll manage to get everyone to agree, and our dragons will be free at last."

Kathleen smiled again, confident, and moved away.

When Sophie returned to the meeting room, everyone was already in their seats, including Kathleen.

"Very well," the president started when Sophie sat down. "Now we must deal with one of the most important topics, perhaps the most important of all. The dragons."

Sophie stiffened into her chair, alert.

"It is obvious to all that dragons are exceptionally intelligent, powerful and therefore dangerous creatures. We believe that for this reason their care cannot be left to your private initiative. Also because they need space, open air, adequate food. You can't give them all this, but I can. For the safety of the community and to let citizens sleep peacefully, you must hand them over to me," Anderson proposed. "I assure you that they will be treated with all honours, with respect to their needs."

"No, we cannot give up dragons," Gregor said. "They have always been ours and must continue to be so."

Kathleen raised an eyebrow: "You know very well that this is unacceptable."

Amanda and Gregor turned to Sophie, waiting.

In this case, it was her who knew what conditions could be accepted.

Sophie drummed her fingers on the table top, trying to think. She didn't want to be separated from Pat, nor did she want the other telepaths to do the same with their dragons, but she too recognized that to take care of them properly they needed resources that they objectively didn't have.

"You said it can't be a private initiative," she said, "but you're a private citizen with a dragon."

"I'm the president!" Kathleen reminded her, apparently surprised to have to point out something so obvious.

"That's true, but you've had him before, as a private citizen, not as a privilege of your office. When your term ends, the dragon will not pass to the next president, or will him?"

Sophie had serious doubts that Anderson had ever planned to leave the presidential office, at least in a short time, but formally there was a term of five years to her term, although it was quite easy to get around. Hartmann, for example, had been in office for more than fifteen years.

"It would seem extremely complicated," Kathleen cautiously replied.

"So, in this case, you are not representing the government, but yourself."

General Chardon and Persson looked at Kathleen, surprised. They had the impression that they had never considered this aspect, taking for granted that Kathleen wanted to put dragons under the control of the government.

Anderson appeared vaguely in trouble for the first time: "I've always given myself to Europa, as you know. Anderson Pharmaceuticals donated the vaccine for free, without profit... I have never made any distinction between myself and my role."

"But we do," Sophie insisted. "We are not all presidents, so, for us, this distinction is very important."

General Chardon spoke for the first time: "This is a matter that hasn't been institutionalized yet, but it is clear that dragons must be subject to government. The plan has always been this, is it not so, Madam President?"

Anderson cleared her throat: "Naturally, this is our proposal," she said. "Can you accept it?"

Sophie smiled to herself: she did not want them to accept either, it was obvious.

She almost wanted to say yes, just to see what she would do... but it wasn't worth it.

She wouldn't risk being separated from Pat over sheer spite.

She decided to play the game along: "Absolutely not, it would be folly," she declared. "As President Anderson herself acknowledged, a solution of this kind would not only be extremely complicated, but impractical, too. By virtue of the bond that is so... um... personal with dragons... well, it has to be a private thing."

"We could find a compromise," Kathleen said after a long pause. "I could establish... a foundation, for example... for the care of dragons and everyone who is in telepathic contact with them would be part of it. In this way the matter would be recognized and regulated by the government," she explained, with a glance of understanding to the Minister of Defence, "but it would allow you infected to actively and constantly participate in the life of your dragons."

As much as she was sorry to admit it, Anderson's idea was good, Sophie thought.

No one, in her place, could have given more, and it was clear that she did so only because she did not want to risk that her own dragon would one day be the subject of unwanted attention from the rest of the government.

"Well, that could do," Sophie nodded.

"We will have to hold a subsequent meeting to discuss the statute of the foundation," Gregor said.

Kathleen nodded: "Of course."

"I think we have dealt with the most important issues," Amanda observed.

"I think you can be very satisfied with the results you have obtained," Kathleen observed. "For you infected this is a great day. But there is one last pending issue that can't be avoided any longer: the underground city must be destroyed."

CHAPTER 20

Erik was astonished when the infected delegation arrived at the government headquarters and Anderson asked him to attend the meeting.

He had already been very surprised that she had agreed to deal with them: Kathleen had never made a mystery of her aversion to those rebels. But the president was a very impartial person, ready to overcome her personal idiosyncrasies for the good of Europa.

However, Erik did not expect that she would also bring him, since he obviously could not give any support to the negotiations.

"Only my dragon would make me feel safe in front of those people," Anderson explained, "my dragon and you."

Erik was still feeling weak because of his recent convalescence and hoped he wouldn't have to take more bullets or do any vaguely physical action, but he felt so honoured by that remark that he didn't even consider the possibility to refuse.

But the unexpected events of that day had not ended there: Amanda Solarin was part of the delegation.

He had not expected it: he had imagined that he would only meet infected people, but then he had realised that she must have been part of the subversive organization for a long time because of her brother.

Strange that she had attended, instead of James: but, during the negotiations, he had the opportunity to appreciate her decisiveness and her willingness to seek compromises.

He wanted to say hi or something else, but everything seemed vaguely out of place under those circumstances, so he had been silent.

He then realized that he also knew the other two infected people: one was Sophie Weber, Solarin's assistant that he had desperately looked for some time before. She really was infected, he thought.

Compared to the photos and videos of her escape, she had changed a lot: back then, she looked so young, barely older than Maja. The woman who was in front of him that day, however, in addition to having scales on her face and hands, had a hard expression that made her look older and more determined. Erik imagined she'd been through a lot since she had run away from that medical centre.

The other infected was also familiar to him: he was the man who had stopped his beating during their attack to the presidential guard. Even though his memories of that moment were confused, he had no difficulty in recognizing his voice and his bare face, with its cadaverous paleness.

He introduced himself as Gregor Horvat.

It was strange to be with people he had met at such different times in his life, he thought.

Throughout the meeting, Anderson had shown a great willingness to cooperate.

Erik was very upset when he heard that the medical police would be dismantled; he had the feeling that his whole life's work had been swept away without thinking twice.

But now his work and his commitment were elsewhere, he told himself: perhaps sometime before he could have seen the end of the war against the infected as his personal defeat, but it was no longer so. What he had seen in the pre-trial detention hospital and during his work for Anderson had made him realize that it was time for the hostilities to end.

When the time came to discuss the situation in the underground city, Kathleen was very firm.

Erik agreed with her: they had made many concessions to the people who had been so violently persecuted by the previous government, however, it was not acceptable that the situation of degradation and crime of the underground city continued to persist.

Her request was met with dismay by the three delegates.

"Where did you think of reallocating all the people who currently live there?" Solarin asked.

"Many have already been directed to the outer rings, where they have been given work and accommodation including board and lodging."

"That sounds suspiciously like a sentence to forced labour," Horvat remarked.

Kathleen shrugged: "For the inhabitants of the underground city any kind of work is forced. All they know is theft and crime."

"Destroying the underground city means that thousands of people who now live there will be on the street," Amanda pointed out. "It would be madness, a social emergency."

"Most of them could be absorbed by the same programme of work and reintegration into the agricultural sector…"

"This definitely sounds like a sentence to forced labour," Gregor Horvat declared in a mockery tone.

Anderson appeared calm, but Erik observed that under the surface she was about to lose her patience: "Excuse me, but what else can you ask for? These people have lived at the expense of society all their lives, should we continue to provide for them indefinitely?"

Solarin sighed: "They would argue that they don't live like parasites, but rather outside the system," she explained.

Kathleen scoffed: "Oh, do they, now? And what do they live off? They don't produce food or any kind of product or service. Everything they use comes from Europa."

"This is also true for many citizens. I didn't think that the Anderson government would label all who don't actively produce as a parasite…"

"You're distorting my words…"

Solarin and Anderson started to argue animatedly.

Erik looked at the other two delegates, who were talking to each other in a low voice. She knew that Weber was a regular citizen before she was infected, and he was pretty sure that the other one used to be, too.

He wondered why no one from the underground city was present at the meeting: did the infected have the power to negotiate for them too? It didn't sound like a very good arrangement.

Weber had been very determined when it came to dragons, so much so that she had made Anderson uncomfortable for the first time, but now she seemed a bit absent, almost bored. The other merely made a few caustic remarks with little conviction.

Erik got the impression that Amanda was the only one who cared what would happen to the underground city.

"What I'm saying is that, yes, it's true, there's definitely a crime problem down there, but it's not at all true that all the people who live there are criminals!" Solarin said. "You can't just clear the area and send them all into the eighth ring, it would be a violation of human rights, which is something you've always said you wanted to defend!"

"Then, pray, tell me where I should put them," Kathleen exclaimed. "I am not going to take away the house of a citizen of Europa to give it to them if that's what you're suggesting."

"For them, it's important to have a territory in which to be autonomous," Sophie Weber unexpectedly said. "You could build a separate community, in which they can have some legislative autonomy. Some people don't share the credit system and want to be able to practice bartering or something like that. They also have a different idea of community," she explained. "Many would be happy to just stay on their own, others would probably integrate."

Kathleen thought about it for a long time and finally sighed tiredly: "This… can be considered…" she finally granted. "We can build a camp…"

"A village, at least, or a town," Solarin replied. "You can't just send them to a campsite."

"Yes, a town. We can identify an area in the outer rings…."

Amanda and Sophie Weber looked at each other nodding, while Gregor Horvat shrugged off. Erik didn't think it made much of a difference to him.

The meeting was over: Anderson planned to meet after two weeks, to define some of the issues left unresolved. In the meantime, there would be a truce: no arrests by the police, no attacks by the rebels.

As Kathleen left the room, Erik suddenly found himself next to Amanda Solarin.

"I'm sorry about your face, Persson," she said in a low voice. "It looks like every time we are in the same room someone beats you up."

"I'm also surprised that my nose is still intact after all these hours," Erik admitted. "It's a particularly risky point when you're around."

Solarin smiled: "I'm glad to see that you're fine. I'm sorry about what happened at the hospital. Sometimes James can be a little rough."

"I noticed. Anyway... it doesn't matter, all is well that ends well. Besides, I don't think you'll have to go to prison after all."

"I certainly hope so!" Amanda exclaimed.

Suddenly Sophie Weber approached her: "Gregor says we have to go. They made a cord around the building, there are security problems."

"Right, I'm coming," she turned again to Erik. "Well, I guess I'll see you soon."

"Yes. See you soon."

Erik followed them to the lobby, where there were still many ministers and various government figures, evidently curious to know how the meeting went.

When the three were in front of Christian Voigt, he saw him pale and begin to shake.

"Voigt," Horvat coldly greeted him. "Long time no see. Damn, you look awful. Your hairline has receded, your belly has grown fat. You're a basically a wreck."

Voigt stammered: "Horvat... I... I... what a surprise, I didn't think you were... here... um... alive..."

"I'm sure you didn't dare to hope," the other replied, holding out his hand to him.

Erik saw the Head of Secret Services hesitate.

"Why, don't you even want to shake my hand? After everything we've been through. You were vaccinated, weren't you?"

Voigt looked around and seemed to notice that many people looked at him perplexed, so, always trembling, he stretched out his hand towards the infected, who squeezed it with force: Voigt withdrew his hand, terrified, and looked at his palm.

Erik wasn't sure, but he thought he saw a little red dot.

"See you soon, Voigt. It's always a pleasure," the infected greeted him in a mocking tone, walking away and out of the building.

The Head of Secret Services did not reply: his face had a greenish tinge.

He looked like he'd just met a ghost.

When Erik looked up to see where the three delegates had gone, expecting to see them walking down the street, he noticed that they had already disappeared.

CHAPTER 21

Sophie, Amanda and Gregor very quickly took off from the crowd in front of the seat of government, taking a side street and, shortly after, entering a manhole.

Sophie felt dazed and excited.

She felt that the meeting had gone well but she was almost afraid to think back on the hours that had just passed.

Gregor pulled out a backpack attached behind a pipe with adhesive tape: "Get changed," he ordered, opening it and pulling out clothes.

"Why?" Sophie asked, perplexed.

"I don't want to take any chances."

"What a pity, I liked this jacket..." Amanda observed, starting to undress.

"Be thankful that I'm not insisting to shave our heads. There are tiny bugs, they can put them anywhere," he mumbled.

"No, thanks, I don't want to adopt your look."

Sophie laughed, putting on a sweatshirt that was a little too big for her, while Amanda was giggling.

The worst part was having to change her shoes because those brought by Gregor were not exactly her size, but they would do to get back to the cathedral.

They put all their clothes in a backpack, which Gregor then threw into a sewer pipe, and walked home.

Sophie felt that the adrenaline that the meeting had given her had not yet vanished, and she realized that it was the same for Amanda: they both laughed nervously about every little thing.

Gregor was harder to read, but from the way he was giving a series of instructions on how to get home without being noticed Sophie was pretty sure that he too was still on edge.

"What did you do to the fat guy?" she asked.

"Who, Voigt?"

"That was Voigt?" Sophie was surprised. She had already heard of him before Gregor told her his story, but she didn't know his face.

"Yes. Nothing, I just gave him a scare," he minimized.

Amanda looked at him: "You wouldn't do anything that might jeopardise the negotiation, would you?"

"Of course not!" he defended himself. "I only pricked him with a pin I had in my jacket, I wanted to see his face."

"Why?" Amanda asked, exasperated.

Gregor shrugged: "Just a whim."

Sophie laughed. At that moment everything seemed so funny. She felt vaguely drunk.

They climbed out of a manhole in the third ring, then took a train, then walked for a long time.

Actually, the cathedral wasn't so far from where they were, but Gregor claimed that it was safer to take a more complicated detour to make them lose their tracks.

When they finally got to Korbinian's area, Sophie was exhausted. After the nervousness given by the meeting and the long walk, she just wanted to lie down on her cot and sleep for twelve hours straight.

But that was not possible: everyone wanted to know what Anderson had said, what they had told her, what arrangements were made, and then to hear the same story again.

It took her more than an hour to reach Pat, who, being very sensitive to her moods, was also agitated.

Sophie hoped to have a few moments to relax with him, but everyone kept following her to ask her a thousand questions about what the president was like, if she had seen Kathleen's dragon, if they had been tortured at the parliament building...

Sophie had lost sight of Amanda and Gregor as soon as they arrived, but she assumed that they too were prey to such curiosity.

To the other infected, Sophie gave a sincere account, but when she found herself in front of Korbinian she realized she didn't know what to say.

"What did you decide? My territory will remain with me, won't it?" he asked, worried.

"Well..." Sophie hesitated. "There will be new territories..."

"But my area will remain mine, right? You told Anderson that?" he insisted.

Sophie wanted to scream out her frustration. How could they expect to bring their territorial quarrels before the government of Europa?

"We didn't get to this level of detail," she admitted, "It was a much more general discussion. Next time we will make more precise arrangements."

"Well, remember that, when they divide the areas, you must make it clear that I have the best part. After all I've done for you, it's the least you can do." Korbinian stared at her. "You'll do it, won't you?"

Sophie realized at that moment that the underground city probably expected very different arrangements from those they had made.

Thankfully, Nadia arrived to take her away from the embarrassment: "There you are, I've been looking everywhere for you! Come with me!"

"Actually, we were..." Korbinian protested.

Nadia looked down on him: "Oh, leave her alone, can't you see she's exhausted?"

When Korbinian had left, looking grumpy, Nadia drove Sophie to the area where the infected had been living.

When they opened the door, Sophie was amazed: there was a very loud noise, which after a few moments she identified as music coming from a snarling loudspeaker.

The cots and sleeping bags had been moved somewhere, and a frightening amount of infected people, probably everyone Sophie had ever seen, were pressed into the room.

Someone must have recovered some bottles because many people drank an unidentifiable liquid from plastic cups.

"We must celebrate!" Nadia exclaimed. "Can you believe that maybe in a week we'll be able to go out again in the open air, walk the street without being in disguise?"

Sophie nodded enthusiastically: "We can take the dragons out! It will be amazing!"

She was very tired and a part of her just wanted to find a place to rest... but she was also happy, she realized, full of optimism for the future.

Suddenly, that impromptu party seemed like an excellent idea.

Trying to get away from the stream of people, they were joined by the other telepaths, Paul, Marie, Heinrich, and Jane. Sophie told them about Anderson's enthusiasm for dragons and how she wanted to protect the personal relationship between humans and dragons.

All of them were thrilled to discover that soon their creatures would be able to enjoy more freedom instead of being locked up in a basement.

Sophie left them to look for a cup of that substance, that she assumed to be alcoholic, which everyone was drinking, but whose source she could not identify.

She saw Amanda and James on the other side of the room talking animatedly, and saw Britt, who for once seemed almost cheerful.

The music, if you could define it so, was very strong and rhythmic, but every now and then she could catch some shred of conversation.

Almost everyone seemed to make plans for their new life within the city.

"I'm going to see my mother..." she heard someone say. "I haven't seen her in ten years!"

"I had a girlfriend before the plague, do you think she still remembers me?"

"I've heard that now there are restaurants, and they have even built parks, with trees and everything..."

She had to smile: it would be nice to see some green. She missed the island where initially she had felt so trapped.

She couldn't figure out where everyone was taking their drinks from, but, at some point, she identified Gregor.

He stood in a corner and also had a cup in his hand, from which he sipped the mysterious drink.

"What is it?" she asked him, taking the cup from him. She drank a sip of it: it had an intense taste that burned her throat, causing her to cough.

"Please, go ahead," he commented, sarcastic. "Try at least not to spit in it, though."

"You steal my food all the time, it's only fair," Sophie replied. "What is it?"

Gregor shrugged: "I'm not sure I want to know. It's strong, got to give it that. It's what it takes after a day like this," he said, taking his cup back and taking another sip with a grimace.

"Where did you get it?"

"Over here."

He turned to the corner of the room and produced an almost full bottle and paper cups as if out of nowhere.

"Cheers," he said, handing a cup over. "To the woman of the hour."

"You mean to Kathleen Anderson?"

"Yes, of course, to Anderson." Gregor finished what was left in his cup, and Sophie drank cautiously from hers. The second sip was not as bad as the first: the taste was still terrible, strong and strangely metallic, but the sensation of heat radiating from her stomach was curiously pleasant.

Gregor said something, and Sophie had to get closer to hear it. The music was loud and there was so much noise that it was impossible to talk unless speaking directly into each other's ears.

"I said that you helped a little, too," Gregor said.

Sophie took another sip, which seemed almost good: that drink was growing on her.

"This music is awful," Gregor complained. "Where did they even get it?"

Sophie listened carefully "Wait, wait, I've already heard this song... wasn't it the theme song of a TV show, or something like that?"

"They all sound the same to me," he said with contempt.

"You don't like music?"

Gregor stared at her: "No, I love it, actually." He drained his cup. "You know, if we'll really get to walk through the city again, the first thing I want to do is go to see a nice concert. The philharmonic, maybe. I want a nice ensemble, strings, horns, timpani, the whole thing. God, I miss that."

Sophie thought he must be a little tipsy because she had never seen him talk so enthusiastically; even his cheeks were red... or rather, they seemed to have a vaguely rosier shade than his usual paleness.

"What are you going to do when you're a free citizen again?" she asked. "Apart from going to concerts, I mean."

"I don't really know," he admitted, filling his cup again. "I don't think I could go back to my old job. I have no living relatives and my friends..." he made a grimace, perhaps thinking of Voigt. "Oh well, I'll figure something out."

Sophie nodded: if there was anyone who would surely get away with any situation, that was Gregor.

"What about you? Are you going back to being a doctor?"

Sophie sneered: "Yeah, right. I'm sure there will be a line to get treated by a doctor with the plague. No, I think I'd like to do something with Pat. You know, someone's going to have to take care of the dragons, if Anderson really is going to build that foundation, so... I mean, why not? Of course, assuming that the whole negotiation goes well," she added.

She hardly dared to make any plans, fearing that they might be wiped away at any moment.

At the same time, however, she felt light-headed, as if she was floating. It was probably the effect of the alcohol.

"If it doesn't work, we're screwed," Gregor said gloomily. "Also because, between us, I believe that as soon as these guys from the underground city know the terms of the agreement, they'll kick us out... if we're lucky, that is."

Sophie felt her stomach turn: she feared the moment when she would have to communicate to the heads of the underground city the solution they had come to.

"Tell me about it… I feel like I've made a big mess."

Gregor grinned: "Of course you've made a big mess! That's all you've done since you started making decisions."

"Well, thank you," Sophie replied, offended.

"But I must give you this: since I was infected, this is the first time I have the impression that we could also live... as in, not only survive."

"Damn!" Sophie laughed. "That almost soundedike a compliment."

She was definitely tipsy, but she didn't care. In fact, she was having a great time.

At that moment, someone who had probably drunk a little too much bumped into Gregor, who was forced to take a step forward, resting his hands on her hips, not to knock her on the floor.

Sophie felt his breath, which was warm and alcoholic, but it wasn't unpleasant… quite the contrary, in fact…

Gregor got closer, perhaps to say something...

"Sophie!"

She realized that Ken was next to her, trying to attract her attention.

Gregor stepped back, and Sophie blinked, trying to figure out what Ken was saying.

Maybe she shouldn't have drunk so much on an empty stomach, she thought.

"You must come immediately," Ken said. "It's about Cain."

Sophie's heart sank: no, she thought, it wasn't fair, not now...

"What happened?" she asked, preparing for the worst.

Ken smiled: "He has woken up."

END OF FIRST PART

SECOND PART

CHAPTER 22

Cain had woken up from the coma a week earlier, but Sophie had only managed to see him a handful of times.

The night Ken announced it, she, Gregor and Famke rushed to the apartment on the surface where Amanda and James had settled.

Although the evening air had cleared her mind of the excessive drinking, she still felt awkward in her movements, as if she was trying to walk in the water.

At that moment, Sophie realized that she had never been there and that she had never visited Cain since the dragons had been moved to the cathedral.

I considered him dead already, she thought, feeling guilty.

Amanda wasn't very happy when she saw all three of them showing up at the door.

"He needs rest, he's still very weak."

Eventually, Sophie convinced her to let them into his room one at a time, for a few minutes.

When it was her turn to do so, she found Cain still lying in bed, his eyes barred, looking dazed.

He had lost a lot of weight and looked like the ghost of himself; his hair had grown back into irregular locks; he had deep dark circles and was mortally pale. His gaze, however, was vigilant.

He looked at her vaguely puzzled, as if he wasn't sure who she was.

"Hi," Sophie said, embarrassed. "I'm happy to see that you're feeling better."

Cain kept staring at her in silence.

Sophie wondered if she should take his hand. She had read that human contact helped healing and brain recovery; she had fantasized, in the previous months, that Cain would wake up and they could finally touch each other without fearing the contagion...

At that time, however, she only felt uncomfortable, and as for him, perhaps he didn't even remember having met her.

"I... well, a lot of things happened while you were in a coma," she continued. "I can't tell you all now but... er... to begin with, I caught the plague, but I survived, and then the dragons..."

Cain suddenly seemed very agitated and started to move in bed, making confused sounds.

Suddenly he seemed terrified of her presence.

Amanda rushed into the room, and James had to keep him down not to let him hurt himself.

"I told you it was too much for the first day," said Amanda, pushing Sophie outside the door. "You better leave now, we mustn't upset him too much..."

After that first meeting, which proved to be vaguely disappointing, Sophie kept her distance and waited for Cain to be able to sustain a conversation.

She had cautiously passed by Amanda's apartment a couple of times but had always found him asleep.

She was told he had confused memories and difficulties in distinguishing fantasy from reality but was recovering well.

He couldn't walk or stand, but he had started talking, he could grasp objects and eat by himself, and he was usually lucid. He even started to ask where he was, and where all the other infected were.

It didn't seem like much to Sophie, but Amanda was very impressed.

"Usually it takes months, even years, to have this kind of improvement, while it only took him a few days," she explained. "It must be something related to the increased resistance of the infected body..."

Since Sophie seemed a little disappointed, she added: "Tomorrow we will start to inform him about the new situation. Ken is pestering me because he says that we can't make arrangements without his approval, now that he's awake..." Amanda sighed tiredly. "To be honest I don't think it's possible that Cain will actively participate in this phase.

As for Anderson, we had agreed to go ahead with the negotiation despite Cain's new health development."

According to Amanda, a normal patient in his condition would take many months to recover sufficient physical and mental faculties to lead a normal life, provided he had not suffered brain damage, which was not entirely certain yet.

In the meantime, they couldn't screw up all the negotiations they had carried on with Kathleen.

To her surprise, the next day Sophie received a message from Amanda telling her that she could visit Cain, and also to bring Gregor.

From the day of the party, she hadn't seen much of him either: he had used some of the channels he still owned in the secret services to verify that Anderson had taken action to define the issues left unresolved, such as the dragon care Foundation or the project for the reintegration of the underground city inhabitants, while she had been busy keeping Korbinian and his cronies quiet, as they were very worried about the imminent agreement.

And rightly so, Sophie thought. She felt very guilty every time she had to talk to them. Rationally, she was convinced that the integration of the population of the underground city and the end of those strange tribal struggles between the various leaders was the best solution, but she felt sorry for Korbinian, who had helped them when they had nowhere to go.

She knew that all criminal leaders would have a fit when they would find out about Kathleen's terms. By then, she'll need to ask Anderson to have an alternative accommodation ready for all of them, otherwise the consequences would have been serious.

Moreover, Pat was becoming more and more difficult to keep under control: since he knew that he could soon go out into the open air, he had grown restless.

Sophie was increasingly impressed by his intelligence and awareness.

When she saw Gregor, he seemed tired but optimistic: Anderson was apparently fulfilling her commitments, despite the contrary opinion of many of her ministers and collaborators.

"But I wouldn't worry too much about that," Gregor added. "You know her, she will do what she wants."

When they arrived at Amanda's, they found Cain sitting in an armchair.

He wore normal clothes instead of the sort of nightshirt he had throughout his convalescence, and he was shaved, apparently fresh from a shower, or more likely from a bath.

He was still very skinny and had a weak, sickly appearance, but he looked more like he was recovering from bad flu than from a coma of several months.

Amanda was right: it was a miraculous recovery.

Cain greeted Gregor with warm camaraderie, then turned to her.

"Hi, Sophie."

His voice was very low and rough, as if making sounds was very difficult for him.

But it was him again, Sophie thought with relief, and he also seemed to remember her, something she had not been certain about the previous time.

His deep gaze was once again his own, and Sophie felt the familiar sensation of being hypnotized by it.

"I almost didn't recognize you."

Sophie flushed, acutely aware of the scales that scarred her face.

"Ah, um, yeah..." she said, instinctively rubbing her cheeks, as if she could hide them. "The plague left me these nice marks..."

He seemed surprised: "Yes, those too... but I meant that you look good. I'm sorry that you've been infected, but it's a pleasure to see that you're alive and well."

Sophie didn't know what to say.

"James told me that you risked your life to save mine," he continued, always talking with laborious effort. "I'm very grateful for that."

Sophie smiled, happy for his words and for the fact that he was so lucid: "Don't mention that... I was so worried about you, it was terrible. First the cut to the throat, then the aneurysm..."

Cain ran a hand on his head, where the scars were still visible: "That was the best thing that ever happened to me."

"What do you mean?"

"Even if I was only barely conscious, I have confused memories... of voices... and the dragon, always in the back of my mind, as it had always been. Then, I remember the convulsions, the noises around me... and finally the feeling of something being cut off, and the dragon was finally silent. I haven't heard from him since. I think it was your surgery that finally freed me. I can't thank you enough."

"Oh," Sophie commented. She didn't know what to think: of course, she was happy that Cain had gotten rid of his personal demon, that her hasty surgery had no serious consequences, and that it had brought an improvement, even. However, now that she too was in telepathic contact with a dragon, she felt an instinctive horror at the idea that such a bond could be severed. It was a sinister thought.

"Since I started to have control of my thoughts again, I have wondered what happened now that Kathleen and that monster have been reunited..." Cain continued.

"Well, uh, about that," Gregor chimed in, "we have some updates to give you."

At that moment, Ken arrived too and greeted Cain with enthusiasm.

Sophie felt vaguely annoyed by his presence, as if he was an intruder; but then she remembered that he had always been in Cain's closest circle, and probably from his point of view *she* was the intruder.

Famke was also part of the trio that accompanied Cain everywhere, but by the time she had begun to take care of Elias Visser's dragon, she had gradually been completely absorbed by the new task. She and the dragon had started to become very close, almost as if they also shared a bond as deep as the telepathic one.

James brought some chairs, and they all settled around Cain's bed for a sort of meeting.

"First of all, as Amanda has already explained to you, the island where we had planned to move was compromised and we could not go there," Gregor began. "So we all moved to the city, where we used the safe houses for a while, until…"

Gregor briefly reported the events of recent months, and Sophie noted that he had avoided mentioning the role of Pat in the agreement with the underground city, nor had he talked about the new arrangements regarding the dragons' care.

Did he want to avoid giving him too much information all at once for fear of upsetting him, or did he prefer someone else to take on the task? Sophie was sure it would be difficult to convince Cain of the benefits of the new solution.

When he came to have to explain the police raids in the underground city, Gregor stopped and Amanda continued in his place: "Cain, I understand this is hard news to digest, so… well, if you start to feel too upset or tired, we can stop and…"

"I think I can do it, thank you," Cain stopped her coldly.

Sophie realized how it bothered him to appear weak: she wondered if the fact that he had not shown up in bed but sitting up, washed and dressed, was an illusion to seem stronger than he really was.

"Anyway," Amanda continued, "after she regained her identity, Kathleen Anderson spread the plague vaccine. Now a large part of the population is vaccinated. This gave her a lot of support and in a few months she took over the government. Now she is the President of Europa, and she has the dragon always by her side."

Cain said nothing, but his jaw stiffened almost imperceptibly. Sophie had the impression that although he was trying to keep a cool façade, the news had shaken him.

"In contrast to the old government, and thanks to the spread of the vaccine, Anderson has proven not to be so averse to the infected. On the contrary…"

"Let me guess," Cain interrupted her. "She proposed to make a deal to make us come out and stop being persecuted?"

Amanda exchanged an uncertain look with James: "Well, um, actually yes, she did."

Cain sighed: "Of course, just as I imagined. I assume we turned the deal down, didn't we?"

An embarrassed silence fell into the room.

Since no one was saying anything, Sophie decided to speak up.

"To tell you the truth, we accepted. We've already started the negotiation."

Cain stared at her.

"'*We*'? Who's negotiating this nonsense?"

Sophie flushed: "Um, Amanda, Gregor and me. And it's a good deal!" she insisted, in a surge of pride.

Cain looked at Gregor accusingly.

"Hey, wait a minute, at least hear the terms..." the latter defended himself.

"Oh, I'm sure they're very advantageous terms," said Cain. "Let me take a wild guess: total immunity, forgiveness for all past crimes, perhaps even the suppression of the medical police? Am I right?"

Amanda was also uncomfortable: "She gave us what we asked for, yes" she confirmed. "Is it such a terrible thing?"

Cain shook his head: "No, you... I understand your position. But you don't know that woman as well as I do. You see, she's made a lot of promises, but she has no intention of keeping them. She only wants one thing: the dragons. I bet they are also part of the agreement, is that correct?"

"We won't give them to her!" Sophie explained. "Kathleen will never control them. Dragons will stay with the humans they are bonded to, they will not be separated," she explained.

Cain, though, seemed horrified from this perspective: "That's even worse! In this way, she will not only have the dragons, but she will already have the means to use them too. That's crazy. No, this agreement must be stopped immediately," he declared.

"That's what I said!" Ken jumped up. "I knew we shouldn't have moved on with it! It's since they've freed the dragons that I..."

"Freed the dragons?" Cain repeated. "What are you talking about?"

"Hang on, wait a minute…" Gregor said in a reasonable tone. "Let's try to go with order, shall we? The dragons have not been 'freed'," he pointed out, miming quotation marks with his fingers. "They are in a safe place, in one of the most remote corners in the underground city. They just have a little more space, that's all," he minimized, watching Ken threateningly, as if to intimidate him. "And we've increased surveillance. Now each of the dragons has a contact person who feeds them, teaches them how to fly and so on. Sophie's got it all worked out, and this system works really well. We used dragons during an attack to the presidential guard's seat, and it all went great. We've been controlling them perfectly. When had we ever succeeded in that before, huh?"

In spite of Gregor's assurances, Cain still appeared suspicious: "I see. It sounds like a good solution," he granted, "as long these people of reference are not their telepaths, right?"

Gregor looked at the tip of his shoes: "Um, well…"

"Of course it's the telepaths, come on!" Sophie snapped. "Who else could do it? When there is such a strong bond you can't try to break, it would be impossible, and it brings nothing but suffering and alienation and…"

"You… you too," Cain whispered with horror. "You too have one of those monsters in your head, don't you?"

"I... well, first of all, they are not monsters and then…"

"I'm so sorry, Sophie. I really am," Cain said, taking her hand. "None of this should have happened."

Sophie was taken aback: part of her would have liked to protest, but she was also acutely aware of the contact between them and of the warmth of his skin against hers, and any objection died on her lips.

"Cain, you look exhausted," Amanda said. "I think you've had enough for today."

Cain nodded, letting go of Sophie's hand: "Just tell me this: at what point are you in the negotiations?"

"We should meet next week to make everything official," Gregor replied.

"So there's nothing final yet?"

"No."

Cain nodded: "Good. Thankfully, we are still in time to stop everything."

Amanda looked devastated: "But… we have worked hard to get to this point… shouldn't we at least try…?"

"I'm sorry, but no negotiations with Kathleen Anderson will ever have any value. You can't agree with a completely unreliable interlocutor," he said.

No one answered, and Sophie realized desperately that that was his final word.

"I don't want you to think that I don't appreciate what you've done," Cain added in a softer tone. "You were in good faith, and the progress you've made is remarkable. But you certainly couldn't imagine how wicked that woman could become. As long as she's in the government, we can't hope for any kind of cooperation."

CHAPTER 23

Two weeks after the meeting with the rebels, everyone in the government had acted to put the changes promised by Kathleen into place.

The most important task was certainly the integration between the medical police and the ordinary police.

In recent times, the former had been so powerful that the latter was almost irrelevant; the news of their dissolution, predictably, had not been taken very well by the highest ranks of the medical police, who in a short time had seen themselves go from respected and important figures to excess personnel who no one knew where to relocate.

Even the medical police officers themselves, despite being assured that they would have a place in the ordinary police and an equal role in their structure, were not very happy to have to study pages and pages of laws, crimes and new procedures to be applied: the ordinary police made fewer on-field actions, but dealt with much more varied issues.

Even the regular police officers, accustomed to their routine and organisation, were not enthusiastic about the imminent expansion.

Kathleen Anderson had attempted to stem the discontent of the parties involved with diplomacy, trying to offer a solution that satisfied everyone: faced with lack of cooperation, however, she ended up entrusting the presidential guard with the task of deciding who would remain in office and who would be relocated somewhere else, and then defining where.

This put Erik in the unpleasant position of having to choose who to keep in charge and who to send away among his old superiors; he had to spend hours and hours a day reading through the personal files of the various officers and determine who would go where. Some were strangers to him, but most he knew at least by name.

Part of him was tempted to take some revenge for past offences, but then decided to strive to be mature and impartial. He had even planned for Hoffman a small promotion in the transition between one armed force and another: in the end, despite his pompous ways, he was a good bloke.

In addition to the new task at work, Erik was also concerned about Peter.

Although he had been in the eighth ring for a few months now, Erik had received few calls, a few messages, all very laconic and difficult to interpret.

Maja was restless too.

"I have the impression that there's something that he doesn't want to say…" she explained.

"Maybe, more simply, working life isn't the exciting adventure that he expected and he's a little disappointed," Erik suggested.

Maja shrugged: "Maybe. But if it was just that, he would go on complaining forever... I don't know, I feel there's something else."

Erik didn't know what to think: he may clash more with Maja, but Peter was the one he found more difficult to understand. He and his daughter were similar, more inclined to speak clearly. Peter, on the other hand, had inherited Thea's tendency to avoid discussions and preferred a shrug to a long discussion.

In the end, Maja had decided to use a few days' leave to visit her brother.

The journey to the eighth ring was long: only a handful of trains a day went there, because they had to cross long expanses of fields and factories, where those who did not work there never visited, and also, once in the eighth ring, you had to have a car or make arrangements with someone to be picked up because there was little public transport. Most of the companies provided minibuses for their employees, but it was all private. Cell phones also had bad reception.

Using his position, he had managed to give Maja a government cell phone, which had signal almost everywhere and allowed encrypted calls, and asked her to give him an update as soon as she spoke to Peter.

Erik looked at the watch and hurried to call a car to go to the government headquarters: that day he would see the three delegates of the infected again.

To his surprise, the infected had made a good impression on him: Sophie Weber seemed a reasonable person and, as much as the other guy was a bit unpleasant, Erik remembered that it was him who had stopped his beating. It was hard to hate someone after that.

Sometimes he remembered the file on Thea and Anderson's words about the fact that they had, in fact, caused her death, involving her in dangerous and illegal activities: but, despite all this, Erik began to have the creeping doubt that his wife might have had her reasons. Was helping the infected really that wrong?

If they were close to concluding a peace that would improve the lives of all the inhabitants of Europa, it was also thanks to what Thea had done while she was alive.

Erik had conflicting feelings: in a way, he regretted the period of his life when he could hate the infected without asking too many questions. Having an enemy to turn against was a lot easier.

In addition to all this, the presence of Amanda Solarin confused him.

All in all, he was happy to see that she was alive and well; and a part of him was happy with the idea that they would soon be on the same side.

He could not deny his admiration for her, and he did not like having to consider her an enemy, which was perhaps paradoxical given that she had committed all sorts of crimes, from subversive activity to escape from a prison hospital, but that was the truth.

When he arrived at the government headquarters, he was surprised at the relative scarcity of security measures: despite the fact that there were many policemen guarding the area and trying to disperse the crowd of demonstrators and onlookers, there were no helicopters or snipers, who were instead present two weeks earlier.

Inside, he found the group of ministers in great ferment: everyone was talking to each other with agitation and running from one meeting room to another.

Erik spotted Voigt and stopped him: "What's going on? Where's the meeting?"

"There won't be any meeting. The rebels rejected the agreement for good!"

Erik was amazed: "But... they seemed so sure, only fifteen days ago..."

"They are unpredictable!" Voigt exclaimed. "They don't think logically, as we do! They could do anything... anything!"

Erik would have liked to say that Amanda Solarin wasn't infected and he was pretty sure that at least she wasn't unpredictable and irrational, but he noticed the crazy note in the Head of the Secret Service and decided to refrain.

Compared to two weeks earlier, Voigt appeared exhausted: his complexion had an unhealthy tinge and seemed to have lost at least ten pounds.

"Are you feeling well?" he asked him.

"Of course, I'm in perfect health!" Voigt snapped. "I was tested for the plague this very morning!"

"I didn't mean the plague, of course... you just look a bit stressed, that's all."

"I'm perfectly well!" Voigt insisted, a shrill note in his voice.

Suddenly, an emergency government meeting was announced, and Erik went to the assembly's meeting room.

Kathleen Anderson was already present: she looked furious.

"As you have probably already heard," she began, once everyone had sat down, "the rebels decided to reject the generous agreement I had offered them. This morning, instead of the negotiation delegates, the following message arrived: 'The coalition of the plague survivors and the underground city refuses to come to terms with the ruling government," she read, her voice vibrant with repressed anger. " 'We ask for the immediate resignation of the President and the taking into custody of the dragon. As long as the criminal Kathleen Anderson is in power, no deal will be considered.'"

She shook her head: "I gave them everything they could wish for peaceful coexistence: respect for their rights, a new opportunity to live within society, peace... but it's now clear that this is not what they want. They only want destruction."

Erik frowned: their behaviour made no sense. Why refuse to negotiate when they'd managed to get so much? The three delegates seemed very cooperative, why this sudden change?

"The underground city may have reacted unfavourably to the proposed agreement and blown up the negotiation," suggested Friedrich Haas, the Minister of the Interior. "The message speaks of a 'coalition', which suggests that they may have a more important role than we had expected."

Kathleen seemed thoughtful: "The message is a direct attack towards me. It even calls me a criminal and asks for my resignation... I don't think this request comes from the underground city. It sounds more like a personal grudge..." she added, as if she was thinking aloud.

General Chardon took the floor: "President, have you considered the possibility of a reversal of power within the rebel group? Perhaps the most moderate faction, which was willing to deal with us, was put aside?"

"By whom? I believe there aren't any other prominent people among the infected... unless..." Anderson shook her head: "No, it's not possible."

"Pardon me, Madam President, but in the past days I took the liberty of carrying out some extraordinary investigations," Voigt said with a fluty voice. "Maybe some of the information I found could be useful to you."

Anderson gestured him to continue.

"I tried to intercept conversations among rebels by placing bugs on the delegates when they came here," he said.

Kathleen seemed surprised: "You didn't tell me about it."

Voigt gave a viscid smile: "Forgive me, Madam President, professional deformation. I already had the feeling then that the negotiations might be more complicated than expected."

"So we have a bug in their headquarters?"

Voigt made a grimace: "Unfortunately not. The three delegates freed themselves from their clothes and bugs shortly after leaving the government seat, and meanwhile said nothing worthy of note. The clothes, however, were abandoned in the underground city, and at least one item of clothing was collected by one of its inhabitants, who, as we know, live by gimmicks and rummage even through the dirtiest garbage," he added, disgusted.

"The words we intercepted are mostly worthless. Mundane conversations, quarrels between family members, a shady business of buying and selling food and small stolen items... However, shortly before the bug was destroyed, presumably accidentally, we heard about the infected. The reception was very confused, but I'm sure I've heard of a figure known to us," Voigt made a pause to effect. "The General."

A disturbed murmur spread in the room.

Kathleen fiercely pursed her lips, and for a moment Erik found her almost frightening.

"Cain..." the president whispered.

Chardon stared at her in amazement: "Cain? Him again? Weren't we certain he was dead? Voigt, you didn't say you had the final confirmation?"

"This input didn't come from my sources" he clarified. "Perhaps, the President..."

Kathleen looked up: "The information came from me. Cain had been seriously injured in an accident during my undercover mission and had gone into a coma. Sometime after, his mind... I stopped receiving information about his vital functions and concluded that he was dead."

"What kind of information?" Voigt asked, puzzled. "Bugs?"

"I have my sources," Anderson snapped. "But not even those are infallible."

Erik had the impression that he was the only one who did not know this Cain very well. He was the General that he had heard so much about in the past years, but he had the impression that rumours were mixed with reality to the point that it was difficult to discern one from the other.

"With Cain at the head of the rebels, what should we expect?" he asked cautiously.

Kathleen turned to look at him: "We can expect nothing but open war. From this moment on, the truce is over."

CHAPTER 24

Cain had not yet left the apartment in which he was staying, yet, since he had woken up, the situation of the infected and the underground city had changed radically.

Korbinian, Misha and the other leaders were shocked when they were told that the negotiations had been skipped.

Korbinian, in particular, was disappointed, and wanted to know more details: perhaps he thought that Sophie had defended his interests and that with Kathleen's relocation he would have a larger territory and particularly advantageous agreements.

In general, they were all very angry to have been cut off from the discussion, and Sophie's attempts to remind them that it was their decision not to attend the meeting were worthless.

Kathleen Anderson had kept her word and had not sent any more raids to the underground city, at least for the time being; however, in a television speech she announced that her generous attempt at peace had been rejected and that she would soon provide for a 'definitive solution'.

From what she heard from those who went to the surface, however, Sophie had the impression that public opinion was still divided: like the demonstrators she had seen at the government seat, many still defended the rights of the infected and condemned the treatment they had suffered.

Many leaders of the underground city, particularly Misha, claimed that it was necessary to strike before she did, taking advantage of the confusion of the moment.

Cain, in any case, had decided to stop any attempt to coordinate the underground city in defence against the government.

That would no longer be the infected's business: it was, in fact, his intention that they would leave the underground city to go to another safe place, in the mountains south of the eighth ring.

It was an area far from the city, formally still within the borders of Europa but closer to the quarantined territories.

Cain had been there in the past, before the rebel group was formed, and considered the area as a backup plan after the two islands that had been discovered by Kathleen. As a precaution, he never talked to anyone about this, not even Gregor.

Sophie felt conflicted about it: on one hand, she was happy to be able to leave those dark tunnels and have the prospect of living in the open air again; on the other hand, she was still disappointed the bad outcome of the agreement with Kathleen.

It seemed almost absurd to her that for a moment she had really believed that she could have a normal life, that she could get back to work, that she could go to the restaurant or the park, even that she could devote herself to Pat in a safe and legal environment.

The little dragon, on the other hand, did not take well to the news that the prospect of going out had been destroyed. Sophie wasn't sure if she'd managed to get him to understand the details of the matter, but Pat understood very well that he would have to stay down there a little longer, and he was disappointed and angry.

He was nervous and often got into fights with Taneen. His bad mood had also infected Sophie, who often felt frustrated without knowing exactly why.

"Soon we will leave anyway," Sophie assured him. "We will go out in the mountains, in the middle of the woods, it will be beautiful!"

The dragon, however, did not let himself be softened: to him, that was a distant, unreal prospect.

Furthermore, Nadia had not received the news of Cain's miraculous awakening with the same enthusiasm as Sophie.

According to her, his return had 'ruined everything' and that they could have lived quietly if it hadn't been for 'that control-freak asshole'.

"Do you know what the problem was with the deal with Kathleen? That he didn't do it! For years he has only managed to get us killed and persecuted, and then you and Amanda arrive and solve all the problems in a few months. He's jealous, that's the truth."

Sophie, however, did not agree: in her opinion, it was not a matter of pride, but of principle.

Cain was absolutely sure that Kathleen would never keep her promises, and undoubtedly he was the person who knew her best, having grown up with her... and yet, with a certain sense of guilt, Sophie couldn't stop tormenting herself with doubt.

Would she really have betrayed them? Arrest and execute all the infected and then keep the dragons, as Cain claimed? What if she really wanted to live at peace with all of them?

Cain saw Kathleen as a sociopath who wanted nothing more than to bring death wherever she went, but Sophie thought her motives were much more definite.

Kathleen wanted her dragon, and she wanted Cain dead. She didn't have any feelings towards the other infected people, she didn't care.

The problem is, Cain isn't dead.

She felt horrible for just formulating the thought: Sophie was happy that he was recovering.

After so many months spent in uncertainty, wondering if he would ever wake up and what condition he would be in, seeing that he had not suffered permanent damage was like an answer to all her prayers.

Of course, he was still weak, but his intense gaze hadn't changed.

Only his voice was different: the cut that Kathleen had inflicted on him must have touched his vocal cords, because it had remained hoarse and raspy, but Sophie found it, if possible, even more fascinating.

When she was in his presence, she was assailed by the familiar feeling of dazedness, as if no one else existed in the room.

She shouldn't have let her disappointment for the deal distract her from what was really important, which was the fact that Cain was alive and awake, she told herself.

Telling Anderson to go to hell had probably saved them all from a horrible fate.

Sophie went to the cathedral as usual to keep Pat company. Her past days had been a little empty. She didn't think she would come to miss the quarrels between the leaders of the underground city, but she did.

She brought food to both her dragon and Famke's, who was busy organizing the movement of all the infected into the mountains, as was as Gregor, Ken and James.

Cain had reconstituted his group of collaborators, or henchmen, as Nadia called them.

Sophie realized that she and Amanda had been left behind.

It was a little strange to be on the side-lines after having been at the centre of all decisions in the last few months.

From Cain's point of view, however, who had not been there, she was still the newcomer.

Sophie heard a noise behind her and saw that Marie had entered the cathedral. Her dragon, Cosette, trotted over to her. Compared to the impetuous personality of Taneen and Pat's enthusiastic one, Cosette was very sweet. Sophie thought it was funny that Marie was the only one to have given her dragon a female name: the dragons had no gender distinction, so the choice was absolutely arbitrary.

A few moments later, Marie approached her: "Sophie, I was hoping to find you here alone. There's something you need to know," she said, in an anxious tone.

"What is it about?"

"The move. Earlier, I was helping Ken to pack up some things, computers, electronic stuff, you know those things he always works with, and…" Marie seemed embarrassed. "Well, it's not that I've been rummaging around, of course, but those papers were there and…"

"I get it, don't worry."

"In any case, I saw sheets with some projects. Basically, as I understand it, we will go to an abandoned village, a bit like it was on the island… but they are also building something else…" Marie seemed desperate. "A bunker."

Sophie did not understand what the problem was: "So what?"

"What do you think they want to put in it?"

Suddenly she was caught by a terrible suspicion: "You think…?"

"Of course!" Marie nodded. "It's for dragons! They want to lock them up again, chain them up... they'll probably forbid us to see them again," she added, her voice trembling with anger and worry.

"No, come on... after all we've done, Cain won't want to go back..." Sophie said, but she didn't go on. She thought back to the last time they had talked of the arrangements for the dragons and recalled that Cain had actually made no commitment in this regard, merely acknowledging the current situation.

Were their successes enough to change his mind about the need to limit contact between dragons and telepaths?

"Will you talk to him? To Cain," Marie implored her. "Maybe if you tried to explain to him, he would listen to you..."

"To tell you the truth, it's not like he ever listened much to me in the past," Sophie pointed out to her, but then she remembered his words back on the pier: *'I thought for a long time about what you told me...'*

It seemed like a lifetime had passed since then.

But maybe he could listen to her again... maybe he would think about what she was telling him and would reconsider the relationship with people and dragons.

"I'll try," she assured Marie. "It's worth a try."

Marie nodded: "Look, I've talked to the others about it, and..." she lowered her voice, "if Cain doesn't change his mind, there's always another possibility."

"What do you mean?"

Marie seemed uncomfortable: "You know... Anderson always said she would welcome any infected person with a dragon. She had already said so in her inauguration speech. If Cain continues to treat us like he did in the past, we'll go with her. That's what you should do, too."

Sophie opened her mouth, shocked: yet she shouldn't have been surprised. Heinrich had already mentioned this possibility in the past and, with Cain's return to power, the prospect became more and more attractive.

If Cain was right, Kathleen just wanted to get the dragons and then who knows what she would do.

"Wait a minute," Sophie said. "Don't do anything hasty, please. I'll talk to Cain, I'll do everything I can. Trust me."

"Oh darling, it's not you I don't trust," Marie said with an indulgent smile. "I know how much you care about Pat. Cain is the problem."

Sophie decided to go talk to Cain right away.

She walked through the tunnels that led to the neighbourhood where the apartment with hesitation, because she was not sure of the way. She realized it was her first time there without Gregor.

She found him already there, discussing with Cain the details of the move.

"I told you," he was saying tiredly. "We only have three more jeeps, we should make a hundred trips back and forth to bring everyone, not to mention the risk of being caught us and..."

"Is it true that you want to build a bunker to lock the dragons in?" she interrupted him, going straight to the point.

"Why, good morning to you too," Gregor replied. "What did you say? Oh, I'm fine, thanks for the interest."

Sophie ignored him and turned to Cain: "Tell me the truth. Do you want to lock up the dragons again?"

Cain seemed taken aback: "How do you know about the bunker?"

"I've heard rumours about it," she answered with a shrug.

"I'm considering the problem of dragons in our next arrangement, yes," Cain nodded. "I don't understand why you're so outraged, though. You didn't think we'd let them flutter around freely, I suppose."

"Well, no, but..."

Actually, if she could have chosen, it was exactly what she would have done. The dragons would never abandon the person they were attached to and there was no need for supervision because the telepaths always knew where they were and what they were doing.

"I think that if they were given more freedom than they had on the island, this would be of great benefit both to them and to us," she went on with passion. "There is something wrong about being locked up all the time... how do you think they feel? And what do you expect them to do as soon as we get them out? There would be no way to control them! If we want them to be an advantage and not a burden, however, we must live with them, and therefore respect their needs."

Cain listened to her in silence, then stood up and approached her. He was moving with difficulty, but confidently.

Sophie for a moment was surprised that he was already able to walk.

"I appreciate you wanting to make your contribution, Sophie," he said to her in a reasonable tone, staring at her intensely. "But it hurts me that you can never trust me. I assure you that I care only about the good of my people, and that includes you and the other telepaths. I would never do anything to cause pain to any of you."

"Then you won't lock up dragons?" Sophie asked.

His speech was encouraging, but she wanted to know something more concrete.

Cain sighed: "I'm considering various options. Believe me, I'm looking for the best solution for everyone, but I must think about safety first. I promise you, however, that I will also evaluate the experiment that has been carried out by you in these months, at the cathedral."

Sophie would have liked to insist and have a certain answer immediately, but she sensed that it was better to wait for the right moment. Cain had had to process a considerable amount of information and change since he had woken up, she thought: the world as he knew it had completely changed, while he was anchored to his beliefs. She supposed it wasn't easy for him.

"Thank you," she said. "I... I know you had a bad experience with dragons and telepathy…"

Cain smiled without joy: "'Bad experience' is a bit reductive."

"Yes. Um. Anyway. Maybe you had the idea that all dragons are the same, that they all have the same personality or the same desires…" she continued, "but you know, they are actually very different from each other! Mine, for example, Pat… he's still a puppy, and he's such a playful little thing! Maybe if you tried to get to know him, to see what he is like, you would realise…"

"Sophie, I don't think it's a good idea," Cain sighed. "I know that your intentions..."

"I mean, if you just tried, if you just give it a..."

"You speak just like my... like Kathleen," he coldly cut her short.

Sophie flushed: "I didn't mean..."

"I know. I got it. Seriously, Sophie, I promise I'll think about it."

She nodded, not entirely convinced.

Cain beckoned her to sit down and then sat down next to her. Their faces were unexpectedly close.

"I don't want you to think I'm trying to put you aside. Gregor told me about everything you did during my period of unconsciousness, and I haven't had a chance to thank you yet, nor to tell you how important it was for all of us."

Sophie would have wanted to say something, but she felt her throat was suddenly dry.

"I'm still trying to understand all that has happened and to adapt to the new circumstances and I hope that you will still want to help me. But I would ask you once again to have some faith in me. I'm sorry that you always jump to the worst conclusion when it comes to my actions. That night on the island, were you really convinced that I would hurt what I thought was a friend of yours? I would never do that."

Sophie felt very embarrassed. It was true, back then she hadn't even stopped to think and had assumed he was guilty.

"Forgive me, please... It's just that Kathleen, or rather Emma, seemed so helpless and in danger..."

"Yes, she did," Cain nodded. "She deceived us all, she turned us against each other. Let's not let it happen again."

Sophie nodded, looking into his deep green-blue eyes. He was so close that she could distinguish every line on his face, the worried furrow between his eyebrows, the trace of beard on his chin and...

"Ahem," Gregor said from behind them. "May I remind you that I am still here? Maybe I'll go now, so you can keep staring longingly into each other's eyes, swearing eternal fidelity or something like that..."

Sophie got up, uncomfortable, and Cain did the same.

Why didn't Gregor ever shut his big mouth?

"No, um, that's ok, I was about to leave, anyway, that is, I'm really about to go."

"Oh, yeah, I get that. You looked like you were leaving," Gregor replied, apparently uncaring of her embarrassment.

"See you soon, Sophie," Cain dismissed her.

As she walked through the door, Sophie had the impression that she could feel his stare burning in the back of her head.

CHAPTER 25

Erik's cell phone rang, and he was shaken when he saw on the display that Maja was calling.

His daughter had left two days earlier, and that was the first call he received.

He tapped on the screen to answer: "Hi! How was your journey? Are you okay? Have you seen Peter?"

"Yes, it's all good!" said Maja's voice, sounding far away. "I had to wait for ages in the sixth ring because I lost the connection," she explained, scoffing. "You should see this place, it's incredible! There are fields everywhere, and there's so much space... The greenhouses are huge, I've never seen anything like it."

"How is Peter?" Erik asked. "Is he with you?"

"No, he's at work. I think he's fine but... he's a little weird."

"What do you mean?"

Maja sighed: "Well, when he talks about work, he sounds quite happy with what he does, but he never mentions any of his colleagues, and sometimes he stops in the middle of a sentence to change the subject suddenly. Peter has always been easily distracted but... not like that," she explained.

Erik thought about it: "You think his colleagues are mobbing him or bullying him somehow?"

"I don't know. Perhaps," Maja said. "I'll try to get something more out of him."

"OK, let me know. If you need anything..."

"I'll call you right away," she assured.

After hanging up, Erik reflected on Peter's situation: his son was smart, but perhaps his strange ideas might have made him an object of ridicule for his colleagues.

This kind of situation could be very stressful; Erik had seen it happen many times in the police.

He wondered if maybe going to the eighth ring in person and trying to get him to talk could help him; at that moment there was Maja, but she would leave soon.

He didn't like the idea of leaving Peter alone and away from home in a hostile environment; he mentally promised himself to take a couple of days off to visit him.

On the computer screen, on the other hand, he received a message from Kathleen Anderson, who wanted to see him that afternoon.

He left the office and told Charles about the change in his program: as usual, the boy stood up as he saw him arrive. After the attack on the presidential guard, Erik had the impression that Charles had become even more nervous and that he occasionally jumped up for no reason. In the end, he had stopped telling him to sit down, and he just tried to ignore his sudden movements.

In front of the government headquarters there was, as had often happened in the past days, a group of demonstrators urging Anderson to recognise the rights of the infected even in the absence of a formal agreement.

Erik saw some signs, which had slogans like 'INFECTED DOESN'T MEAN CRIMINAL' or 'EUROPA IS NOT A POLICE STATE'.

The majority of the population, however, was happy that Kathleen had not granted an amnesty to the infected rebels, and, apparently, the average citizen did not wish to be confronted with an infected person in their daily lives.

When he arrived at Anderson's office, he found Zoe Hernandez in front of the closed door.

"She's making private calls and she's asked me to leave the room."

Erik wondered for the first time what was in Kathleen Anderson's private life, if she had one: even when he was taking care of her security, he had almost always seen her at work, or, at least, in the company of her frightening dragon. He had never met anyone in her family or friends who were not closely linked to Anderson Pharmaceuticals or, lately, to the political environment.

He felt a little sad for her, but then he realized that the same could be said of him.

Since he didn't bring his kids to work, no one knew much about his private life.

"I see," he told Zoe. "How's it going, apart from that? Any other strange behaviours in there…" he nudged towards Kathleen's office, "or did you find the headset she uses to make phone calls," he joked.

Hernandez answered with a tight smile: "Very funny."

Erik realized that Hernandez did not look good at all. She appeared stressed and had deep dark circles under her eyes.

"Something wrong?" he asked.

Zoe looked away: "Look, I know you will turn a deaf ear to this, but…" she stepped closer to him and lowered her voice. "There's something wrong with that woman."

Erik opened his mouth, ready to answer, but Hernandez anticipated him: "Please listen to me. You know I'm on her side. I've always been, I think she's doing some wonderful things for this city…" she bit her lower lip. "But sometimes, when she's alone in her office and I'm out here, I hear her arguing with someone. She's not on the phone, I'm sure!" she said before Erik could object. "Sometimes she slams objects on the ground and when she comes out, her eyes… Erik, I'm scared," she whispered.

"Zoe…"

Suddenly the door opened, and Kathleen Anderson emerged from the office.

"Who are you talking to?" she asked in a sharp tone, so different from her usual.

For a moment, he really thought something was disturbing about her expression, the hard line of her mouth and her flaming eyes.

But then Anderson saw him and her face softened: "Persson, come in, I was waiting for you," she said, stepping aside to make him walk through the door.

Hernandez gave him one last desperate look, then the door closed behind him.

"I called you to talk about the situation of the medical police," Anderson continued. "I hope you weren't too disappointed to find out that the deal is off and all your work on integrating the two police forces had been in vain."

"It was a little discouraging," Erik admitted.

As he saw her sitting at her desk and flipping through the files, he told himself that the moment of disconcertment he had before must have been dictated by his imagination. There was nothing strange about President Anderson: she was always the usual, polite woman he knew, at most a little more tired than usual. The weight of the responsibilities associated with her office couldn't be easy to carry.

Kathleen laughed: "Then I have good news for you. I decided to integrate ordinary police and medical police anyway, regardless of the demands of the rebels."

Erik was surprised: "I see. Forgive me if I dare, but… this decision perhaps has something to do with the pressure from the demonstrators?"

"Oh, no, of course not," Kathleen replied. "That handful of slackers doesn't bother me at all. The truth is that I would never have accepted Solarin's request if it hadn't been something I had planned to do anyway."

He should have guessed as much, Erik thought. Maybe Anderson was born as a scientist, but by now she had become a real politician.

"Having two separate police forces is confusing and inefficient," she continued. "But this doesn't mean that there will be no one left to deal with the issue of the infected."

"Are you going to entrust the matter to some department of the new unified police?"

"No," Anderson replied. "I will entrust it to you."

"Me?" Erik repeated, confused.

Kathleen nodded: "I want the hunt for the rebels to be handled directly by the presidential guard. I've already wasted too much time with Seidel's obstructionism and his stupid bureaucracy," she shook her head. "No, I want to have more direct control over this whole affair. I want to take a hard line, and I want to do it immediately."

Erik was happy about this sign of trust from her, but the last words of the president had disconcerted him: it seemed paradoxical to him that the hunt for the infected would intensify when they were so close to making peace...

He saw Amanda Solarin's face before his eyes. Was she an enemy again?

"I see you're worried, Persson, what is it? You don't feel your men are up to the task?"

"No, they won't have any problems," Erik replied. "I was just wondering if the possibility of a future peace had completely disappeared."

"I'm afraid so," Kathleen sighed. "I wanted to believe until the last moment that there was hope for them, but now I realize that I was delusional. I don't think this story will be over until each one of them has been imprisoned or executed."

Erik was upset: "I don't think all the rebels want to oppose the government in principle. We have found out that there is a faction that wanted to make a deal with you... If it really was this Cain who regained power, it doesn't mean that he has no opposition from within..."

"Persson, trust me. I know Cain well, and I know that as long as he's alive, he can get the rebels to do whatever he wants."

Erik thought back of Elias Visser's body swinging from the ceiling of his cell, his empty eyes... that too was Cain's work, he remembered. Even then, he had no qualms about killing one of his own, when he feared that he might betray him.

"Listen to me, Erik," Anderson continued. "If we don't take a hard-line right away, they'll force us to do it. That... creature," she spat out with contempt, "is capable of anything. Don't get me wrong, I feel sorry for everyone else, too. Sophie Weber, for example... who knows if Cain spared her," she added in a melancholic tone.

Erik trusted Kathleen's judgment, as always, but a part of him was reluctant to unleash his men, many of whom he knew could be very violent, against people guilty only of having to follow a ruthless leader...

Suddenly, Anderson's phone rang, then the landline phone did the same; a moment later, Erik's phone also began to vibrate in his pocket.

From the corridor, he could hear frightened voices.

"Anderson," Kathleen answered, while Erik instinctively checked the door and windows and led the president into the most sheltered corner of the room.

When she turned towards him, he saw that she was pale and looked dismayed.

"I understand, I do... of course. Send me an update as soon as possible."

Kathleen closed the call and looked at Erik.

"Four homemade bombs exploded at the medical police station. Looks like it was the rebels," her eyes became shiny. "The rescuers say that there are no survivors."

CHAPTER 26

The news of the terrorist attack on the medical police station had caused mass hysteria in the underground city.

Korbinian, showing a little initiative for once, had set up a meeting with the main leaders, and the infected had also been called to attend.

Cain had decided to participate in person: he still had difficulty walking, but, after all, he used crutches even before the accident.

His arrival had caused a moment of silence from the representatives of the underground city: although they were used to seeing the survivors of the plague, Cain's appearance was always somewhat alien.

Sophie had to insist on participating and had to remind Cain that the underground city was used to dealing with her, because his idea was to handle everything personally, accompanied only by Ken and Gregor.

All the groups accused each other of the attack: Lisica said that it was Fa'r that placed the device, Fa'r said that it was Sinsonte, Sinsonte accused Misha, and Misha claimed that it was the infected.

"No, the attack is not our work," Cain replied, unblinking.

"Oh, isn't it?" Misha asked. "And how do we know that?"

Cain pierced him with a cold glance: "Because I just told you."

"Misha, it was we who opposed the use of these devices when you wanted to put bombs at Anderson's house!" Sophie, exasperated, reminded him.

"Oh, and isn't that convenient? A classic diversionary tactic," Misha replied, triggering a murmur of approval from others.

Sophie was about to answer, but Cain put a hand on her arm: "Let it go, Sophie," he whispered, "It's not worth wasting time, we've already told them what we think."

Sophie thought it was Misha himself who placed the bomb, it was what he had wanted to do from the first moment; she was annoyed by the scene he was putting on to blame the infected, also because she had realized that the other leaders of the underground city seemed inclined to believe him.

Ironically, the only thing that was managing to unite those litigious people was their hatred of the infected.

However, she had to trust Cain, as it was him who dictated the line now.

And she thought the skin on her arm was tingling where Cain had touched her.

"We are tired of having you here in our territory, dictating the law and never consulting us about anything!" Fa'r exclaimed at some point. "Remember that if you have a place to hide is only thanks to our generosity!"

"True, true!" Korbinian nodded. "Don't forget who has helped you so far."

"You, Cain, refused Anderson's agreement at the last moment without even deigning to ask our opinion," Lisica accused him. "What if we wanted to accept, eh?"

Cain raised his eyebrows: "Would you have wanted Anderson to move you all to a village in the eighth ring with any activity strictly controlled by the police? Those were the terms."

Sophie startled: she had carefully avoided giving them the details until then.

Predictably, Korbinian pointed his finger at her and Gregor: "You wanted to accept!" he squealed. "You wanted to sell us out to Anderson, you bastards!"

"We just..." Sophie began, but she was interrupted by insults from all the other leaders.

Fa'r made menacing gestures, while Lisica spat on the floor in front of her.

"Ah, yes, I missed the spitting," Gregor sighed.

Sophie realized that the situation was rapidly deteriorating.

"It's clear that we can't trust these creatures!" Misha thundered, receiving general approval. "I'll be damned if I'll ever listen to an infected again!"

"As you please," Cain said menacingly, and unexpectedly the leaders went quiet. "In any case, we will leave by tonight," he continued. "We thank you for your hospitality."

He got up to leave.

"What makes you think that I will let you go so easily?" Korbinian threatened, beside himself with anger.

"Oh, you will," Cain smiled. "You wouldn't risk having the position of your precious territory revealed to the real police, do you?"

Korbinian went pale: "You wouldn't dare..."

"And why not?" Cain replied. "Now get out of the way," he ordered, then walked towards the exit.

Korbinian still seemed upset, but that didn't stop him from grasping Sophie's arm: "As for you, and your friend who looks like a living dead," he whispered, gesturing towards Gregor, "if you only dare to show your face around here, I will get you, I will tear you to pieces and I will hang each of your bloody limbs at the entrances of my territory, so everyone will know what happens to those who try to betray Korbinian," he said.

"What a picturesque idea, you should consider a career in interior decoration," Gregor replied. "A simple farewell would have done too, you know"

Sophie yanked her arm, and Korbinian let her go; however, he kept staring at her with hatred until he disappeared from her sight.

Once they had left the meeting place, they headed towards the surface, into the seventh ring.

Cain and Gregor had somehow managed to find an empty freight train that would carry them to the edge of the eighth ring. From there, they could use the few cars they had and get other vehicles to get to the chosen place.

Sophie wondered if she could fly with Pat, once away from the city: it would be fun, and also comfortable. She decided she would propose it once the train had arrived at its destination.

She had reassured Marie and the other telepaths that Cain was more inclined to listen to their proposals, and that she was confident that they would find a solution that would respect both the security needs and those of the dragons. She had decided not to talk to him about Marie's threat to leave them, otherwise she was certain that there would be unpleasant consequences for all of them.

For the moment she had appeased them, and there had been no more talk of surrendering to Anderson, but Sophie could only hope that Cain would keep his word, or the crisis would break out again.

"You should take one for the team and fuck him once and for all, so maybe he'll leave Pat and all of us alone," Nadia had suggested.

Sophie had told her to go to hell, blushing so violently that her ears were burning.

When they were away from Korbinian and had left the underground city, the infected went to retrieve a large car with tinted windows.

Sophie sat in the back seat, and Ken did the same.

After a few minutes of watching the city flow through the window, she closed her eyes, almost dozed off.

Suddenly she heard Gregor, who was at the wheel, talking to Cain, who was sitting in the seat next to him: "Was it really necessary to treat those guys like that?" he asked in a low voice.

"What do you mean?" Cain asked.

"Don't get me wrong, I don't like those fuckers any more than you do," he said, with a grimace of disgust, "but they were the only allies we had, and now they hate us."

Sophie kept her eyes closed, but she kept listening.

"We don't need allies like that," Cain replied. "Turning to them was a good idea, given the circumstances," he granted. "In any case, this alliance would not have lasted long, you know that. It was an impossible coexistence, we'll be much better off on our own."

"Well, yes, that's what I believe too," Gregor admitted. "But we could have been more diplomatic, couldn't we? I could have done with another support in the city, it has been useful in recent months. Then, let's be honest, the only time that some government has at least pretended to take us seriously was when we all got together and..."

"Are you questioning my decisions?" Cain interrupted him.

"Of course not!" the other exclaimed. "It's just that Sophie's strategy of collaboration has borne some fruit and perhaps we should have continued to listen to her, after all, when she made some decisions..."

Cain cut him short again: "You know, it's nice that you were infected, pun not intended, by this pacifist spirit and this nice idea of being all friends," he hissed coldly. "Although isn't it a little hypocritical coming from the person who spent years plotting revenge and claiming that we should start planning mass contagion?" he accused him. "Remember when you were so reckless that you almost got yourself killed? Who helped you back then? Or remember how many victims you made trying to get to Voigt. Who put up with you and covered up your suicide-homicidal manias for years? And now you're telling me that you're all about collaboration and negotiation... Please, spare me this shit," Cain scoffed. "And we still haven't talked about that crazy idea of handing yourself over to the government, but don't believe that I've forgotten it. I can understand that Sophie believed in Anderson's good faith, she's a newbie. You, on the other hand… What were you even thinking?"

Through her semi-open eyelids, Sophie saw Gregor stiffen up, but he didn't reply.

The rest of the journey by car was spent in silence.

Sophie was upset by Cain's words: had Gregor really wanted to infect masses of innocent people, who would mostly die? It was a psychopath's idea.

Was that really the person that she had come to consider her friend? It seemed impossible.

 Yet she remembered that the first time she met him she had the feeling of being in front of a deeply dangerous individual... but unstable, even?

Sophie reflected on the depression that many, almost all, went through after surviving the infection; in her case, the presence of Pat had made the difference, but it was a very rare occurrence.

For most infected people, along with the relief of not being dead, there was usually the despair of not knowing what to do with their lives. James had also told her about the deep state of prostration that he had only overcome when he had joined Cain's group of rebels.

Had it been the same for Gregor? And was that stupid practical joke to Voigt enough to give him closure?

Once they had reached the train depot, Sophie pretended to wake up and hurried to reach the wagon where the wooden crate containing Pat had been loaded.

The dragon was very restless, much more than all the others, because it was the first time he had been locked up in something like a cage. Sophie concentrated on sending him comforting thoughts.

It's just for the journey, she told him, *soon we will be free, we will be able to fly in the open air.*

The other dragons occupied an entire wagon each, but since Pat and Taneen were smaller, their crates were loaded together.

Sophie and Nadia were able to spend the trip together, keeping the box doors open, so that the dragons did not feel as if they were suffocating in the cages.

Nadia told her that she thought Karla was upset about her deepening bond with Taneen.

"She said that I'm obsessed, that I'm not being myself anymore," she explained, shaking her head. "You can't get it if you're not in it."

"Isn't that weird for railway staff to see a ghost train pass?" Sophie asked when they passed by a station.

"Oh no, Ken hacked the route management system and changed all the timetables. I heard that from Marie. Must have been a lot of work," Nadia explained.

From the inside of the freight cars, it was not possible to see the landscape, but, after several hours of travel, Sophie realized that the temperatures had dropped abruptly.

After a while, the train stopped, and the doors opened.

Sophie and Nadia put the dragons back in the crates, then they came out.

Instead of the plain that stretched as far as the eye could see in Europa, in front of them there were hills that after a few miles became snowy mountains.

A damp slush was falling from the sky.

Sophie wasn't cold, not really: since the plague, her temperature had never fallen below forty-two degrees.

However, at that time she was happy with her new condition because she was certain that a normal human being would have needed many layers to warm up.

She was pleased that Amanda had decided to stay in the city. At first, she was shocked by her friend's decision.

"Do you want to stay here? Why?"

Amanda had shaken her head: "That's not the place for me," she said. "I can't do anything relegated to a small town without medical equipment and without the possibility of doing research. And Cain doesn't need my advice," she had added, slightly bitter. With Cain's awakening, she had found herself abruptly side-lined and had been very disappointed by the end of negotiations with Anderson, even more so than Sophie.

"I'll have Anderson Pharmaceuticals hire me and work on the research for the cure," she joked. Or maybe not.

"What about James?"

"I'll see him every now and then when he comes to town, as we've always done."

"Everyone knows your face, Anderson will have you arrested in no time."

Amanda had shaken her head: "You'd be surprised by what a fake document and a new haircut can do. You'll see, I'll be fine."

Sophie was disappointed, but deep down she understood Amanda's decision. After all, she could hope to rebuild her life, and that was only fair.

It was clear that the train could no longer continue: the track ended in nothing.

A few cars were unloaded; they were to be used to reach the abandoned village where they were to settle.

Sophie felt hungry, even though she had just eaten: it took her a few moments to understand that the feeling came from Pat.

She went to Famke to ask her for food, but she shook her head: "I'm sorry, we no longer have meat. It's very hard to find, and the one we had is finished."

"Then what should I give Pat, a salad?" Sophie protested.

Famke shrugged: "I thought he'd eaten enough before he left. Maybe when we get there someone will be able to hunt some wild animal."

Sophie bit her lip, thoughtful. She could feel that Pat was hungry, he was suffering. Plus, since they would have to hunt, why not start right away?

She spotted Cain at the top of the train, as he was about to mount on one of the jeeps.

"My dragon is hungry, and there's no more meat. There are forests in these mountains, I could take him to hunt and then reach you at the village," she proposed.

Cain seemed scandalized: "Sophie, I think that would be way too reckless…" he replied. "We are still close to the fields of the eighth ring... if it ran away…"

"Pat wouldn't do that," Sophie explained. "I can control him, I assure you, as I did during the attack to the building of Kathleen's guard. Trust me."

Cain shook his head, and Sophie was sure he was going to say no again, when Gregor pointed out: "Well, this would solve the problem of transporting dragons. They can't go on jeeps. It's better to make them fly than leaving them here for the night as we'd decided. And then they carry seven people, it means almost two rounds by car."

"Exactly," Sophie nodded. "Pat has to eat something, I'll take care of it, but the others could fly in a group to the village. That would be the easiest solution. I'm sure Famke would have no problem coordinating it."

Cain looked to her and then to Gregor, then finally sighed: "Alright... let's do this experiment. Get a map from Gregor and get one for Famke too."

"Will do!"

"Remember, maximum caution!"

Sophie smiled: "Thank you, you won't regret it."

"I hope not."

Nadia and the other telepaths were very happy with the news, and Sophie was satisfied: she felt confident that, in the end, they would be able to find a mediation with Cain.

An hour later, she was finally flying with Pat. The air was cool and brisk, completely different from both the one in the city and the salty air that she had breathed on the island.

Despite the snow that was wetting her hair and creeping into the collar of her shirt, Sophie felt excited; Pat seemed beside himself with joy to finally be able to spread his wings.

Sophie directed him into the woods, and after a few minutes, Pat smelled prey.

"Which way?" Sophie asked him, trying to follow the flow of his thoughts.

It was very difficult: hunting made the dragon faster and more instinctive, and its reflexes were better than Sophie's human ones.

When Pat dived into one of the trees, Sophie had to hold him back, and, after a few moments, they lost the animal's smell.

Pat's thoughts became frustrated.

"I'm sorry," she apologized. "You have to go slower, I'm scared!"

There's no need to be scared.

After a few minutes, Sophie felt the smell of another animal.

Pat went after it very fast. Too fast for Sophie.

The air hissed around her, slapping her face with icy blows, while snow covered her eyes and numbed her hands. She had to stop, she knew, or she'd crumble to the ground.

Let me go, please, let me go...

Sophie felt the will of the dragon, strong, unstoppable. He was hungry, *very* hungry, and the food was so close... he just had to go a little further.

Sophie closed her eyes...

The prey was there, a few meters below. It ran, but it was still slow, too slow.

The wind supported his wings and, in fact, this inclination made him go even faster.

The foliage hit his snout, but it didn't matter: the animal's smell was warm, inviting, delicious.

He sank his claws with one last leap and in a moment he was on top of it. The first bite made him sink his teeth in the fur. He pulled it out to get to the flesh. The first bite was as tasty as he had imagined, and, finally, the meat came to placate his stomach. It was satisfying, juicy, a true delight... he wanted more.

He threw himself on the carcass again, sinking his teeth again and...

Sophie jolted and opened her eyes: she was next to Pat, intent on eating the corpse of a hare, the snout dirty with fresh blood.

How did she get there? She remembered the intoxication of hunting, the wild smell of the animal, the hunger...

Sophie shivered: she had allowed the dragon to take control, she had lost herself in his will.

Nothing had happened, she told herself, everything was fine.

Yet she couldn't even convince herself.

She stood up and began to walk around nervously. Pat didn't pay any attention to her, too busy with his meal.

Despite her always high temperature, she suddenly felt cold.

She couldn't believe she'd completely lost control for so long... several minutes, at least. Or maybe more?

Of one thing she was certain: Cain nor anyone else should ever know.

CHAPTER 27

A light but persistent rain fell on the park in front of the government headquarters, where President Anderson was giving a commemorative speech for the victims of the attack to the medical police station.

Hundreds of dark caskets were arranged in rows in front of her: the flag of Europa had been draped on each of them, and a photo of the victim stood next to them.

They were not great photos: for some, their family had provided a nice picture or even a professional portrait, but for many, in the absence of anything better, the photo on the badge had simply been printed in a larger format.

Erik looked at the picture on Lara Meyer's casket, an ugly photo that was too grainy to do justice to the beautiful, intense face she had in life.

Next to her, not far away, he could also distinguish the photos of Laurent and Janssen.

We should have had a beer together, Erik thought stupidly.

He'd always postponed, and now it was too late.

Hoffman, contrary to what he expected, was alive: on the day of the attack, he was outside the station, coordinating missions for some operational teams.

He really had a stroke of sheer luck, since it was rare for him to leave the office.

At that moment, he was on stage next to Anderson, but he didn't seem to enjoy the moment of sad fame: he still seemed to be in shock, as if he didn't understand the danger he had escaped.

The caskets, like the photos, were only props: recomposing the bodies after the explosion was practically impossible, and, for many agents, only fragments had been found.

Erik imagined a lot of those caskets were empty.

According to the police report, three rudimentary devices had exploded simultaneously or almost so: one had been placed in the basement of the building, one on the tenth floor and one on the twentieth.

The point where the police station stood a few days before was now only a heap of ruins.

Fortunately, the task of analysing the crime scene had been entrusted to the police and forensics, and the presidential guard didn't have to intervene. Erik had gone to the site of the tragedy but was advised not to go in, and, all in all, he was convinced that it was for the better.

The image of the gutted and burning building was already haunting his nightmares, and he was happy not to have seen the torn bodies or what was left of them.

Zoe Hernandez was next to him: she was not on duty that day. Anderson had given her a few days off after the tragedy.

Erik thought the girl looked shocked and sad, but not as sad as he did.

But after all, it was normal, he thought: she had been a member of the medical police for a couple of years, while for him, after more than twenty years of service, it was a second family.

A family that he had no qualms abandoning, he thought with a great deal of guilt; it was a stupid notion, and he knew it. If he hadn't left the medical police, perhaps he too would have been in one of those empty caskets that day, or more likely his remains would have been collected by forensics while his kids cried on an empty grave.

Part of him, however, continued to feel guilty, as if not having been at the side of his lifelong companions at the most difficult time made him responsible for their deaths.

He was certain that the psychologist who treated him after Thea's death would speak pompously of survivor's guilt, or something like that, an expression he had heard too many times during his service; he preferred to consider it a final act of solidarity with his companions.

He longed for a cigarette. Even if he hadn't decided to quit smoking, since Anderson was in power she had banned smoking almost anywhere because, according to her words, it was 'disgusting and poisonous,' and she had also waged a war against the tobacco black market.

Erik rationally agreed with her... however, he thought that if he had had that little comfort, maybe that day would be easier to bear.

From what little he had heard, the President's speech had been as touching and dignified as ever, but that day he had not been able to concentrate.

Erik continued to think back on his colleagues, of their time together, and the image of Lara's hair dancing on her back as she walked.

After the ceremony, Kathleen Anderson approached Erik. Hernandez quickly disappeared after a few circumstantial greetings.

Even the president was shocked by that violent act of terrorism: she appeared pale and tormented, with deep dark circles.

"I wanted to express my condolences to you again, Erik," she said. "I know how much the medical police meant to you."

"Thank you, Madam President."

"I know that all words are meaningless at a time like this, but I promise you that this horrific act will not be left unpunished. We'll do everything we can to find the rebels and make them pay for what they did."

Erik nodded with little conviction. He felt empty. Nothing they did could bring Meyer or the other agents back to life. It was all useless, so useless...

He said goodbye to Laurent's widow and gave her his condolences. He realized he'd never met anyone from Lara's or Janssen's family.

There were many other people he knew, friends and family of his colleagues, but he realized he didn't want to talk to anyone.

His pocket vibrated and Erik took his cell phone, which showed an incoming message.

Maja had just returned from her journey in the eighth ring. During her last phone call, she seemed restless, and evidently there was something she didn't want to talk about on the phone.

She asked him to see her as soon as possible.

Grateful to have an excuse to get away from the funeral, Erik told her to go to his house, which was much closer than Maja and Marc's apartment.

When Maja arrived home, she hugged him: "I'm so sorry about your colleagues, Dad."

"Thanks."

She looked around, vaguely intimidated. Erik remembered that she hadn't been there since Thea had died.

Maja ran a hand on an armrest of the sofa: "Nothing has changed here," she said, with the shadow of an embarrassed smile.

"Your room is still how you left it. You can come back whenever you want, you know."

Maja shrugged, and Erik understood that it probably would never happen: by now, her life had gone on, she had a job, a new home and a boyfriend with whom she might start a family of their own.

He was happy for her, but at that moment, for some reason, the thought made him even sadder.

"There's something urgent I need to talk to you about. It's about Peter and what's going on in the eighth ring."

Erik sat on the couch and Maja did the same.

"Is that what we thought? His colleagues are giving him a hard time?" he asked.

Maja shook her head: "No, they are quite nice actually, and he likes the work." She sighed, uncomfortable: "It's... what he saw in the fields."

"In the fields," Erik repeated. "What could he possibly have seen? Corn, wheat...?"

She rolled her eyes: "Look... you don't know anything about the arrests they made in the underground city, do you?" she asked. "It's not the presidential guard that's taking care of it?"

"The arrests? Well... we did a couple of them last week..." he replied, taken aback.

Only a few days had passed since Anderson had entrusted the presidential guard with the task of dealing with calming the revolt, and, to tell the truth, Erik had not yet done much about it, also because the assignment coincided with the attack to the headquarters of the medical police.

He had sent teams to patrol areas of the underground city that were now under their control, and they had arrested some people who had been so reckless as to go there.

Erik had the impression that, compared to the period before the truce negotiations, the rebellion had lost coordination: nobody had chased them in the tunnels or had pushed them to turn around in circles in a labyrinthine path as it happened before.

Anyway, during those days he had other things to think about.

"No, I meant what happens to the people of the underground city after they are arrested."

"We hand them over to the police, who formalize the arrests and send them to trial."

Anderson had passed a law that allowed court proceedings with minimal waiting times, so as to speed up and make the entire process more efficient.

"And then?"

Erik shrugged: "I don't know in detail. They'll be working in factories, in fields, stuff like that. Why?"

"So you have nothing to do with what happens to the prisoners?" Maja insisted. "Do you promise?"

"What the... yes, all right, I promise!" he exclaimed. "But what does this have to do with Peter?"

Maja leaned closer and lowered her voice: "Peter works with them..." she whispered. "Actually, some of them are in his building. And..." his daughter suddenly seemed scared, "they're keeping them in terrible conditions. They're worse than in prison... Anderson wants to exterminate them," she murmured.

Erik was speechless. He thought it was one of Peter's ridiculous conspiracy theories.

"Maya... I think there's been some misunderstanding. Are you sure that Peter...?" he began, in a reasonable tone.

"That's what I thought too, but then I saw them!" she heated up. "Dad, we can't let this thing go on, we have to do something to stop Anderson and...."

"Stop Anderson?" Erik interrupted her. "What are you even talking about? Kathleen Anderson is our only hope, she is the person who is changing the city, she is improving our life..."

"Yes, but at what price?" Maja exclaimed. "I... Dad, you have not seen the conditions... there is nothing that can justify all this, nothing! They're innocent people and..."

"Innocent?" he yelled. "*Innocent?* Today I was at the funeral of three thousand five hundred people! People I knew, my colleagues, my friends! People they have killed!"

He thought of the headquarters building reduced to rubble, the row of dark caskets, his desk in his old office. And that ugly picture of Lara Meyer next to the flag, her eyes...

That rebellion had already taken away enough from him: first his wife, then his friends... and now he should help the rebels, fight for them? No way.

"I'm sorry for your colleagues, you know that!" Maja said, almost in tears. "But those are civilians, they have nothing to do with the attacks... please, Dad, we have to do something. We should talk to the press! I have evidence, I have taken pictures and..."

"No... That's enough. We won't do anything at all," Erik said in a definitive tone. "Anderson knows what she's doing. If those people, those murderous parasites were arrested and imprisoned, they only got what they deserved."

For the first time since the attack, Erik felt other feelings beside pain: anger, indignation, desire for revenge. It was like Anderson said, someone had to pay, and he couldn't stop until all the rebels and the infected had been arrested.

His kids were probably making more of a scene than it was necessary, and in any case... only Anderson had always been on their side. He had to trust her.

Maja looked at him like she didn't recognize him.

"But Dad...."

"You won't talk to the press. If you or Peter try anything like this, I will silence everything. You know I can do that," he threatened.

Maja stared at him for a long time, with an expression that Erik could not decipher, and then she left without saying a word.

When he heard the door slam, Erik realized that what he saw on his daughter's face was fear.

CHAPTER 28

The village where Cain had brought all the infected was cold and dilapidated, but, according to Sophie, it had an undeniable charm.

It was surrounded by mountains, and, in the centre, the houses were made of wood and stone, perched on steep streets made of cobblestone. Over the years, the vegetation and debris had invaded most of the houses and alleys, and to be able to circulate they had to spend much of the day eradicating dry shrubs and move stones and piles of ice and snow.

However, Sophie liked that village: she thought that the sloping roofs full of snow, the shapes of the ice stalactites, and the clear and briskly air on sunny days were enchanting.

When it was late at night, as it was in that moment, the expanses of fresh snow lit by the moon made her feel wonderfully relaxed, at peace.

To be honest, she was rather convinced that if she hadn't had the plague and her body was the same as it used to be, she would have found the constant cold unbearable. One of the few advantages of the disease, however, was the fact that she could be relatively comfortable in the winter, in the high mountains, with only a light jacket on.

Next to the village were bizarre twisted buildings, high metal poles with long cables hanging at the ends, and crumbling seats emerging here and there from the piles of snow.

"The remains of a ski resort," Gregor explained, "people would sit on the chairlift, be taken up, and then ski down."

Sophie found the idea of people being lifted with those unstable-looking pulleys bizarre: wasn't it dangerous?

From Gregor's words, however, it seemed to be considered a rather amusing activity.

The most appreciated aspect of the new accommodation, in any case, was the fact that she could let Pat fly in the open air.

Cain had kept his word, and the dragons were no longer chained.

Sophie had identified a large underground space in what must have been a hotel: in the basement, there were the remains of a swimming pool and other rooms with strange equipment that had been obsolete for centuries.

Pat, Taneen and Paul's dragon, Osiris, were placed there, being the youngest, while the others were in an abandoned warehouse near the old ski slopes.

During the day they were told not to let them out, but they had a couple of hours during the night to be able to hunt; the meat had run out sometime earlier, and they had not yet found another food that the creatures fed on.

Pat and Taneen were instinctively very good at hunting, helped by their agility and small size.

The older ones, however, sometimes managed to catch a deer or a roe deer, but most nights they returned empty-handed, so the loot of the other dragons had to be divided.

The dragon that Famke was taking care of, whom she had called Baldur, almost never managed to hunt anything, and he just sat in the snow looking at the others with big sad eyes.

Taneen was reluctant to share his game with the others, while Pat didn't seem to care; he enjoyed running after hares and boars more than he liked their flesh, and he was happy that he was allowed to do so for the other dragons as well.

Sophie had stopped accompanying him during the hunt, preferring to stay at the edge of the woods and see him return with the game in his fangs.

The episode of loss of consciousness that occurred on their arrival had initially frightened her, but in the days that followed she had convinced herself that it was not so serious. She couldn't have left Pat in control of her mind for more than a few minutes. In any case, she didn't want to take any more risks, so she decided to leave him to the excitement of the hunt without her.

Taneen was first to glide into the clearing where Sophie, Nadia and Paul were, carrying the fresh carcass of a wild boar between his jaws, and then began to devour it.

Paul pulled out a thermos and some plastic cups: "Do you want some tea? That's what you need with this cold."

Both Sophie and Nadia accepted with pleasure.

The tea was strong and invigorating on that icy night.

"Nice game, eh?" said Paul, pointing to Taneen's wild boar. "You know how good that one there would be if cooked in the oven? Marinated overnight in red wine, then baked with carrots, onions and herbs... ah!" he exclaimed, with a chef's kiss. "A delicacy!"

"Stop it, Paul, I'm already hungry!" Nadia protested, giving him a nudge. "I swear if I see another can of beans I'll freak out."

The main flaw of the new arrangement, besides the cold, was the lack of food.

When the snow would thaw, they'd be able to plant vegetables as they had done on the island, Famke had explained, but not while snow covered everything.

Another possibility was to take the food from the loads to the city, as they used to do. However, this was apparently harder than expected, even if they were close to the eighth ring, the area that supplied the whole city.

"It took me years of work to hack into the warehouse system near the island!" Gregor had said, exasperated by the constant requests. "You have to falsify the inventories, corrupt the stewards... it is not something that can be done overnight."

For the moment, therefore, they had to rely on supplies.

"Around here they used to make cheese, you know?" Sophie suddenly said. "There are old signs everywhere and in one of the buildings near the road I saw the equipment. It would be nice to recover it, right? I love cheese!"

"To make cheese you need cows, for the milk. Where would you find a cow around here?" Paul objected.

Sophie shrugged: "Dunno, we had some on the island, they must have brought them from somewhere."

"No, we found those already there," Nadia said. "There was a small herd of cattle, survived in the wild in the countryside. Here they must have all died of hunger and cold, as we will. What a stupid idea to come up here and freeze our asses," she mumbled gloomily, sipping her hot tea.

Sophie rolled her eyes.

Despite Cain's demonstration of goodwill in loosening the security on dragons, Nadia's opinion of him hadn't changed, and she never missed an opportunity to let people know what she thought of his decisions.

Osiris landed in the clearing, without any prey. Paul's dragon was small but stocky; he didn't have the same ability as Pat and Taneen to slalom through the trees, which disadvantaged him when hunting.

He began to fly around Taneen, stretching towards the carcass of the wild boar.

Even if he didn't speak, the message was clear: he was hungry, and he wanted that meat. He may not have been a champion in hunting, but, in hand-to-hand combat, he would have had an undeniable advantage over Taneen.

But the younger dragon did not want to share the food with him and began to growl threateningly, protecting what was left of the boar with his wings.

"Hey, Osiris, leave him alone, go, go," Paul tried to distract him, but to no avail.

The call of hunger was too powerful.

Osiris dived on Taneen, grazing him with his claws. The smaller dragon locked itself inside his wings, trying to shelter himself.

"Leave him alone!" Nadia yelled. Seeing Taneen in distress, she threw herself against the other dragon, hitting him with her fists.

Osiris, probably already nervous because of the hunger, turned against Nadia and tossed her to the ground, immobilizing her with his claws; he opened her jaws, producing a puff of dark smoke.

If he started spitting fire, he'd burn Nadia alive in seconds, Sophie thought.

"What are you waiting for?" she told Paul, who was watching the scene, apparently incapable of reacting. "Call him back, do something!"

Paul exhorted the dragon to get off of Nadia, trying to pull him away by the tail, an almost impossible task: even if Osiris was not a particularly imposing specimen, his weight was far greater than that of a human being.

At that moment, Taneen fell over Osiris and snatched him away from Nadia; the two dragons began to fight.

"Enough, stop it now!" Nadia ordered, but neither of the creatures listened to her.

Trying to divide them was unthinkable: they were both angry, and they tried to hit anything that was in their range.

Osiris managed to bite into Taneen's neck, who moaned with pain; he clawed at Osiris' eye, who became even angrier, and gave a howl that made Sophie shiver.

"Osiris, stop it, let him go!" Paul screamed.

Suddenly, Sophie heard a hissing in the air, and the dragons were hit in the neck by two syringes.

A moment later, they fell asleep on the ground.

Sophie turned and saw Famke coming, with the gun still in her hand... and Cain was walking next to her, she noticed with worry.

He seemed very angry and headed towards them with all the speed that his crutches allowed him.

"What happened? Didn't you say you could control them?" he asked.

"It was just a little food fuss."

"It seemed much more than that!" Cain thundered. "I could hear their roars from miles away" Now tell me how I can let them go free when as soon as I turn around, they start to slaughter each other!"

"They weren't slaughtering each other, it was just a little quarrel! These things happen, they're still puppies!" Nadia exclaimed.

Cain threw her a murderous glance: "How come every time there are problems, you're involved?"

Nadia was beside herself with anger: "How come every time you open your mouth, bullshit comes out?"

Cain's eyes widened in surprise and even the bystanders remained frozen.

No one had ever dared address Cain like that.

Sophie had the impression that Paul wanted to laugh but was too upset to do so.

"Enough with this shit," Cain murmured and turned to Famke. "Have the dragons brought into that sort of dungeon and lock them up. I don't want them to come out as long as they continue to show signs of aggression," he ordered.

"Hey! Taneen didn't do anything, he was attacked and...." Nadia protested, following Cain, who turned to look at her.

"If you say one more word, I'll lock you up too," he threatened. "Give me an excuse, just give me a reason to do it, I can't wait to."

Nadia's jaw stiffened, but, with what seemed like a superhuman effort, she remained silent.

At that moment, Pat descended into the clearing, carrying a large bird between his teeth.

He approached Sophie, who put her hand on his snout.

Why is everyone angry?

"Shhh..." said Sophie, stroking him.

Better not to attract attention, she thought.

Pat trotted away and began to feed on his find.

Cain left, and Nadia kicked a pile of snow, shouting with frustration.

"I hate him," she murmured. "If I could see him dead, I… I…"

Nadia looked at Sophie: "I'm seriously considering joining Anderson."

Sophie spent the rest of the night trying to convince Nadia of the absurdity of the notion.

Of course, Kathleen Anderson made great promises, but would she keep them?

What could guarantee Nadia that the president would not take the dragon and then get rid of her?

And wasn't she thinking about Karla? Maybe Anderson would welcome Nadia and the dragon, but what could she offer to other infected?

Nadia eventually seemed quite dissuaded, or maybe she was just tired and had begun to agree with Sophie just to get rid of her. Sophie wasn't sure.

In any case, she was certain that she had to try to convince Cain to change his attitude towards Nadia and the other telepaths, before losing their support for good.

If Kathleen had eight dragons and the way to use them... Sophie didn't even want to think about it.

She spent the morning sleeping: she was exhausted, but her sleep was tormented by frightening nightmares. Sleeping in the daytime and taking Pat out to hunt at night always made her feel a little dazed.

In the afternoon, she went to find Cain.

She found him in the large hotel that served as the operational centre of their community.

The village must have been a touristy place because there were several hotels and large wooden houses divided into small apartments. The accommodation was ideal for them, since it allowed them to have an individual space.

This was a novelty that Sophie appreciated very much, especially after her time in the underground city, where her privacy did not extend beyond the edges of her sleeping bag.

Cain was in the large hall, where tables had been set up to serve as desks, computers and the escort of handhelds and mobile phones for missions in the city.

Sophie was alarmed to notice that there were also several weapons in the room, including rifles with tranquillizers that were used on dragons.

Hanging on the walls were photos and cards of some people who seemed vaguely familiar to her: watching more closely, she read that they were Kathleen Anderson's bodyguards.

Was Cain considering trying to murder her?

At that moment, however, Sophie had other things to think about.

"Hello there," Cain greeted her with a smile. "Are you looking for something in particular?"

"Yes, I was looking for you."

Sophie always found it a little alienating how kind Cain could be to her while he was so hateful towards Nadia or anyone who contradicted him. It was something that always caught her off guard.

"Let me guess... it's about the dragons, isn't it?" he asked tiredly, letting himself fall on a chair.

"Um... well, yes. I know I'm repeating myself, but..." Sophie wondered if she could speak clearly to him. She didn't want to accuse her companions, but it was necessary for Cain to understand the gravity of the situation.

"I wish you had a little more confidence in our ability to keep dragons in check."

Cain raised an eyebrow: "This morning..."

"It was really just a minor scuffle," Sophie continued. "They are big aggressive beasts, it's true, and sometimes they bite each other. We can't deny their nature, but that doesn't mean we have to keep them in a cage all the time."

"Sophie, I'll be sincere..." Cain sighed, "I'm worried about this dependence on the dragon that all of you seem to have. From the outside, you... don't be offended, but you look like a sort of sect of madmen. I know how strong and aggressive a dragon can be. I'm only afraid that they're controlling you and not the other way around."

"No, they're not!" Sophie exclaimed. For a moment she thought back to that night in the forest, to the hunt, the sense of abandonment, of loss of herself... No, it was just an accident, she told herself, chasing the thought away.

"You mustn't think that it's a constant battle of authority over each other," she tried to explain. "It's more... how can I say? A symbiosis. The dragon is not an animal to train, he's a part of me."

Cain stared intensely at her: "Kathleen said very similar things," he pointed out.

"Well, perhaps the bond that we have is somewhat similar," she granted, "but we are not Kathleen, and not all dragons are as evil as hers. They're as different from each other as people are. I'm sorry you had to put up with an evil entity in your mind... but believe me, they're not all like that. Pat, for example, most of the time just thinks about playing, chasing animals, things like that. He's not an evil creature, he's just a puppy."

"And what about when it's a puppy anymore? What if it starts to get stronger? Sophie, I've seen it happen with my own eyes. Kathleen got lost, she was obsessed with the idea of finding the dragon, she sacrificed everything..."

"But that's precisely why you should not separate us from the dragons. It's something that's going to haunt us forever. Being away from them is like... I don't know, physical pain. And this is also why Nadia is so protective of Taneen. Damn, if I thought that something could hurt Pat, or even kill him..." Sophie shook her head. "If something like this happened, I think I'd die. I'm not saying this to be melodramatic, I mean from a medical point of view. I don't think my mind could handle that kind of shock. And for dragons it's the same: look at Baldur, the dragon who was... what was his name... Elias...?"

"Elias Visser."

"Yes, him. It was a hard blow. Now since Famke follows him more closely he seems to be better but..." Sophie shook her head. "I don't think he'll ever recover completely."

Cain remained silent for a while, intent on pondering her words.

"I'm sorry there's this, um, friction between you and Nadia. Actually, she's really smart..." Sophie said cautiously.

"I'm sure she is," Cain commented with a grimace. "I always try to be polite with her, but then… I don't know how she does it, but she always manages to say that one thing that I find unbearable!" he admitted. "Has that ever happened to you?"

Sophie nodded, thinking of Fa'r: "Oh yes, I understand perfectly!"

There was something comforting about thinking that even Cain was not as rational and cold as he seemed on the outside.

"There is also another question..." Sophie continued, uncertain. "There is always Kathleen's offer at stake. A lot of people are starting to think that... well, that she might be able to offer a better alternative.

We can't lose the dragons, but that's exactly what will happen if you don't make some concessions."

Cain stood up and paced through the room, stopping in front of the pictures of Kathleen's bodyguards, as if he could find the answer in their faces.

His expression was illegible.

"Please, if you can't tell me something now, at least promise me you'll think about it."

Cain walked back to her and took her hand: "I'll do it, I assure you. Thank you for trusting me. You've really given me so much to think about."

CHAPTER 29

Erik silently watched the line of people who were loaded onto the vans of the presidential guard to be taken to the police station.

Since he had personally taken charge of the management of the arrests, they had increased exponentially within a few weeks.

He believed that the police had sent the officers in a disorderly, unorganized manner, and he had seen not to make the same mistake: he ordered for maps of all the known areas, and he had recovered the ancient schemes of the subway and its ventilation ducts and wiring diagrams from the archives.

Even though the inhabitants of the underground city had dug some new tunnels over the centuries, they had mostly relied on the pre-existing structure: once that had been decoded, it was not difficult to encircle and narrow them down.

There had been resistance, of course: when he entered the heart of the underworld territories, he had not expected anything different.

Erik had ordered his men not to hesitate, and to use every possible means to bring every man and woman to justice.

He didn't know exactly which of them had organized the attack to the medical police station; from what he had understood, there were several scattered clans within the underground city, and they almost never managed to act in a coordinated manner; when in doubt, he wanted to be sure that none of them escaped.

One way or another, the guilty would pay.

When the presidential guard had managed to penetrate their territories, they had found different situations from those they had imagined. Some clans were organized as large extended families, with many small houses that branched off from the central home of the elders who ruled that area. Others, on the other hand, had built small villages using the old metro lines or created houses inside the trains that still lay in the middle of the tracks.

He had imagined misery and degradation, and, in many cases, this was exactly what he found; surprisingly, however, in many areas, those little makeshift houses had appeared clean and tidy, and he had found people who were well-nourished and who did not seem to have experienced any particular deprivation.

When frightened children were taken out, he was amazed at how well looked after they seemed, though mortally pale because they had probably never gone out into the light of day.

The thought gave him the creeps.

Those strange families weren't the only discoveries they had made: in many of their bosses' shelters, Erik's men had found all sorts of weapons, from rudimentary knives made from salvaged materials to guns, machine guns and lots of explosive material.

Erik shuddered every time he was told about these findings: if only the police had moved earlier, if they had been stronger instead of getting lost in all those useless raids... maybe the attack to the police headquarters would have been foiled in time.

Probably not, the answer was clear: the percentage of the territory purged was still less than half of Europa's surface, and therefore presumably of its equivalent underground. There was no way of knowing if the organisers of the attack were still at large.

Kathleen Anderson was very satisfied with the progress but was impatient because the infected had not yet been found.

"We must recover their dragons," she kept saying. "Remember, they are our priority. We can't let them remain at Cain's mercy for much longer." The President seemed increasingly stressed, and there was a note of despair in her demands.

Did she fear that the rebels would use dragons against the city?

Erik had done everything he could to identify the group of rebels, but without success, at least for the time being.

He asked Zoe for constant updates on Anderson's state of health, but he didn't get much out of it: after the terrified request for help she made to him the day of the attack, she had become strangely reticent about Kathleen's alleged mental disorder.

"Sorry, boss, I must have been wrong," she just mumbled.

Erik wasn't satisfied with this answer: he had begun to wonder if it was Hernandez who was having difficulty managing the stress and physical fatigue that her work entailed.

He should give her some time off: a few weeks of rest would do her a great deal of good.

As soon as he had overcome the crisis of the underground city, he would take care of finding a suitable substitute who could replace her. He wasn't convinced that Alan was the right guy, and, in any case, he needed at least two people to cover all the shifts.

Maja and Peter were less enthusiastic about his new job: they had not closed communications as they had previously done, but there was a new, palpable coldness in their relationship.

Maja simply called him on a regular basis, giving him updates on her work, and talking to him prudently and politely; Erik had asked Peter if he wanted to go back to the city, where he would surely be able to find a better job or go back to school, but he had firmly refused.

Erik couldn't help but wonder bitterly if they would continue to talk to him just because they were afraid that if they didn't, he could have them controlled in another way.

That was a very sad thought.

What did his own children think of him? There was nothing in the world that was more important to him, and if he tried to protect them it was only for their own good.

He had to eradicate the creeping evil that threatened the city so that they could live safely... how could they not understand it?

Maja and Peter were young and easily impressionable, he thought: the conditions of inmates in any prison, even those with low security, were probably enough to make them cry out in scandal.

He was certain that Anderson was dealing with the matter with the rationality and efficiency that distinguished her; the images of sad-looking prisoners meant nothing, but they would be a handhold to which the press and her enemies would cling with all their might.

He tried to explain this to Maja, but she always ended the conversation very quickly.

That moment of crisis would pass, Erik told himself; in the meantime, he had to continue with his work.

Luckily, that's what filled his days.

He didn't spare himself and spent the whole day between the tunnels under the city and in his office.

He had often fallen asleep at his desk, exhausted, or snuck in a few hours of sleep on the couch of his meeting room.

Not that he could sleep much even at home, anyway: he had nightmares about the explosion, and he had to watch helplessly while all his friends burned and screamed, and screamed...

Charles, his assistant, called him.

"Director, I've just received an update from one of our teams operating on-field," he said. "Apparently a certain Misha, a figure who enjoys a certain authority within the underground city, has been captured."

Erik nodded.

"A lot of explosive material, like the ones used for the bombs that exploded at the police headquarters, were found in his shelter. They're taking him to the police station right now."

"Very well," Erik answered.

Since he had started studying the situation of the underground city in-depth, the name of this Misha guy had come up very often. Putting him under arrest was a great result.

Could he really have been behind the bombing? He certainly had the means...

"Wait a minute," he told his assistant. "Tell the team not to take him to the police, but to our headquarters. I want to question him personally."

Erik had a car called to be taken to the guard's headquarters.

The interrogations were not normally carried out there, so there were no rooms dedicated to the purpose. In the absence of a better option, he had Misha taken to his office.

He turned out to be a tall, corpulent man, with a thick brown beard that covered most of his face. He defiantly stared at Erik.

Erik found him instinctively detestable. He found he wanted to get him out of his face as quickly as possible.

He kept his assistant Charles in the office, in charge of recording the interrogation, and two other security agents.

"During our operation, we found in your shelter material to build explosive devices, like those used during the terrorist act at the headquarters of the medical police. Did you set it up?" he asked coldly.

Misha looked at him: "You from the city above say so much shit," he said in a deep voice. "How come you call what you do 'operations' and when we defend ourselves then it's a 'terrorist act'?"

"We carry out arrests, we do not take it out on innocent people," Erik exclaimed.

He knew he shouldn't argue with that man, but he couldn't help himself.

"Oh, don't you, now? You come into our house to steal everything we have and throw that toxic gas at us as if we were fucking animals. Since you started with these arrests, I have seen nothing but destroyed lives, separate families, children taken away by their parents. And you also have the nerve to tell us your bullshit about the common good and peace in Europa." Misha spat on the ground. "You disgust me."

One of the guards hit him in the back of the head. Under normal circumstances, Erik would have told him not to do so, but at that moment it seemed right to show that criminal that he could not address them like that.

Erik was getting nervous: "Answer my question," he ordered, watching the stain of saliva spreading on the carpet. "Was it you who put those bombs? How did you get into the station?"

"We didn't do it," Misha replied. "Just think, what if it was your infected friends? Oh, spare me that outraged expression: you were all best friends until some time ago, ready to get along and set us up."

"Were the infected who organized the attack?" Erik asked, puzzled. Nothing during the negotiations had made him think that they could do such an action. Could his judgment have been so wrong?

Misha shrugged: "And why not? They keep saying one thing and then do another, those reptile bastards. Good thing they're gone."

"They're gone? Where?"

That was interesting information. The infected were no longer in the underground city... This was an update that Kathleen would be happy to receive. Or maybe not, since Erik didn't know where they were, but it was a step forward.

Misha made a face: "You're all the same, you and the infected. All hypocrisy and bullshit. You have no honour."

"Honour?" Erik repeated, anger mounting in his chest. "Was it an act of honour to kill more than three thousand people, blown up or burned alive? People who had done nothing but go to work that day..."

"I told you, it wasn't us!" Misha repeated.

"So what about those explosives we found in your shelter?"

Misha looked away, and, with a lightning-fast gesture, he grabbed the framed photo of Maja and Peter that was on Erik's desk.

"What a beautiful little family," he commented. "How would you feel if they came to take them and took them away... "

"Don't you even dare to mention my kids," Erik growled, snatching the picture from Misha's hand. "So, where did you plan to put the next bombs?"

"Are you forgetful as well as deaf?" Misha replied. "We use the explosive to blow up the tunnels."

Erik had a painful flash of Lara telling him that she had gotten lost in the meanders of the underground city: 'Last time I got lost in a tunnel and it took five people to get me out, it was so embarrassing…'

The memory of her voice infuriated him even more: "So it's only a coincidence that the explosive used at the police station was of the same type as yours. Don't make fun of me!"

Misha shrugged: "The fuck do I know? You're the experts. The other clans have explosives too, we all used them."

"Was it another clan who organised the attack? Which one?"

"I don't know, I told you," Misha replied. "Do you think they would come up and tell me? You don't know shit about us."

Erik wished to wipe that mocking expression off his face.

"So you're telling me that you have no authority over the underground city decides to do..."

"Hey, fucking asshole, how dare you?" Misha exploded. "Do you question my authority? No one talks to me like that, no one!"

"If you are so powerful, then how come you know nothing?" Erik challenged him.

This seemed to infuriate Misha even more: "I already told you who I think did it, the infected!" he thundered. "And when I learned about it, I got angry, because they shouldn't have done it without telling us anything. But you know what, now I'm glad that they put those bombs," he spat out. "I'm just sorry that I couldn't see all those bastards being blown up. But we still have a lot of explosives down there, don't we? And trust me, we'll use them. Maybe they will be the next," he said, pointing at the photo of Maja and Peter.

Erik had the impression that a black fog was falling over his eyes, and a moment later he found himself over Misha, violently punching him in the face.

He felt something hard and slippery under his knuckles and he continued to hit, and to hit, warm splashes over his face… He couldn't stop, he didn't *want* to…

Suddenly he felt strong arms pulling him away, and he wriggled for a few moments, before realizing that it was his two agents, who were removing him from Misha's still body.

"Calm down boss…" one of them said. "It's alright."

Erik saw with horror that the face of the criminal was a bloody mask.

Did he kill him?

No, no, he was still breathing… but he was unconscious, and his nose and other bones in his face were probably broken.

"I… I'm fine…" he said, trying to convince the two agents, or maybe himself.

Suddenly, he noticed that Charles was still in the room, staring at him with real terror.

"It was an accident..." he said, but the words sounded empty even to himself.

He left the office and rushed to the bathroom, where he leaned against the sink.

He was nauseous, and his head was spinning.

When he looked up at the mirror, he had the impression of staring at the face of a stranger.

CHAPTER 30

Sophie entered the lobby of the old hotel that had been occupied by Cain and his most trusted collaborators.

That day, Cain had called many infected people stating that he had to make an announcement: there were his henchmen, as Nadia called them, as well as all the telepaths and even a large number of people that Sophie had never seen.

There were a lot of infected people who never took part in any decision and seemed quite happy to mind their business and move where they were told.

At first, Sophie was a little surprised that many people would delegate decisions about their future to others, but, lately, she had started to regard them with a certain envy.

Most of the infected people didn't spend their time struggling for their condition or making wars and alliances: they tried to settle in the place where they were, they organized themselves, they went on with their lives. Maybe they were right, after all, Sophie thought.

She noticed Nadia and Karla at the back of the room and joined them.

"Do you know what our great leader wants to tell us this time?" Nadia scornfully asked, gesturing towards Cain.

"I have no idea," Sophie replied.

"Maybe we're moving again!" suggested Karla, hopeful. "Perhaps to a place where there's more food and it's warmer, maybe to the west?"

"The temperature's starting to rise, don't you think?" Sophie asked. It was true: she had begun to notice a thaw, especially during the hottest hours of the day. The meadows and fields were still covered with snow, but here and there she could see the tiles on the roofs of the houses, and often there were streams of melted snow that slid down the streets.

"I still think it's bloody cold," Nadia answered, shrugging.

Cain stood on the other side of the room, where a raised floor area looked like a kind of stage. Behind him, there were screens on which Gregor was tinkering.

Sophie noticed that Ken was missing, which was very strange because since Cain had woken up he seemed never to leave his side.

His little dog, Nadia called him with contempt.

Sophie reflected on the fact that Cain had recovered very well from his prolonged coma: he seemed to be stronger every day, and he had also begun to gain some weight again. He was still skinny, but he didn't look like a skeleton anymore.

The room shut up when he took the floor.

"I've called all of you here to tell you some news I just heard. Apparently, Kathleen Anderson discovered that we are no longer in the underground city and began researching areas outside the eighth ring. They are using ground forces, helicopters and even drones."

Gregor pressed some buttons, and, behind Cain, the screens projected images of the presidential guard and the army in patrol.

Sophie's heart missed a beat, and, around her, the other infected began to murmur.

"For the moment they are still far away, but sooner or later they will come here. In the meantime, we must be very careful: in particular, we must eliminate all forms of artificial lighting at night, which would be easily detected."

Considering that the sun was rising around seven in the morning and setting at five and a half in the afternoon, staying in the dark for all those hours would be very boring, Sophie thought. However, they could not take risks.

"In any case, I don't want us to stay here waiting for us to be found," Cain explained. "Anderson has forces that can hunt us down for years, and I really believe that she intends to use them. We can't hide forever. We're not going to die like rats! We won't sit here and wait for each other to get chased down like animals in their lair. I'm going to counterattack and do it soon."

An enthusiastic buzz spread in the room.

"Kathleen Anderson has a very efficient personal security service, where nothing is left to chance."

On the screens, images of the president, surrounded by policemen and agents of the presidential guard, began to scroll.

"Wherever she goes, she always has a team of agents to protect her, as well as two personal bodyguards who never leave her. The buildings she's usually in, like the government seat, the headquarters of Anderson Pharmaceuticals and her own house are equipped with bulletproof glass, surveillance cameras, and even helicopters that often patrol the perimeter of the area. Kathleen Anderson is virtually unattackable," Cain declared, "but no security system is perfect."

Everyone in the room held their breath.

"Ken was able to hack into the server that controls the data of the surveillance cameras, and all the info of the movements of the agents. We will introduce the order of an unscheduled shift change while Anderson is moving between buildings and, taking advantage of the confusion, we will shoot her."

Sophie felt disconcerted. Although part of her hated Kathleen, the idea of a bullet planted in her forehead gave her the creeps. But she recognized that it was necessary. Cain was right, as long as she was alive, none of them would ever have had peace.

Everyone else also seemed to approve the plan and watched Cain with enthusiasm and admiration.

"My plan is to sneak into the city using what remains of the tunnels of the underground city," Cain explained. "The police took almost half of it, but once they cleared the previous occupants, they didn't bother to patrol the area, which is now mostly empty…"

Cain started to divide the people summoned into several teams and explain who would take care of what, when Sophie, unable to keep silent, stood up.

"Why do we have to go back down there? It's long and dangerous. Can't we just use dragons to fly into Kathleen's residence? Look, we won't have to face anyone, just land from above…" she insisted, indicating the map on the screen. "And we won't even run the risk of running into some officer of the police or the presidential guard in the tunnels, or someone from the underground city, which might be even worse since they want us dead now."

"It's true," Famke nodded. "It wouldn't be difficult to get in from above without being seen, especially on a cloudy day."

"Yes, we can do it!" said Marie.

Cain shook his head: "No way."

"I admit that it would be a faster system," Gregor said. "And it would minimize the potential losses."

Cain looked him askance, then returned to address Sophie: "I understand your reasons, but I don't want to run the risk of insubordination. It's a very delicate a moment and..."

"Insubordination? No, we already used dragons in action, they behaved very well, you'll see that..."

"I'm not talking about the dragons," Cain interrupted her. "It's the telepaths I do not trust. That's why I sent Ken to take the dragons into custody."

Suddenly, Sophie received a flash of bewilderment from Pat, a pang of concern and disbelief.

Focusing on his thoughts, she received confusing information: *strangers were coming, someone was taking away Taneen and Osiris...* She felt that Pat was wriggling, trying to free himself, and then, suddenly, she felt a great torpor that turned into a deep sleep. They must have hit him with tranquillizers, she thought, upset.

Nadia must have somehow witnessed a similar scene through Taneen.

"You bastard!" she cried, while Karla kept her from attacking Cain. "You brought us all here to distract us... to leave our dragons... You are an asshole and a traitor!"

"Traitor?" Cain exclaimed. "You have a nerve calling me traitor! As if you hadn't been conspiring for months, all of you, to deliver the dragons to Anderson!"

Famke went pale, incredulous: "That's not true, we never did anything like that!"

"No, *you* didn't," Cain granted. "And neither did Sophie. That's why I didn't touch your dragons. They're still where you left them, even if Ken had orders to put them to sleep if they got too worked up. But as for you," he said, addressing Nadia, Marie, Paul, Heinrich and Jane, "I know what you are planning to do and I am not going to allow it."

Chain nodded to James, who along with other infected people approached the telepaths and cuffed them.

James is involved, too, Sophie thought, disappointed.

She could not believe that he, Amanda's brother, who had always supported them during negotiations with the president, had decided to continue to follow Cain blindly.

"No, wait, that's not necessary..." Sophie tried desperately.

The telepaths protested, but Cain's men immobilized them.

"Hey, wait a minute!" Gregor said. "Is this really necessary? And why didn't I know anything about this plan?"

Cain shot him a murderous glance: "I had to make sure that the information did not leak."

"Leak... what... what are you saying? You don't trust me anymore?" Gregor asked, appearing wounded.

"Let's not talk about this right now."

Heinrich had almost managed to break free, but one of Cain's men hit him in the back of the head, making him fall to the ground.

Jane screamed, and Paul kicked one of the henchmen in the shin, getting an elbow back in his face.

The other infected seemed confused by what was happening, and Cain quickly gestured to James that the meeting was over.

"That's enough, we'll continue the meeting later!" James shouted, while some others opened the doors of the hall and pushed all the bystanders out.

Sophie saw that the other telepaths had been taken away.

With a few pushes, she managed to get back in the room and reach Gregor, who was trying to talk to Cain, even if the latter was about to leave the room: "How can you ask me to follow your orders if you don't even inform me...?"

"That's enough!" Cain cut him short, turning to face him. "I don't owe you any explanation, especially after the last events. You're telling me I can trust you, aren't you? Are you sure you wouldn't have said anything to anyone?"

He shut up abruptly when he saw Sophie coming, as did Gregor. Clearly, they didn't want to argue in her presence.

"Cain, why did you do that?" Sophie exclaimed.

"I had to," he replied. "You were the one who warned me of the danger yourself, remember? You certainly knew that I would take some precautions."

"Yes, but not this!" she exclaimed. "I wanted you to give them more freedom, not to take it away completely!"

He sighed: "It's complicated. Now excuse me, but we have a lot to do if we want to attack Anderson before she finds out about it."

Having said that, he walked down the corridor.

"No, wait, now you'll listen to me!" Sophie yelled, following him. "I trusted you! I told you that some people had been talking about joining Kathleen because I thought you'd trust me back!"

"I trust you. I didn't take your dragon, remember?"

"But you locked up all the others and, as if that wasn't enough, you even imprisoned all my friends! How could you think that this was the best solution?"

"Because it's the safest!" Cain shouted back at her and slammed the door with violence. Sophie realized at that moment that the corridor had ended and that they had entered what had to be his room.

"You may think that a dragon is a cute little puppy you can teach funny tricks to. 'Oh, look, he can hunt bunnies. Look, he's taking me on his back to attack the police!'" he mocked her. "Wake up! They are evil and powerful creatures, very powerful. Before you know it…"

"What? What do you think is going to happen?" she interrupted him, beside herself. "Are you scared Pat will make me become a madwoman who wants to kill everyone? You don't know anything about Pat or me…"

Sophie felt the familiar feeling of unstoppable anger mounting in her chest.

"I know dragons," Cain exclaimed, threateningly stepping closer. "I had to endure one inside my head all my life, and I assure you, I've seen terrible things. They are not only wicked but also intelligent, they have a strategy, they can deceive you and..."

"You are paranoid!" Sophie spat out. "You can't bear that we were succeeding where you failed!"

Fury continued to rise inside her... it could explode at any moment.

"Paranoid?! You're the one who's deluded!" Cain accused her. "You only see what you want to see... You should trust me instead, I know dragons like no other!"

He was so close that she felt his breath against her face.

I could attack him, she thought angrily, *I could hit him, hurt him, I could...*

She couldn't hold back: she extended her hand towards him, sure that she would hit him... instead she pulled him close and bent down to press her lips on his.

She pushed his tongue into his mouth, biting him, and felt the ferrous taste of blood.

Cain was paralysed by surprise, but after a moment he returned the kiss with the same passion.

Sophie pushed him against the closed door, sinking her teeth into his neck, perceiving the scent of his skin in her nostrils, as warm and attractive as she remembered it, which completely enveloped her, while the principle of a beard on his chin scratched her cheek.

The uncontrollable anger of a moment before had turned into a burning and violent desire.

She could not have stopped even if she had wanted to; she felt a kind of thirst that continued to mount rather than extinguish. Cain's hands ran under her clothes, which suddenly seemed heavy and unbearable to her, a weight from which to free herself as soon as possible.

When she finally felt his skin against her own, she let go of all thought, abandoning herself to her body and the fire that burned her.

It was only at the end, when she found herself panting in Cain's arms, lying on the floor, that Sophie realized what she had just done.

She felt tremendously embarrassed... what the hell was wrong with her?!

She looked at Cain's face, who seemed as breathless as she was, and noticed a stream of blood coming from his mouth.

"I bit your lip," she said, worried. "I'm sorry."

He brought his hand to his mouth: "Oh. I didn't even notice," he smiled.

Sophie made a face, while the details of what just happened became less hazy.

"I basically jumped you," she realized. "I'm sorry... I assure you that usually I don't..."

"I don't mind!" Cain hurried to interrupt her. "In fact, you know what, I hereby give you permission to jump me anytime you want. A little notice could be useful, I admit, but I can do without too."

Sophie laughed, while the embarrassment of a few moments before turned into a pleasant feeling of satisfaction.

Despite his recent convalescence, Cain's arms were as solid and warm as she had always imagined.

Their bodies were so strange, she thought, looking at their skin: her own scales were dark and vivid, while Cain's looked like scars, discoloured by time.

She instinctively tried to cover herself with the clothes she found.

Cain looked at her: "Are you OK?"

"I don't think I'll ever get used to seeing the signs of the plague on me," Sophie admitted.

"The scales?" he asked, apparently puzzled. "I like them. They look good on you."

Sophie kissed him on the mouth: "Thank you, that's a nice thing to say, but I don't think..."

"No, I mean it!" Cain insisted. "They look like tattoos or something like that. They make you look…fierce."

"Shut up," she replied, but she laughed.

"This one is my favourite," he continued, pointing to a strip of scales that climbed from her knee to her thigh. "It has such a beautiful shape."

His lips rested on her knee, then began to rise along the line drawn by the scales, and Sophie felt a pleasant sense of expectation...

A knocking on the door interrupted them.

"Cain? Are you in there?" Gregor's voice asked.

Cain cleared his throat: "Yes, I'm here" he said, resuming his usual tone of command.

"Weren't we supposed to review the attack plans and divide the teams? Everybody's waiting for you here," Gregor, bored, informed him.

"OK, I'll be right out. I'll see you there."

Gregor's steps moved away from the door.

"I must go," Cain said apologetically, while Sophie could not hold back a sigh of disappointment.

While Cain was putting his shirt back on, which was missing a few buttons, Sophie remembered why she had originally been in that room.

"As for the dragons…" she began cautiously. "I wanted to tell you that…"

Cain took her hand: "It doesn't matter. I'm glad you decided to listen to me. Trust me," he said, and then kissed her on the lips.

As Cain left the room, Sophie realized with anguish that they would never agree on dragons.

CHAPTER 31

"What do you mean, we haven't found them? Where the hell are they?!" President Anderson yelled, throwing the cup in her hand to the ground.

The porcelain broke on the floor with a sharp noise, and everyone went silent.

Erik was in the President's council chamber, along with Voigt and the closest circle of ministers.

She had not taken the news about the lost traces of the infected very well.

Anderson had a red face and ferocious eyes, injected with blood. Erik had never seen her so angry before.

"I... we... we... do not have definitive information on the matter yet," Voigt stammered. "We are trying to follow various paths, using a network of informers..."

"You're saying that you don't have the faintest idea, in short," Anderson interrupted him.

"Well... we're working on it..." Voigt replied.

Unfortunately, Kathleen was right: they had absolutely no idea where to look for the group of rebels.

After Misha's interrogation, Voigt's agents also confirmed that the infected were probably no longer in the underground city; Erik had sent his men to search the most remote areas of the city, even beyond the eighth ring.

Kathleen had said that, before her incognito mission, the infected had settled on an island and lived more or less autonomously. For this reason, he had begun research from the south-west, in the area that had once been the south of France: the climate there was mild and, although the soil and water sources had been irreparably contaminated during the atomic war centuries earlier, certainly the rebels could have easily found shelter and food.

It was the perfect place to hide, and Erik was sure the rebels would think about it too; he had been so sure... but he was wrong. They found no sign of the rebels in any of the areas they searched.

He had ordered to continue to search all the areas closest to the quarantined territories, but it was a long job and, unless they incurred in a stroke of luck, it could take months to get a result.

"You must find the infected as soon as possible!" the President shouted, a shrill note in her voice. "This is our number one priority! How can I make you understand that?!"

"We know very well," Friedrich Haas assured her, calm. "All our forces are deployed precisely to hunt them down. They won't escape us much longer."

Anderson, apparently calmer, let herself fall on her chair.

"Let me bring to your attention another problem that we are encountering in the agricultural areas of the eighth ring, particularly in the facilities created for the detention of the underground city inhabitants."

"What is this about?" Anderson asked, without particular interest.

"Apparently there are... um, complaints about the conditions of the prisoners, which would be defined" Haas read from a piece of paper in front of him, "'unacceptable', 'inhumane' and 'a source of shame for the whole Europa'. It seems that many of the prisoners went on hunger strike to protest against the overcrowding, the overworked shifts, the less than precarious hygienic conditions and the scarcity of food distributed to them."

Erik had an unpleasant feeling in his stomach when he heard these words: it was precisely what Maja had tried to tell him.

From Haas's words, it seemed that there was some truth in it and that it was not the rant of a couple of easily impressionable children. Had he been wrong in ignoring her?

Anderson shrugged: "They want to fast? Go ahead. The food they don't eat will be distributed to others and there you go, the lack of food is resolved."

Haas gave an incredulous giggle as if the words of the president had been a joke: "Well, my staff and I wanted to suggest investing more money in these facilities, and maybe consider some initiative for the reintegration of these people in the society, considering a reduction of the sentence in case of good conduct..."

"I'm not going to spend money to improve the quality of life of people who stole and lived at the expense of honest citizens. Or should I remind you what they did to the medical police station? It was the bloodiest episode since the end of the Great War. And you would like to see Europa pay to give them better food and more luxurious accommodation?"

Haas flushed: "No, of course, I just meant..."

"The conditions of the inmates from the underground city are the least of our problems," Anderson cut him short. "Rather, are these socially useful work centres ready to welcome the inmates from the new wave of arrests?"

"Theoretically, yes," Haas admitted, "but since the current situation, we must consider the problem of overcrowding..."

"Overcrowding… please," Kathleen exclaimed. "Those people lived like rats in holes in the ground. And now they're complaining!" She made a contemptuous grimace. "They have some nerve!"

Chardon and some other minister gave a polite laugh.

"The fact is that even the people who work in the eighth ring are complaining," Haas insisted. "They seem upset by what they see, they talk about joining the strike... I don't think we should underestimate…"

"If they don't want to work there they are free to leave," Anderson interrupted him, "Surely they will have no difficulty finding another job. For the first time in years, we have a dropping unemployment rate. Remind them of this next time they intend to protest," she snapped. "That's enough, I don't want to waste any more time on this. Tell me about more serious matters. Have we had any other sightings of dragons?"

Erik felt a creeping discomfort about the president's attitude: her words had confirmed to him that he had undoubtedly done well not to encourage Maja in her useless battle for a non-existent cause... yet... perhaps he would have preferred Anderson to pay more attention to the matter, instead of dismissing it in two words. Wouldn't he have liked to see a more sensitive leader in her place?

He mentally called himself a fool for his unfair thoughts: it was these people who had planted the bombs that had killed most of his friends they were talking about. If they were locked up in a cell and working in the fields, they only deserved it, he thought.

President Anderson, moreover, must have been going through a moment of great stress: she looked more and more tired, the dark circles under her eyes deeper and deeper, and she had begun to show a nervous movement in her hands when she appeared particularly under pressure.

"We must find the infected, we must find the dragons," she had repeated before the meeting, in a feverish tone. "I know Cain, he is preparing to attack me. I know, I'm sure! And the dragons aren't safe with him... not even mine is... if we don't stop him, if we don't..."

Erik assured her that they were doing everything they could and, to be safe, he decided to increase the president's personal security and put additional agents at the government headquarters and Anderson's mansion. He didn't think a huge fire-breathing monster actually needed an escort, but if that made Kathleen feel better, it certainly couldn't hurt.

Anderson concluded the meeting by urging all of them to find the rebels, adding in a vaguely threatening tone that she would otherwise have to take care of it herself. Was she planning to fire them all? Erik didn't think it was likely, but the possibility seemed to worry Voigt.

He seemed to have been constantly upset for months, at least since they met the rebels' delegation to negotiate the now discarded agreement: since then, he had lost weight very quickly, so that his skin seemed to hang from his bones; his hair was whiter and thinner, and he looked positively frightened. Erik had heard him talk to his doctor on the phone on more than one occasion, asking for more tests.

"Are you not feeling well?" he had asked him one day, more out of politeness than real interest.

"There's something wrong with me," he had admitted, perhaps eager to confide in someone. "But I don't understand what. I can't find any symptoms; my values are fine... I don't understand, I don't sleep at night anymore..." he added in a desperate tone.

"Um… but if you have no symptoms or results from the tests… maybe you're fine?" Erik cautiously suggested.

Voigt had stared at him: "I know there's something wrong with me, I know it! I'm not a fool!"

"No, of course, I didn't mean that." Erik had mentally taken note never to come back to this subject again.

Maybe Voigt too had some trouble dealing with stress.

Back in his office, Erik began to think about how to find the rebels that worried the President so much.

He knew that they were not in the underground city, and they were not in the most obvious places where they could hide.

So where were they? And how did they get there? Erik kept reflecting, walking back and forth in his office.

There were almost a thousand infected in the group led by Cain: the transfer must have left traces. It was now clear that the infected had some form of network of contacts within the city: it was not likely that they would do it all by themselves.

There had to be citizens, perhaps friends or family, who actively helped them, as Amanda Solarin had done... as Thea had done, he thought, with the now-familiar pain that accompanied every thought of his wife.

Erik produced the file about her from a drawer in his office.

Sometime before, he had done some research on all the people who were mentioned that he did not know personally, but nothing worthy of note had emerged.

He opened the page about Dr Cohen, the psychiatrist who had treated her.

Apparently, he was a model citizen: he was married, had a son who worked as an engineer in the railway company, never a crime or a fine, no kind of involvement in suspicious activities.

And yet there was something that didn't make sense to him... something that seemed familiar to him, but that he couldn't identify.

He saw his pictures again: a man in his fifties with glasses.

He was often portrayed next to the hospital where he worked or near home. A cottage in a nice neighbourhood, Erik noticed, in the second ring. Houses like this were hard to find by now.

He assumed that a psychiatrist like him, who had graduated before the spread of the plague which had caused most public institutions, including universities, to fall apart, would earn quite a lot of money. His generation... Erik stopped, struck by a sudden thought.

He went to pick up Dr Cohen's resume and observed his course of study.

Prior to his specialisation in psychiatry, he graduated in medicine and surgery... just like Amanda Solarin.

He remembered reading a lot of information about her when she was detained in the custody hospital... Erik did a brief search from his terminal and found Solarin's resume.

The university and the year of graduation coincided; the two of them knew each other, he was sure of it... it could not be a coincidence!

It was Cohen who recruited Thea and made her a spy, he understood.

And now he'd take him right to the other rebels.

CHAPTER 32

Sophie had returned to the basement of the abandoned hotel, where she found Pat asleep, with a syringe still planted in the point of his long neck where the scales were thinnest.

She took it out gently and sat down next to him.

His chest rose and fell rhythmically; he did not seem to be in pain, only immersed in a very deep sleep. Sophie leaned against his back thinking about the events of that day.

She was happy about what had happened with Cain... and yet, she couldn't help but think about the fact that he had just had her friends and their dragons locked up, even though they had done nothing.

Was it her fault for telling him that some people had considered Anderson's proposal? Maybe she had been naïve to trust Cain... No, she told herself, she shouldn't think like that.

She had jumped to the wrong conclusion about him once before and she didn't want to make the same mistake again.

Perhaps he was too cautious and obsessed with control, but it was also understandable given all that he had gone through... and she could not deny that she was still intoxicated by the scent of him that still hovered over her skin.

Pat's regular breathing was strangely relaxing, and, after a while, Sophie slipped into sleep. She woke up with a jolt a few hours later.

What's the matter? Where's everybody else?

Pat jumped up and looked around terrified.

"It's OK, don't worry," Sophie tried to calm him down, rubbing her eyes. It was the middle of the night.

Who were those people? Why did they hurt Taneen?

"Well... it's complicated to explain..." Sophie began. "But don't worry, he's fine, he's just somewhere else..."

He is in pain. I can feel it.

Sophie frowned, surprised by that information: "Can you hear him? Can you communicate with each other?"

But Pat was too agitated to think coherently and began to pace around the room from side to side, waving his tail threateningly and emitting puffs of smoke.

Where were you? Why didn't you stop them?

"I didn't know they were coming here!"

It's not a safe place, it's not a safe place... Pat thought, turning on himself, obviously very upset.

"Believe me, you can rest easy, no one's after you, they won't come for you. Cain assured me..."

He's a bad man! We have to go away, go far from here...

Sophie was starting to worry: despite her efforts and the most reassuring thoughts she was trying to convey to him, Pat was getting more and more scared, and seemed to be in a panic attack.

Let's go, let's go!!!

"That's enough! Calm down," Sophie ordered in a firm voice.

No!

"Pat, stop it now!" she yelled, now upset too. "If you don't stop it, I... I...." she hesitated, not knowing how to end the sentence. What could she possibly do against a two-hundred-pound, fire-breathing beast?

The threat, however incomplete, seemed to scare Pat even more.

Sophie was struck by a stream of intense and unstoppable emotions: terror, anguish, distrust, compassion towards other dragons in chains, sense of abandonment.

She moved to get closer to Pat, but he wriggled out and hit her with a blow of the tail, throwing her on the floor.

Then he threw himself against the low and wide windows near the ceiling of the room and, with a blaze, set fire to the planks that had been nailed on top.

"Pat, no!" Sophie screamed, but the dragon didn't listen.

He slammed into what was left of the boards and flew out the window.

"Wait, come back!" she shouted, to no avail.

From the window, she could see the silhouette of Pat, who was moving faster and faster towards the woods.

Where are you going? Please, come back!, she projected mentally, but received no response.

Pat seemed to have deliberately cut off all communication with her.

She didn't even know that was possible to do; she'd never done it before.

With her heart in her throat, she ran out of the building, but by then there was no trace of Pat in the sky.

She looked around in a panic. Where was he going? What if Kathleen's men spotted him? Or worse, if he was captured or... shot down?

She had tears in her eyes: *Pat, where are you?!*

She had to find him, run after him... but how? By now he was far away, she needed some means of transport, at least a car...

She couldn't take one of the jeeps without Cain's permission. And that meant having to explain to him Pat's panic crisis and his escape... What would happen next?

No, she couldn't tell Cain.

Could she steal one of the cars? The problem was that she didn't even know where they were; somewhere in the old hotel, she assumed, but she wasn't sure.

She needed help: Nadia would know what to do, she would understand... but Nadia had been arrested by Cain's henchmen that very day. Sophie wondered where they had her locked up.

Not knowing what else to do, she headed to the old dilapidated hotel.

Sophie knocked on the door vigorously, wondering if that was the right one.

The hotel was quite large, and all the floors were very similar, especially those that were still in passable condition. If she'd pulled the wrong person out of bed... well, it would have been a little embarrassing, but she could make up some excuse.

When she didn't receive an answer, she began to storm the door with fists: "Hey, are you there?"

After a few moments, she heard steps approaching, and the door opened: "Sophie? What the hell do you want at this hour?" Gregor, his voice groggy with sleep.

"I need your help," she said urgently, "I've lost Pat."

"It's fucking... three a. m.," he informed her. "I went to sleep only two hours ago and... wait, what do you mean you lost Pat?" he exclaimed.

"Not so loud!" Sophie implored him, looking around. "If anyone hears you...

Gregor sighed, perhaps abandoning the idea of going back to bed: "Come on, get in," he told her. "Now tell me what happened."

Sophie entered the room, closing the door behind her, while Gregor sat on the bed, holding his head in his hands.

"When the effect of the tranquillizer ended, he woke up in a panic: he wanted to know what had happened, why the other dragons were locked up... and he was afraid that they would come back for him," Sophie explained very quickly. "I tried to reassure him, but there was nothing to do... He flew away and I can no longer hear him and I am very worried, because, you know, what if he flies too far, like to the city? What if someone sees him? Ah, I'd rather find him before Cain notices. I mean, it's not that I don't want to tell him anything as if it were a lie, only that I thought it would be better to solve the situation before, you know, the psychological effect of saying there was a problem but we solved it rather than..." she stopped. "Are you listening to me?" she asked, since Gregor was unusually quiet.

"Yeah..." he mumbled, yawning. "I got it."

Sophie noticed that he was wearing only a grey T-shirt and shorts that made him look even more skeletal than usual. He was so pale he almost glowed in the dark, she thought.

When he raised his face, she saw that the dark circles under his eyes were particularly deep.

"Look, I know that you need to get a good night's sleep," she went on, feeling vaguely guilty, "but I don't know what to do, I thought we could take a jeep and try to find him and..."

"Yeah, fine, OK…" he interrupted her tiredly, standing up with what seemed like a great effort of will. "Did you see which way he went, at least?"

"Yes, he went north."

Gregor scratched his head thoughtfully: "If I remember correctly, fentanyl leaves the dragons very weak, perhaps he'll want to hunt to get back in strength... with any luck, we could still find him in the woods munching on a deer, or something like that."

"You're right... it's a good idea," Sophie nodded, beginning to feel a little more confident. "Let's go!"

"Yay, I can't wait to run in the woods, exhausted, in the middle of the night, with twenty degrees below zero temperatures," Gregor commented. "Can I at least have a minute to get dressed or do I have to come in my underwear?"

"Yeah, sorry, go ahead. Oh and... thank you. You're a real friend," she added sincerely. "I really appreciate that you..."

"Yes, yes, I know, I'm a gem," Gregor said, bored. "Please just shut up for a minute."

They left the hotel as quietly as possible; fortunately, Gregor remembered that one of the jeeps was in the abandoned warehouse where the biggest dragons used to be, so they could leave without waking anyone up with the noise of the engine.

They had to proceed with their lights off, but it was a clear night and the moon illuminated the road well enough.

Of course, Gregor kept complaining for the whole trip, but Sophie found his sarcastic quips almost comforting, as they distracted her from her worry about Pat, who was all alone, frightened, angry, and possibly in danger.

After a few kilometres through the snow-covered trees, they saw a half-eaten carcass of a marmot on the ground and a trail of blood on the white snow.

"That's gross," Gregor commented with a grimace. "But looks like we are on the right track."

They went on for a few more minutes until they found signs of struggle in the snow.

Then, finally, Sophie saw the dragon.

"Up there," she exclaimed, pointing to a tree on which he was perched, biting the remains of a no longer identifiable animal.

Gregor braked abruptly, and Sophie rushed out of the vehicle.

"Come here, Pat. Let's go home," she urged him.

The dragon just turned his head the other way, ignoring her.

"I'm sorry I raised my voice," Sophie said. "Believe me, no one wants to hurt you... please, let's go back."

Pat gave a mocking bark and got up in the air.

Sophie got back on the jeep as fast as she could, and they went in pursuit of the dragon.

"Faster, we're losing him!" Sophie yelled.

"If I go any faster, we'll end up crashing. Don't worry, he won't get far."

Pat, please, stop! Sophie mentally implored him.

With relief, she felt his presence on the edge of her own consciousness: he had not completely blocked their mental communication.

I know you're scared. It must have been awful seeing those guys taking your friends. But I won't let anything happen to you. Trust me.

She felt a breach in Pat's armour of thoughts, a weakness that revealed his fear and frustration.

She could reach him, she realised, she just had to make a little effort, a small step forward...

Sophie closed her eyes and had the feeling of jumping from a great height, until...

The air was cold, but this was pleasant after spending so many hours in that room.

He felt better flying: there he could defend himself, while the small spaces made him feel like he was going to suffocate.

He wanted to keep going, to fly, to get away from those evil men, especially their boss. A horrible man, a monster. Taneen had explained that he must be careful with him.

Despite this, he began to breathe more deeply and to slow down his run.

Everything was fine, something inside himself said, no one would hurt him.

He wasn't sure... could he believe it? His pack had told him to run, and he was. Yet that calm and reassuring presence within him made him feel at peace.

Slowly, he glided towards the ground.

The panic he had felt moments before began to seem distant, alien.

Maybe he could go home for now. If something happened, he could leave again. But for the time being, he was safe.

"Sophie! Sophie! Wake up!" Gregor said, shaking her by the shoulders, "Sophie!"

Sophie blinked and looked around, confused.

"What are you doing?" she asked.

Gregor sighed with relief: "You're back... Damn, you scared me!"

"Where is Pat?" she asked. "Have we lost him?"

"No, look, he's over there" he informed her, pointing outside the jeep. The dragon had curled up next to the car, apparently quiet and tame.

"He landed on his own and sat there... It's you I'm worried about! You fell on the seat, your eyes were turned upside down and you kept shaking..." Gregor shivered. "It wasn't a pretty sight, I tell you. Now tell me what happened."

Sophie didn't know what to say. She was certain that those who had no experience of that bond wouldn't understand that communion of conscience with the dragon... damn it, even she, who was inside it, found it difficult to accept. But Gregor had seen it, she could not deny what had just happened.

"Um... nothing, you know, I gave Pat a little nudge, let's say. I just focused really hard."

"You…? What kind of bullshit is this? When you focus, you don't have an epileptic seizure. If it's one of your telepathic bullshit, I…"

"It's not bullshit!" she protested. "It's just…I don't know how to explain it to you. You wouldn't understand."

"That's right, I don't understand," Gregor said, "and if you don't want to explain it to me, you leave me no choice but to tell Cain about this nice out-of-town trip we've made."

Sophie went pale: "No!" she exclaimed, then took a deep breath "Ok, look... I'll try. Now, sometimes it's like I can get into Pat's head. Like I was… him," she said.

Gregor stared at her with an unreadable expression: "So you control his movements and actions?"

It wasn't exactly like that: in those moments there was no difference between the will of the dragon and her own, but perhaps it was better not to point out this detail.

"Something like that," she nodded instead.

Gregor leaned his head against the back of the seat: "Sophie, I don't know... I don't like this."

"I know it sounds scary from the outside but... really, it sounds worse than it is," she assured. "That's how I brought Pat back, isn't it? He didn't get down on his own."

"Then why didn't you stop him right away?" he objected.

"It's not that simple. It's not a switch that I turn on or off when I want."

Gregor sighed. He seemed very conflicted.

"I hope you know what you're doing," he said at last.

"I do, I assure you," Sophie lied.

They returned to the village with the jeep, while Pat flew behind them, apparently fearless.

The sky was no longer so dark, and, to the east, the horizon had begun to brighten up. Soon the sun would come up.

Gregor parked the car where he had found it, and Sophie got off, looking forward to getting a good night's sleep. After everything that had happened that day (or was it the day before now?) she was exhausted. Pat followed her... when suddenly a big net fell on him.

The dragon began to wriggle, to no avail, while infected with rifles emerged from behind the building.

Sophie saw that Cain was in their midst.

"What are you doing?!" she shouted. "You told me you wouldn't touch Pat!"

Cain looked at her with a sorry expression: "You said you could control him."

"I can!"

He shook his head: "No, you can't. I saw him running away from my window and then I heard you coming here... why didn't you come to me?" he asked.

"Because I knew that you would take it the wrong way!" Sophie exclaimed, exasperated. "And that's exactly what you did!"

Cain sighed: "After all this time you still do not trust me. I will now take custody of your dragon and lock it with the others. I don't intend to hurt it, don't worry, but I can't let it free to leave whenever it wants. It's too dangerous, for all of us."

"But he didn't leave!" Sophie protested. "He just went alone to the woods, where I always take him hunting, he was just hungry..."

"It's true, Cain, he hasn't gone very far," Gregor confirmed. "We found him right away."

"I'll deal with you later," Cain snapped.

"Wait..." Sophie said. "Let's talk about it for a moment..."

Cain took her hand, a gesture that at that moment she found annoying: "Not now, Sophie. Have faith in my decision, at least this time. It's for the best; in time you'll see it, too."

Sophie couldn't help but watch as Pat was being taken away. From inside the net, he cried a last, desperate lament at her.

CHAPTER 33

Dr Cohen's tailing immediately brought some results.

According to Erik's instructions, Voigt had his house under surveillance and all his communication devices under control.

After a week, he was told that the psychiatrist had met in the sixth ring with a tall, black woman with long black hair. It wasn't difficult for Erik to recognize Amanda Solarin in a wig from the photos that had been shown to him.

He felt vaguely uncomfortable when he gave the order for her to be followed too. He remembered her face in the pre-trial custody hospital cell, and those two horrible agents who tortured her... was that what he was about to inflict to her again?

He shouldn't even think about it: Erik held Amanda Solarin in great esteem on a personal level, but he couldn't overlook the fact that she was connected to a ruthless terrorist organization, as well as her psychiatrist friend.

This connection would have been enough to get Cohen arrested, but Erik had decided to wait.

Getting Amanda tailed proved more difficult than expected. In a few hours, in fact, she had managed to get away from Voigt's men. However, that little time had been enough to intercept a call from her cell phone. When she used it, Voigt had intercepted a signal from beyond the eighth ring, from the south, in the middle of the mountains.

Erik was thrilled: he had found out where the infected were hiding, he was sure of it.

Voigt asked him if he should arrest Solarin, but he told him to wait. For the moment, it was better to keep her free and under control; if the track had proved unsuccessful, their best hope of finding the rest of the rebels was still following her.

However, Erik was intimately convinced that he was not mistaken. Those damn infected had hidden well; without the cell phone trace, it would have taken a long time to locate them in the mountains. Erik would never have thought of going there to look for them, not in that impervious, icy area.

He also decided to wait to arrest Cohen: Erik wanted to face him, ask him how had he dared to recruit Thea, how could he take advantage of her weakness and guilt... or maybe it was her who discovered his connection with the rebels and asked him to participate in the resistance?

It was hard not to become obsessed with these thoughts, but he had to stay focused on the goal. Cohen's arrest would alarm Amanda Solarin, and, as a result, he could blow up the entire operation.

Erik was going to bring Kathleen Anderson his result and ask her how she wanted to act. The rebels had certainly taken the dragons with them, and he was convinced that their army, however numerous and well equipped, could be in trouble against seven of those creatures especially because, contrary to what had happened in the past, when the infected had attacked the seat of the presidential guard, they seemed perfectly capable of exploiting the war potential of the dragons.

It was the evening, and Kathleen Anderson was at her house. Erik sent her a message to let her know he was coming.

Under normal circumstances, he would have waited until the morning to talk to her about state matters, but certainly the president would have liked to know the news as soon as possible.

Her villa was surrounded by many security agents, as always. Erik narrowed his eyes, trying to see Kathleen's great dragon, but without success. Maybe he was asleep, hidden among the trees in some corner of the large park.

When Erik arrived, the president was in the kitchen, pouring herself a glass of water.

She never drank alcohol, Erik remembered, nor had he ever seen her eat anything slightly unhealthy. It looked like Anderson was immune from vices.

"Madam President, forgive me for the late hour, but I have to tell you something that couldn't wait," he began. "We picked up a signal from the south, in the Alps. Now, my intention is to attack as soon as possible. I don't think they can move very often, because of the dragons, but on the other hand…"

Suddenly, Erik realized that Kathleen hadn't had the reaction he expected: she almost looked like she wasn't listening to him. She was sitting at the kitchen table, staring with big, empty eyes at the glass of water she had poured.

For a brief, disconcerting moment, she did not look like the charismatic leader he had always admired, but as an elderly and frightened woman.

"Madam President, are you alright?" he asked.

"I…" she stammered, with a trembling voice. "I'm sorry Persson, but I don't feel like myself. I haven't felt myself for a long time."

Erik frowned: "Excuse me…?"

Kathleen looked up at him, and Erik noticed that her face was full of terror: "We must be quiet, very quiet. Now he's asleep, but it never lasts long. He almost doesn't sleep anymore."

"What is he… who doesn't sleep? Someone in your home? They're threatening you?"

Anderson gestured him to keep quiet: "Shh, don't talk so loud!" she said, looking around like a trapped animal. "He will hear us… he… he always hears. At first, I thought he was giving me strength, that I was using him to be a different person, someone more intelligent, more determined…" she shook her head, and her eyes became shiny. "Now I know he's using me."

Erik was confused and frightened at the same time: it looked like President Anderson, the same woman he had been trusting in a minute before, had gone mad. Is that what Zoe had tried to tell him?

"I don't understand."

"There's no time. There's no more time," she exclaimed, walking back and forth through the room.

Erik didn't know what to do: Anderson evidently had reached the breaking point. Too much stress, too much responsibility, he imagined.

He put his hand on Kathleen's shoulder and gently piloted her to a chair.

"Madam President, please, sit down for a moment and drink your water. Tomorrow you can take a day off, to rest, we'll tell your staff that..."

"Rest?!" she hissed. "Don't you understand? He never leaves me! He's always here, in my head! There's no way out, you understand?"

Erik saw that her eyes were bloodshot. She did look like a crazy old lady at that moment.

Kathleen stood up again, and went to the door, leaning her ear on it to listen better.

"Did you hear that?" she whispered. "Did you?"

"No," Erik said tiredly. "I haven't heard anything."

"He's moving. He'll soon wake up... I can't run away, it's over, it's over!" she moaned, clawing at her hair with his hands.

Erik kept staring at her, feeling strangely detached: was the government of Europa really in the hands of such a clearly disturbed person? And most of all, who had allowed it? Was it his fault, too? He preferred not to dwell on that thought.

"Soon he will have what he wants," she whispered. "Now that you found the other dragons..."

The other dragons, thought Erik, beginning to understand.

He stepped closer and grabbed her wrists, stopping her from pulling her hair out.

"No, don't..." he urged her. "Stop, look at me. Are you talking about the dragon?" he asked her. "Is he the one taking control?"

Anderson nodded.

In the past, she had very often spoken about the bond that was established between humans and dragons, Erik recalled, and Sophie Weber, during the meeting, had also confirmed the intensity of that relationship.

That must have been the problem: an overly intense connection that was getting out of hand.

It was a sinister thought, but somehow it seemed preferable to the idea that the President of Europe was a paranoid schizophrenic.

"When I find the other dragons and the infected... it will be terrible," Anderson went on, almost speaking to herself. "He just wants to kill, and that's what he'll do, all those people! I thought I could hold him back, I thought..."

"But..." Erik was confused. "I didn't think you were so worried about the fate of the infected. I'm not saying that I thought you wanted to kill them all but..."

"Kill?" Anderson repeated. "I never wanted to kill anyone... it wasn't me... those bombs, all those people..." she hid her face in her hands. "My God, all those people."

Erik left her hands, shocked.

The bombs at the police headquarter... it wasn't the underground city, it wasn't the infected either. It was her... or rather, it was the dragon, who, from what he had understood, was devouring her mind more and more every day, leaving her only flashes of consciousness.

All the hatred he felt for Misha, for the underground city... Erik felt like he was about to faint. He didn't want to listen to Maja... he was so blinded by anger that he didn't notice what was happening right under his nose.

What kind of person had he become?

"How can we stop him?" he whispered.

Kathleen lifted her tears-streaked face: "No one can stop him. Maybe another dragon..." she shook her head. "No, that's impossible."

"Look, let's talk it through," Erik said in a reasonable tone. "The dragon is right here, we can simply..."

Suddenly, Kathleen grabbed his arm: "Persson, leave. Take your kids and leave as far away as possible. Go away!" she screamed. "Go! Go!"

Erik stepped back but stumbled into a chair and fell to the ground.

Suddenly, something in Anderson's expression changed: her frightened gaze became determined, her whole face lifted, her eyes began to burn once again.

She cleared her voice: "Persson, are you hurt? What happened?" she asked, in her usual friendly tone.

"I... I..." Erik stammered.

Anderson kept watching him with an interrogative expression.

"I stumbled..." he said at last. "I shouldn't... I shouldn't have... I'm sorry I disturbed you at this hour"

"That's hardly a problem, I haven't gone to bed yet. Please, go ahead," she urged him.

"Um, it was just… just a false alarm. I have to go now."

Erik turned around and left the president's villa, trying hard not to walk too fast.

When he looked towards the park, he saw a large dark silhouette hanging over the side of the house.

With his heart pounding in fear, he told the driver to start the car.

Amanda Solarin was walking down a road in the sixth ring, her hair covered by a wig, wearing a light raincoat. She looked very different from how Erik last saw her at the government sear. The long hair softened her features, making her blend in with the crowd. If he hadn't seen her in the photos, Erik probably could have crossed her way without recognizing her.

When she passed by, Erik pulled her into the badly lit alley where he was, trying to hold her by the arms.

Amanda reacted quickly, wriggling out and trying to escape his grip.

"It's me, it's not..." he tried to say.

"Let me go, asshole!" she yelled. "Help!"

"Wait, wait, it's me, it's Erik," he told her, getting away just in time from her knee, dangerously addressed to his groin.

Amanda widened her eyes in surprise: "Persson? What...?"

For a moment their faces were very close, and Erik was surprised to stare into her dark, deep eyes; then he recovered, and took a step back, letting her go.

"Listen to me, we don't have much time," he said, looking around. "There are people who are looking for you, people from the secret service who..."

"You mean those two guys with dark glasses, not suspicious-looking at all, that followed me the other day?" she replied, smoothing the cloth of the raincoat on her sleeves.

"Not just them, actually, but... look, let's not waste time," Erik continued. "I think Anderson is going crazy," he confessed.

"Oh, really?" she replied. "And I was considering voting for her at the next elections, if we'll ever have any."

"No, I meant..." Erik caught his breath, "the dragon is taking control of her mind. Most of the time, it's not her who decides what to do, it's that creature. I know it sounds crazy but... I've seen it, and I assure you, I was scared, she..."

"I understand," Amanda interrupted him. "And I believe you. In fact, Cain said something like that could happen."

Erik sighed in relief. The part of that meeting that worried him the most was the possibility that Amanda would take him for a lunatic.

"Then maybe you can help me. Help the whole city," he continued. "You must kill the dragon. I know you may not believe me, but Anderson is just as much a victim as the rest of us, maybe the biggest victim. Without the dragon, she'd be free again."

Amanda stared at him: "Why do you think you need us?"

"Kathleen said... well, suggested... in short, she was confused, but she thinks that only another dragon has a chance to kill it. You still have at least one dragon, don't you?"

"Yes, of course we do, but..."

"All then you have to try. I will relax the security protocols during the night and leave the south corner of the perimeter of Anderson's villa uncovered. From there you can enter the park and... well, it's there."

Amanda looked away, reflecting.

"How do I know it's not a trap?"

"It's not," Erik said, "I already know where the infected are, and Voigt knows it too. They're in the south, in the Alps. Isn't it right?"

Amanda didn't answer, but Erik noticed that her posture had stiffened.

"I can keep this information confidential for a few days, a week at most," he insisted. "Then Anderson will send the army to strike. You have to do something before then."

Solarin remained silent.

"Amanda, you know me by now," Erik said softly. "It's not a trap. I wouldn't do it."

"I'll talk to Cain," Solarin said, after a few moments. "I'll see what he thinks about it. You take some security out of Anderson's mansion in the meantime."

"I'll do it," he nodded. "You must go now. You managed to leave those two guys behind, but Voigt is getting the whole area checked, you better change ring as soon as possible."

"I'll keep that in mind," Amanda assured him, walking down the alley. Erik turned to leave in the opposite direction.

"Oh, one more thing."

Erik turned around, surprised.

"Thank you, Persson," she said, then left.

CHAPTER 34

Sophie's gun fired and missed once again. The big bird, maybe a pheasant, flew away.

"Damn it!" she exclaimed.

Famke approached. She hadn't managed to catch anything either.

"It's no use," she said. "We're both hopeless at this. We'll never be able to catch anything."

"We must improve, then," Sophie replied.

Famke looked at her indulgently, then picked up her rifle and walked away.

Since dragons could no longer hunt on their own, feeding them had become complicated.

During the first few days, they had used the frozen meat that Sophie had set aside during Pat's most successful hunting trips. But the stock had quickly run out.

Getting closer to the edge of the city had become increasingly dangerous because of the troops patrolling the outer border of the eighth ring; the presence of the armed forces had intensified considerably since they left the city.

Trying to buy meat, or stealing it from a farm, was therefore not possible.

Fortunately, Gregor found an old food distribution depot, now in disuse: it contained a large quantity of indefinable canned meat. Sophie found its very smell simply revolting, but the dragons seemed to stomach it. It wouldn't last long, though.

Sophie had decided to try to hunt for Pat: unfortunately, she had soon discovered that she did not possess his talent.

With rising temperatures and as the snow was beginning to melt, many animals had begun to show up in the trees, but Sophie still didn't manage to shoot them.

She tried to use the telepathic link to get help from Pat, but without success. After the first days in which he had fretted and tried to escape, now the dragon seemed to have fallen into a kind of resigned torpor. Sophie suspected he had been given some kind of tranquillizer.

Sophie would have liked to ask Gregor for help because at least he knew how to shoot well.

However, after he had helped her recover Pat from his escape, Cain had assigned him a lot of long and tedious tasks, probably as a form of punishment, such as trying to restore the hotel boilers or compiling endless translations of all intercepted communications of soldiers stationed in the valley below. Also, Gregor was also always in the company of Ken or some other henchman, and even getting a few minutes in private with him was getting harder and harder.

"He'll get over it," he had said, shrugging, on one of the few occasions on which they had managed to speak. "Cain can hold his grudge as long as he wants, but he needs me, and he knows it."

Sophie had avoided Cain as much as possible since Pat had been locked up. She was mad at him: she could not forgive what he had done, first arresting Nadia and the other telepaths because of something she had privately told him, then confining her dragon in a cramped basement where he could not even spread his wings.

A part of her knew that Cain was doing this because he thought it was the best for everyone that he held all responsibilities towards the infected and that he didn't want to put them in danger... but even so, Sophie felt betrayed.

She didn't want to think about the moments of intimacy they had spent together: they made her feel confused and even more angry, especially because a part of her only wanted Cain to come back to her, apologize for his misdeeds and kiss her like he did that night.

But that never happened.

Cain seemed to have accepted her distance without making any comments or objections, and Sophie didn't know whether to feel relieved or disappointed.

She had to admit that shooting was strangely cathartic, and somehow made her feel better; of course, she would feel even better if she managed to get something to feed Pat.

A couple of days earlier, she had shot a small white animal with a soft fur. She wasn't able to tell what kind of animal it was. Seeing it there, a bloody stain on the immaculate the snow, had made her feel nauseous. For a moment, she hated herself for having to kill something so beautiful and innocent.

When Pat had devoured it in two mouthfuls and looked at her hopeful and still hungry, Sophie felt even worse.

Suddenly, she saw Ken approaching them.

"Cain wants to see you. Amanda called; she has some important news to share with us."

"OK, thank you," Famke answered coldly, setting to follow him.

As Sophie climbed the snow-covered hill, she fantasized about how it would feel to shoot one of those bullets in Ken's back.

Since Cain's awakening, he had all but gloated every time he had opposed Sophie and any decision she had made in the past, looking smug.

Sophie couldn't believe that she had thought he was so nice at first, and that Gregor was the asshole.

Now she saw that Ken was just a bootlicker and Gregor... well, Gregor was a bit of an asshole, she had to admit, but not of the worst kind.

When they arrived in the hotel lobby, Sophie saw Amanda's face appearing on a screen and that she was communicating with a camera, presumably connected to her computer.

Also in the room were James, Gregor and, of course, Cain.

When Sophie and Famke arrived, he addressed them with an impersonal gesture of greeting.

Sophie just nodded and sat on the other side of the table.

"Hi, Amanda!" she said instead, facing the camera above the screen.

"Hello!" she answered with a smile. At least someone seemed happy to see her, Sophie thought.

"I was just waiting for you two. How are your dragons feeling?"

Sophie and Famke exchanged a perplexed look: "Nervous and tired of being indoors, but, apart from that, they are fine," Sophie said. "Why do you ask?"

"That's great!" Amanda exclaimed. "Persson said that only a dragon has the ability to stop Anderson's one and…"

"Hold on, what are we talking about?" Famke interrupted her.

"Amanda received a message from her favourite little policeman friend…" Gregor began.

"He's actually the head of the presidential guard, and he's not my friend," Amanda pointed out.

Gregor shrugged: "Anyway. This guy says that Anderson's dragon has started to make her go mad, he, like, completely hypnotized her."

Sophie fretted in the chair, uncomfortable. Was that something that could happen?

"So, he too wants to get rid of it, but he doesn't know how. Anderson, in a rare moment of lucidity, apparently said that only a dragon could win over another, and that's where we enter the scene."

"Instead of trying to kill Kathleen, we should try to suppress the dragon," James explained. "That way, there would be no power vacuum, no risk of civil war… Anderson would return to be a normal person, probably much more reasonable and less charismatic. She might lose her grip on the government and, well, let's just say the games would reopen. Sounds like a good plan to me."

"The idea was to go to Anderson's villa, where the dragon is, with Pat and… what's your dragon's name, Famke?" Amanda asked.

"Baldur."

"Yes, Baldur. We could try to narcotize the dragon and then…um, finish it. If it resists… Pat is small and agile, and Baldur is big and strong. They're a good team. Anderson's dragon is huge, but in my opinion two of them could overwhelm it quite easily," Amanda proposed. "What do you think?"

Sophie was about to answer that it sounded like a good idea, both because it was less reckless and suicidal than the plan to assassinate the President and because she agreed with the fact that only one dragon could stop another. Observing Pat and Taneen, especially, she had reflected on the fact that in nature, they likely would have lived in herds and...

Before she could give voice to these thoughts, Cain, who had not opened his mouth until then, prevented her.

"No way," he said.

Everyone looked at him, not daring to speak.

"Can I ask you why?" Amanda asked, obviously annoyed.

"You know why," Cain replied. "I don't trust dragons. Although I'm not opposed to the idea of killing Anderson's, and I intended to do it anyway, our first target is her."

"Hold on, when James talked about a possible civil war..." Gregor started, but Cain didn't let him go on.

"Killing a person is simple, a trivial matter. Killing a dragon, on the contrary, is a difficult, long and complicated operation. And what's our lifebelt supposed to be?" Cain shook his head. "No, it's madness. No way. We'll go ahead with our plan: we'll kill Kathleen, and then we'll deal with the dragon."

"Didn't you think about the consequences of this action?" Amanda shouted. "Kathleen Anderson is loved by the citizens of Europa. Some oppose her, yes, but most people adore her, they see her as the saviour of the city. What do you think is going to happen when they find out that she was murdered by the infected? They'll hunt you down even more than before! It's never going to end!"

"When Kathleen is dead, it will be over," Cain replied.

"For you maybe, but for the others? Damn Cain, don't you think about your people, about my brother?" she accused him. "You can't sacrifice everyone for your thirst for revenge."

Sophie saw Cain's jaw stiffen.

"It's not about revenge," he replied, slowly. "You don't know what you're talking about. Using dragons on such a dangerous and delicate mission is suicide. And trying to kill a dragon, just like that, on the spot, it's harder than it looks. Believe me, it's not that I've never tried."

"I agree with Amanda!" Sophie exclaimed. "I trust Pat. And Famke has perfect control over Baldur. We can do it, I'm sure!"

Cain looked at her coldly: "Thank you for your opinion, but I won't change your mind."

"Cain, you've known me for years, you know I wouldn't lie to you," Famke said, almost begging. "I also think we can control them. It's worth a try, isn't it?"

"No," Cain replied. "If this attempt is not successful, as it most likely would happen, even the original plan would be jeopardised. I can't take that chance."

"Wait a minute..." Amanda objected, but Cain pressed a button and the screen went out.

"Enough, I don't want to hear any more about this."

Sophie looked around: Gregor was leaning against the window with his arms crossed, looking down; James was playing with a pen, uncomfortable; Famke seemed very disappointed.

At that moment, she was certain that everyone in that room, except perhaps Ken, was sure that they had just been recruited for a suicide mission.

They could not miss that opportunity to solve their problems, to have the prospect of a new life and, also free Europa from a powerful and evil creature, all because of Cain's obstinacy.

If they continued to follow his orders, they would become increasingly weaker, isolated, always on the run. And Pat and the other dragons would always be treated like ferocious and irrational animals until they eventually would become so.

No, she couldn't let this happen.

With a heavy heart, she realized that she knew what to do.

That night, Sophie knocked on Cain's door. She felt nervous, her stomach in turmoil, and began to doubt her decision.

"Come in," Cain said.

Sophie opened the door and saw that Gregor was with Cain, showing him something on a handheld. She would have preferred to find him alone, she thought with disappointment.

"Hi," she greeted him, embarrassed.

When he saw her on the threshold, Cain smiled at her: "Hello Sophie," he said, with that beautiful, rough voice that always made her knees tremble.

She could still change his mind, Sophie thought desperately, she could still let it go…

For a moment the temptation to turn around and give up on her plan was almost irresistible.

But it was too late. Behind her, Nadia kicked the door open and pointed the gun at Cain.

"Now put your hands on the desk," she ordered, while the other telepaths raided the room.

"What's going on?" Cain asked, appearing confused and helpless for a moment.

Gregor stood up, trying to reach the crates with his weapons on the other side of the room, but Heinrich blocked his way.

"I'm sorry…" Sophie said. "I'm really sorry. I just wanted to…"

"It was you," Cain murmured, looking at her as if she was seeing her for the first time. "I should have imagined."

"Look, it's not like you think," she started to say, as reasonably as she could. "It's just that we can't go on with that suicide plan of yours, you know that, right? And you never want to listen to us…"

Suddenly, Gregor was behind her, and, with a quick move, pushed Sophie against the wall.

"What the hell are you doing?" he confronted her, his face a few inches from hers. "Have you gone mad? Why did you free these fanatics?"

"We can't assassinate Anderson… you don't want to do it either!" Sophie replied, trying to free herself from his grip.

"No, but that doesn't mean I approve of this stupid mutiny!" Gregor exclaimed. "Sophie, this is a mistake. Don't do it," he continued, almost imploring.

"I must... Gregor, you know it too, I must do it!" she insisted, looking for a glimmer of understanding in his cold, clear eyes.

Before Gregor could answer, Paul grabbed him and pulled him away from Sophie.

"It's not about Anderson, is it?" Cain said in a harsh voice. Sophie saw that Nadia had cuffed him. "You don't give a damn about that woman, or about any civil war, or about the other infected. You did it to free your dragon," he sneered. "It's always about those damn dragons. By now I should have learned."

Sophie put a hand on his arm: "Please listen to me," she desperately said. "You left me no other choice. I just want us to fix this situation, and when the crisis is over..."

"That's why you slept with me," Cain continued, undaunted. "You know, I didn't really think you could be so opportunistic. Apparently, I was wrong. Did you have to think about that fucking dragon to pretend you liked it?"

Sophie flushed, while everyone went silent.

Heinrich looked away, holding back a giggle, while Gregor simply stared at her, unable to react.

"Wow, that was awkward," Nadia said at last.

"That's enough," Sophie said in a resolute tone, then turned to Cain. "Whatever there is between us has nothing to do with this, and you know it too. If we've come to this point, it's because you've never wanted to listen to anyone's opinion except yours."

Cain didn't answer but looked at her with a stare so full of hatred that Sophie shivered.

"We'll lock you up in a dungeon to starve, so you'll know what those dragons you hate so much have gone through."

"Shut up," Sophie sighed exasperatedly. "We won't do anything like that! Just lock him in one of those rooms down the hall, they are identical to this one but without computers and weapons," she ordered.

Nadia made a theatrical puff of disappointment, then gave Cain a push to make him walk.

"Please believe me," Sophie whispered to him when he passed by her. "I just want you to be quiet for a while, until we have killed Kathleen's dragon. I wish there was another way..."

"You'll regret this," Cain hissed, before Nadia pushed him out of the room.

A few moments later, only Sophie and Gregor remained in the room. He was carefully avoiding to look her in the eyes.

"Say something," Sophie snapped at last.

Gregor looked up. He seemed saddened.

"I don't know what to say. You can't turn back from this."

That said, he walked away, leaving her alone in the now empty room.

CHAPTER 35

After meeting Amanda Solarin, Erik kept his word and left the southern corner of Anderson's villa considerably unprotected.

He had taken a surveillance shift off the night and disabled a surveillance camera, always uploading the same footage to the guard's monitor.

Solarin hadn't contacted him, and Erik wasn't sure when the attack would take place.

It would have been kind of the rebels to give him a little notice, but he didn't think it was likely to happen.

He was very upset after seeing Anderson's mind collapsing in front of him. Was it possible for a dragon to creep so deep into a person's consciousness?

Or was it just a schizophrenic delirium generated by Kathleen's disturbed mind?

Either way, Erik felt he was in danger. Anderson had almost absolute power throughout the city, and by now he had no idea how she was going to use it.

Europa, the new Europa that Kathleen had built, now felt like a dangerous, hostile place: he could no longer see the safe and almost crime-free city that he had appreciated until a few days earlier, but a place where everyone was constantly monitored, and where Anderson's anger could mean the end for millions of people.

He remembered her last words before recovering from the crisis: Kathleen had ordered him to take his kids and leave.

The idea that his kids, like everyone else, were subject to the will of an unstable and unpredictable leader frightened him: Peter was probably safer, as he was in a remote, not very densely populated place, surrounded by fields, but Maja... no, Maja was too close to the danger. He couldn't bear to have her stay there.

In his mind, a plan had begun to emerge: together with his daughter, he would join Peter in the eighth ring, and there he would wait for the outcome of the rebels' attack.

If the killing of the dragon really brought about a sudden change from Anderson, then the danger would be averted; otherwise... Erik had to admit the possibility that the President was completely crazy. In that case, he should inform the rest of the government and take action.

He had considered turning to Chardon or Voigt and informing them of what he had seen, but the truth was that he didn't trust them. Chardon was very loyal to Kathleen, and Erik doubted that his word would suffice to make him doubt her sanity; the most likely consequence was that he would have Erik locked up somewhere in a straitjacket.

When Zoe had tried to warn him, Erik himself hadn't even believed her.

As for Voigt, he would surely use that episode to undermine Kathleen's trust in him and gain some personal advantage.

He only knew the other ministers superficially and had no idea who might believe him.

For the time being, his priority was to keep Maja and Peter safe.

He had tried to explain to Maja that she had to get as far away as possible from the city centre, but she had not been very receptive about it.

"Dad, I assure you that I am very well and that there is no danger where I live," she had sighed tiredly. "I'm not going anywhere."

"Maja, you must listen to me," he had tried. "Trust me when I tell you that..."

"No," she had interrupted him. "I'm sorry, but by now I can't really trust you," she had said, closing the communication.

Erik almost threw the phone across the room in frustration: why did no one ever listen to him?!

In any case, they would leave, he decided.

He spent the next few days making feverish preparations: he told his subordinates that he would take a few days' leave, and he sent a communication to Anderson.

Then he packed his luggage: he took his warmest and most practical clothes and also collected what he could find for Maja. For Peter, he didn't pack much, since he had become much taller than the year before, and he doubted that his old clothes would still fit him.

He was now more likely to wear Erik's.

For safety's sake, he also collected several water bottles and a stock of non-perishable supplies that would last them about a week.

If his involvement with the rebels emerged for any reason, he wanted to make sure he had a few days to get organised without needing to see anyone.

It was now evening, and Erik was ready to go and pick up Maja to explain her the situation in person, when his cell phone rang.

"Persson," he replied.

"It's Kathleen Anderson," the formal voice of the president said. "I would like you to come to my house immediately because there are some urgent issues I would like to talk to you about."

Erik silently cursed.

"Madam President..." he tried. "I'm actually on vacation right now. I've taken a few days off and I'm leaving shortly..."

"Yes, I'd like to discuss that. I haven't given you my permission to be absent. On the contrary, I actually received your notice only now. Please, come here at once," she ordered, closing the communication.

Erik for a moment only stared at his cell phone.

Of course, he could have Maja picked up and taken away, even against her will if necessary, but... well, it would be a much less terrifying experience if he was there.

He went to Anderson's villa, ready to try everything and convince her that he really needed a short holiday. He feared that his behaviour, in retrospective, would appear very suspicious when the attack occurred, but thought it was worth the risk.

This time he didn't find her in the kitchen, but in the large, elegantly furnished sitting room.

Her appearance could not be different from that of the frightened old woman he had seen only a few days earlier: that day Kathleen Anderson sat with an impeccable posture on one of her expensive sofas, looking calm and self-confident.

"I hope I didn't interrupt your preparations for the holidays, Persson," she said to him with a polite smile.

"Well... actually, yes, that's what I was doing," Erik admitted.

Kathleen sighed: "See, I was very surprised when I found your request. Why this sudden decision to leave, with so little notice?"

"It's about my son," Erik replied. "As I've told you, he has just started working away from home, and he seems to be upset. I would like to go and visit him."

"Ah yes, I remember," Anderson said. "Family always comes first, don't you think?"

Erik shrugged: "Well, yes, I mean, when you become a parent..."

"Oh, but I know well," she replied. "I also have children."

"You do?" Erik asked, interested despite himself. Her official biography did not mention it, he was certain, nor had she ever talked about them.

The president stood up: "Of course. Life is so empty without the prospect of leaving anything of yourself in the world, don't you think?"

"Um, I don't know…" he replied, confused. He never thought of it that way, actually.

"The fact is, Persson," Anderson continued, pacing distractedly through the room, "is that I have always considered you a person of absolute trust, my rock. And then, I discover that you want to do this sudden trip eighth ring, something so spontaneous, so unlike you..."

Erik felt cold sweat down his back: "It's just a small holiday. I'll be gone barely more than weekend..." he minimized.

Kathleen smiled: "Of course. I certainly don't want to deny my employees the chance to take some well-deserved rest. But it is curious, in my opinion, that this 'holiday' coincides with the cancellation of a surveillance shift from my house," she said, looking him in the eye. "What is it, even your men need a holiday? Is there is an epidemic of chronic fatigue in my presidential guard?!"

"It must be a mistake...." Erik stammered, aware that he was shaking. "I can explain..."

"Oh no, my dear, you *must* explain," Anderson continued, opening the door of the living room and nodding to someone. "And to be sure that your explanations are satisfactory, I thought to give you a little incentive."

Her bodyguard, Alan, pushed someone into the room.

"Oh, no..." Erik mouthed, recognizing Maja.

His daughter looked terrified and had a big bruise on her forehead.

"Maja, are you all right?" he asked.

"They came to pick me up at home," she said in a trembling voice. "They hit Marc..."

Kathleen Anderson took the gun the agent handed her and pointed it at the girl's head, then closed the door.

"I'm waiting for your explanations," she reminded Erik.

"Wait a minute, calm down," Erik began. "No need to threaten or..."

"I'm very calm," the president replied. "And I don't like to wait," she continued, arming the gun.

Maja sobbed and Erik felt his heart missing a beat.

"I had the guard removed from the south side of the villa. I had staffing problems to cover the shifts and I thought..."

"Don't make fun of me, Persson," Anderson warned him, not even looking like herself anymore. Her face was fierce, transfigured. It was the face of someone who would stop at nothing. The face of a murderer. And Maja was there, in her clutches...

"The rebels want to kill your dragon!" Erik confessed. As long as she left Maja alone, he would give her anything...

"I promised I'd loosen the security, to help them...to..."

"Why?" Anderson roared, pushing the barrel of the gun against Maja's forehead. "Why would you do that? Tell me!"

"For you! To free you!" Erik shouted.

Kathleen's face seemed to soften for a very brief moment, then it twisted into an unprecedented ferocity: "I am free," she whispered.

Her finger slowly pressed the trigger.

Erik heard a shot and shouted, desperate.

A moment later, however, he saw that the president had dropped the gun, and she was holding her hand, covered in blood. Erik turned and saw Zoe Hernandez in the door, with the weapon she had just fired in her hand.

Maja threw herself into his arms, and Erik held her with relief.

If Zoe had arrived just a moment later…

While Erik still felt unable to move, Zoe approached Anderson and hit her with the kick of the weapon, making her unconscious.

"We must leave, Erik!" Hernandez told him.

"T-thanks Zoe…" Erik stammered, realizing that he had tears in his eyes. "I'm sorry, I should have believed you when you tried to tell me…"

"It's ok, it doesn't matter now!" she said, stealthily checking the corridor. "I made Alan leave, telling him that this wasn't his shift, but it won't take long for him to return."

Erik followed Hernandez into the corridor, dragging Maja, who kept on sobbing.

"How did you know that…Anderson, and Maja…?" Erik stammered.

"I heard her talking to Alan. She waited for me to leave, but I went back because I had forgotten my keys and…" Zoe shrugged. "I couldn't let her threaten you or your family."

Erik still felt numb.

"A bunch of agents will be here any minute. Let's go!" Hernandez urged him.

Erik gave one last look at Kathleen's unconscious body then moved away.

If everything went according to the plan, she'd soon be back to herself, he thought.

CHAPTER 36

Sophie had spent the last few hours feverishly organising Kathleen's rescue mission.

She preferred to think in these terms rather than focusing on killing a dragon, which would surely cause Kathleen an unsustainable shock. But if the alternative was to leave Europa in the hands of a bloodthirsty beast, she supposed she had no choice.

Although she still felt guilty about removing Cain from his role, she could not deny that it was nice to finally be able to make some decisions and see that the situation was moving in the right direction.

She had freed the dragons, and the other telepaths had spent a lot of time making sure that they were strong and able to go into battle. Sophie had decided to strike in force: she would bring all the dragons. She thought that together they'd have a better chance of defeating Anderson's great dragon.

She had the impression that most of the infected (except Ken, who had been shocked to learn of the power shift and had more or less voluntarily locked himself in his room) were secretly happy that Cain was no longer in charge. The atmosphere was more hopeful, light-hearted, even playful. They would make it, very soon they would have a new, rich and full life.

Sophie believed it too with all her might.

Nadia was particularly excited about the idea of going into battle and, Sophie suspected, about having gotten rid of Cain.

The downside of it was that she had started mercilessly teasing Sophie.

"I can't believe you actually slept with Cain. I mean, that's gross," she said with a grimace of horror, for what Sophie thought was at least the tenth time. "And you defend him too! All in all, it was less disturbing to think that you had sacrificed yourself for Pat."

Sophie rolled her eyes: "Ha. Ha. Very funny."

"I understand that maybe you were desperate," Nadia continued. "But... honestly, Cain?" she shook her head. "You absolutely must find a better boyfriend. You know, meet new people, something like that."

"Ah, yeah, nothing could be easier. Ninety per cent of the population considers us murderous monsters... the ideal situation for romantic encounters," Sophie mumbled.

"Try to see the bright side of it, all your potential partners are right here with you!" Nadia pointed out. "For example... James! Why not? He's tall, handsome, you already know the family..."

"Stop it, I don't want to date James! Give me a break."

The truth was that she hoped that, once the situation had resolved and Cain's anger had cooled down, maybe they would talk about it calmly and make peace.

She had gone to see him in the room where he had been locked up and tried to talk to him... but to no avail.

She got nothing out of him but a few sharp remarks, and eventually she gave up.

Now Cain felt humiliated, but Sophie was sure that when it all worked out for the best, he would understand... he had to.

"OK, not James. But you should expand your circle of friends because you never hang out with any potential boyfriends," Nadia continued in a knowing tone, then she counted on her fingers: "Heinrich is with Jane, so no. Don't even think about Paul, two girls have been fighting over him for years, and he's basically dating both of them... I know, who would have thought?" she commented, in response to Sophie's disconcerted expression. "Absolutely not Ken, since you hate each other and anyway he's a creep... let's see... well, of course not Gregor, he's almost uglier than Cain and he's really too old for you, he's at least sixty or so."

"I'm fifty-four, thank you," Gregor commented, popping out of nowhere as usual.

"Really? You look much older," Nadia went on, with no trace of embarrassment. "Do tell me what you use for your skin, so I'll remember to avoid it carefully."

He ignored her and turned to Sophie: "I got a message from Amanda. She says that Persson kept his word and removed the guards on the south side of the villa two nights ago," he informed her.

Sophie nodded: "Then we must hurry. We're ready. We can do it tonight."

"Great!" Nadia exclaimed. "I'm going to prepare Taneen" she said, moving away.

Sophie turned to Gregor: "I thought that you could lead the team that will arrive by land," she proposed, hesitant.

He looked at her with a severe expression, then shook his head: "Sophie, I'm sorry. I don't want to participate."

Sophie had to hold back a curse. She had expected it: Gregor had never made a mystery of disapproving of her choice to put Cain aside, which was a bit disconcerting since the latter had been treating him like crap since he had woken from his coma.

But, apparently, that wasn't enough to shake his loyalty.

"I need you over there. I don't trust anyone else."

Gregor looked away: "James can take care of the ground team. He already has all the information and will have no problem keeping in touch with Amanda…"

"I thought you were in favour of killing that dragon…" Sophie insisted. "Why don't you want to try to help us now?"

"Don't be melodramatic now, of course I will help you," Gregor replied, acidic. "I don't want to abandon you to die there. One of my contacts sent me a route through the underground city that won't let James run into the presidential guard, and if you want, I'll help you coordinate the attack from here. But I'll be honest, I don't like your plan, and I don't like what you did to Cain."

"What else could I do, Cain never wanted to listen to anyone…"

"And you?" Gregor interrupted her. "Whose opinion are you listening to? In the end, you're doing your own thing, too, and…"

"That's unfair!" Sophie exclaimed. "I've always trusted you and I've always listened to your opinion…"

"You want to listen to my opinion?" he asked. "Splendid. You know what to do. Release Cain, come to an agreement, and you two come up with a common plan. Put together your strengths instead of going against each other."

Sophie rolled her eyes: "Oh, yeah, right. I'm sure he'll be wonderfully collaborative…"

"I'm not saying he won't be hostile at first, but in time…"

"We don't have time, we have to do it tonight! They've cut down on surveillance, but it's not going to last forever. We can't miss this opportunity, don't you see?"

He stepped closer, looking her straight in the eyes: "Sophie, what if Cain is right? I think you rely too much on being able to control the dragons…" he lowered his voice. "What about what happened in the forest? What if it happened again during the battle…?"

"It won't happen, not against my will," Sophie replied.

Gregor took a step back: "Fine. Whatever. If you say so," he said. "I will help you as I can from here, because I don't want to lose a single infected in this operation, but you can't ask me to actively participate in a mission in which I don't believe."

Sophie nodded: "Alright. I don't want to force you."

Gregor moved to leave.

"Wait!" Sophie exclaimed, without being able to hold back. "Please, don't look at me like that. I'm not proud of what I've done. I never wanted to betray Cain's trust, I just wish that… I don't know, that he and all of us…" she hesitated, not being able to find the right words. "I'm just trying to make you see that concert you were telling me, sooner or later."

Gregor smiled without cheerfulness: "I know, Sophie, I know. I just hope you're right."

The dragons left at sunset. The team that would arrive by land, however, had left the village several hours earlier, since it would take them longer to get to the city.

Luckily the evening was cloudy, and for Sophie it was not difficult to direct Pat above the clouds. The dragon always knew perfectly well where he was. In any case, she had a position detector inside her suit, and every now and then Gregor gave her directions on where they were during the journey from the headset she was wearing.

The cold air lashed her face, and when she passed inside a cloud, she felt her cheeks covered with a light frost. It wasn't an unpleasant feeling: the thrill of speed was exhilarating, and she didn't remember a more beautiful sight than seeing the sunset from above the clouds. She certainly had never seen a sky this clear.

Pat, free after his brief but painful imprisonment, seemed to go mad with joy. From him, she continued to receive intense amounts of enthusiasm, fun and love.

"I love you too," she said, caressing his head with affection.

After a few hours, she knew she was above Anderson's villa and received a confirmation from her headset.

Pat stopped, flying in a circle to maintain the position.

After a few moments, she was joined by Heinrich, Jane, Marie, Paul, Famke and Nadia.

"We are in position," Sophie said. "I recommend that you respect the plan. If for some reason you start to notice that you have difficulty directing the dragon, get away as soon as possible, and take them away until they have calmed down," she reminded them, addressing especially Famke who, being deprived of the intense telepathic bond with her dragon, seemed the most fragile element of the team. "Gregor will tell you where to go."

"James is in position," his voice confirmed from the headset. "Start the descent in a minute."

"Let's get into formation," Sophie ordered, and the other dragons were arranged in a semicircle.

Now that the time had come, she felt nervous.

On the back of Taneen, Nadia approached Sophie.

"We'll do it," Nadia reassured her with a confident smile, then twisted her hand in hers and pulled her closer to press her forehead against Sophie's. "Let's go kick that scaly ass," she exclaimed, then put herself in position.

Sophie laughed tensely.

"Begin to descend in ten... nine... eight..." the headset communicated.

Sophie looked down, where she could see the intense lights of the city through the blanket of clouds.

"Seven... six... five... four..."

Around her, the other telepaths seemed excited but determined. Sophie knew that only they could understand how she felt at that moment, when every emotion was reflected and amplified by the dragon's mind.

"Three... two... one... GO!"

Sophie felt the cold hair slap her face while Pat plunged down.

CHAPTER 37

Erik left Anderson's villa with Maja and Hernandez; the guards at the door did not stop them, just politely greeted them.

There was nothing strange about it: clearly, Kathleen didn't have the time to give the order to arrest them.

However, they had to get out of the city as soon as possible: it was only a matter of minutes before Alan or someone else found the unconscious President and gave the alarm.

"Did you get a car?" Erik asked Zoe.

"Unfortunately not," she replied. "I came by train, as usual."

Erik nodded. He had arrived there by car but using a presidential guard's vehicle was too risky: it would only take a few minutes to locate them.

"OK, let's go to the nearest station."

He glanced at Maja, who still looked visibly in shock; she could only imagine how terrified she had to be at seeing Anderson's guards break into her apartment to take her away.

Luckily nothing had happened, he told himself. Maja would recover from the fright; but if Zoe had pulled the trigger a second later...

"Look!" Maja exclaimed in a shaky voice.

Erik followed her gaze and had to hold back a frustrated exclamation: a photo of himself had been projected on the screens above the station (he recognized the picture on his badge), and the warning indicated that he was wanted for high treason and attempted murder of President Anderson. In rotation, photos of Maja and Zoe also appeared.

As if that wasn't enough, some cops were standing at the entrance to the station.

"We can't take the train, they'd find us right away."

Erik wanted to scream: "Where can we get on foot? We must reach the eighth ring; Peter is in danger and..."

Zoe thought about it: "We could steal a car, a taxi for example," she proposed.

Erik sighed: "I don't know… that might be an idea…"

"No," Maja replied. "It would only take them a few minutes to find it, all taxis have a position detection system."

"Oh," Erik was disappointed. He ran a hand through his hair: how could they reach Peter? Every minute his situation became riskier. If the news already had his image, then his son was probably under arrest…

"We have to pass through the underground city," Maja suddenly said. "It's the only passage that is still free."

Erik objected: "There are guards everywhere…"

"We can find out where they are," Zoe said. "Can you check it from your handheld?"

"Yes, I can do that." Erik pulled out the device and did a quick check. "OK, there's a free entry point right behind us," he said, looking around.

He memorized the map and took some quick notes on a sheet of paper; then, reluctantly, he dropped his handheld into a trash can, as well as his mobile phone.

They were useful, but the first thing the police or the presidential guard would do was using them to check their position.

Zoe did the same, while Maja had nothing with her.

With circumspection, they reached the entrance to where the underground city had been.

Walking all together was a risk, as they were all wanted: alone they would attract less attention. However, after everything that had just happened, Erik just couldn't bear to be far from Maja, even if only for a few minutes.

Luckily it was late at night, and the few passers-by didn't seem to pay any attention to them.

When they passed through the police security tape and forced the door open, they found a dirty, badly lit tunnel.

Zoe looked around and found a flashlight, probably left by some agent.

"We must go on for a few miles, then we will find a detour on the right..." Erik began, but he was interrupted by the sound of someone approaching.

Hernandez looked around feverishly, looking for a hiding place, but there was none.

"We're in position, I repeat, we're in position."

"You said there were no guards here," Zoe whispered.

"There were not supposed to be! Let's go before they see us!"

Erik pushed Maja towards the door from which they had just come down, but before he could climb the short metal staircase, a familiar voice behind them said: "Everyone stop or I'll shoot."

Erik slowly turned around and, to his great surprise, he found himself in front of James Solarin, surrounded by about twenty people with weapons and protective helmets.

"You're here for the dragon!"

One of the men next to James looked at him askance.

"So much for the element of surprise," he commented.

James gestured for him to calm down: "It's all right, he's our contact in the presidential guard," he said, a little reluctantly, as if he had preferred anyone else to be in his place.

"Oh," the other exclaimed, as if remembering something all of a sudden, "your sister's little policeman friend."

"I'm not her little friend," Erik objected, feeling Maja's perplexed gaze on him.

"Absolutely not," James confirmed, shuddering, and looked at him with suspicion. "How's the nose going?"

"You know what, it was pretty good until one of your colleagues in the underground city broke it again."

Hernandez's gaze ran from one to the other: "I wouldn't want to interrupt your lovely get-together, but can someone explain what's going on?"

"I'd like to know, too," Amanda Solarin sad, annoyed, coming from the bottom of the row. "What are you doing here? That was not the plan."

Erik was surprised to see her: would she also be part of the attack to the dragon?

She was wearing a jumpsuit like the others and had a weapon on her side.

He realized that until then he had taken it for granted, perhaps erroneously, that she would simply pass on information to the infected without acting in person.

She wasn't wearing her wig, and Erik fleetingly thought that her natural short grey hair suited her much better.

"Anderson discovered the plot and threatened my daughter," he replied, "Zoe shot her in the hand," James turned to look at Hernandez with admiration, "but the police are looking for us already, so I think she's woken up. You must act quickly, before she has time to reorganize the entire security of the building."

"Shit, if that's the case, maybe it's better to stop the whole thing," James commented, then he started to tinker with the headset. "Gregor, there's a problem, looks like Anderson knows about the attack…." there was a pause and James suddenly look worried. "I understand… Yes, we are in position… ok, we'll wait for your signal."

James closed the communication, then sighed.

"Sophie and the others are already there. We can no longer postpone, we have to go ahead with the plan."

Amanda was upset: "Jamie, no!" she exclaimed, grabbing his arm. "Warn Sophie, tell her to come back and…"

"They can't go back, it's too late," James replied. "If we postpone now, we won't have another chance, the surprise effect…"

"We've already lost the surprise effect!" Amanda interrupted him. "Don't you understand? It will be carnage and…"

James gestured her to be quiet and brought his hand to the headset.

"We are out in thirty seconds," he said, then turned to his sister. "Sophie and her team are already inside. We have to go… you're right though, it's dangerous, so I want you to stay here."

The rest of the infected started climbing out of the trapdoor.

Maja flattened herself against the wall, looking terrified.

"Don't worry, honey, they won't hurt you," Erik reassured her.

"It's not that," Maja replied. "It's just that I'm not vaccinated and..."

Erik was shocked: "W-what do you mean you're not vaccinated?"

Maja shrugged apologetically: "Um... Peter and I always thought that..."

She could not finish the sentence because her voice was covered by Amanda, who was fighting with her brother.

"Don't you even try, the plan was that…"

"As you rightly said before, the plan has changed," James replied, then looked at Erik. "Don't let Amanda join us."

Erik was taken aback: how exactly did James expect him to stop Amanda from following him?

"Um..." he began.

"Don't even try to play the protective brother, because you know I won't fall for it," Amanda snapped.

"He's not wrong, though," Erik objected. "I saw Anderson, and I assure you... she's not herself anymore. I believe that the dragon, or her psychosis, or whatever, has taken complete possession of her. She won't stop at anything... staying here is not only safer for you, but it's also reasonable for someone to stay and arrange for a possible retreat," he said, trying to sound sensible.

"Exactly what I meant," James exclaimed, then kissed his sister on the forehead. "See you soon."

That said, he followed the last of his men out of the hatch and closed it behind him.

"If you think I believe this paternalistic bullshit for just a second..." Amanda started, reopening the hatch.

"Wait a minute..." Erik began, holding her by the arm. "Not to diminish your contribution, but it would really be useful if someone stayed here in case it was necessary..."

"I can't leave my brother!"

"Look, shouldn't we go?" Zoe cautiously intervened. "There's police everywhere in this area, and if they keep seeing people coming out of this door, that should theoretically be sealed, it won't take long for them to send someone down to check."

"I agree," Amanda stated. "I'm going with the others and you follow that tunnel and go your way."

She opened the door and went out.

"Amanda, no!" Erik exclaimed and climbed to follow her.

When he went outside, he found her motionless next to the hatch.

"Please go back inside..." he began, then followed her gaze and gaped.

A giant black cloud was approaching.

It was like a dark, hot wave that filled the streets and incinerated everything it found on its way.

For a moment, Erik remained paralyzed by horror, then he realized they had to move.

"Come, let's go!" he said, shaking Amanda, who seemed to have been equally shocked.

With their hearts in their throats, they returned to the manhole, but Amanda didn't manage to close the door behind her.

"Leave it, we have to go!" Erik urged her.

He pushed her to the bottom of the tunnel, then ran to Zoe and Maja.

"Go, go!" he yelled, gesturing to the depths of the tunnel.

There was not a minute to lose, they had to leave as soon as possible, but, after a few steps, a sudden pang of pain in his side forced him to slow down.

A moment later, a blaze invaded the tunnel, and Erik threw himself over Maja, covering her with his own body, while the clothes on his back caught fire.

CHAPTER 38

Pat landed lightly on his hind legs, and Sophie felt a jolt when he touched the ground.

Kathleen Anderson's house's park was large and quiet, with wide, well-kept lawns and even a pond. In the dim light of the lamps, it was an idyllic landscape.

Sophie had a pang of regret, thinking of the now-discarded project to create a similar place for all dragons. It didn't matter, she told herself; after all, it had never been a real project, just a bait from Anderson to lure them into her deception.

At the end of the garden, there was a large wooden building, halfway between a barn and a hangar; the dragon had to be there.

"We're in," she said to the headset.

Next to her, the other dragons had landed.

"This way," she told Nadia, who followed her.

The others placed themselves around them, their weapons flattened, waiting for an attacker.

Sophie and Nadia headed towards the south side of the garden, which, as promised, was unguarded.

There was a small security gate: nothing to do with the sumptuous entrance gate on the other side of the house; this was probably used by gardeners or maintenance workers.

It was still enough to get James and the others through.

The headset gave a buzz: "Sophie," said Gregor's crackling voice. "James says that Anderson knows about the attack, get away as soon as possible."

She looked around: the park continued to be quiet.

"But we're already here, and there's no one," Sophie replied. "We're about to open the door for James."

"It could be a trap, let's abort the mission," Gregor insisted.

"No," Sophie decided. "We are so close, and there is no guard in sight. It must be a false alarm."

Nadia forced the lock of the metal door, which opened effortlessly. A few seconds later, James appeared with about twenty infected.

Sophie watched them closely.

"Where's Amanda?" she asked.

"She stayed behind."

"What? But..."

Sophie didn't have time to finish her sentence.

When the last infected had walked through the door, blinding lights lit up all around the perimeter of the garden, and, suddenly, armed officers appeared all around them.

"Lower your arms and surrender," a voice ordered from a megaphone.

Sophie held back a curse.

"What do we do?" Famke asked.

Sophie looked around feverishly, then took a decision.

"All dragons to the hangar, cover us!" she ordered, addressed to James.

They had seven dragons and many armed men: they were so close to the target... they could still make it.

"Sophie, get the hell out of there!" Gregor shouted in the headset.

She decided to ignore him. She squeezed under Pat's wing, protected from the bullets hissing at her side.

The dragons sat in front of the door of what had to be the dragon's lair, and those who rode them harnessed the guns loaded with tranquillizers.

First, they would narcotize the creature, then they'd finish it.

Sophie looked back: James was doing well; his men were covering them.

"What's going on?" Gregor asked in the earpiece. His frustration was perceptible.

"We're in front of the barn," Sophie replied.

In front of her, the entrance to the hangar was dark. She thought she could see a large mass inside, breathing slowly.

She remembered the night that Kathleen had cut Cain's throat, and how she thought she had seen something similar. She stepped closer to the entrance, looking through the viewfinder of the rifle, ready to fire, when a blaze lit the inside of the hangar, and the creature came out.

Sophie was breathless: it was simply huge, frightening.

It had to be at least twice the size of Baldur, their biggest dragon, but this one looked much more ferocious and terrifying. Its snout was full of thorns and pointed scales, and its jaws were as sharp as razors.

Its big, scarlet eyes were flaming.

She didn't need a telepathic bond to know it was furious.

The dragon gave a great roar and spit a powerful blaze at them.

Sophie escaped just in time, helped by Pat's enhanced reflexes.

She realized that the blaze had gone beyond the wall of the garden and had hit the road behind it, which now appeared charred: the street lamps had been bent by the burning flames, and there were several scorched cars.

From afar, she heard Kathleen's voice give orders into the megaphone.

"Protect the dragon!" she screamed. "Do not waste time!"

"Let's surround it!" Sophie ordered, then mounted on Pat's back, who immediately took off.

The other telepaths did the same, and the seven dragons flew around Anderson's.

"I've got its neck at gunpoint," Nadia informed her.

"Go!"

Nadia fired a syringe and hit the neck of the dragon, just below its jaw.

The creature snatched it away with a paw before it could fully stick, and gave an outraged roar, trying to hit Nadia.

But Taneen turned downwards, dodging the claws of the beast.

Sophie and Pat flew around the dragon, looking for a clear spot in the neck, but it wasn't easy: despite its size, the dragon moved very fast.

Suddenly she saw that Famke had managed to get very close to the animal's neck and was about to shoot: Sophie held her breath. Famke was the one with the best aim, definitely the one with the highest chances of hitting it effectively.

Sophie was so close that she could see her finger pull down on the trigger... when, suddenly, her dragon Baldur shook and threw her off, making her fall to the ground.

A moment later, Sophie felt a lot of pain in her temple, and a feeling of anger, pain and frustration.

Pat started to wriggle as if he was trying to shake her off.

"Stop, you'll make me fall!" she screamed. "No!"

Pat gave a stronger blow, and Sophie lost her grip, collapsing on the ground.

The impact cut off her breath, and she hit her head.

She moaned and brought her hand to her ear. The earpiece had gone, she realized, and the gun had fallen somewhere she couldn't see.

Her head was spinning.

When she tried to get up, she saw that others had also fallen like her.

What was going on?

"Pat, come here!" she called, but the dragon did not move, continuing to stare at her with big, strangely empty eyes.

She tried to send him a telepathic command and perceived a sad, almost resigned thought.

I have to obey. I have no choice.

"What does that mean?"

She closed her eyes, trying to reach Pat as she had done in the forest, but found a hostile wall that bounced her back.

Sophie sensed a blaze not far from her and turned just in time to see Baldur immobilize Famke with his paws and spit a powerful jet of fire at her.

Sophie cried out in horror as Famke twisted inhumanly while her skin, muscles and bones lit up like a torch.

A moment later, all that was left of her was a pile of twisted, charred bones.

Anderson's great dragon roared with satisfaction, while Baldur went to lie down next to him.

He was the one who ordered him to do it, Sophie understood. He was the leader of the pack, and the others had to obey him.

"Go away! Get away from the dragons!" she ordered the others.

With great effort, she got up and tried to run away, without knowing where to go.

Running, she saw Paul fall beside her, and Osiris fire at him.

It's not possible, it's not possible!

She couldn't accept what she was seeing.

Their bond so powerful, so intense... could the mere appearance of a more powerful dragon cut it off?

Sophie reached the corner of the big hangar and hid on the other side.

Powerless, she saw her friends fall one after the other: Heinrich was killed by his dragon while trying to protect Jane, who was burned alive a few moments later.

Marie tried to calm down her dragon Cosette, but without success; she closed her eyes while she was being hit by the blazing jet.

A second later, there was nothing left of her but an unrecognizable smoking mass on the ground.

Sophie realized that she had tears in her eyes: it was her fault, it was she who had led them to die in such a horrible way.

She trusted the dragons, and they had betrayed them to follow their leader.

How could she not have foreseen this?

"Taneen, don't do it," said Nadia's voice nearby.

Her dragon loomed over her. She had fallen and had no chance of getting back up and escape.

No, not Nadia... at least she had to survive, she couldn't die like that...

"Taneen, it's me," her friend tried to coax him, with a reasonable voice. "It's Nadia. Don't you remember? I came to see you when they had you locked in that mountain, when you were just a puppy..." she reminded him. "I have always been with you whenever I could... I tried to free you, to get you out, to take you to hunt..."

The dragon lowered his head, and Sophie was sure that he had changed his mind... when the great dragon glided, powerful and commanding, next to him.

Taneen raised his snout and reluctantly spit a blaze of fire which burned Nadia on the spot.

"No!!!" Sophie shouted, while her friend was melting and twisting in the flames.

Sophie was in shock, motionless.

Nadia, Nadia was dead.

She was there a second before... right there...

By now Anderson's dragon was surrounded by the other smaller ones, that obsequiously fluttered around him.

He spat a flame in the courtyard, and burned a handful of men alive, infected and officers, without distinction.

The other dragons imitated him, attacking whatever was moving.

It was carnage, she realized, with horror... she had to leave. With her heart pounding in her chest, she walked along the back of the building, until she turned the corner... and found herself in front of Pat.

Her puppy was unrecognisable, with an empty expression and unsheathed jaws.

"Wait... Pat, listen to me."

It had to work, he must listen to her... they were always together, they were one.

And yet it hadn't worked out for Nadia. Taneen had killed her.

"Pat, please... I know you don't want to do this..." Sophie said in the most calming and persuasive voice she could manage, even though she only seemed to emit squeaky wheezes.

The puppy shook his head like he was in pain.

"Pat... please... it's me..." she said, not being able to hold back the tears. "We've always been together... why do you want to abandon me?"

The dragon roared and spat a fiery jet.

Sophie closed her eyes, resigned to the worst...

The flames, however, hit the wooden wall next to her, which caught fire like a torch.

Pat gave her one last grief-stricken glance, then turned around and took off to reach the rest of the pack.

Sophie stood still, shaking, for a few minutes.

When she managed to get herself together, she got out in the park, where she found an apocalyptic scene.

In the garden, now reduced to a desert, lay the dark piles of charred bones that had been people until a few minutes before.

There was no way to know if they had been infected or officers: the dragons had killed everyone, without distinction.

Sophie saw Kathleen on the horizon. She was riding her giant dragon, who drove the rest of the pack out of the park, towards the city.

Then, apparently without warning, they began to spit fire on the streets, devastating everything they found.

Sophie looked helpless, while Europa was being reduced to a pile of ashes.

CHAPTER 39

When Erik exited from the underground city, he found himself staring at piles of rubble.

At first, he thought she had gone the wrong way: they had walked a long way, following Amanda's directions through the tunnels, and she was not confident of her sense of direction.

And yet they had taken the right path. The fire wave that chased them underground hadn't been the only one.

They had waited a long time before coming out, hearing noises of explosions above their heads, of falling objects, even screams, which became more and more dim and distant as they entered the deserted meanders of the underground city.

It had been difficult to convince Amanda to flee: she wanted to go back and look for her brother, but when she tried to return into the tunnel leading to the exit that the infected had used, she found nothing but flames and molten metal.

That way was blocked: Amanda had insisted on waiting and looking for another way to reach James, but all the attempts they had made to get out had led them to a hell of fire and destruction.

Erik was walking with difficulty because of the painful burns on his back and neck from the first great flame. Amanda, Zoe and Maja, fortunately, were mostly unharmed, apart from a few minor burns. He desperately wanted painkillers, but there was no way to get them, so he had no choice: he had to keep walking.

They had walked on for what had seemed like hours, until they had found an exit; and now there was nothing but a heavy, unnatural silence.

Maja looked around: "What happened here?"

"I don't know," Erik replied. He didn't know for sure, but he imagined that the rebels' plan to kill the dragon had had an unexpected outcome. That couldn't have been the work of bombs. Only one dragon, or more than one, could have destroyed the city with such ferocity.

They must have been in the third or fourth ring, he evaluated, observing the skeletons of the buildings that remained standing, empty and devastated. It was a horrible sight... but never as bad as the charred bones scattered in the street. They were mostly just indistinct piles, but in some cases it was still possible to recognize human silhouettes.

He would have told Maja not to look, but it didn't make sense: they were everywhere, all around them. They couldn't avoid them.

Zoe looked around with a horrified expression.

Amanda was desperately trying to operate the communicator she had in her suit.

"Hello? Jamie, it's me, pick up, please. Jamie...."

Her voice had a hysterical tone now.

"We must reach the eighth ring to get to Peter," Erik stated.

Maja's eyes became full of tears: "What if there's no longer an eighth ring? If Peter...?"

"No," Erik shook his head. "I don't even want to think about it. The eighth ring is far away, they must have had a warning, to hide..." he said with certainty, because the alternative was unthinkable.

"I have to go back," Amanda said, "James could still be alive, I must help him, I must..."

Erik and Zoe looked at each other, uncomfortable.

"He could still be alive," Amanda insisted.

"Amanda, you saw that fire too..." Erik began cautiously, but she interrupted him.

"Don't say it! Don't even say that! He could have hidden, he could have left..." her voice broke. "You shouldn't have stopped me, I should have been with him!" she shouted at him. "Why did you stop me? It's all your fault!"

Erik didn't know what to say. Amanda's accusations were obviously meaningless, but the pain on her face was all too real.

"I'm sorry," he said at last. He wanted to put his hand on her shoulder as a comforting gesture, but she wriggled away.

"Don't touch me."

Erik remained silent. There was nothing he could do for her at that moment.

"I'm going to find a car," Zoe said at last.

While Amanda continued to fruitlessly tap on the communicator, Maja sat on the edge of the sidewalk, staring at the gutted buildings.

Erik sat down next to her.

"Do you think Marc is safe?" Maja asked.

Erik sighed: "I have no idea."

The true answer was no, but he didn't feel like telling her.

"We should go and look for him," Maja said. "We're not that far away."

"First of all, we have to go to get Peter," Erik objected. "We must look for an area where water, food and structures have remained intact, and I believe that the eighth ring is our best bet. The then we will organize a rescue. If Marc is alive, we'll find him," he said, with a confidence he didn't really feel.

"I know you never liked him very much," Maja said with a broken voice. "But... he's really a good guy, you know. I thought we could... I thought..."

Erik would have liked to say something consoling but all the words seemed empty; he was very happy when Zoe interrupted them, arriving in a hurry.

"I found a way out of here," she said, in a panting voice.

"Are there cars?"

Zoe shook her head: "Even better. There's a helicopter."

The chopper found by Hernandez had belonged to the medical police and had recently been taken by the ordinary police.

The symbol of the medical police had been covered with a hasty coat of paint, and it was still visible up close.

It was in an underground hangar, where it had probably sat unused for months, and, for this reason, it was miraculously intact.

"Do you know how to fly it?" Erik asked.

Hernandez nodded: "I asked to be trained when I was downgraded. Sounded like a better prospect than spending all my time checking people at the stations," she explained.

"How many times have you piloted a real one, outside the simulator?"

"Never!" she answered. "But it should be more or less the same thing, right?"

"Er... I guess."

They didn't have many other options after all.

Next to the helicopter, there were some trolleys to move it, and Erik and Zoe mounted them under it, to take it outside.

Amanda seemed to have desisted from using the communicator, and she let herself be led into the helicopter without protesting. She looked dazed, just like Maja.

Erik, feeling almost grateful for the diversion, sat in the co-pilot seat, next to Hernandez, trying not to lean on his burnt back.

In the compartment, he found a first aid kit that contained, as he enthusiastically discovered, also a pack of paracetamol. He took three pills, swallowing them without water.

Zoe started the helicopter, which shook at first, swaying heavily.

After a few minutes, however, she managed to find a regular pace.

Seeing the city out of the window, Erik realized that the situation was even worse than he had imagined. The entire city centre, in the distance, shone as if submerged in a sea of fire, flowing through the streets like molten lava. There were fires in the outer rings, too, and everywhere he could only see ruins.

Erik closed his eyes, feeling that the painkiller was starting to take effect, and, thanks to fatigue and medication, he fell asleep.

The helicopter's impact with the ground woke him up with a jolt.

Erik took a few moments to figure out where he was: Hernandez had landed the helicopter on a clearing in front of what must have been a large building, perhaps a factory.

All around there were wheat and corn fields as far as the eye could see.

"This is the place, isn't it?" Zoe asked.

Maja got out of the back seat: "Yes, Peter works here. The staff's apartments are... they were... over there," she said, pointing to a heap of rubble.

Erik got out of the helicopter and ran towards what was left of the building.

"Is anyone there?" he screamed desperately. "Peter! Peter!"

He looked around: the whole place was completely deserted.

Suddenly, some figures began to emerge from the fields: about ten people, then more and more came along.

Erik stepped closer to them: "Have you seen my son? His name is Peter... he works here, have you seen him?" he asked, looking all those who were near him in their eyes.

Suddenly a silhouette made its way through the tall ears of corn.

"Dad?!"

Peter emerged running from the field, and Erik hugged him hard.

He clung to him, breathing in the familiar scent of his skin.

"Peter!" Maja shouted, joining them.

He's alive, he's alive, Erik thought, sinking his face into his son's blonde hair. He felt as if a knot melted in his chest.

"We received an alarm signal from the city, they said that the dragons were destroying everything... when they arrived here, we hid in the fields," Peter said. "Luckily, they burned only the houses and the factories. They wanted to kill people, they didn't care about the fields."

Erik wiped from his face tears of relief and began to look around more calmly.

There were people who were dressed normally, like Peter, but most wore a uniform similar to that of the inmates of the pre-trial detention hospital.

They were very emaciated, and their hair was shaven or very short.

Everyone looked at the newcomers with curiosity, perhaps wondering if more help would arrive.

"Who are these people?" he asked his son.

"They come from the prison that was over there," he replied, pointing in a direction where nothing could be seen anymore. "Luckily we managed to free them in time."

"It was this young man who convinced the guards to let us go," a middle-aged woman with a pale and hollowed-out face said. "If it hadn't been for him, we would all still be in there."

"Bravo, little brother!" Maja exclaimed while Peter shrugged.

Another guy asked: "Will they evacuate us to a safe place in the city?"

Erik looked at their hopeful faces, then shook his head.

"There's no one left... no city," he said.

The woman who had spoken about Peter brought a hand to her mouth, shocked.

"Look, this is the safest place right now. We must secure the remaining food, make sure that there is a source of drinking water and..."

"The dragons have come here twice already!" one of the prisoners exclaimed. "We must leave before they come back again!"

Erik cursed: he had hoped that the attacks were over, but, apparently, those creatures could come back at any time.

He wondered what had become of Kathleen Anderson: had the dragon killed her too? Or was she herself, or at least her body, leading the attacks?

A man broke away from the group and headed towards Erik.

"I'd like to say one thing," he mumbled.

"Yes?" Erik asked.

Without warning, the man punched him in the face.

Erik staggered backwards and Peter pushed the inmate.

"Hey, leave my dad alone!"

Two more people intervened to separate them.

"That was for the interrogation, asshole!" the prisoner who had hit Erik spat out.

Erik looked at him more closely and widened his eyes in surprise: they had cut his hair and beard, and he weighed at least fifteen kilos less than the last time he had seen him, but it was undoubtedly Misha.

"I thought it was strange that I've spent all this time with you without you being punched by anyone," Amanda commented in an absent tone.

Despite the pain in his face, Erik was relieved. That was the first thing she'd said since they got on the helicopter.

After Misha's arrival and finding out who Erik was, the ex-prisoners became very hostile towards him. Apparently, they were all from the underground city, and they didn't have much sympathy for the director of the presidential guard, the law enforcement agency that had chased them and taken them there.

Zoe's attempts to organize the distribution of the remaining food and some form of first aid were met with little cooperation: they had been hungry for months, so now they wanted to get back on their feet and wouldn't hear of rationing.

"They're not entirely wrong," Zoe admitted. "Many of them are basically reduced to skeletons. But this way we will never be able to have some form of organization, let alone organise rescuing."

"We should get out of here," Erik agreed. "But to go where?"

"I think there is some military base, a few hundred miles from here," Peter said.

Erik looked at him: "There is no base in this area, I'm sure."

"There is something," the boy insisted. "Once I took a ride on the aeroplane they use to spread the fertilizer... relax, I was with an experienced pilot!" he added, in response to Erik's horrified glance. "I'm sure I saw something, but the pilot kept saying that he could not go there, that they were quarantined territories with a risk of contamination, and that there were only ruins anyways. They didn't look like ruins, though."

"We cannot go into quarantined territory!"

"Of course we can," Amanda unexpectedly said. "The values of radiation are the same inside and outside Europa. Jamie always said so..." she added, looking away.

"Ha!" Peter exclaimed, apparently unaware of Amanda's evident upset. "We can go, it's perfectly safe!"

Erik sighed: "Peter, if this is another one of your inventions, I..."

"Come on, Dad, trust me, at least this time," his son insisted. "We have nothing to lose anyway, right?"

Erik thought about it: Peter was not wrong.

"Zoe, what do you think?"

The officer looked reluctant but nodded: "I guess there's no alternative."

"Ok, then," Erik resolved. "We'll take the helicopter and go and have a look. Maybe it's a top-secret base that's not on the maps."

Once he could have asked for confirmation from Chardon, but who knows what happened to him. He was probably dead, too.

Erik suggested that Amanda should go with them. He wouldn't leave her alone there with those angry, hostile people. She nodded, without much enthusiasm. She was still in shock, but she would recover, Erik told himself.

Peter, despite the circumstances, seemed excited by the fact that they were going to look for the military base.

"Maybe we'll find some experimental weapons that will kill all the dragons and we'll save what's left of the city!" he said enthusiastically, settling into the helicopter.

Erik didn't have the heart to tell him there wasn't much left to save.

Hernandez flew the helicopter in the direction indicated by Peter.

For many miles, they found nothing but endless expanses of fields, and then only rocks, desert, a sterile and inaccessible landscape.

"We're in the quarantined territory," Zoe informed them.

Erik had a shiver: those areas had been contaminated by nuclear war hundreds of years earlier. They said that entering the area could lead to fatal damage, blood diseases, horrible skin growths, cancer consuming people from within... Whatever Amanda said, he wasn't entirely sure that the area was safe. What did James Solarin know, anyway?

"We don't have much fuel anymore," Zoe informed them, turning abruptly.

"Wait, why did you turn around?" Peter protested. "I think it was that way..."

Hernandez sighed: "It's this way, trust me."

"How would you know?" Erik asked.

Zoe didn't answer.

"Look, over there!" Peter said, pointing towards something on the horizon.

There was something... at the beginning, it was just a metallic glimmer, but as they approached, Erik distinguished something that looked like a building...

"It's a wall..." Maja said, perplexed. "Looks like there is a wall in the middle of the mountains..."

"Maybe the military base is inside, so it can't be bombed!" Peter suggested.

Erik was amazed as what was unequivocally a military construction emerged in front of them. As he approached, he could see figures running frantically on top of the wall and snipers at the ends.

Zoe landed the helicopter in the clearing in front of the base.

When they came out, several lights were turned on, pointing at them.

A voice on a megaphone said: "Stop right there!"

Erik frowned: the voice had a bizarre accent, and for a moment he had to concentrate to understand what it was saying.

He raised his hands. Amanda, Maja and Peter did the same.

Zoe instead took a few steps forward: "It's Hernandez, I'm here to report."

Erik was speechless: he watched his colleague, or former colleague, approach the soldiers, who gave a sign of recognition.

Others approached him instead, keeping him under fire with sniper rifles.

Their weapons seemed lighter and more advanced than those he had seen so far, and their uniforms did not belong to any armed force he knew.

Peter stared at a point on the wall and murmured dreamily: "I knew it…"

Erik followed his gaze.

When he read the sign, he was shocked: 'Union of the Republics of Southern Europe – Border.'

CHAPTER 40

Sophie finally saw the village on the horizon.

In the last two days, she had crossed what remained of the city, first on foot and then in a car, when she had found one. The vehicle, however, was designed for the city's asphalt, not for the rough terrain of the quarantined territories, and she had to abandon it miles earlier.

Often, she had to hide to avoid the incursions of dragons, who still raged against everything they saw in motion. She had recognized Taneen and Osiris but hadn't seen Pat since he had escaped to reach the rest of the pack. Maybe it was for the best.

In her thoughts, she felt nothing but a barrier, like a buzzing background noise that prevented her from discerning the emotions of the dragon. Every now and then, she felt some intense pang: pain, fear, frustration. However, those were isolated episodes, nothing to do with the constant exchange she was used to.

She had imagined that crossing the enormous territory of Europa would be a very long and almost impossible task, but she had discovered that, in the absence of the traffic she had always seen around her, it was much quicker than expected.

She had met a few survivors, who, seeing her scales, had run away when they saw her. The buildings were completely destroyed, but some people who were in basements had made it.

Estimating how many could still be alive was impossible.

Sophie felt a kind of numbness as she headed like a zombie to the only place she could consider home. An empty house now: no more Nadia, no more Pat, no more of her friends. But it was still a goal: concentrating on her return was better than retracing the events that had brought her there. But she couldn't help but think of the terrible moment when the dragons had attacked their telepaths, Nadia's skin melting under Taneen's burning fire, that short but intense smell of burnt flesh... Sophie rubbed her eyes, trying to drive away those thoughts.

She was almost there. The village was just around the corner.

She was tired, exhausted; her eyes burned with dust, her muscles went on by inertia.

Her clothes were torn in many points because of the fall from Pat's back, her face was burned by the sun and the flames that in some cases she had to cross.

She could only thank her infected body, stronger and more resistant than a normal one: she was aware that as a human she would never be able to get there.

When she finally reached the steep streets of the village, she saw a series of people carrying crates and loading the remaining jeeps. Clearly, they were preparing to leave.

Of course, Sophie thought, there was no way to know how much Kathleen knew about their position.

Amanda had said that her contact at the presidential guard knew where they were, but they didn't know if he had shared this information with Anderson before his betrayal.

In doubt, it was safer to move while they were in time.

She walked the first few meters without anyone noticing her, but then some infected people began to point at her, speaking softly to each other. They looked suspicious, vaguely hostile.

It wasn't exactly a triumphant return, Sophie thought bitterly.

She had lost everything: the chance to kill Anderson, all the people who had followed her and even the dragons. She couldn't have done worse than this.

She thought that she could live with their disapproval until suddenly she found herself in front of Karla.

The girl's eyes were red for crying, and she seemed to have aged ten years in a few days.

She looked her in the eyes with anxiety and hope at the same time: "Nadia?" she asked, hesitant.

Sophie shook her head: "I'm sorry, she... everything happened so quickly and... "

"How did it happen?" Karla asked, her voice hard. "Who was it? One of Anderson's men?"

Sophie hesitated. The truth was even harder to accept, but Karla deserved it.

"It was her dragon," she answered with an atonal voice. "They revolted against us."

Karla sobbed.

"You couldn't leave them alone, could you?" she whispered. "Nadia was fine before you arrived. Her dragon was kept at a safe, harmless distance, and she would visit him whenever she wanted. It was a safe situation, under control... But no! You had to change everything! You had to stay with those damn beasts, dedicate your whole life to them, and now... now..." she burst into uncontrolled hiccups.

Sophie felt compelled to answer but couldn't find a word. Karla didn't understand that Nadia would never be happy separated from Taneen, and yet she was right. If Sophie had not insisted... if she had not brought Kathleen among them... if she had never arrived on that island...

"Sophie," said a cold voice behind her. "I was told about your return."

She turned around: it was Ken, accompanied by two other men with a shotgun flattened before her. He had an almost triumphant expression.

Sophie laughed, though there was nothing remotely cheerful about it. Ken had finally got what he wanted.

"Are there other survivors besides you?" Ken asked.

"No."

He sighed: "We'll take you to see Cain now."

Sophie nodded, preparing to follow them.

Karla gave her one last look of despair, which made her feel even worse.

The two infected kept holding her under fire, as if she could do something abrupt at any moment.

I can hardly walk, she wanted to tell them. She couldn't hurt anyone anymore. She just wanted to drink some fresh water and curl up somewhere.

She followed Ken into the hotel that served as headquarters and saw that Cain had regained his position of command. He was giving orders to a group of infected people carrying crates of arms.

Where is Gregor? she wondered, puzzled.

When he saw her, Cain just stared at her.

"Leave us alone," he told the others.

She stood in the middle of the room, which seemed curiously empty, like after a hurricane.

Cain didn't tell her to sit down.

"Gregor told me that you lost the connection shortly after the beginning of the battle," he said. "What happened?"

"Anderson ambushed us. She knew we were coming," Sophie said tiredly, without looking at him. She was pretty sure that Cain knew exactly what had happened, but he wanted to make her say it, force her to relive those moments.

"When James and his team entered the park, Anderson's guards closed all the exits, and they attacked us," she continued. "We tried to reach the dragon and kill him, but..."

"Why didn't you come back, when you realized it was a trap?" Cain asked, tough.

Sophie gulped: why didn't she do that? It had been madness, the gesture of a fanatic... yet she had felt so safe, so determined when she was riding Pat, as if nothing could stop her...

"We could not escape without leaving James and the others in the hands of the enemy. It was too late. When we arrived in front of the dragon, however, the others recognized him as their leader, and began to follow his orders," she said, trying to hold back the tremor in her own voice. "They turned against us and killed all those they could find. I managed to get away from them, but when I got out... there was no one left. Anderson's dragon drove the others against the city and they destroyed everything."

"What happened to James?" Cain asked.

Sophie shook her head: "I don't know, I didn't see him but... well, as I told you, there were no survivors."

"What about Amanda?"

"I don't know."

"Famke?" Cain insisted. "Paul, Marie? Nadia? Where is Nadia?"

Sophie looked up: "Stop it. You know what happened. They're all dead. Why do you have to keep on torturing me?"

"Ah, now I'm the one torturing you?" Cain made a contemptuous face. "I tried in every way to dissuade you from this stupid and reckless mission that you wanted to set up, but you didn't want to hear reasons. You even had me arrested so you could make yourself comfortable."

"I thought... There was no way to predict..."

"There was no way?! That's exactly what I've been telling you all along! You can't. Trust. Fuckin. Dragons!" he yelled.

Sophie looked away. Cain was right. She had ignored everything he had said because she thought he was obtuse and unreasonable, but, above all, because she wanted to trust Pat, the bond they shared. It seemed so natural, so right... how could have she been so wrong?

"And now millions of people have died because you didn't want to listen to me," he continued. "How do you feel, having them on your conscience? How does it feel?"

"Stop it."

"Stop it? After all you've done, you don't even want to face the consequences of your actions?"

"I tried to do what I thought was right!" Sophie defended herself.

"Now, thanks to you, Anderson has a herd of dragons, and I have no idea how we can stop them, assuming it's still worth it, since there's nothing to save anymore. Are you happy now?"

Sophie didn't answer and kept looking down.

There was nothing to add.

"I should have arrested you too, along with the others," Cain, murmured bitterly. "I should have curbed this madness long ago when I still could. I wanted to believe the best of you, but I won't make this mistake a second time."

Sophie felt a chill running down her back, as she realized the implications of Cain's words.

"Are you going to execute me?" she asked, surprised at how steady her voice sounded.

But perhaps she had got to a point beyond fear: she was just very, very tired, and all she wanted was to forget what she had done.

"No," Cain replied. "Don't get me wrong, it was an option, and there are those who supported it. But unlike you, I'm not entirely without a conscience," she looked her in the eyes, without a trace of emotion. "But I want you to leave. We are about to leave this village, and you will not follow us."

"Where should I go?" Sophie replied. "There's no longer a city. There's nothing left."

Cain shrugged: "I have been told that parts of the underground city have been saved."

Sophie laughed bitterly.

"I can't go to the underground city. They hate me, remember?"

She surely remembered Korbinian's look of hatred and his promise of revenge. No, she definitely couldn't be seen there anymore, especially alone, without a dragon.

Cain turned his back on her: "It's your problem," he replied, "I don't care what you do, as long as you stay away from us."

Sophie turned him around, to face him: "Look, do you want me to tell you that I'm sorry, that you were right?" she said. "Do you want me to implore your forgiveness? Yes, you were right, I was wrong! You know that if I could go back..."

"It's not about that," Cain answered. "You think that the problem is my wounded pride, but that's not the case. The fact is, you're a person without conscience, without morality, you're a loose cannon. For you, that dragon will always come first. You'll betray me and all of us for that beast, and you'd do it again and again. I don't care about anything you say, because it's just empty words."

Sophie didn't know what to say.

No, I'm not like that, she wanted to say, but she knew that in Cain's words there was a core of truth. As much as she could try to deny it, her connection with Pat was far too real and could not be erased. If she was in the situation of having to choose between protecting him and any other person...

But it was not a problem anymore: Pat had abandoned her and she had lost everything, him, her friends and now also her home.

"Don't follow us," Cain continued. "I don't want to see your face ever again, ever. If you just try to get close to us, I'll have you shot on sight."

It was useless to try to change his mind, she realized.

In his eyes, there was no more anger, hatred, or resentment, just that implacable coldness.

She would almost have preferred that he reproached her for betraying him, that he accused her of hurting him... everything, except that hostile void.

Sophie wanted to cry, but she wouldn't give him that satisfaction, she thought.

"You're taking everything from me," she said in a flat voice. "You're killing me."

Cain stared at her with something that could look like regret but, she realized, it was just indifference.

"Kill yourself, then," he replied. "But don't blame me. You did it all with your own hands."

He gave her half an hour to gather her belongings and leave.

Sophie went to her room and packed the few objects she had in a backpack: warm clothes, a torch, a bottle of water and canned food. She had not been allowed to take arms, but she found a pocket knife and took it.

She didn't have much else. She had already lost everything that mattered to her.

When she left, Cain was waiting for her outside the building, along with the infected who would escort her out of the village. Sophie saw Ken, then her heart lurched when she recognized the silhouette next to him: it was Gregor.

He stood in a corner, with his arms crossed, as if folded back on himself.

Of course, he must have regained his place in Cain's circle: after all, why wouldn't he? He never had anything to do with the plot to get him out of power.

She shouldn't have been surprised by his presence there but seeing him together with Cain and the men who were driving her out of the village upset her.

When she passed by him, close enough to touch him, he didn't even look at her face.

She had managed to get everyone to hate her, she thought. Even Gregor, who had always helped her, who had helped her searching for Pat, who had drunk with her that evening in the underground city...

When they reached the edge of the village, Sophie looked back one last time.

Cain stood still, with a hard and unshakable expression, his arms crossed over his chest.

How was it possible that those were the same arms that had embraced her, that that mouth closed in a thin line was the same one that had kissed her?

It had happened a few days earlier, but it seemed like a century had passed.

She didn't want to think about it, yet at that moment she couldn't help but remember his eyes when he smiled at her, his scent, the warmth of his naked skin against her own.

How could he be the same person who was now looking at her like she was a stranger?

Sophie turned to leave, but at that moment the shoulder strap of her backpack suddenly loosened, and the bag fell. The content spread out over the ground.

Sophie knelt to collect the objects that rolled around, while Cain let out a puff of impatience.

"I'll take care of it," Gregor said, bored.

Always without looking into her eyes, he picked up a handful of clothes and slipped them abruptly into the backpack, then closed it and placed it on her shoulders, tightening the strap more tightly.

At that moment, Sophie felt something slip into the pocket of her trousers.

"Don't move," Gregor whispered against her ear, so quietly that she could barely hear him. "It's a cell phone. Call me if you're in trouble."

His hand squeezed her shoulder almost imperceptibly, a gesture that at that moment she found incredibly comforting.

For the first time, Sophie felt a tear of relief rolling down her cheek.

Gregor didn't hate her. For the moment, it was the most reassuring thought she could articulate.

She walked on the steep road towards the city.

After all, there was only one place where she could go.

EPILOGUE

Kathleen Anderson was on the balcony of her villa, one of the few buildings, perhaps the only one, that remained standing in the city centre.

Her great, terrible dragon was standing in the garden, surrounded by the other creatures, who seemed docile, servile.

Around what had been the boundary wall of her property, a river of metal and molten asphalt flowed, creeping as far as the eye could see among the ruins of what had been the homes of her neighbours.

What had she done? she wondered as she ran a hand through her hair. Her hand was wounded and already medicated, she noticed. She didn't remember any of that.

The memories of that day were confusing, as if it was a bad dream from which she could not wake up.

She had found herself on the back of the dragon, feeling invincible, excited, happy... then she had looked below and had seen the devastation they had caused.

She had almost fainted for the shock.

Everything she had ever known in her life had been destroyed. She had destroyed it.

She had led a pack of dragons who had ferociously annihilated millions of people, mercilessly and for no reason, for the sheer sake of doing so.

That's what we wanted, you knew it too.

No, she never wanted to kill those people. She wanted to help them, rule them, build the dream of a different, peaceful city. A city without crime, without degradation, a city where to live with dignity.

How could this happen, she wondered, looking at the hell that was burning around her. What have we done?

It was necessary. We never needed those people. They were an obstacle, an unnecessary setback.

But why kill them? We could have ignored them, left them to their fate, we could have...

No. I've wanted to do this for a long time. Their lives mean nothing. We are more, much more...

He wanted to reunite his family for a long time.

He had laid his eggs over the years, confident that they would hatch at the right time and that this would create his army, perhaps small, but unstoppable. He wasn't wrong. He was never wrong.

He looked to his children, not entirely satisfied with what he saw: they had been locked up for a long time, and some of them were weak, unhealthy, like plants grown without sunlight.

They would recover, however: they would feast on the flesh of the creatures that had enslaved them, and they would become strong and proud.

He looked at the youngest one: he was the most physically promising, strong, quick, with lean, powerful muscles; but he was also the most undisciplined, the only one who had tried to question his authority.

He will learn, he thought. Over the last few days, he'd had to put him back in line several times.

The temptation to get rid of a problematic element was strong, but he could not afford to lose a single dragon. The little one had to learn.

Now that he had been reunited with his clan, there was nothing left to stop them.

He proudly observed what he had done to that dirty, noisy city: now it was perfect, purified, free. He would take his work even further and extend his dominion over everything he wanted.

All he had to do was to perfect his army, train them, and they would be invincible.

Kathleen heard a sudden noise coming from the entrance and shook herself from the torpor.

Who could that be? Maybe someone had survived?

Her heart was filled with hope: perhaps not everything was lost.

What remained of the large decorated gate creaked shakily, while a familiar figure entered hesitantly: "Kathleen?"

Kathleen Anderson smiled, drying the tears that had rolled through her face: "Sophie..." she exclaimed. "I knew it... I knew that you would come back to me."

THE END

Did you like this book?

If so, I'd be grateful if you took the time to leave a review. Reviews are incredibly important for indie authors like me!
Let's keep in touch at:
www.facebook.com/themantovanisblog
www.themantovanis.blog

Acknowledgment

I would like to thank all the people that helped me in this project, especially my sister Maria Carla, fantastic alpha reader and editor, and my friend Hannah Ross for her encouragement.

A huge thanks also goes to my wonderful beta reader Amanda Brogan: you're a real star!

I'd also like to give a shout-out to my beloved family: Dario, Giacomo, Samuele, my mum Piera and my parents-in-law Graziella and Piero. Thank you!

Printed in Great Britain
by Amazon